The Bennett family has a secret:
They're not just a family, they're a pack.
Wolfsong is Ox Matheson's story.

Praise for *Wolfsong* and the Green Creek series

"An exciting start to the [Green Creek] series." —*Library Journal*

"*Wolfsong* is so well-written that I'm in awe of TJ Klune's talent. The primary character, Ox, has huge feelings he can't articulate. But we know all of them, and we love him. The complex and startling world of Green Creek is the perfect setting." —Charlaine Harris

"One of my new all-time favorite books!" —Giana Darling

"It's a flawless book and shows that you can take the fantastic and make it so very human. I thought the supernatural would be what grabbed me, but instead it's Ox's humanity and humility and loyalty. I hope there will be more. Wildly recommended."

—Mary Calmes

"The prose reads like a simple, placid little pond, and then you jump in and realize it's MILES DEEP. So to conclude this terrible non-review, FIVE BAJILLION STARS." —Emma Scott

"The best part of this book is the pack mentality and how strong of a bond everyone has with each other. Beautiful and I highly recommend!" —K. Webster

"Beautiful, poetic, unbelievably compelling. ALL the stars."

—Juliette Cross

Praise for *The House in the Cerulean Sea*

"It's a witty, wholesome fantasy that's likely to cause heart-swelling."
—*The Washington Post*

"I loved it. It is like being wrapped up in a big gay blanket. Simply perfect."
—V. E. Schwab

"Sweet, comforting, and kind, this book is very close to perfect. *The House in the Cerulean Sea* is a work of classic children's literature written for adults and children alike, with the perspective and delicacy of the modern day. I cannot recommend it highly enough."
—Seanan McGuire

"It will renew your faith in humanity."
—Terry Brooks

"*1984* meets *The Umbrella Academy* with a pinch of Douglas Adams thrown in. Touching, tender, and truly delightful, *The House in the Cerulean Sea* is an utterly absorbing story of tolerance, found family, and defeating bureaucracy."
—Gail Carriger

"*The House in the Cerulean Sea* is a modern fairy tale about learning your true nature and what you love and will protect. It's a beautiful book."
—Charlaine Harris

Praise for *Under the Whispering Door*

"*Under the Whispering Door* is a kind book. It broke my heart with its unflinching understanding that grief never goes away. And then it healed me in the next breath."
—Cassandra Khaw

"There is so much to enjoy in *Under the Whispering Door,* but what I cherish the most is its compassion for the little things—a touch, a glance, a precious piece of dialogue—healing me, telling me that for all the strangenesses I hold, I am valued, valid—and maybe even worthy of love."

—Ryka Aoki

Praise for *In the Lives of Puppets*

A *New York Times, Sunday Times,* and indie bestseller!
A #1 Indie Next Pick!

"*In the Lives of Puppets* is glorious, a thoroughly entertaining and deeply stirring journey through a world of extraordinary robots. The characters here are so vibrant, and the story proves that love stretches well beyond the world of humans."

—Chuck Tingle

"*In the Lives of Puppets* is a powerful story of humanity and what survives after we're gone. TJ Klune has created an enchanting tale of Pinocchio in the end times, offering up hard truths alongside humor, kindness, love, and, most important, hope."

—P. Djèlí Clark

"Literature at its very best opens up the potential of a better world than the one we're currently in. Klune's vision of a more considerate and compassionate society is immensely powerful. One can't help but fall in love with this book."

—T. L. Huchu

TJ KLUNE

WOLFSONG

GREEN CREEK BOOK ONE

TOR

TOR PUBLISHING GROUP
NEW YORK

For Ely, because of all those Tumblr links.

You know the ones.

The thirst is real.

WOLFSONG

Copyright © 2016 by Travis Klune
Exclusive *Wolfsong* short story copyright © 2023 by Travis Klune

A Tor Book
Published by Tom Doherty Associates / Tor Publishing Group
120 Broadway
New York, NY 10271

www.tor-forge.com

Tor® is a registered trademark of Macmillan Publishing Group, LLC.

The Library of Congress has cataloged the hardcover edition as follows:

Names: Klune, TJ, author.
Title: Wolfsong / TJ Klune.
Description: First Tor hardcover edition. | New York : Tor, Tor Publishing Group, 2023. | Series: Green Creek ; book 1
Identifiers: LCCN 2023007929 (print) | LCCN 2023007930 (ebook) | ISBN 9781250890313 (hardcover) | ISBN 9781250906205 (hardcover) | ISBN 9781250292407 (international edition) | ISBN 9781250890320 (ebook)
Subjects: LCSH: Shapeshifting—Fiction. | Werewolves—Fiction. | LCGFT: Paranormal fiction. | Werewolf fiction. | Gay fiction. | Novels.
Classification: LCC PS3611.L86 W65 2023 (print) | LCC PS3611.L86 (ebook) | DDC 813/.6—dc23/eng/20230223
LC record available at https://lccn.loc.gov/2023007929
LC ebook record available at https://lccn.loc.gov/2023007930

ISBN 978-1-250-89033-7 (trade paperback)

Our books may be purchased in bulk for promotional, educational, or business use. Please contact your local bookseller or the Macmillan Corporate and Premium Sales Department at 1-800-221-7945, extension 5442, or by email at MacmillanSpecialMarkets@macmillan.com.

First Tor Paperback Edition: 2024

Printed in the United States of America

0 9 8 7 6 5 4 3 2 1

Oh please don't go—we'll eat you up—we love you so!

Maurice Sendak,
Where the Wild Things Are

MOTES OF DUST / COLD AND METAL

I was twelve when my daddy put a suitcase by the door.

"What's that for?" I asked from the kitchen.

He sighed, low and rough. Took him a moment to turn around. "When did you get home?"

"A while ago." My skin itched. Didn't feel right.

He glanced at an old clock on the wall. The plastic covering its face was cracked. "Later than I thought. Look, Ox . . ." He shook his head. He seemed flustered. Confused. My dad was many things. A drunk. Quick to anger with words and fists. A sweet devil with a laugh that rumbled like that old Harley-Davidson WLA we'd rebuilt the summer before. But he was never flustered. He was never confused. Not like he was now.

I itched something awful.

"I know you're not the smartest boy," he said. He glanced back at his suitcase.

And it was true. I was not cursed with an overabundance of brains. My mom said I was just fine. My daddy thought I was slow. My mom said it wasn't a race. He was deep in his whiskey at that point and started yelling and breaking things. He didn't hit her. Not that night, anyway. Mom cried a lot, but he didn't hit her. I made sure of it. When he finally started snoring in his old chair, I snuck back to my room and hid under my covers.

"Yes, sir," I said to him.

He looked back at me, and I'll swear until the day I die that I saw some kind of love in his eyes. "Dumb as an ox," he said. It didn't sound mean coming from him. It just was.

I shrugged. Wasn't the first time he'd said that to me, even though Mom asked him to stop. It was okay. He was my dad. He knew better than anyone.

"You're gonna get shit," he said. "For most of your life."

"I'm bigger than most," I said like it meant something. And I was. People were scared of me, though I didn't want them to be. I was big.

Like my daddy. He was a big man with a sloping gut, thanks to the booze.

"People won't understand you," he said.

"Oh."

"They won't get you."

"I don't need them to." I wanted them to very much, but I could see why they wouldn't.

"I have to go."

"Where?"

"Away. Look—"

"Does Mom know?"

He laughed, but it didn't sound like he found anything funny. "Sure. Maybe. She knew what was going to happen. Probably has for a while."

I stepped toward him. "When are you coming back?"

"Ox. People are going to be mean. You just ignore them. Keep your head down."

"People aren't mean. Not always." I didn't know that many people. Didn't really have any friends. But the people I *did* know weren't mean. Not always. They just didn't know what to do with me. Most of them. But that was okay. I didn't know what to do with me either.

And then he said, "You're not going to see me for a while. Maybe a long while."

"What about the shop?" I asked him. He worked down at Gordo's. He smelled like grease and oil and metal when he came home. Fingers blackened. He had shirts with his name embroidered on them. *Curtis* stitched in reds and whites and blues. I always thought that was the most amazing thing. A mark of a great man, to have your name etched onto your shirt. He let me go with him sometimes. He showed me how to change the oil when I was three. How to change a tire when I was four. How to rebuild an engine for a 1957 Chevy Bel Air Coupe when I was nine. Those days I would come home smelling of grease and oil and metal and I would dream late at night of having a shirt with my name embroidered on it. *Oxnard*, it would say. Or maybe just *Ox*.

"Gordo doesn't care" is what my dad said.

Which felt like a lie. Gordo cared a lot. He was gruff, but he told me once that when I was old enough, I could come talk to him about a job. "Guys like us have to stick together," he said. I didn't know what he meant by that, but the fact that he thought of me as anything was good enough for me.

"Oh" is all I could say to my dad.

"I don't regret you," he said. "But I regret everything else."

I didn't understand. "Is this about . . . ?" I didn't know what this was about.

"I regret being here," he said. "I can't take it."

"Well that's okay," I said. "We can fix that." We could just go somewhere else.

"There's no fixing, Ox."

"Did you charge your phone?" I asked him because he never remembered. "Don't forget to charge your phone so I can call you. I got new math that I don't understand. Mr. Howse said I could ask you for help." Even though I knew my dad wouldn't get the math problems any more than I would. Pre-algebra, it was called. That scared me, because it was already hard when it was a *pre*. What would happen when it was just algebra without the *pre* involved?

I knew that face he made then. It was his angry face. He was pissed off. "Don't you fucking get it?" he snapped.

I tried not to flinch. "No," I said. Because I didn't.

"Ox," my daddy said. "There's going to be no math. No phone calls. Don't make me regret you too."

"Oh," I said.

"You have to be a man now. That's why I'm trying to teach you this stuff. Shit's gonna get slung on you. You brush it off and keep going." His fists were clenched at his sides. I didn't know why.

"I can be a man," I assured him, because maybe that would make him feel better.

"I know," he said.

I smiled at him, but he looked away.

"I have to go," he eventually said.

"When are you coming back?" I asked him.

He staggered a step toward the door. Took a breath that rattled around his chest. Picked up his suitcase. Walked out. I heard his old truck start up outside. It stuttered a bit when it picked up. Sounded like he needed a new timing belt. I'd have to remind him later.

.   .   .

Mom got home late that night, after working a double in the diner. She found me in the kitchen, standing in the same spot I'd been in when my daddy had walked out the door. Things were different now.

"Ox?" she asked. "What's going on?" She looked very tired.

"Hey, Mom," I said.

"Why are you crying?"

"I'm not." And I wasn't, because I was a man now.

She touched my face. Her hands smelled like salt and french fries and coffee. Her thumbs brushed against my wet cheeks. "What happened?"

I looked down at her, because she'd always been small and at some point in the last year or so I'd grown right past her. I wished I could remember the day it happened. It seemed monumental. "I'll take care of you," I promised her. "You don't ever need to worry."

Her eyes softened. I could see the lines around her eyes. The tired set of her jaw. "You always do. But that's—" She stopped. Took a breath. "He left?" she asked, and she sounded so *small*.

"I think so." I twirled her hair against my finger. Dark, like my own. Like my daddy's. We were all so dark.

"What did he say?" she asked.

"I'm a man now," I told her. That's all she needed to hear.

She laughed until she cracked right down the middle.

.   .   .

He didn't take the money when he left. Not all of it. Not that there was much there to begin with.

He didn't take any pictures either. Just some clothes. His razor. His truck. Some of his tools.

If I hadn't known any better, I would have thought he never was at all.

.   .   .

I called his phone four days later. It was the middle of the night.

It rang a couple of times before a message picked up saying the phone was no longer in service.

I had to apologize to Mom the next morning. I'd held the handset so hard that it had cracked. She said it was okay, and we didn't talk about it ever again.

.   .   .

I was six when my daddy bought me my own set of tools. Not kids' stuff. No bright colors and plastic. All cold and metal and real.

He said, "Keep them clean. And God help you if I find them laying outside. They'll rust and I'll tan your hide. That ain't what this shit is for. You got that?"

I touched them reverently because they were a gift. "Okay," I said, unable to find the words to say just how full my heart felt.

    . . .

I stood in their (*her*) room one morning a couple of weeks after he left. Mom was at the diner again, picking up another shift. Her ankles would be hurting by the time she got home.

Sunlight fell through a window on the far wall. Little bits of dust caught the light.

It smelled like him in the room. Like her. Like both of them. A thing together. It would be a long time before it stopped. But it would. Eventually.

I slid open the closet door. One side was mostly empty. Things were left, though. Little pieces of a life no longer lived.

Like his work shirts. Four of them, hanging in the back. *Gordo's* in cursive.

Curtis, they all said. *Curtis, Curtis, Curtis.*

I touched each one of them with the tips of my fingers.

I took the last one down from the hanger. Slid it over my shoulders. It was heavy and smelled like *man* and *sweat* and *work*. I said, "Okay, Ox. You can do this."

So I started to button up the work shirt. My fingers stumbled, too big and blunt. Clumsy and foolish, I was. All hands and arms and legs, graceless and dull. I was too big for myself.

The last button finally went through and I closed my eyes. I took a breath. I remembered how Mom had looked this morning. The purple lines under her eyes. The slump of her shoulders. She'd said, "Be good today, Ox. Try to stay out of trouble," as if trouble was the only thing I knew. As if I was in it constantly.

I opened my eyes. Looked in the mirror that hung on the closet door.

The shirt was too large. Or I was too small. I don't know which. I looked like a kid playing dress-up. Like I was pretending.

I scowled at my reflection. Lowered my voice and said, "I'm a man."

I didn't believe me.

"I'm a man."

I winced.

"I'm a man."

Eventually, I took off my father's work shirt and hung it back up in the closet. I shut the doors behind me, the dust motes still floating in the fading sun.

CATALYTIC CONVERTER /
DREAMING WHILE AWAKE

G ordo's."

"Hey, Gordo."

A growl. "Yeah? Who's this?" Like he didn't know.

"Ox."

"Oxnard Matheson! I was just thinking about you."

"Really?"

"No. What the fuck do you want?"

I grinned because I knew. The smile felt strange on my face. "It's good to hear you too."

"Yeah, yeah. Haven't seen you, kiddo." He was pissed at my absence.

"I know. I had to . . ." I didn't know what I had to do.

"How long has it been since the sperm donor fucked off?"

"A couple of months, I guess." Fifty-seven days. Ten hours. Forty-two minutes.

"Fuck him. You know that, right?"

I did, but he was still my daddy. So maybe I didn't. "Sure," I said.

"Your ma doing okay?"

"Yeah." No. I didn't think she was.

"Ox."

"No. I don't know."

He inhaled deeply and sighed.

"Smoke break?" I asked him, and it hurt, because that was familiar. I could almost smell the smoke. It burned my lungs. I could see him if I thought about it enough, sitting out behind the shop. Smoking and scowling. Long legs stretched out, ankles crossed. Oil under his fingernails. Those bright and colorful tattoos covering his arms. Ravens and flowers and shapes meant to have meaning that I could never figure out.

"Yeah. Death sticks, man."

"You could quit."

"I don't quit anything, Ox."

"Old dogs learn new tricks."

He snorted. "I'm twenty-four."

"Old."

"Ox." He knew.

So I told him. "We're not doing okay."

"Bank?" he asked.

"She doesn't think I see them. The letters."

"How far behind?"

"I don't know." I was embarrassed. I shouldn't have called. "I gotta go."

"Ox," he snapped. Crisp and clear. "How far?"

"Seven months."

"That fucking bastard," he said. He was angry.

"He didn't—"

"Don't, Ox. Just . . . don't."

"I was thinking."

"Oh boy."

"Could I . . . ?" My tongue felt heavy.

"Spit it out."

"Could I have a job?" I said in a rush. "It's just we need the money and I can't let her lose the house. It's all we have left. I'd do good, Gordo. I would good work and I'd work for you forever. It was going to happen anyway and can we just do it now? Can we just do it now? I'm sorry. I just need to do it now because I have to be the man now." My throat hurt. I wished I had something to drink, but I couldn't get my legs to move.

Gordo didn't say anything at first. Then, "I think that might be the most I've ever heard you talk at one time."

"I don't say much." Obviously.

"That right?" He sounded amused. "Here's what we're gonna do."

He gave my mom the money to get the mortgage caught back up. Said it would come out of the pay he'd give me under the table until I could legally work for him.

Mom cried. She said no, but then she realized she couldn't say no. So she cried and said yes and Gordo made her promise to tell him if it got bad again. I think she thought he hung the moon and might have tried to smile a little wider at him. Might have laughed lightly. Might have cocked her hips a bit.

She didn't know that I'd seen him once with another guy when I was six or so, holding his elbow lightly as they walked into the movies. Gordo had been laughing deeply and had stars in his eyes. I didn't think he'd be interested in my mom. I never saw the man with Gordo ever again. And I never saw Gordo with anyone else. I wanted to ask him, but there was a tightness around his eyes that didn't use to be there before and so I never did. People don't like to be reminded of sad things.

The threatening letters and phone calls stopped coming from the bank.

It only took six months to pay back Gordo. Or so he said. I didn't understand how money worked all that well, but it seemed like it should have taken longer than that. Gordo called us square and that was that.

I never really saw much of the money after that. Gordo told me he'd opened an account for me at the bank where it would accrue interest. I didn't know what *accrue interest* meant, but I trusted Gordo. "For a rainy day," he said.

I didn't like it when it rained.

.   .   .

I had a friend, once. His name was Jeremy and he wore glasses and smiled nervously at many things. We were nine years old. He liked comic books and drawing, and one day he gave me a picture he'd done of me as a superhero. I had a cape and everything. I thought it was the neatest thing I'd ever seen. Then Jeremy moved away to Florida, and when my mom and I looked up Florida on the map, it was on the other side of the country from where we lived in Oregon.

"People don't stay in Green Creek," she told me as my fingers touched roads on the map. "There's nothing here."

"We stayed," I said.

She looked away.

.   .   .

She was wrong. People *did* stay. Not a lot of them, but they did. She did. I did. Gordo did. People I went to school with, though they might leave eventually. Green Creek was dying, but it wasn't dead. We had a grocery store. The diner where she worked. A McDonald's. A one-screen movie theater that showed movies that came out in the seventies. A liquor store with bars on the windows. A wig store with mannequin heads in the windows, draped with red and black and yellow hair. Gordo's. A gas station. Two traffic lights. One school for all grades. All in the middle of the woods in the middle of the Cascade Mountains.

I didn't understand why people wanted to leave. To me, it was home.

. . .

We lived back off in the trees near the end of a dirt road. The house was blue. The trim was white. The paint peeled, but that didn't matter. In the summer, it smelled like grass and lilacs and thyme and pinecones. In the fall, the leaves crunched under my feet. In the winter, the smoke would rise from the chimney, mixing with the snow. In the spring, the birds would call out in the trees, and at night, an owl would ask *who, who, who* until the very early morning.

There was a house down the road from us at the end of the lane that I could see through the trees. My mom said it was empty, but sometimes there was a car or a truck parked out in front and lights on inside at night. It was a big house with many windows. I tried looking inside them, but they were always covered. Sometimes it would be months before I'd see another car outside.

"Who lived there?" I asked my dad when I was ten.

He grunted and opened another beer.

"Who lived there?" I asked my mom when she got home from work.

"I don't know," she said, touching my ear. "It was empty when we got here."

I never asked anyone else. I told myself it was because mystery was better than reality.

. . .

I never asked why we moved to Green Creek when I was three. I never asked if I had grandparents or cousins. It was always just the three of us until it was just the two of us.

. . .

"Do you think he'll come back?" I asked Gordo when I was fourteen.

"Damn fucking computers," Gordo muttered under his breath, pushing another button on the Nexiq that was attached to the car. "Everything has to be done with computers." He pressed another button and the machine beeped angrily at him. "Can't just go in and figure it out myself. No. Have to use *diagnostic codes* because everything is automated. Grandpap could just *listen* to the idle of the car and tell you what was wrong."

I took the Nexiq from his hands and tapped to the right screen. I pulled the code and handed it back to him. "Catalytic converter."

"I knew that," he said with a scowl.

"That's going to cost a lot."

"I know."

"Mr. Fordham can't afford it."

"I know."

"You're not going to charge him full price, are you." Because that was the kind of person Gordo was. He took care of others, even if he didn't want anyone to know.

He said, "No, Ox. He's not coming back. Get this up on the lift, okay?"

Mom sat at the kitchen table, a bunch of papers spread out around her. She looked sad.

I was nervous. "More bank stuff?" I asked.

She shook her head. "No."

"Well?"

"Ox. It's . . ." She picked up her pen and started to sign her name. She stopped before she finished the first letter. Put the pen back down. She looked up at me. "I'll do right by you."

"I know." Because I did.

She picked up the pen and signed her name. And then again. And again. And again.

She initialed a few times too.

When she was done, she said, "And that's that." She laughed and stood and took my hand and we danced in the kitchen to a song neither of us could hear. She left after a little while.

It was dark by the time I looked down at the papers on the table.

They were for a divorce.

She went back to her maiden name. Callaway.

She asked if I wanted to change mine too.

I told her no. I would make Matheson a good name.

She didn't think I saw her tears when I said that. But I did.

.   .   .

I sat in the cafeteria. It was loud. I couldn't concentrate. My head hurt.

A guy named Clint walked by my table with his friends.

I was by myself.

He said, "Fucking retard."

His friends laughed.

I got up and saw the look of fear in his eyes. I was bigger than him.

I turned and left, because my mom said I couldn't get in fights anymore.

Clint said something behind me and his friends laughed again.

I told myself that when I got friends, we wouldn't be mean like they were.

No one bothered me when I sat outside. It was almost nice. My sandwich was good.

.   .   .

Sometimes I walked in the woods. Things were clearer there.

The trees swayed in the breeze. Birds told me stories.

They didn't judge me.

One day, I picked up a stick and pretended it was a sword.

I hopped over a creek, but it was too wide and my feet got wet.

I lay on my back and looked at the sky through the trees while waiting for my socks to dry.

I dug my toes into the dirt.

A dragonfly landed on a rock near my head. It was green and blue. Its wings had blue veins. Its eyes were shiny and black. It flew away, and I wondered how long it would live.

Something moved off to my right. I looked over and heard a growl. I thought I should run, but I couldn't make my feet work. Or my hands. I didn't want to leave my socks behind.

So instead, I said, "Hello."

There was no response, but I knew something was there.

"I'm Ox. It's okay."

A huff of air. Like a sigh.

I told it that I liked the woods.

There was a flash of black, but then it was gone.

When I got home, I had leaves in my hair and there was a car parked in front of the empty house at the end of the lane.

It was gone the next day.

That winter, I left school and went to the diner. I was on break for Christmas. Three weeks of nothing but the shop ahead, and I was happy.

It started snowing again by the time I opened the door to Oasis. The bell rang out overhead. An inflatable palm tree was near the door. A papier-mâché sun hung from the ceiling. Four people sat at the counter drinking coffee. It smelled like grease. I loved it.

A waitress named Jenny snapped her gum and smiled at me. She was two grades above me. Sometimes, she smiled at me at school too. "Hey, Ox," she said.

"Hi."

"Cold out?"

I shrugged.

"Your nose is red," she said.

"Oh."

She laughed. "You hungry?"

"Yeah."

"Sit down. I'll get you some coffee and tell your mom you're here."

I did, at my booth near the back. It wasn't *really* my booth, but everyone knew it was.

"Maggie!" Jenny said back into the kitchen. "Ox is here." She winked at me as she took a plate of eggs and toast to Mr. Marsh, who flirted with a sly smile, even though he was eighty-four. Jenny giggled at him, and he ate his eggs. He put ketchup on them. I thought that was odd.

"Hey," Mom said, putting coffee down in front of me.

"Hi."

She ran her fingers through my hair, brushing off flecks of snow. They melted on my shoulders. "Tests go okay?"

"Think so."

"We study enough?"

"Maybe. I forgot who Stonewall Jackson was, though."

She sighed. "Ox."

"It's okay," I told her. "I got the rest."

"You promise?"

"Yes."

And she believed me because I didn't lie. "Hungry?"

"Yeah. Can I have—"

The bell rang overhead. And a man walked in. He seemed vaguely familiar, but I couldn't think of where I'd seen him before. He was Gordo's age and strong. And big. He had a full, light-colored beard. He brushed a hand over his shaved head. He closed his eyes and took a deep breath. He let it out slowly. He opened his eyes and I swear they flashed. But all I saw was blue again.

"Give me a second, Ox," Mom said. She went to talk to the man and I did my best to look away. He was a stranger, yes, but there was something else. I thought on it as I took a sip from my coffee.

He sat at the booth next to mine. We faced each other. He smiled briefly at me. It was a nice smile, bright and toothy. Mom handed him a menu and told him she'd be back. I could already see Jenny peeking out from the kitchen, watching the man. She pushed her boobs up, ran her fingers through her hair, and grabbed the coffee-pot. "I got this one," she muttered. Mom rolled her eyes.

She was charming. The man smiled at her politely. She touched his hand, just a slight scrape of her fingernails. He ordered soup. She laughed. He asked for cream and sugar for his coffee. She said her name was Jenny. He said he would like another napkin. She left the table looking slightly disappointed.

"Meal and a show," I muttered. The man grinned at me like he'd heard.

"Figure out what you want, kiddo?" Mom asked as she came back to the table.

"Burger."

"You got it, handsome."

I smiled because I adored her.

The man looked at my mom as she walked away. His nostrils flared. Looked back at me. Cocked his head. Nostrils flared again. Like he was . . . sniffing? Smelling?

I copied him and sniffed the air. It smelled the same to me. Like it always did.

The man laughed and shook his head. "It's nothing bad," he said. His voice was deep and kind. Those teeth flashed again.

"That's good," I said.

"I'm Mark."

"Ox."

An eyebrow went up. "That so?"

"Oxnard." I shrugged. "Everyone calls me Ox."

"Ox," he said. "Strong name."

"Strong like an ox?" I suggested.

He laughed. "Heard that a lot?"

"I guess."

He looked out the window. "I like it here." So much more was said in those words, but I couldn't even come close to grasping any of it.

"Me too. Mom said people don't stay here."

He said, "You're here," and it felt profound.

"I am."

"That your mom?" He nodded toward the kitchen.

"Yeah."

"She's here, then. Maybe *they* don't always stay here, but some do." He looked down at his hands. "And maybe they can come back."

"Like going home?" I asked.

That smile came back. "Yes, Ox. Like going home. That's . . . it smells like that here. Home."

"I smell bacon," I said sheepishly.

Mark laughed. "I know you do. There's a house. In the woods. Down off McCarthy. It's empty now."

"I know that house! I live right near it."

He nodded. "I thought you might. It explains why you sme—"

Jenny came back. Brought him his soup. He was polite again, nothing more. Not like he'd been with me.

I opened my mouth to ask him something (anything) when my mom came back out. "Let him eat," she scolded me as she placed the plate in front of me. "It's not nice to interrupt someone's dinner."

"But I—"

"He's okay," Mark said. "I was the one being intrusive."

Mom looked wary. "If you say so."

Mark nodded and ate his soup.

"You stay here until I'm off," Mom told me. "I don't want you walking home in this. It's only until six. Maybe we can watch a movie when we get home?"

"Okay. I promised Gordo I'd be at the shop early tomorrow."

"No rest for us, huh?" She kissed my forehead and left me to it.

I wanted to ask Mark more questions, but I remembered my manners. I ate my burger instead. It was slightly charred, just the way I liked it.

"Gordo?" Mark asked. It was almost a question, but also like he was trying out the name on his tongue. His smile was sad now.

"My boss. He owns the body shop."

"That right," Mark said. "Who would have thought?"

"Thought what?"

"Make sure you hold onto her," Mark said instead. "Your mom."

I looked up at him. He seemed sad. "It's just us two," I told him quietly, as if it were some great secret.

"Even more reason. Things will change, though. I think. For you and her. For all of us." He wiped his mouth and pulled out his wallet, pulling a folded bill out and leaving it on the table. He stood and pulled his coat back over his shoulders. Before he left, he looked down at me. "We'll see you soon, Ox."

"Who?"

"My family."

"The house?"

He nodded. "I think it's almost time to come home."

"Can we—" I stopped myself because I was just a kid.

"What, Ox?" He looked curious.

"Can we be friends when you come home? I don't have many of those." I didn't have any except for Gordo and my mom, but I didn't want to scare him away.

His hand tightened into a fist at his side. "Not many?" he asked.

"I speak too slow," I said, looking down at my hands. "Or I don't speak at all. People don't like that." Or me, but I had already said too much.

"There's nothing wrong with the way you speak."

"Maybe." If enough people said it, it had to be partially true.

"Ox, I'm going to tell you a secret. Okay?"

"Sure." I was excited because friends shared secrets so maybe that meant we were friends.

"It's always the ones who are the quietest who often have the greatest things to say. And yes, I think we'll be friends."

He left then.

I didn't see my friend again for seventeen months.

· · ·

That night as I lay in bed waiting for sleep, I heard a howl from deep in the woods. It rose like a song until I was sure it was all I could ever want to sing. It went on and on and all I could think of was *home, home, home*. Eventually, it fell away and so did I.

I told myself later it was just a dream.

. . .

"Here," Gordo said on my fifteenth birthday. He shoved a badly wrapped package into my hands. It had snowmen on it. Other guys from the shop were there. Rico. Tanner. Chris. All young and wide-eyed and alive. Friends of Gordo's who'd grown up with him in Green Creek. They were all grinning at me, waiting. Like they knew some big secret that I didn't.

"It's May," I said.

Gordo rolled his eyes. "Open the damn thing." He leaned back in his ratty chair behind the shop and took a deep drag on his cigarette. His tattoos looked brighter than they normally were. I wondered if he'd gotten them touched up recently.

I tore through the paper. It was loud. I wanted to savor it because I didn't get presents often, but I couldn't wait. It only took seconds, but it felt like forever.

"This," I said when I saw what it was. "This is . . ."

It was reverence. It was grace. It was beauty. I wondered if this meant I could finally breathe. Like I had found my place in this world I didn't understand.

Embroidered. Red. White. Blue. Two letters, stitched perfectly.

Ox, the work shirt read.

Like I mattered. Like I meant something. Like I was important.

Men don't cry. My daddy taught me that. Men don't cry because they don't have time to cry.

I must not have been a man yet because I cried. I bowed my head and cried.

Rico touched my shoulder.

Tanner rubbed a hand over my head.

Chris touched his work boot to mine.

They stood around me. Over me. Hiding me away should anyone stumble in and see the tears.

And Gordo put his forehead to mine and said, "You belong to us now."

Something bloomed within me and I was warm. It was like the sun had burst in my chest and I felt more alive than I had in a long time.

Later, they helped me put on the shirt. It fit perfectly.

.   .   .

I took a smoke break with Gordo that winter. "Can I have one?"

He shrugged. "Don't tell your ma." He opened the box and pulled a cigarette out for me. He held up the lighter and covered the flame against the wind. I took the cig between my lips and put it toward the fire. I inhaled. It burned. I coughed. My eyes watered and gray smoke came out my nose and mouth.

The second drag was easier.

The guys laughed. I thought maybe we were friends.

.   .   .

Sometimes I thought I was dreaming but then realized I was actually awake.

It was getting harder to wake up.

.   .   .

Gordo made me quit smoking four months later. He told me it was for my own good.

I told him it was because he didn't want me stealing his cigarettes anymore.

He cuffed the back of my head and told me to get to work.

I didn't smoke after that.

We were all still friends.

.   .   .

I asked him once about his tattoos.

The shapes. The patterns. Like there was a design. All bright colors and strange symbols that I thought should be familiar. Like it was on the tip of my tongue. I knew they went all the way up his arms. I didn't know how far they went beyond that.

He said, "Everyone has a past, Ox."

"Are they yours?"

He looked away. "Something like that."

I wondered if I would ever etch my past onto my skin in swirls and colors and shapes.

.   .   .

Two things happened on my sixteenth birthday.

I was officially hired at Gordo's. Had a business card and everything. Filled out tax forms that Gordo helped me with because I didn't understand them. I didn't cry that time. The guys patted me on the back and joked about how they no longer worked in a sweatshop with child labor. Gordo gave me a set of keys to the shop and smeared some grease on my face. I just grinned at him. I didn't think I'd ever seen him so happy.

I went home that afternoon and told myself I was a man now.

Then the second thing happened.

The empty house at the end of the lane was no longer empty and there was a boy on the dirt road in the woods.

TORNADO / SOAP BUBBLES

I walked down the road toward the house.

It was warm, so I took off my work shirt. I left the white tank top on. A breeze cooled my skin.

The keys to the shop were heavy in my pocket. I pulled them out and looked at them. I'd never had that many keys before. I felt responsible for something.

I put them back in my pocket. I didn't want to take the chance of losing them.

And then he said, "Hey! Hey there! You! Hey, guy!"

I looked up.

There was a boy standing in the dirt road, watching me. His nose was twitching and his eyes were wide. They were blue and bright. Short blond hair. Tanned skin, almost as much as mine. He was young and small and I wondered if I was dreaming again.

"Hello," I said.

"Who are you?" he asked.

"I'm Ox."

"Ox? Ox! Do you smell that?"

I sniffed the air. I didn't smell anything other than the woods. "I smell trees," I said.

He shook his head. "No, no, no. It's something *bigger*."

He walked toward me, his eyes going wider. Then he was running.

He wasn't big. He couldn't have been more than nine or ten. He collided with my legs, and I barely took a step back. He started climbing me, hooking his legs around my thighs and pulling himself up until his arms were around my neck and we were face to face. "It's you!"

I didn't know what was going on. "What's me?"

He was in my arms now. I didn't want him to fall. He took my face in his hands and squished my cheeks together. "Why do you smell like that?" he demanded. "Where did you come from? Do you live in the woods? What are you? We just got here. *Finally.* Where is your house?" He put his forehead against mine and inhaled deeply. "I don't get it!" he exclaimed. "What *is* it?" And then he was crawling up and over my shoulders, feet pressed against my chest and neck until he clambered onto my back, arms around my neck, chin hooked on my shoulder. "We have to go see my mom and dad," he said. "They'll know what this is. They know *everything*."

He was a tornado of fingers and feet and words. I was caught in the storm.

His hands were in my hair, pulling my head back as he said he lived in the house at the end of the lane. That they had just arrived today. That he had moved from far away. He was sad to leave his friends behind. He was ten. He hoped to be big like me when he grew up. Did I like comic books? Did I like mashed potatoes? What was Gordo's? Did I get to work on Ferraris? Did I ever blow up any cars? He wanted to be an astronaut. Or an archeologist. But he couldn't be those things because one day he'd have to be a leader instead. He stopped talking for a little while after he said that.

His knees dug into my sides. His hands wrapped around my neck. The sheer weight of him was almost too much for me to take.

We came upon my house. He made me stop so he could look at it. He didn't get down from my back. Instead, I hitched him up higher so he could see.

"Do you have your own room?" he asked.

"Yes. It's just me and my mom now."

He was quiet. Then, "I'm sorry."

We'd just met. He had nothing to apologize for. "For?"

"For whatever just made you sad." Like he knew what I was thinking. Like he knew how I felt. Like he was here and real.

"I dream," I said. "Sometimes it feels like I'm awake. And then I'm not."

And he said, "You're awake now. Ox, Ox, Ox. Don't you see?"

"See what?"

He whispered, as if saying it any louder would make it untrue, "*We live so close to each other.*"

We turned toward the house at the end of the lane.

The afternoon was waning. The shadows were stretching. We walked among the trees, and up ahead, there were lights. Bright lights. A beacon calling someone home.

Three cars. One SUV. Two trucks. All were less than a year old. All had Maine license plates. Two thirty-foot moving trucks.

And the people. All standing. Watching. Waiting. Like they knew we were coming. Like they'd heard us from far away.

Two were kids. One was my age, the other maybe a little younger. They were blond and smaller than me, but not by much. Blue eyes and curious expressions. They looked like the tornado on my back.

There was a woman. Older. The same coloring as the others. She held herself regally, and I wondered if I'd ever seen anyone more beautiful. Her eyes were kind but cautious. She was tense, like she was ready to move at any moment.

A man stood next to her. He was darker than the rest, more like me than the others. He was fierce and foreboding and all I could think was *respect, respect, respect*, though I'd never seen him before. His hand was on the woman's back.

And next to them was . . . oh.

"Mark?" I said. He looked exactly the same.

Mark grinned. "Ox. How lovely to see you again. I see you've made a new friend." He looked pleased.

The boy on my back wriggled his way down. I let his legs go and he dropped behind me. He grabbed my hand and started pulling me toward the beautiful people like I had a right to be there.

He started spinning his storm again, voice rising up and down, words forcefully punctuated without pattern. "Mom! *Mom*. You have to *smell* him! It's like . . . *like* . . . I don't even know what it's like! I was walking in the woods to scope out our territory so I could be like Dad and then it was like . . . *whoa*. And then he was all standing there and he didn't see me at first because I'm getting *so* good at hunting. I was all like *rawr* and *grr* but then I *smelled* it again and it was *him* and it was all *kaboom*! I don't even know! I don't even know! You gotta *smell* him and then tell me why it's all candy canes and pinecones and epic and *awesome*."

They all stared at him as if they'd come across something unexpected. Mark had a secret smile on his face, hidden by his hand.

"Is that so?" the woman finally said. Her voice wavered like it was a fragile thing. "*Rawr* and *grr* and *kaboom*?"

"And the *smells*!" he cried.

"Can't forget about those," the man next to her said faintly. "Candy canes and pinecones and epic and awesome."

"Didn't I tell you?" Mark said to them. "Ox is . . . different."

I had no idea what was going on. But that wasn't anything new. I wondered if I'd done something wrong. I felt bad.

I tried to pull my hand away, but the kid wouldn't let go. "Hey," I said to him.

He looked back at me, blue eyes wide. "Ox," he said. "Ox, I have *got* to show you stuff!"

"What stuff?"

"Like . . . I don't . . ." He was sputtering. "Like *everything*."

"You just got here," I said. I felt out of place. "Don't you need to . . . ?" I didn't know what I was trying to say. My words were failing me. This is why I didn't talk. It was easier.

"Joe," the man said. "Give Ox a moment, okay?"

"But *Dad*—"

"Joseph." It almost sounded like a growl.

The boy (*Joe*, I thought, *Joseph*) sighed and dropped my hand. I took a step back. "I'm sorry," I said. "He was just *there* and I didn't mean anything."

"It's okay, Ox," Mark said, taking a step down from the porch. "These things can be a bit . . . much."

"What things?" I asked.

He shrugged. "Life."

"You said we could be friends."

"I did. It took us a bit longer to come back than I thought it would." Behind him, the woman bowed her head and the man looked away. Joe's hand slowly slid back into mine, and it was then I knew they'd lost something, though I didn't know what. Or even how I knew.

"That's Joe," Mark said, pushing through. "But I think you know that already."

"Maybe," I said. "Didn't get his name. He was talking too much."

Everyone looked at me again.

"I wasn't talking too much," Joe grumbled. "*You* talk too much. With your face." But he didn't leave my side. He kicked the dirt with his sneakers. One of his shoes was about to become untied. There was a ladybug on a dandelion, red and black and yellow. A breeze came and it flew away.

"Joe," I said, trying out the name.

He grinned as he looked up at me. "Hi, Ox. Ox! There's something I—" He cut himself off, sneaking a glance up at his father before he sighed again. "Fine," he said, and I didn't know who he was talking to.

"Those are his brothers," Mark said. "Carter." The one my age. He grinned at me and waved. "Kelly." The younger of the two. Somewhere between Carter and Joe. He nodded at me, looking a little bored.

That left two others. They didn't scare me, but it felt like they should. I waited for Mark, but he kept quiet. Eventually, the woman said, "You're an odd one, Ox."

"Yes, ma'am," I said, because my mom taught me respect.

She laughed. I thought it beautiful. "I'm Elizabeth Bennett. This is my husband, Thomas. You already know his brother, Mark. It looks as if we're to be neighbors."

"Pleased to make your acquaintance," I said, because my mom taught me manners.

"What about *my* acquaintance?" Joe asked me, pulling on my hand.

I looked down at him. "Yours too."

That smile returned.

"Would you like to stay for dinner?" Thomas asked, watching me carefully.

I thought *yes* and *no* at the same time. It made my head hurt. "Mom's coming home soon. We're eating dinner together tonight because it's my birthday." I winced. I hadn't meant to say that.

Joe gasped. "*What*? Why didn't you tell me! Mom! It's his *birthday!*"

She sounded amused when she said, "I'm standing right here, Joe. I heard. Happy birthday, Ox. How old are you now?"

"Sixteen." They were all still staring at me. There was sweat on the back of my neck. The air was hot.

"Cool," Carter said. "Me too."

Joe glared at him, baring his teeth. "I found him first." He stood in front of me, as if blocking Carter from me.

"That's enough," his father said, his voice a bit deeper.

"But . . . but—"

"Hey," I said to Joe.

He looked up at me with frustrated eyes.

"It's okay," I said. "Listen to your dad."

He sighed and nodded, squeezing my hand again. His shoelace came untied as he kicked the dandelion.

"I'm ten," he muttered finally. "And I know you're old, but I found you first so you have to be my friend first. Sorry, Dad."

And then he said, "I just want to get you a present," so I said, "You already did," and I didn't think I'd ever seen a smile as bright as his at that moment.

I said good-bye then and I knew they watched me as I walked away.

.   .   .

"People moved in?" Mom asked me when she got home.

"Yeah. The Bennetts."

"You met them?" She sounded surprised. She knew I didn't talk to people if I could get away with it.

"Yeah."

She waited. "Well?"

I looked up from my history book. Finals were next week and I had tests I wasn't ready for. "Well?"

She rolled her eyes. "Are they *nice*?"

"I think so. They have . . ." I thought on what they had.

"What?"

"Kids. One's my age. The others are younger."

"What's that smile for?"

"A tornado," I said without meaning to.

She kissed my hair. "And here I thought you being older would mean you'd make more sense. Happy birthday, Ox."

We ate dinner that night. Meatloaf. My favorite, just for me. We laughed together. It was something we hadn't done in a while.

She gave me a present wrapped in Sunday comics from the newspaper. A 1940 Buick shop manual, old and worn. The cover was orange. It was musty and wonderful. She said she saw it at Goodwill and thought of me.

There were some new pants for work. My others were starting to fall apart.

There was a card too. A wolf on the front, howling at the moon. Inside, a joke. *What do you call a lost wolf? A where-wolf!* Underneath she'd written seven words: *This year will be better. Love, Mom.* She drew hearts around the word *love*, little wispy things that I thought could float away if they but caught on my breath.

We washed the dishes as her old radio played from the open window above the sink. She sang along quietly as she splashed me with water, and I wondered why I smelled like candy canes and pinecones. Of awesome and epic.

There was a soap bubble on her nose.

She said I had one on my ear.

I took her by the hand and spun her in a circle as the music picked up. Her eyes were bright and she said, "You're going to make someone very happy someday. And I can't wait to see it happen."

I went to bed and saw the lights on in the house at the end of the lane through my window. I wondered about them. The Bennetts.

Someone, my mother had said. *Make* someone *very happy.*

Not a *her*. But *someone*.

I closed my eyes and slept. I dreamt of tornadoes.

WOLF OF STONE / DINAH SHORE

Rico said, "Looking good, papi," when I came to work the next day. "What's got you going with that spring in your step?"

It was Sunday, the Lord's Day as I was taught, but I figured the Lord was okay with me coming to this house of worship instead of one of his. I'd learned my faith at Gordo's.

"Must be some pretty girl," Tanner called from where he was bent over some ridiculous SUV that could be turned on by the sound of your voice. "He's a real man, now. You get some sixteen-year-old strange last night?"

I was used to the crude. They meant no harm. That didn't stop me from flushing furiously. "No," I said. "No, it's not like that."

"Oh," Rico said, slinking over to me, hips rolling so obscenely. "Look at that *blush*." He ran his hand through my hair, his thumb against my ear. "She pretty, papi?"

"There's no girl."

"Oh? A boy, then? We don't discriminate here at the Casa de Gordo."

I pushed him off and he laughed and laughed.

"Chris?" I asked.

"Seeing the moms," Tanner said. "Stomach thing again."

"She okay?"

Rico shrugged. "Maybe. Don't know yet."

"Ox!" Gordo shouted from the office. "Get your ass in here!"

"*Oye*," Rico said with a small smile. "Careful there, papi. Someone's in a mood today."

And he sounded like it. Voice strained and harsh. I worried. Not for me. For him.

"He's just pissed off because Ox needs the next week off for school," Tanner muttered. "You know how he gets when Ox isn't here."

I felt awful. "Maybe I could—"

"You hush that mouth of yours," Rico said, pressing his fingers against my lips. I could taste oil. "You need to focus on school and Gordo can just deal with it. Education is more important than his little bitch-fests. We clear?"

I nodded and he dropped his fingers.

"We'll be fine," Tanner said. "Just get through your tests and we'll have the whole summer, okay?"

"Ox!"

Rico muttered something in Spanish that sounded like he was calling Gordo a fucking dickhead dictator. I'd learned I was adept at picking up curses in Spanish.

I walked to the back of the shop, where Gordo was sitting in his office. His brow was lined as he did his one-finger typing thing. Tanner called it his hunt-and-pecker. Gordo didn't think that was funny.

"Close the door," he said, without looking up at me.

I did and sat in the empty seat on the other side of his desk.

He didn't say anything, so I figured it was up to me to start. Gordo was like that sometimes. "You okay?"

He scowled at the computer screen. "I'm fine."

"Awfully twitchy for fine."

"You're not funny, Ox."

I shrugged. That was okay. I knew that about myself.

He sighed and ran a hand over his face. "Sorry," he muttered.

"Okay."

He finally looked up at me. "I don't want you here next week."

I tried keeping the hurt from my face, but I don't think I did very well. "Okay."

He looked stricken. "Oh, Jesus, Ox, not like that. You have your finals next week."

"I know."

"And you know part of the deal with your ma is that your grades don't suffer or else you can't work here."

"I *know*." I was annoyed and it showed.

"I don't want . . . just . . ." He groaned and sat back in the chair. "I suck at this."

"What?"

He motioned between the two of us. "This whole *thing*."

"You do okay," I said quietly. This *thing*. My brother or father. We didn't say it. We didn't have to. We both knew what it was. It was just easier to be awkward about it. Because we were men.

He narrowed his eyes. "Yeah?"

"Yeah."

"How are the grades?"

"Bs. One C."

"History?"

"Yeah. Fucking Stonewall Jackson."

He laughed, long and loud. Gordo always did laugh big, rare as it was. "Don't let your ma hear you say that."

"Never in your life."

"Full-time this summer?"

I grinned at him. I couldn't wait for the long days. "Yeah. Sure, Gordo."

"I'm gonna work your ass off, Ox." The lines on his forehead smoothed out.

"Can I . . . can I still stop by next week?" I asked. "I won't . . . I just . . ." Words. Words were my enemy. How to say that here was where I felt the safest. Here was where I felt most at home. Here was where I wouldn't be judged. I wasn't a fucking retard here. I wasn't a waste of space or time. I wanted to say so much, *too* much, and found I couldn't really say anything at all.

But it was Gordo, so I didn't have to. He looked relieved, though he kept his voice stern for appearances. "No working in the shop. You come in here and you study. No dicking around. I mean it, Ox. Chris or Tanner can help you with fucking Stonewall Jackson. They know that shit better than me. Don't ask Rico. You won't get anything done."

The tightness loosened in my chest. "Thanks, Gordo."

He rolled his eyes. "Get out of here. You have work to do."

I saluted him, which I knew he hated.

And since I was in such a good mood, I pretended not to hear him when he muttered, "I'm proud of you, kiddo."

Later I'd remember I forgot to tell him about the Bennetts.

.   .   .

I walked home. The sunlight filtered through the trees, little shadows of leaves on my skin. I wondered how old the forest here was. I thought it ancient.

Joe was waiting for me at the dirt road where he'd been the day before. His eyes were wide as he fidgeted. His hands were hidden behind his back. "I knew it was you!" he said. His voice was pitched high and triumphant. "I'm getting better at—" He cut himself off with a cough. "Uh. At doing stuff. Like . . . knowing . . . you are . . . there."

"That's good," I told him. "Getting better is always good."

His smile was dazzling. "I'm always getting better. I'll be the leader, one day."

"Of what?"

His eyes went wide again. "Oh crap."

"What?"

"Uh. Presents!"

I frowned. "Presents?"

"Well, *a* present."

"For what?"

"You?" He squinted at me. "You." He blushed fiercely. It was splotchy and went up to his hairline. He looked at the ground. "For your birthday," he mumbled.

The guys had gotten me presents. My mom had. No one else ever really did. It was something friends did. Or family. "Oh," I said. "Wow."

"Yeah. Wow."

"Is that what you're hiding?"

He blushed harder and wouldn't look at me. He nodded once.

I could hear birds above us. They called out long and loud.

I gave him the time he needed. It didn't take long. I could see the resolve flood into him, steeling his shoulders. Holding his head high. Marching forward. I didn't know what he'd be a leader of one day, but he would be good. I hoped he would remember to be kind.

He held out his hand. He had a black box with a little blue ribbon wrapped around it.

I was nervous for some reason. "I don't have anything for you," I said quietly.

He shrugged. "It's not my birthday."

"When is it?"

"August. What are you even—*geez*. Take the box!"

I did. It was heavier than I thought it would be. I put my work shirt over my shoulder and he stood close. He took a deep breath and closed his eyes.

I untied the ribbon and remembered a dress my mother had worn once on a picnic in the summer when I turned nine. It'd had little ribbons tied in bows along the edges and she had laughed as she handed me a sandwich and some potato salad. After, we lay on our backs and I pointed out shapes in clouds and she said, "Days like this are my favorite," and I said, "Me too." She never wore the dress again. I asked her about it one day. She said it'd accidentally gotten ripped. "He didn't mean it," she said. I'd felt a great and terrible rage then that I didn't know what to do with. Eventually, it went away.

And now this ribbon. I held it in my hand. It was warm.

"Sometimes people are sad," Joe said, leaning his forehead against my arm. A whine sounded like it came from the back of his throat. "And I don't know how to make it go away. It's all I ever wanted. To make it go away."

I opened the box. There was a black felt cloth carefully tucked and folded inside. It felt like a great secret lay hidden underneath and I wanted to know it more than anything else in my life.

I unfolded the cloth and inside was a wolf made of stone.

The detail felt miraculous on such a small and heavy thing. The bushy tail curled around the wolf as it sat on its haunches. The triangular ears that I thought should be twitching. The individual paws, sharp toenails, and black pads. The tilt of the head, exposing the neck. Eyes closed, snout pointed up as the wolf howled a song I could hear in my head. The stone was dark and I wondered briefly what color it would be in real life. If it'd have white spots on its legs. If its ears would be black.

The birds had stopped singing overhead and I wondered if it were possible for the world to hold its breath. I wondered at the weight of expectations.

I wondered many things.

I picked up the wolf. It fit perfectly in my hand.

"Joe." I sounded gruff.

"Yeah?"

"You . . . this is for me?"

"Yeah?" Like it was a question. Then, more sure, "Yeah."

I was going to tell him it was too much. That he needed to take it back. That there was nothing I could ever give him that would be so beautiful because the only things I had that were beautiful were not mine to give away. My mother. Gordo. Rico, Tanner, and Chris. They were the only beautiful things I had.

But he was waiting for that. I could see it. He was waiting for me to say no. To give it back, to tell him I couldn't accept it. His hands were twitching and his knees were shaking. He was pale and he gnawed on his lip. I didn't know what else to say, so I said, "It's probably the nicest thing anyone has ever given me. Thank you."

"Really?" he croaked.

"Really."

And then he laughed. His head rocked back and he laughed and the birds came back and laughed right along with him.

. . .

That day was the first time I went inside the house at the end of the lane. Joe took me by the hand and talked and talked and walked and walked. He didn't even pause as we came up to my house. We passed it right on by without a single stutter to our steps.

The moving trucks were gone from the front of the bigger house. The front door was open, and I could hear music coming from inside.

I came to a stop as Joe tried to pull me up to the porch.

"What are you doing?" Joe demanded in that way I already recognized.

I didn't quite know. It felt rude to just walk into someone's house. I knew my manners. But even the bottoms of my feet were itching to take a step and another and another. I was often at war with myself over the little things. What was right and wrong. What was acceptable and what wasn't. What my place was and if I belonged.

I felt small. They were rich. The cars. The house. Even through the windows I could see nice things like dark leather couches and wooden furniture that had no scuffs or cracks. Everything was sweet and clean and so wonderful to look at. I was Oxnard Matheson. My fingernails were gritty and black. My clothes were streaked with grime. My boots were scuffed. I didn't have much common sense, and if my daddy was to be believed, I didn't have much in the way of anything else. My head didn't know its way out of my heart and I was poor. We weren't on-the-county poor, but it was close. I couldn't bear the thought that this was charity.

And I didn't know them. The Bennetts. Mark was my friend, and maybe Joe too, but I didn't know them at all.

But then Joe said, "It's okay, Ox," and I said, "How did you know?"

He said, "Because I wouldn't have given my wolf to just anyone."
He blushed again and looked away.

And I felt I'd missed something greater than his words.

.   .   .

Elizabeth was singing along with an old Dinah Shore song that spun
on an ancient record player. It was scratchy and the song bumped
and skipped, but she knew the exact places it did and would pick up
the song right where it began again. "I don't mind being lonely," she
sang in a breathy voice, "when my heart tells me you are lonely too."

My God, I ached.

She moved about the kitchen, her summer dress spinning around
her, light and airy.

The kitchen was lovely. All stone and dark wood. It'd been recently cleaned and everything shone as if brand new.

I could hear the others moving around out in the backyard. They
laughed and I felt almost at ease.

Dinah Shore stopped being lonely and Elizabeth looked over at
us. "Do you like that song?" she asked me.

I nodded. "It hurts, but in a good way."

"It's about staying behind," she said. "When others go to war."

"Staying behind or getting left behind?" I asked, thinking of my
father. Elizabeth and Joe stilled, their heads cocked at me almost in
the same way.

"Oh, Ox," she said, and Joe took my hand back in his. "There's a
difference."

"Sometimes."

"You're staying for Sunday dinner," she said. "It's tradition."

I didn't have many traditions. "I wouldn't want to bother anyone."

She said, "I see you opened your gift," like I hadn't spoken at all.

Joe grinned at her. "He *loved* it!"

"I told you he would." She looked back at me. "He was so worried."

Dinah Shore picked up again in the background as Elizabeth began
to cut a cucumber into thin slices.

Joe flushed. "No, I wasn't."

Carter came in through the back door. "Yes, you were." His voice
went high and fluttery. "What if he *hates* it? What if it's not *cool*
enough? What if he thinks I'm a *loser*?"

Joe scowled at him and I thought I heard a rumble come from deep inside him. "Shut *up*, Carter!"

"Boys," Elizabeth warned.

Carter rolled his eyes. "Hey, Ox. Do you have an Xbox?"

Joe laughed. "Ha! Rhymes. Ox and Xbox." He let go of my hand and began to pull silverware from a drawer near the stove.

I rubbed the hand against the back of my head. "Uh. No? I think I have a Sega."

"Dude. Retro."

I shrugged. "Don't have much time for it."

"We'll make time," he said. He took plastic cups down from a cupboard. "I need to ask you about school, anyway. Kelly and I will be starting up with you next year."

"I wish I could go," Joe grumbled.

"You know the rule," Elizabeth said. "Homeschooled until you're twelve. It's only one more year, baby."

This did nothing to ease his mind. But I'd never been homeschooled before, and I didn't know if it was a good thing or a bad thing.

"Ox, invite your mother, would you?" Elizabeth asked as she spun back and forth between the countertops. Back and forth.

"She's at work," I said, unsure of what I should be doing. They all moved like they'd lived here forever. I was the elephant in the room. Or the Ox. I wasn't sure which.

"Next time, then," she said, as if there would *be* a next time.

"Because it's tradition?"

She smiled at me and I saw Joe in her. "Exactly. You catch on fast."

I was suddenly very aware of my appearance. "I'm not exactly dressed for this." I brushed a hand through my hair and remembered my fingers were dirty.

She waved a hand at me. "We're not formal, Ox."

"I'm dirty."

"Well-worn, more like. Take this out back, would you? Thomas and Mark will be glad to see you." She handed me a bowl of fruit and I held it along with the box that carried the stone wolf. Joe tried to follow me out, but she stopped him. "You stay here with me for now. I need help. Ox, away with you."

"But *Mom*—"

I walked through the back door. A large table had been set up in the grass. It was covered in a red tablecloth held down by old books set on the corners. Kelly was unfolding chairs around the table. "All right, then?" he asked me as I set the fruit down.

"Things happen . . . fast here," I said.

He laughed. "You don't know the half of it." And as if proving my point, "Dad wants to talk to you."

"Oh. About what?" I tried to think back if I'd done something wrong already. I couldn't remember everything I'd said yesterday. It wasn't much. Maybe that was the problem.

"It's okay, Ox. He's not as scary as he looks."

"Liar."

"Well, *yeah*. But it's good you know that already. It'll make things easier." He suddenly laughed, as if he'd heard something funny. "Yeah, yeah, yeah," he said, waving his hand at me.

They were grilling, Mark and Thomas. I wanted desperately to go stand by them. Shoot the shit. Talk like I belonged. I gathered up my courage.

Only to have Mark turn and walk toward me. "We'll talk later," Mark said, squeezing my shoulder before I could say anything. He left me with Thomas. Thomas had at least three inches on me and maybe forty pounds in his chest and arms and legs. I was bigger than most, even at sixteen, but Thomas was bigger still.

He eyed the box in my hand. "Joe tied the ribbon himself," he said. "Wouldn't let anyone else help."

Honesty, maybe. "I almost told him I couldn't take it."

An eyebrow rose. "Why is that?"

"It seems . . . precious."

"It is."

"Then why?"

"Why what?"

"Why would he give it to me?"

Maddeningly, "Why not?"

"I don't have precious things."

"I understand you live with your mother."

"Yes." And then I knew what he meant. "Oh."

"We're all allowed to have certain things that are just ours." He motioned for Kelly to come to the grill. "Walk with me, Ox."

I followed him. He led me away from the house. Into the trees. A man I'd met only the day before. And yet I felt no hesitation. I told myself it was because I was starved for the attention and nothing more.

"We used to live here," he said. "Before you. Carter was only two when we left. It wasn't meant to be for as long as it was. That's what is so funny about life. And so scary. It gets in the way and then one day, you open your eyes and a decade has passed. Even more." He reached out and brushed his hands along score marks in the trunk of a tree. His fingers fit them almost perfectly and I wondered what could have caused such scrapes. They looked like claw marks.

"Why did you leave?" I asked, though it was not my place.

"Duty called. Responsibilities that couldn't be ignored, no matter how hard we tried. My family has lived in these woods for a very long time."

"It must be good to be home."

"It is," he said. "Mark kept an eye out every now and then, but it wasn't the same as touching the trees myself. He's quite taken with you, you know."

"Mark?"

"Sure. Him too. You think you hide, Ox, but you give so much away. The expressions on your face. The breaths you take. Your heartbeat."

"I try not to."

"I know, but I can't figure out *why*. Why do you hide?"

Because it was easier. Because I'd done it for as long as I could remember. Because it was safer than being out in the sun and letting people in. It was better to hide and wonder than reveal and know the truth.

I could have said that. I think I had the capacity and I could have found the words. They would have come out in a stutter, halted and choked and bitter, but I could have forced them out.

Instead, I said nothing.

Thomas smiled quietly at me. He closed his eyes and turned his face up toward the sun. "It's different here than anywhere else," he said, inhaling deeply.

"Mark said that when we met. About the smells of home."

"Did he? In the diner?"

"He told you?"

Thomas smiled. It was nice, but it showed too many teeth. "He did. He seemed to think you were a kindred spirit. And then what you did with Joe."

I was alarmed. I took a step back. "What did I do? Is he okay? I'm sorry. I didn't—"

"Ox." His voice was deep. Deeper than before, and when his hands came down on my shoulders, it felt like a command, and I relaxed even before I knew it was happening. The tension left like it had never been there at all and I tilted my head back slightly, like I was exposing my neck. Even Thomas seemed surprised. "What is your last name?" he asked.

"Matheson." There was an undercurrent of panic, but his voice was still deep and his hand still on my shoulders and the panic wouldn't bubble toward the surface.

He opened his mouth to speak but then closed it again. Then each word came, deliberate and careful. "Yesterday, when Joe found you. Who spoke first?"

"He did. He asked if I smelled something." I wanted to take the stone wolf out of the box and look at it again.

Thomas stepped back, dropping his hands. He shook his head. There was a small smile on his face that looked almost like wonder. "Mark said you were different. In a good way."

"I'm not anyone," I said.

"Ox, before yesterday, we hadn't heard Joe speak in fifteen months."

The trees and the birds and the sun all fell away and I was cold. "Why?"

Thomas smiled sadly. "Because of life and all its horrors. The world can be a terrible place."

. . .

It can be. The world. Terrible and chaotic and wonderful.

People could be cruel.

I heard it when people called me names behind my back.

I heard it when they said the same things to my face.

I heard it in the sound the door made when my father left.

I heard it in the crack of my mother's voice.

Thomas didn't tell me why Joe stopped talking. I didn't ask. It wasn't my place.

People could be cruel.

They could be beautiful, but they could be cruel too.

It's like something so lovely can't just *be* lovely. It also has to be harsh and corroding. It's a complexity I didn't understand.

I didn't see the cruelty when I sat down at their table the first time. Mark sat to my left, Joe to my right. The food was dished but nobody lifted a fork or spoon, so I didn't either. All eyes were on Thomas, who sat at the head of the table. The breeze was warm. He smiled at each of us and took a bite.

The rest of us followed.

I kept the box with the wolf of stone in my lap.

And Joe. Joe just said things like *I like it when things blow up in movies like* boom *and stuff* and *What do you think happens when you fart on the moon?* and *One time, I ate fourteen tacos because Carter dared me to and I couldn't move for two whole days.*

He said:

Maine was Maine. I miss my friends but I have you now.

That's not even funny! I'm not *laughing!*

Can you pass me the mustard before Kelly uses it all like a jerk?

He said:

One time, we went to the mountains and went sledding.

I suck at video games, but Carter said I'll get better.

I bet I can run faster than you.

He said:

Can I tell you a secret?

Sometimes I have nightmares and I can't remember them.

Sometimes I can remember all of them.

The table went quiet, but Joe only had eyes for me.

I said, "I have bad dreams too. But then I remember I'm awake and that the bad dreams can't follow me when I'm awake. And then I feel better."

"Okay," he said. "Okay."

. . . .

I passed all my finals. Fuck Stonewall Jackson.

PRETTY BOY / FUCK OFF

My mother met the Bennetts halfway through summer at one of the Sunday dinners. She was nervous, like I'd been. She ran her hands along her dress, smoothing it out. She curled her finger in her hair. She said, "They seem so fancy," and I laughed because they were and they weren't.

My mom smiled anxiously when Elizabeth hugged her. Later, they were in the kitchen drinking wine and Mom giggled, her face a little flushed with drink and happiness.

. . .

Thomas worked from home. I never understood what he did exactly, but he was always on the phone in his office late at night, calling people in Japan or Australia, and always early in the morning with New York and Chicago.

"Finances," Carter told me with a shrug. "Money something something blah blah boring. You can't die on this level, Ox. It's too easy."

. . .

Elizabeth painted. She said that summer she was in her green phase. Everything was green. She'd spin a record on the old Crosley and say things like "Today, today, today" and "Sometimes, I wonder," and then she'd begin. It was always a controlled chaos and every now and then she'd have paint in her eyebrows and a smile on her face.

"Apparently she's good," Kelly told me. "Has shit hanging in museums. Don't tell her I said this, but I think it all looks the same. I mean, I can splash paint on a canvas too. Where's my money and fame?"

. . .

I walked down the dirt road after work and Joe was waiting for me. "Hey, Ox," he said, and he smiled so very, very big.

. . .

Sometimes they had days when I wasn't allowed to go over. Two or three or four days in a row. "It's family time, Ox," Elizabeth would say. Or, "We're keeping the kids in tonight, Ox," Thomas would say. "Come back on Tuesday, okay?"

I understood, because I was not part of their family. I didn't know what I was to them, but I forced the hurt away. I didn't need it. I had too many of my own to add more on top. They didn't mean it in a bad way, I didn't think. I'd find Joe waiting for me on the road a few days later and he'd hug me and say, "I missed you," and I'd follow him home and Elizabeth always said, "There's our Ox," and Thomas always said, "You all right?" Then it would be like nothing had happened at all.

I'd lie in bed those nights, lost in my thoughts, hearing far-off sounds I would have sworn were wolves howling. The moon would be fat and full and would light up the room as if it were the sun.

They never came inside my house. I never asked and neither did they. I never really thought about it.

"You still cutting out early today?" Gordo asked me one humid day toward the end of August.

I looked up from the alternator repair I was doing. "Yeah. Registration. Already." I'd brought a change of clothes so I didn't go stinking of metal and oil.

"Your ma's working?"

"Yeah."

"You want me to go with?"

I shook my head. "I got this."

"Junior year. It's tough."

I rolled my eyes. "Shut up, Gordo."

"You going to take that pretty boy with you, papi?" Rico shouted from across the shop.

I flushed, even though it was nothing.

Gordo's eyes narrowed. "What pretty boy?"

"Our big boy has got himself some prime real estate," Rico said. "Tanner saw them out a couple of nights ago."

I groaned. "That's just Carter."

"*Carter,*" Tanner sighed, his voice all breathy.

"Carter?" Gordo asked. "Who is he? I want to meet him. In my office so I can scare the shit out of him. Goddammit, Ox. You better be using fucking condoms."

"Yeah," Chris said. "Make sure you get the fucking condoms instead of the regular ones. They're better. For the fucking."

"Ba-*zing!*" Rico cried.

"I hate all of you," I muttered.

"That's a lie right there," Tanner said. "You love us. We bring you joy and happiness."

"So you're fucking him, then?" Gordo said with a scowl.

"Jesus, Gordo. No. We were getting pizza to take back to his little brothers. We're friends. They just moved here. I'm not into him like that." Though I didn't think it would be that hard to be. I did have eyes, after all.

"How'd you meet him?"

Nosy bastard. "They moved into the old house next to ours. Or back into the house. I don't know quite which yet. The Bennetts. Heard of them?"

And then a funny thing happened. I'd seen Gordo pissed off. I'd seen him laugh so hard he pissed himself a little. I'd seen him upset. I'd seen him sad.

I'd never seen him scared. Of anything.

Gordo didn't get scared. Never once since I'd first met him when my daddy took me to the shop one day and Gordo had said, "Hey, guy, heard a lot about you. What say you and me go get a pop out of the machine?" Never once. If asked, I would have said Gordo didn't get scared at all, even if I knew how ridiculous that sounded.

But Gordo was scared now. Eyes wide, blood draining from his face. It lasted ten seconds. Maybe fifteen or twenty. And then it was gone like it'd never been there at all.

But I'd seen it.

"Gordo—"

He turned and walked into his office, slamming the door behind him.

"What the fuck?" Rico asked succinctly.

"Jealous prig," Tanner muttered.

"Shut the fuck up, Tanner," Chris warned, glancing over at me.

I just stared at the closed door.

.   .   .

"I'm sorry," I told Gordo later. "For whatever I did."

He sighed. "It's not on you, kiddo. I need . . . Can you find different friends? Why aren't we enough?" He sounded miserable.

"It's not the same."

"You need to be careful."

"Why?"

"Forget it, Ox. Just watch yourself."

.   .   .

"Got a strange call from Gordo," Mom said one night.

"What?"

"Wanted me to keep you away from next door."

"*What?*"

She looked confused. "Said they were bad news."

"Mom—"

"I told him to leave it alone."

"Something crawled up his ass," I said.

She frowned. "Watch your mouth. You're not at the shop."

.   .   .

I burst through the office door. "What the hell is your problem?"

"You'll thank me one day," he said. He didn't look away from the computer. Like he didn't have the fucking time of day.

"Too bad she doesn't give a shit what you think. She said I'm old enough to make my own choices."

That got his attention. He was pissed.

I stormed out.

.   .   .

He wanted to drive me home every day after work. I laughed and told him to fuck off.

.   .   .

"Ox! Look how many french fries I can fit in my mouth!" Joe then proceeded to shove at least thirty into that gaping maw, making little snarly sounds as he did.

"Gross," Carter groaned. "This is why you don't get to go out in public."

Kelly snorted. "You're just trying to impress the waitress."

Carter punched him on the shoulder. "She's *hot*. She go to our school, Ox?"

"Think so. Senior."

"I am so going to hit that this year."

"Ah, the joys of young love," Mark sighed. "Joe, don't put french fries up your nose."

"*Hit* that?" Kelly asked, incredulous. "Dude. Gross."

"Oh, I'm sorry if I offended your delicate sensibilities. I meant *make love to*."

"Please don't tell Thomas or Elizabeth anything about this," Mark begged me. "I'm a good uncle, I swear."

"Ox, hey, Ox! I'm a french-fry walrus. Look! Look—"

They all stilled at the same time. Mark's hands curled into fists on the table. "Stay here," he growled. He was up and out the door before I could speak.

"What the hell?" I asked.

Kelly tried to follow him, but Carter held him back. "Let me go, Carter!"

"No," Carter said. "We stay here. Ox and Joe. You *know* this."

Kelly nodded and stood next to the table, arms crossed, like he was guarding anyone from coming over.

I looked out the window of the diner.

Mark was across the street. With Gordo. They were not happy to see each other.

"Motherfucker," I muttered.

I pushed my way out of the booth. Kelly grabbed my arm and said, "*No*, Ox, you can't just—" but I snarled at him something fierce and his eyes went wide and he stepped back.

"Joe, you stay here," I snapped over my shoulder.

Joe's eyes narrowed and he opened his mouth to retort, but I cut him off, telling Kelly to watch him. Carter was up and followed me out the door without a word.

I only caught bits and pieces of the conversation as I approached. There was no context, no way for me to understand. I saw the look of fury on Gordo's face. The harsh set of Mark's jaw.

"Gordo, it's *not* the same—"

"You *left*. I kept this town safe and you fucking *left*—"

"We had to, we couldn't—"

"I'll put up wards around him. Strengthen the ones around his house. You'll never—"

"It's *his* choice, Gordo. He's old enough to—"

"You leave him out of this. He is *not* part of this."

"You know what happened to Joe. He's helping Joe, Gordo. He's *fixing* him."

Gordo took a step back. "You fucking bastard. You can't *use*—"

"Gordo!"

He looked over at me, eyes wide. "Ox, you get your ass over here. Now."

"What the fuck is your problem, man?" I asked him. I pushed past Mark and stood in front of Gordo, inches from him. I'd never used my size to intimidate anyone before.

But that's okay because Gordo wasn't intimidated, even when we both seemed to realize at the same time that I'd grown taller than him over the last few months. He had to look up at me now. "You need to get behind me, Ox. Let me deal with this."

"With what? You didn't tell me you knew them. What's going on?"

He took a step back. His hands were fisted at his sides. His tattoos looked brighter than normal. "Old family drama," he said through gritted teeth. "Long story."

"I get this, okay?" I said, motioning between the two of us. "I get this. But you can't tell me what to do. Not about this. I'm not doing anything wrong."

"It's not *about* you—"

"Sure as hell seems like it."

He closed his eyes. Took a deep breath. Let it out slowly. "Ox. I need you safe."

"Why wouldn't I be?" I didn't understand.

"Shit," Mark muttered. "He's your tether." He chuckled darkly. "Oh, the fucking irony."

Gordo's eyes flashed. He tried to step around me, but I wouldn't let him. "Take a walk, man," I told him. "Cool off."

He snarled at me but turned and walked away.

I whirled on Mark. "What the hell was that?"

He was watching Gordo walk away. "Old family drama."

"What?"

"It doesn't matter, Ox," he said. "Ancient history."

. . .

I asked Gordo to explain. I asked him how he knew Mark and the others. Why he had lied to me and acted like he didn't know them at all.

He just scowled until I walked away.

. . .

I asked Mark how he knew Gordo. Mark looked sad, and I couldn't handle that so I told him I was sorry and never brought it up again.

It was the last Sunday dinner before school started. Joe and I sat on the porch watching the trees.

"I wish I could go with you," he muttered.

"Next year, yeah?"

He shrugged. "I guess. It's not the same. You won't be around as much."

I put my arm over his shoulder. "I'm not going anywhere."

"I'm scared."

"Of?"

"Things are changing," he whispered.

I was too. More than he could ever know. "They will. They have to. But you and me? I promise that won't ever change."

"Okay."

"Happy birthday, Joe."

He laid his head on my shoulder and his nose brushed my neck. He breathed me in as we watched the sunset. It was pink and orange and red and I couldn't think of a single place I'd rather be.

. . .

"Fucking retard," Clint sneered at me the second day of school. Because that was his thing.

I ignored him, as I always did, shoving books into my locker. It was easier.

Apparently not for Carter, though. He grabbed Clint by the back of the head and threw him against the row of lockers, pressing his face against the cold metal. "You talk like that to him again and I'll rip your fucking heart out," he hissed. "Tell everyone that Ox is under Bennett protection and if anyone so much as *looks* at him funny, I'll break their arms. Don't fuck with Ox."

"You didn't have to do that," I said quietly as Carter and Kelly pulled me away. Carter had his arm around my shoulders and Kelly held my elbow. "They go away eventually."

"Fuck that," Carter snarled.

"They don't touch you," Kelly growled. "Ever."

. . .

They came into the school with their fancy clothes and their perfect faces and their secrets and everyone talked about them. The Bennett boys.

High school is the same wherever you go.

It's rumors and clichés and innuendo.

They're in a gang, people whispered.

They're drug dealers.

They had to leave their other school because they killed a teacher.

They take turns fucking Ox.

Ox fucks them both.

I laughed and laughed.

We sat in the lunchroom and I had friends. Sometimes, I wanted to talk. Sometimes, I had nothing to say and opened my book. They always stayed.

They always sat on the same side of the table as me, crowding in close.

.   .   .

They were physical. The whole family.

A hand in my hair.

A hug.

Elizabeth's kiss on my cheek.

Joe on the dirt road as I walked in the sun. His hand would go into mine and he would lean up against me as we headed home.

Kelly bumped my shoulders as we passed each other in the hallway.

The weight of Carter's arm on me as we walked to class.

Thomas's hand shaking mine, the grip strong and callused.

Mark's thumb against my ear.

At first it was just me.

But as winter approached, they started to include my mother.

.   .   .

Gordo told me about Joe. Part of it, anyway.

And I hated him for it.

"You have to be careful with him," he said. We were on a smoke break, even though I didn't smoke anymore.

"I know," I said.

"You don't. You don't know the first thing." He touched the raven on his arm. Smoke curled up around his fingers.

"Gordo—"

"He was taken, Ox."

I stilled.

"They took him. In the middle of the night. To get back at his father. His family. They hurt him for weeks. He came back and he was broken. He didn't even know his *name*—"

"Shut up," I said hoarsely. "You shut your fucking mouth."

He must have realized he'd gone too far. He closed his eyes. "Shit."

"I love you," I told him. "But I hate you right now. I've never hated you before, Gordo. But I hate you so fucking bad and I don't know how to stop."

We didn't say anything for a very long time.

. . .

And then everything changed.

OR NEVER / EIGHT WEEKS

Chris's mom died and it was bad.

He cried in the middle of the shop, and I put my head on his shoulder. Rico touched his neck. Tanner laid his head on Chris's back. Gordo ran his fingers over his buzzed hair.

He went away for a while.

He came back with Jessie. His little sister. She'd just turned seventeen and was going to live in Green Creek with him.

She looked like her brother. Brown hair and pretty green eyes. Fair skin with little freckles on her nose and cheeks and one on her ear that fascinated me. He brought her to the shop and she smiled quietly as he introduced her.

"And that's Ox," he said, and I walked into a wall.

The guys all stared at me.

"Did he just . . . ?" Gordo asked.

"This is awesome," Tanner said.

"Hi," I said. My voice was much deeper than it'd ever been before. "I'm Ox. Oxnard. Call me Ox." I tried to pose against a 2007 Chevy Tahoe but I slipped and skinned my elbow. I pulled myself back up. "Or Oxnard. Whatever."

"Oh boy," Rico said. "This is so awkward to witness. We should save him. Or leave."

No one saved me. Or left.

"Hi, Ox," Jessie said. "It's nice to meet you." She grinned and it was a mischievous thing with a hint of teeth. My mouth went dry because her lips were pretty and so were her eyes, and I thought, *Well, that's just fine.*

"You . . . ah. You too?"

"Maybe Ox can show you around school next week when you start," Chris said.

I dropped a socket wrench on my foot.

．　　．　　．

Jessie started school on a Tuesday in the spring. I was awkward, unsure, even when she laughed after I told a joke I didn't mean to tell.

It was low and throaty and I thought it was one of the nicest sounds I'd ever heard.

Carter and Kelly seemed to like her well enough, but they refused to leave my side between classes and crowded me more than usual at lunch. I suppose it must have looked odd to anyone else, seeing three big guys on one small bench while a girl sat opposite them with all the room in the world. She cocked her eyebrow at us, but Carter and Kelly refused to move and I explained to her later that's just how they were.

"Protective?" she asked, eyeing the two of them.

"You could say that. Guys, come on."

They glared at me before glaring at her.

She laughed at them.

Later, she walked with me to the shop after school and I turned red when her arm brushed mine. I held the door open for her, and she called me a gentleman. I tripped over my feet at that and almost knocked her to the ground. Rico said in a very loud voice that it must be love.

. . .

The sun was setting when I walked home, thoughts of pretty girls and brown hair swirling around in my head.

Joe was waiting for me, a smile on his face. The smile faded as I got closer.

"What is that?" he asked as I reached him.

"What?"

"That smell."

I sniffed the air around me. It smelled the same. The forest and leaves and grass and blooming flowers, all sharp and heady. I told him so.

He shook his head. "Never mind." The smile came back and he took my hand and we walked toward home. He told me about all he'd learned, how he couldn't wait until he got to go to school with me and Carter and Kelly, and didn't that tree look like a lady dancing? Did I see that rock with the crystal strip running down its side? Had I seen the commercial for that new superhero movie that we just *had* to go see this summer? Did I want to stay for dinner? Did I want to read comic books tonight?

"Yes, Joe," I said.

Yes to it all.

It was a Thursday that I finally worked up the nerve.

"She's going to look at me weird and I won't remember how to breathe!" I groaned to Carter and Kelly.

"You don't have to do anything you don't want to," Kelly said.

"But I *want* to."

"Are you sure?" Carter asked, sounding dubious. "You're not acting like it. Maybe think on it a few more days?"

"Or weeks," Kelly said.

"Or years," Carter said.

"Or never," Kelly said.

"She's coming!" I said. I might have squeaked.

"Hey, guys." Jessie flashed a smile as she sat down at the lunch table.

"Jessie." Carter sounded bored out of his mind.

"How nice to see you again." Kelly didn't sound like he meant that at all.

They both crowded me closer. I could barely breathe.

"Hi," I said. "You look . . . swell."

Kelly snorted.

"Thanks," Jessie said.

"So," I said.

They all looked at me.

"There's . . . stuff. Happening. This weekend."

"Is there?" Carter asked like a jerk. "What *kind* of stuff is happening this weekend, Ox?"

"Things." I kicked him under the table. He didn't even flinch.

"Stuff and things?" Jessie asked. "Exciting."

"Maybe . . ."

"Maybe what?"

"Maybe you'd want to . . . do? Stuff and things? With me."

Kelly groaned.

Jessie grinned. "Why, Oxnard Matheson. You devil. I can't Saturday because Chris and I have to go do some work on Mom's estate. How about Sunday afternoon?"

"He can't," Carter said.

"I can't?" I asked.

"Sunday dinner," Kelly reminded me.

"Oh. Well. Maybe I can miss it? This once? It's not like I can't go next Sunday."

Carter and Kelly stared at me.

"Sounds good," Jessie said. She was blushing and I thought, *Wow*.

"You have to be the one to tell Joe," Carter said.

"Seriously," Kelly agreed. "I don't even want to be in the same room."

"Joe?" Jessie asked.

"Little brother," Carter said, like it should have been obvious.

"Ox's best friend," Kelly said, like it was a challenge.

"He's awesome," I agreed, and I felt the first stirrings of guilt and didn't know why.

"Where is he?" she asked.

"Homeschooled," I said. "He'll be here next year." And I couldn't wait.

"How old is he?" she asked. She sounded confused.

"Eleven."

"Your best friend is an eleven-year-old?"

Carter and Kelly tensed on either side of me, coiling like spring-loaded traps.

"That's so sweet," Jessie said. She smiled at the three of us.

"Whatever," Carter mumbled.

"Don't forget to tell Joe," Kelly said.

.   .   .

I forgot to tell Joe.

I didn't know why. Maybe it was work. And school. And the fact that I was going on my first date with a pretty girl. Maybe it was because I was distracted by the joyous ribbing the guys gave me at the shop when they found out ("Make sure you wrap it up, papi," Rico said. "Chris will come after you with a shotgun if you don't." Chris had looked horrified and then threatened me with bodily harm if I even *thought* about sex in *any* way, shape, or form. Tanner and Gordo just laughed and laughed. Gordo seemed especially pleased by all of this).

(Chris came in on Saturday with a box of condoms and told me never to speak of it again. I threw them in the dumpster behind the shop so Mom wouldn't find them at home. I was mortified.)

But I forgot to tell him.

Jessie smiled at me when I knocked on the apartment door. Chris did his best to scowl at me, but I knew him too well. He rolled his eyes and ruffled my hair and told us to be good.

And we were.

She told me stories over lasagna that was too dry, like how when she was seven, she was riding a horse that got spooked by a snake. It took off with her on its back and didn't stop for almost an hour. She didn't ride horses anymore, but she thought snakes were okay.

She took a drink of water that was in a wineglass, like we were adults. Like it was wine and we were adults and doing adult things. I thought her foot touched mine.

She said, "We knew she was going. We'd known it for a long time. But when she took her last breath, it was still such a surprise that I thought I would break. It got easier, though. Much quicker than I thought it would."

I opened my mouth to give her a tragedy for a tragedy, to tell her about Dad walking out on us one random day, but I couldn't find the words. Not because they weren't *there*, but because I couldn't find a reason to give them to her. She was open and kind and I didn't know what to do with that.

We got ice cream as the sun set.

We walked around the park, the paths lit up with white lights.

She reached out and held my hand and I stuttered over my words and tripped over my feet.

It was perfect. It was so perfect.

And then she said, "How's Joe doing?"

And I said, "Oh shit."

I took her back home. I apologized because I had cut our first date short. She was puzzled but nice about it. She said I could make it up to her next time and my face felt hot. She laughed again and before I knew it was happening, she leaned up on her tiptoes and kissed me softly. It was sweet and kind and I hoped Joe was okay.

"See you tomorrow?" she asked when she pulled away.

"Yeah," I somehow managed to say.

She smiled at me and went inside.

I touched my lips because they tingled and then I remembered myself.

Home was two miles away. I didn't have a cell phone. We couldn't afford one.

I ran the whole way home.

The lights were on in the house at the end of the lane.

The door opened even before I got to the porch.

Thomas stood in the doorway. Carter was at his side. Both looked like they were ready to attack. Thomas took a step onto the porch. His nostrils flared, and for a moment, I thought his eyes flashed impossibly, but I told myself it had to be the light. Nothing more.

Carter was on me in a second, rubbing his hands over my head and neck. "Are you okay?" he said, his voice deep. "Why are you so scared? What happened?"

It was then I realized I *was* scared. Because I had let down my friend.

"No one followed him," Thomas said, stepping beside his son. I could feel the heat off both of them.

"He's not injured," Carter said. He put his hands on my shoulders and looked me in the eyes. "Did someone hurt you?"

I shook my head. "Joe," I said. "Joe. I forgot. He—"

"Ah," Thomas said. "That explains it."

Carter dropped his hands and took a step back. Now he only looked annoyed. "You're an asshole, Ox."

"Carter," his father snapped as I recoiled. "That's enough."

"But he's—"

"*Enough.*"

With that one word, all I wanted to do was make everything better. To do whatever Thomas told me to do. And I couldn't figure out why.

Carter sighed. "Sorry, Ox. It's just . . . Joe, man. He's Joe."

I hung my head.

"Dad," Carter said quietly. "Don't you think he should know already? He's pack."

"Inside," Thomas said.

Carter didn't say another word. He was back up the porch and inside, shutting the door to the Bennett house.

"Is he okay?" I asked Thomas, unable to look at him.

"He will be," Thomas said.

"I didn't mean . . ."

"I know, Ox."

I looked up at Thomas. He wasn't angry. He was just sad. "I'll walk you home."

I thought to argue. To tell him I just wanted to see Joe for a minute, to tell him I was sorry. But his tone left no room for argument, so I just nodded and followed him, feet dragging in the dirt.

"Is she nice?" Thomas asked.

"Who?"

"The girl."

I shrugged. "She's okay. She seems like a good person."

"And you haven't had many of those," Thomas asked. It was not a question.

"I do now," I said honestly. Because I did.

"You do," he said. "Sometimes I forget you're only sixteen. You've got an old soul, Oxnard."

I didn't know if that was good or bad, so I said nothing.

"Do you like her?"

"I guess."

"Ox."

"Yes, I do."

"Good," he said. "That's good. Elizabeth and I met when I was seventeen. She was fifteen. There has never been another one for me."

"But . . . Joe. He's . . ."

"Joe . . ." He sighed. "Joe was upset. I'm not saying that to make you feel bad, Ox, so please don't misinterpret my intent. Joe is . . . different. After everything that has happened to him, he can't be anything *but* different."

"Gordo said—" I stopped myself, but the damage was done.

Thomas cocked his head at me. "And what *did* Gordo say?" he asked, sounding more dangerous than I'd ever heard him.

"That someone hurt him," I whispered, looking down at my hands. "I didn't let him tell me any more."

"Why?"

"Because . . . it wasn't his right to tell me. It's not my right to be told anything at all. And honestly? I don't know if I care. And not because I don't care about him. But because I want to be his friend no matter how he needs me." I scuffed the dirt a bit with the tip of my boot. "And I'll be his friend as long as he lets me."

"Ox, look at me."

I did. I couldn't have stopped it even if I'd wanted to.

His dark eyes were bigger than I'd ever seen.

And he spoke, his voice even and soft. Words that washed over me like a river and I couldn't stop him, no matter how much I wanted to. No matter how hard I wished he would shut his fucking mouth.

Joe had been taken by a man who'd wanted to hurt Thomas and his family. The man had kept him for many weeks. He'd hurt him. Physically. Mentally. Broke his little fingers. His little toes. His arm. His ribs. Made him cry and bleed and scream. He would call them sometimes. The bad man. He would call them and they would hear Joe in the background saying that he wanted to come home. All he wanted to do was come home.

Eight weeks. It took them eight weeks to find Joe.

And they did. But he wouldn't speak.

He knew them. His family. Mostly. He cried silently, his arms and shoulders shaking.

But he wouldn't speak.

Even when his nightmares were at their worst and he would wake screaming in the night, thrashing on his bed, trying to escape the bad man, he still wouldn't speak.

They tried therapy. It didn't take. Nothing would make him speak.

"Not until you," Thomas said.

I must not have been a man yet, because under all that rage, a tear worked its way out and rolled down my cheek. "Who?" I asked, and that one word sounded like an earthquake.

"A man who wanted something he couldn't have," Thomas said.

"Did you kill him?"

His eyes grew darker. "Why?"

"Because I will if you didn't. I will break him and make him suffer."

"You would?"

"For Joe? Yes."

"You are so much more complex than you first appear," Thomas said. "These layers of yours. Just when I think I've reached the bottom, it falls away and goes even deeper."

"Can I see him?"

"Give him a couple of days, Ox." Thomas touched my shoulder, squeezing it gently. "He'll find you when he's ready. And you take care of your girl. She deserves it."

I flushed. "She's not my girl," I muttered.

"She could be."

"Maybe. Am I part of your pack?"

For the first time since I'd known him, I had caught Thomas Bennett by surprise. His eyes went wide and he took a step back and said, "What?"

"Your pack. Or whatever Carter said."

He said nothing and I wondered if I'd crossed a line I didn't know existed.

"I didn't mean . . ." I trailed off, unsure how to finish.

He said, "What do you think pack means?"

"Family," I said promptly.

Thomas smiled. "Yes, Ox. You are part of my pack."

. . . .

Carter and Kelly weren't at school the next day. I worried. Usually, I rode with them. But they weren't there in the morning and I was almost late after Mom gave me a ride.

"I'm sure it's fine," Jessie said, squeezing my hand while we sat at lunch. I did my best to smile at her as she talked. About how she liked Green Creek more than she thought she would. About how she couldn't wait for summer. About how she missed her mom. She wondered how long it would hurt and I told her I didn't know, even though I wanted to say it would probably hurt forever.

She kissed me on the cheek before I went to work.

. . . .

The guys gave me shit at the shop. Chris said Jessie had gotten home the night before and was all swoony.

"Ox is so *dreamy*," he breathed in a high falsetto. "His *eyes* and his *smile* and his *laugh*. O. M. G.!"

I blushed furiously and tried to focus on an oil change.

"Look at him!" Rico said gleefully. "He's like a tomato!"

"Our precious baby boy is growing up," Tanner sighed.

I said, "Where's Gordo?" His office was dark.

"Day off," Rico said. "Had some business to take care of."

"What business?" I didn't remember him saying anything. He never took Mondays off.

"Don't you worry your pretty little head about it," Tanner said. "You just worry about trying to impress your girlfriend."

"She's not my girlfriend!"

"Yeah," Chris said. "Try telling *her* that."

.   .   .

Joe wasn't waiting for me on the dirt road. The house at the end of the lane was dark, like no one was home. I thought about knocking on the door, but I went home instead. In my room, the stone wolf sat on a shelf. I held it and realized that Thomas had never answered me about the bad man who had hurt Joe. If he was still alive.

.   .   .

A horn honked outside the house the next morning. Carter and Kelly waited in the car. I was nervous.

"Hey, Ox," they said when I got in the front seat. Kelly sat behind me.

"Hey," I said back. I wrung my hands together.

"He's okay," Carter said as we bumped down the dirt road.

I let out a breath. "You sure?"

"He will be."

Kelly said, "We'll make sure of it."

And I said, "Your dad says I'm part of your pack," because I wanted to make sure they thought so too.

Carter hit the brakes suddenly. The seat belt pulled against my chest. Kelly's arms came around my front, clasping tightly. Carter leaned over and rubbed his forehead against my shoulder. "Of course you are," he said, and Kelly hummed his agreement, arms tightening.

We didn't say much after that and that was okay.

Carter laughed at something Jessie said. Even Kelly smiled. I was in a daze.

.   .   .

Gordo was at the shop. The moment I walked through the door, he was in front of me.

There were bags under his eyes, and he looked pale. Even the tattoos on his arms looked faded.

"You okay?" I asked him.

He nodded. "Yeah. You?" He sounded pained.

"You weren't here yesterday."

"I know."

"Maybe you should go home, man. You don't look well."

"I'm feeling better now," he said, and then he hugged me.

We didn't do this often, so I was surprised. But I hugged him back anyway because he was Gordo. I put everything I could into it because I needed to.

"I'm getting you a phone," he muttered. "Cell phone. I'm pissed off that you don't have one. Couldn't even call you."

"Hey, no. You don't need to—"

"Shut up, Ox."

And so I did.

Joe wasn't waiting for me on the dirt road. The lights were on in the house at the end of the lane. I was pack now, but I went home instead.

I slept with the stone wolf in my hand.

Carter and Kelly smiled at me when I got into the car the next morning. I wanted to ask them about the eight weeks Joe was missing, but the words stuck in my throat. Both of them found some way to touch me. A clap on the back. A pat against my chest.

It should have been obvious. It should have been obvious what they were, but then I wasn't looking for the incredible buried in the ordinary.

"How's Joe?" Jessie asked at lunch, and Carter and Kelly froze.

"Haven't seen him," I muttered.

She looked confused. "Why not?"

"He's been sick," Carter said before I could speak, and Kelly squeezed my leg underneath the table. They still crowded on either side of me while we ate.

"Oh," she said. "I'm sorry to hear that. I hope he gets better."

"He will," I said. I must have put too much emphasis on the words because she looked at me funny.

Carter and Kelly pushed against me and I knew what they were trying to say.

Gordo handed me a cell phone. It wasn't fancy. It was functional. It was awesome. He had programmed his number, the shop's, the diner's, and the rest of the guys' into it.

"You keep this with you, okay? But don't you dare use it in class unless it's an emergency."

I nodded, touching the screen lightly. "I have my own phone number?" I asked in awe.

And he smiled at me. That little smile I knew was for me alone. "Yeah, man. You got your own number."

I said, "Thanks, Gordo," and I hugged him again.

He laughed in my ear and I forgot that I had hated him for a little while.

. . .

It was Wednesday and Joe wasn't there.

. . .

Carter and Kelly made me put their numbers in my new phone. They gave me their parents'. And Joe's, because apparently he had one too, even though he was only eleven. I didn't know why little kids needed phones, but as soon as I had his number, I stared at it. I couldn't figure out how to do a text message, so I didn't do anything at all.

. . .

Chris told me that Jessie was hinting at him that I should ask her out again. I rolled my eyes when they laughed and whistled.

. . .

I walked down the road to the house. Dirt bloomed up in little clouds as I dragged my feet. The sky was gray and the clouds were threatening rain.

And there he was. Standing there. Wide, bright eyes.

I'd known him for almost a year. He'd grown during that time. His brothers still called him a runt, but I didn't think it'd be true that much longer. He'd be big like the rest of them. He was a Bennett, after all.

His eyes never left me as I walked forward slowly, unsure of my place. He didn't reach out for my hand when I got close. Part of me wanted to be angry, to say, *It was just one fucking dinner, it was just one day that I missed, it's not fair, it's not fair, you can't be like this.* It was a small part, but it was there and I hated myself for it.

And then he said, "Hey, Ox," in a small voice so unlike him that it all just went away.

So I said, "Hi, Joe," and I sounded kind of rough.

He looked like he wanted to reach out and touch my hand but stopped himself. I waited, not wanting to push.

He said, "I wanted to see you." He looked down at his feet and kicked a dried-out leaf. Somewhere, a bird sang a song that ached.

I said the only thing that came to mind. "I got a cell phone. I have your number. I don't know how to text. Can you teach me? Because I want to text you things and I don't know how."

He looked up at me with those big eyes and his bottom lip was trembling. "Yeah. Yeah, I can teach you. It's not hard. Do you love her?"

I said, "No. I don't know her like that."

And he jumped into my arms then, wrapping himself around me and crying into my neck. I held him tightly, and I guess I wasn't a man yet because my eyes leaked too. I told him I was so sorry I hadn't been there for Sunday dinner and that it would never happen again because he was Joe and I was Ox and that was how things went.

He shook and sobbed and my neck felt sticky, but eventually he calmed and curled up against my chest. Once settled, he took a deep breath, like he was inhaling every part of me. I carried him home.

.   .   .

They were all waiting for us when we got to the house at the end of the lane. Joe was asleep, his face in the crook of my neck, his arms dangling at his sides.

"He was tired," I said by way of explanation, and I thought, *pack*.

"He missed you," Elizabeth said, her voice warm. "We did too."

"I'm sorry," I said.

"You have nothing to be sorry for," Mark said.

I frowned. "That's not true. I—"

"Ox?"

I looked back at Elizabeth. "You're sixteen," she said. "You're allowed to go on dates. Just maybe give Joe a heads-up?"

I nodded.

"You hungry?" she asked.

I nodded again, even though I really wasn't. I just wanted to go inside with all of them.

"Why don't you take him upstairs and I'll heat up some leftovers. Then you can tell us about this pretty girl of yours."

I followed them inside.

I stayed with Joe. For a little bit. Just to make sure he didn't have bad dreams.

The next day, he taught me how to text. He was my first.

hi joe its ox texting you thank you for helping me

It took me five minutes to type because my fingers were too big. I wouldn't let him read it while I fat-fingered it out.

When I'd finished, his phone pinged almost immediately and I marveled just how quickly words could be sent. It was a scary thought.

He read the message and laughed so hard he fell down, tears in his eyes.

Later that night, I got my first text:

You help me too

CLAWS AND TEETH / LAUGH OUT LOUD

I turned seventeen and said good-bye to my junior year. Three solid months of work and pack and Jessie stretched out before me. I didn't quite believe things were happening the way they were. It seemed too good. Too much like a dream.

Things were normal for a while.

Gordo said, "It'll be good to have you back here all day again."

Mom said, "Think we should talk about getting you some wheels? I'm sure Gordo could help us out."

"Happy birthday!" they all said.

Carter said, "I really need to get laid."

Kelly said, "That's something I never wanted to hear."

Tanner said, "Can you call Mrs. Epstein and let her know the Jeep's finished? I fucking busted my knuckle and it's bleeding all over."

Elizabeth said, "I've moved on from my green phase. It's time. I'm thinking Picasso and blue. What do you think, Ox?"

Rico said, "I'm glad you're back full-time, papi. Gordo is much nicer when you're here."

Thomas said, "Do you know about Plato and the allegory of the cave? No? That's okay. Just don't believe the shadows are all that's real."

Chris said, "She likes you, Ox. She likes you a lot. Don't break her or I'll have to break you. Or if she breaks you, tell me and I'll kick her ass. You don't fuck with family."

Mark said, "Every day, you're making him just a little bit better. Ox, I am so glad we found you."

Joe said, "Ox! Hey! You *have* to come with me *right this second*. I found these . . . like . . . these *trees* and they're *crazy* and I think they could be a fort or something. I don't even know! You just have to come *see* them."

Jessie said, "I think we should have sex."

.   .   .

I stared at her. "What?"

"We should have sex."

I said the first thing that came to mind. "Your brother will *murder* me."

She rolled her eyes and brought her feet up onto my bed. She had slender toes. I don't know why they fascinated me. They were painted red. Some shade of red that I thought was sexy.

"We're old enough to make our own mistakes," she said.

"Uh. We're seventeen. And I don't know if the best way to seduce me is to call it a mistake."

She laughed and punched my arm. "Seduce. Oh, Jesus."

"So," I said.

She arched an eyebrow.

"Maybe?" My palms were sweaty and my throat was dry. "But maybe not."

"That's . . . clear. As always."

"I'm not . . . good. At things."

She said, "That's not true at all."

And I was seduced.

•   •   •

After, we lay in my bed, sweaty and sated. My mouth had done things to her and her mouth had done things to me, but we didn't have condoms so not much else was done. It didn't matter because my mind was blissed out and blank. It reminded me of the old TV my dad had kept in the garage. It only showed static. White noise. I was a forgotten, broken television buried under years of memories. I laughed at this, and when she asked me what was so funny, I just said, "Nothing."

"What's that?" she asked.

I couldn't see where she was pointing. "What?"

"That dog thing." She pushed herself off me.

"Hmm?" I said, channels still trying to come in clear. I needed to wrap tinfoil around my rabbit ears.

"It's heavy," she said quietly.

And everything was razor sharp. I sat up quickly and snatched it from her hands.

"Ox," she said. She sounded confused.

"It's . . . I don't . . ." I didn't want her to touch it. I never wanted anyone else to touch it. I just couldn't find the words (reasons) to say that.

"It looks old," she said finally.

"Joe gave it to me. For my birthday."

"Joe," she sighed. "Am I ever going to meet him?"

"Maybe."

"Maybe? He's your best friend, Ox. I'm your girlfriend. I introduced you to my friends." And she had. Some girls at our school she'd met in class. Cassie and Felicia and something something something. I didn't do well with new people. They seemed nice, but I could see them flitting their eyes back and forth between Jessie and me and thinking, *Really?*

"You know Carter and Kelly."

"Ox."

"He's . . . Joe."

"I know."

"He's not in a good place all the time."

"I know that too. That thing that no one will tell me about."

I swallowed to keep my anger in check. At her. "You don't need to know."

She winced. "I'll pretend you didn't sound like an asshole right then. Why doesn't he ever come over here? Why don't any of them come to your house?"

"It's easier to go over there."

"That's weird, Ox."

I put down the stone wolf and sighed.

·   ·   ·

"She wants to meet you."

Joe said, "Oh."

"She knows how much you mean to me."

Joe said, "Really?"

"I won't let anyone hurt you."

Joe said, "I know."

"You can say no."

He looked up at me. The sunlight hit his face through the trees as we walked down the dirt road. His hand was warm in mine. "Do you care about her?"

"Yes."

"Do you care about me?"

"*Yes.*"

"Okay," he said.

"Okay?"

He shrugged. "Okay."

.   .   .

She came to Sunday dinner at the beginning of July. She was nervous. I told her she didn't need to be. She looked pretty in her summer dress. It was yellow and she was golden. I touched her hair. She looked so small next to my hand.

"But they're your *family*," she said as we walked toward the house at the end of the lane, and that filled me with so much warmth that I could hardly breathe.

"You met my mom," I managed to say.

"That's different and you know it."

The front door to the Bennett house opened even before we reached the porch, like it always did, like they always knew I was coming.

Joe ran out the door. His smile was bright when he saw me. He glanced over at Jessie and something much more complex stuttered across his face that I couldn't even begin to understand. His left hand curled into a fist and then it relaxed.

"Hey, Ox," he said.

"Hi, Joe."

He didn't hug me like he normally did. He stayed on the porch. He looked unsure.

I dropped Jessie's hand and took a step forward.

He jumped off the steps and crashed into me, his nose in my neck. I laughed and held on tight. "Okay?" I whispered.

He shrugged. Then nodded. Rubbed his forehead on my shoulder.

Jessie started to take a step forward but I shook my head and she stopped.

Eventually, Joe slid down. He gripped my hand and stood rigidly at my side.

"Hi," he muttered at Jessie. He glanced up at her face, then away. Then down.

"Hi, Joe," Jessie said. "I've heard so much about you. I'm glad to finally meet you."

"Me too," he said and then he grimaced because he didn't sound like he meant that at all. "Sorry."

"It's okay," she said. "Nothing to be sorry for."

He pulled me into the house, and Jessie followed behind.

* * *

I could see Jessie didn't understand the Bennetts. Not like I did. They touched me. All of them. Hugs and hands on my neck and hair and arms and back. I was used to it. She was not.

Thomas and Elizabeth smiled warmly at her but did not touch her. No hands were offered. No kiss to the cheek.

It wasn't rude. Or reserved. They laughed with her during dinner. Encouraged her to tell stories. Brought her in on the conversation. Made sure no inside family (pack) jokes went too far so she wouldn't get lost.

But they did not touch her.

I took my usual place next to Joe. Jessie sat on my other side, the place normally reserved for my mother.

Sometimes Joe spoke. Sometimes he looked distant. I thought I heard him growl once, but he looked away. His hands were fists at his sides. Then they relaxed. His shoulders were hunched and he grimaced like he was in pain.

"What's wrong?" I asked with a frown.

"Just stiff," he muttered. His voice sounded low and scratchy.

"You sick?"

He shook his head.

Mark, Elizabeth, and Thomas were watching us when I looked up. Carter and Kelly were talking to Jessie. The three adults gave me answers with their vibrant eyes that I didn't understand.

Joe took a breath and let it out slowly.

And then he smiled. He had many teeth.

* * *

"They're . . . strange," Jessie said before she got into her car.

I scowled. "No, they're not."

"Ox, they kind of are."

"Be nice."

"I'm not being mean. I know you're protective of them, but they give off this . . . vibe. I don't know how else to explain it."

"They're my pack."

Her brow furrowed. "Pack?"

"I meant family."

She kissed me on the lips. "Joe is pretty great," she said quietly.

"I know."

"He doesn't like me very much, though."

I frowned. "He liked you fine. He's just been through a lot."

"You can't see it, can you?" She sounded amused.

"See what?"

"He's very protective of you."

"He's my friend."

"Ah," she said. She smiled softly. And then she left.

• • •

I knew how to text now.

Wednesday:

> hi i am at work
>
> Hi, Ox! How long did it take you to type that lol
>
> whats lol
>
> Laugh Out Loud
>
> oh i am not good at this lol
>
> You're doing good. I promise

Friday:

> Want to watch a movie tonight with us?
>
> can't jessie wants to go out
>
> Oh. Okay!
>
> you come too
>
> You want me to go with you?
>
> yes
>
> I'll ask mom!! =D
>
> whats that
>
> Smiley Face
>
> lol

Thursday:

> Mom wanted me to remind you its family time. Won't be around for a few days
>
> ok
>
> I wish you could come with us
>
> me too
>
> One day. I promise <3
>
> whats that
>
> Never mind. I'll talk to you later.

Sunday:

> We're back!
>
> good you safe
>
> Yes. I'm not a little kid Ox
>
> you are a little kid
>
> Whatever. You coming for dinner?
>
> its sunday of course i am
>
> You bringing Jessie?
>
> no she has stuff to do

Tuesday:

> what do you want for your birthday
>
> It's still over a month away!
>
> so what you want
>
> Caveman
>
> joe tell me what you want
>
> Everything!
>
> ok i can do that <3
>
> What
>
> Ox.
>
> Ox!

    •   •   •

It was two in the morning when my phone rang.

"Huh?" I said into it.

"Ox." Mark sounded stressed.

Sleep was gone instantly. "What happened?"

"It's Joe."

I was up and already scrounging for the shorts I'd left on the floor. "Is he okay?"

"No. He had a nightmare. We can't get him calm. I think he needs you."

"Okay. On my way."

Carter met me at the door. He didn't even get a chance to open his mouth before I heard a loud cry come from inside the house. I pushed passed him, saying, "Joe," calling out, "*Joe.*"

I was on the stairs when I heard him again. "No! Don't let the man take him. *Please*, Mom! Please don't let him take Ox away." Joe's voice was broken and wet, and my heart cracked in my chest.

Mark was at the door with Kelly. They both stared at me with wide and tired eyes. I ignored them because I had to get to him. I had to see him and—

He was on his bed. Thomas and Elizabeth were curled on either side of him. His face was in his mother's neck and he was *shaking*, and it was so *violent*, and his hands were gripping her tight as he cried out again, and I said, "Oh, Joe."

I didn't think of it too much when I reached down between the two of them and lifted him up. They didn't snap at me for handling him in such a way. They didn't try to stop me. Thomas's face was tight with worry. Elizabeth was crying, great globular tears that tore at my chest.

For a moment, Joe tensed in my arms, and then he held on as if his life depended on it, legs latching on around my waist, hands pulling at the back of my head.

Thomas and Elizabeth stood up from the bed. They touched my arm and Thomas whispered they would tell my mom where I was. They shut the door behind them.

I moved us to the side of the bed and sat on the floor, my back to the mattress. I moved Joe around until he was resting against my chest.

Eventually, he said, "I had a bad dream."

I said, "I know."

He said, "It's always the same. Most of the time. He comes for me and takes me away and does . . . things."

I wanted to scream out my horror, but I kept it in and said, "I'm here."

Joe said, "Sometimes, he takes my mom. Or my dad."

I put my hand in his hair.

Joe said, "This time, he took you, and if he can find you in my dreams, he can find you in real life."

I said, "I'll protect you," and I'd never meant anything more in my life.

He fell asleep as the sun began to rise.

I didn't sleep for a long time.

.   .   .

After that, anytime he had a bad dream, he asked (cried, *screamed*) for me and I always went to him.

He would shake and sob, his eyes half-crazed with the trappings of his nightmare. But then my hands would be on his back, rubbing soothing circles, and he would quiet until there was nothing left but shuddery breaths and a wet face.

Three weeks later, I found out their secret.

MOON

O x."

"G'way."

"Ox, wake the fuck up!"

I opened my eyes. It was still night, the only light coming from the full moon high in the sky.

There was someone else in the room, shaking me.

"The fuck?" I said.

"Get dressed."

"Gordo? What the hell is—"

He stepped back, eyes narrowed. "You need to come with me."

My heart was in my throat. "My mom—"

"She's *fine*, Ox. She's asleep. She won't hear anything. She's safe."

I threw on a shirt and some discarded cargo shorts. Gordo waited for me at my bedroom door. I followed him down the hall toward the stairs. My mother's door was partway open and I could see her sleeping. Gordo tugged on my arm.

We were outside before he spoke. The night air was warm against my skin. Everything felt too loud.

"There are things," he said, and through my haze of sleep, I tripped over his words and couldn't process them. "Things you're going to see tonight. Things that you've never seen before. I need you to trust me. I won't let anything hurt you. I won't let anything happen to you. You are *safe*, Ox. I need you to remember that."

"Gordo, what's going on?"

His voice cracked when he said, "I didn't want you to find out this way. I thought we'd have more time. If you ever had to find out at all."

"For what?!"

A howl rose from deep in the forest and I felt chilled to the bone. It was a song I'd heard before, but it sounded distressed.

"Fuck," Gordo muttered. "We have to hurry."

The house at the end of the lane was dark.

The moon was fat and white overhead.

There were stars. So many stars. Too many. I'd never felt so small in my life.

We entered the woods at a quick pace.

I was half listening to Gordo, trying to avoid tripping over tree roots and stumps. He was sputtering his words, false starts and syllables that died before they could combine into something more. He was nervous, terrified, and it affected his speech.

And then it wasn't quite as dark anymore.

"It's like. You see. There are *things*."

"Gordo?" I interrupted.

"What."

"Your tattoos are glowing."

Because they were. The raven. The lines. The swirls and whorls. All up and down both of his arms, they glimmered and shifted like they were alive.

He said, "Yeah. That's one of the things."

I said, "Okay."

He said, "I'm a witch."

And I said, "That makes sense," because I thought there was a very real chance I was caught in a dream.

He laughed, but it sounded like he was choking.

I was distracted and my shin caught something solid. The pain was bright and glassy, and it shot through the fog. It was only then that I realized I'd never felt pain in a dream before and that I'd read somewhere it was impossible to actually feel pain in a dream.

"Fuck," I said. "You're a *what*?"

"Witch."

"For how long?"

"My whole life."

"*What?*"

Another howl. Closer now. We'd gone at least half a mile into the woods. Maybe farther. There was nothing but forest that went on for thousands of acres ahead of us. I'd gotten lost in it plenty of times. "What was that?"

"Your pack," he said, and his words were so bitter I could taste them.

"My . . . I don't . . ." Dreaming, dreaming, dreaming. It had to be, even with the pain. My leg was sore, but maybe I'd just *wished* it so and therefore it was.

"I tried to keep them away from you," he said. "I really did. I didn't want this life for you. I didn't want you to be a part of this. I wanted to keep you clean. To keep you whole. Because you are the only thing in my life worth that."

"Gordo."

He said, "Listen to me, Ox. Monsters are real. Magic is real. The world is a dark and frightening place and it's *all real.*"

"How?"

He shook his head. "Don't be afraid."

A cloud slid over the moon and the only light was the shifting kaleidoscope that rolled up his arms. Prisms of colors, all blues and greens and pinks and reds.

"Does it hurt?" I asked.

"What?"

"The colors."

"No. It pulls and I push and it crawls along my skin, but it never hurts. Not anymore."

"Where are we going?"

"To their clearing," he said, and the howl picked up again, but now there was more than one. There were many, and they mingled and rose together, the song hidden within a half-step above and below, off key until it wasn't. And then it was *beautiful.*

"Who?" I asked as I itched all over because I felt *something.*

Instead, he said, "I tried to stop this," and he was *desperate* and *pleading* but they were *singing* above him and—

come, the song said. *hurry come now. here. please. hurry hurry hurry because you are us and we are you.*

He said, "I tried to tell them to stay away. To leave you out of this."

Ox. it's Ox it's him and he's here and he is ours. smell him taste him he is ours and we need because he hears our song.

"But by the time I found out you knew who they were, that they were back in Green Creek, it was already too late."

"They're calling me," I said, and my voice sounded light and airy.

"I know," Gordo said through gritted teeth. "Ox, you can't trust them. This."

"I can," I said, even though I didn't know who he meant. "Don't you hear it?"

Ox Ox Ox Ox. bring him food rabbits fowl deer. show him we can provide because he is PackOursMineBrotherSonLove.

"Yes," Gordo said. "But not like you can because I'm not pack. Not anymore."

Pack.

Oh God. Pack.

I started running.

"Ox!" he roared after me.

I ignored him. I had to get closer because my chest felt hot like burning, my skin itching until I thought it would drive me insane. Wind roared in my ears and the cloud left the moon and it was almost as bright as day, and they *howled*. They *sang*. The song was *alive* and *vibrant*, and it was all I could do to keep from tilting my head back and crying out soul-struck melodies—*I hear you I know you I'm coming for you I love you*—for all the forest and moon to hear. My heart was a drum and the beat pounded in my chest. I thought I could shatter and the pieces would fall among the trees and all that would be left would be little fractals of light from the moon as it reflected off the shards that had been my whole.

OX OX OX OX OX OX

Tree branches slapped my face. My arms. Little flickers of brief pain before the song took over.

HERE HERE HERE HERE

I thought of my father, and he said, "You're gonna get shit. For most of your life."

OURS OURS OURS OURS OURS

I thought of my mother, and she laughed, "There's a soap bubble on your ear."

HOME HOME HOME

I thought of Gordo, and he whispered, "You belong to us now," and did I? Did I really?

YES YES YES YES YES

I thought of Joe, and it was in *song*, in *concert* with all the howls that were *just beyond the tree line and I just had a few more steps and I needed to be there I needed to see what there was to see and I I I—*

I came into the clearing.

I stopped.

I fell to my knees.

Closed my eyes.

Fell back on the heels of my feet.

Turned my face toward the moon.

They *sang.*

And then it echoed away.

I took a breath.

Opened my eyes.

Before me stood the impossible.

A white wolf. Smatterings of black on its chest. Legs. Back.

Its eyes were red, flashing in the moonlight.

It was the size of a horse, its paws twice the size of my hands. Its snout was as long as my arm. There was a hint of teeth like spikes.

There was movement behind it, but I couldn't look away.

The wolf walked toward me and I could not move.

"This is a dream," I whispered. "Ah, God, this is a dream."

It stood before me. Lowered its head. Sniffed along my neck, slow, deliberate breaths that were hot against my skin. I thought I should be scared, but I couldn't find a reason to be.

The wolf exhaled along my throat. My hair. My ear.

In my head, I heard whispers of *OxPackOxSafeOxOxOx.*

I knew that voice. Those voices. I knew them all.

I reached up. My hands slid into soft hair, grazing along the hide underneath.

And then, a cold splash of something like reality. "Ox!" a voice shouted from behind me.

The wolf growled over my shoulder. A warning.

"Oh, fuck off, Thomas," Gordo said. I could hear him coming up behind me. "You don't know shit. The wards are holding."

Thomas. Thomas. Thomas. "Thomas?" I sounded broken.

The wolf looked back down at me, eyes flashing red. It (*he*) pressed its (*his*) nose against my forehead and *huffed.* "My," I choked out. "What big eyes—"

He bumped his snout against my head and I took that for what it was.

The wolf (*Thomas Thomas Thomas*) took a few steps back and sat down on his haunches. He towered over me, waiting. For what, I didn't really know.

I stood slowly and I wondered if he was going to eat me. I hoped it would be quick.

The wolf (*THOMAS THOMAS THOMAS*) cocked his head at me.

And I said, "So, this is a thing."

Gordo snorted behind me.

"I don't think I'm dreaming," I said.

"You're not," Gordo said.

"Okay. You have shiny arms because you're a wizard." I didn't look away from the wolf, who huffed again, like I'd said something funny.

"Witch," Gordo said. "And I don't have *shiny arms.*"

"That's a lie," I muttered. "You're like your own flashlight."

"This is what you're focusing on? You find out the Bennetts are werewolves and you think about my *shiny arms*?"

"Werewolves," I breathed. "That's . . . whoa."

The wolf shook his head, almost as if he was amused.

"Jesus Christ," Gordo muttered. "Thomas, get the rest of your mutts over here to do your ass sniffing. I'll make sure everything is still holding."

Thomas growled low in his throat. His eyes went red again.

"Yeah, yeah. Your Alpha shit doesn't work on me. I could fry the hair off your ass in a heartbeat. You dog dick."

He pushed past us and his tattoos shimmered up and down his arms.

I looked back up at Thomas. "I . . ." didn't know what to say.

He looked over his shoulder and rumbled deep in his chest. There was a loud yip and then two smaller wolves bounded over, one slightly bigger than the other. They rubbed themselves all over me, their heads butting against my chest and head. The bigger one was a dark gray with little flecks of black and white on his hind legs. The smaller one had similar coloring, but his white and black splotches started on his face and went back to his shoulders.

Their eyes flashed bright orange as their tongues dragged along my skin.

"Gross," I said mildly.

They laughed. Not out loud, but they laughed and the familiarity caused me to ache.

"Carter," I said. "Kelly." I sounded just *stupid* with awe.

They laughed at me again and bounded around me, hopping like they were puppies. They nipped at my clothes and fingers and *I wasn't dreaming.*

I touched their backs and moonlight filtered through my fingers onto their skin. They were happy. Somehow, I knew they were happy. I could feel it in my head and chest and it was so *bright.*

I looked back to Thomas and saw a large brown wolf sat at his right side, watching me closely. He wasn't anywhere near as big as Thomas, but his eyes kept lighting up like Halloween, all fiery and warm. He huffed at me, and I saw the curve of a secret smile.

I said, "Mark."

He leaned over and rumbled in the back of his throat, his nose drifting along my face, tongue trailing.

"So licking is something you do," I told them. "You're going to be embarrassed later. I'm not going to lick you right now." I paused, considering. "Or probably at all."

None of them seemed to care. I didn't know if they understood me. I didn't even know if this was real.

Gordo came back, and his tattoos had quieted down. They were still illuminated, but they didn't seem to shift as before. He was pale, and his eyes looked sunken in their sockets.

He looked up at Thomas and said, "It won't take. He can't attach himself to any of you. His tether won't affix." Then his voice grew hard. Accusing. "And I think you knew that before."

A sound came then. It was wet and snapping and horrible, and there was a groan of muscle and skin, and white fur rippled and receded. It only took seconds, but where there'd once been a wolf, now stood Thomas. He was still an animal, or at least partway, caught between man and wolf. His fingers ended in black claws and his face was slightly elongated. There were teeth, sharp teeth, and his eyes were red.

And he was naked, which just made everything all that more surreal.

"We knew this was a possibility," he told Gordo, his voice a deep rumble, the words slightly lisped because of the fangs. The *fangs.*

"How is this fair to Ox?" Gordo asked bitterly. "You didn't give him a choice."

"And you did?"

The tattoos flared on Gordo's arms. "It's not the same and you know it."

"You're not a stupid boy," Thomas snapped. "Don't act like you are. These things choose themselves. Your father, regardless of what he turned into, taught you better than that."

"Don't you *dare* bring him into this. Ox isn't—"

"I'm standing right here," I somehow managed to say.

They looked over at me, surprise on their faces, like they'd forgotten I was there.

And it hit me.

"Joe," I said. "Where's Joe?"

Carter and Kelly whimpered at my sides, brushing up against me.

Thomas sighed. "It's his first shift. He's not . . . handling it very well."

Fear ran through me. "Where is he?" I demanded.

Gordo stepped forward. "Ox, you need to understand. You *always* have a choice. This isn't set in stone."

"I don't care. I don't care what's going on. I don't care if I'm dreaming or awake or if I've lost it. Fucking wolves and witches and I don't fucking care. *Where the fuck is Joe?*" My hands were fists at my sides. Carter and Kelly laid their ears flat against their heads and slunk down, trying to make themselves smaller.

Thomas said, "He needs your help."

And Gordo said, "Fuck that. You don't put that on him."

But then Thomas had him by the throat and he was more wolf than man, though he still stood on two legs. The white hair had returned, and the claws had extended. His teeth were bigger, like fat nails, and the noise that spilled from him caused gooseflesh along my arms and neck.

"You are here," Thomas snarled at him, "because I respected your father and the covenant. Or at least what he once was. Don't mistake that for anything more. You are not pack by your own choice."

"And yet you call me for this?" Gordo snapped, struggling in Thomas's grasp. "And I *came.* I'm not bound for *shit* and I *still* came."

"He is my *son.* And the next Alpha. You will show *respect.*"

"Fuck you," he wheezed.

And I said, "*Stop.*"

And they did.

Gordo fell to the ground, sucking in air.

Thomas breathed heavily, eyes red, growling low.

And then I saw it. Behind them. In the clearing. In the moonlight.

A dark shape, curled on the ground. A flicker of light rose up around it. Green, maybe. Deep green, but it was gone before I could be sure.

I pushed past Gordo and Thomas. I didn't have time for them.

Carter and Kelly were at my sides, tongues lolling from their mouths. Mark was behind me, his nose pressing against my back.

Another wolf lay on the ground, almost as big as Mark, and I thought *Elizabeth*. She was colored like her sons, grays and blacks and whites. She raised her head at my approach and her eyes were the same, so beautiful and blue, and I remembered her telling me how she was done with her green phase. She had laughed and spun me in a circle, flecks of paint on her hands.

They were the same, but I could see the sadness in them.

"I don't . . ." I shook my head.

"She can't hear you," Gordo said quietly from behind me. "There's an earth ward around them infused with silver. It blocks out all sound and smells." There was another flash of green, and in the moonlight I could see slashes in the earth forming a circle around Elizabeth.

"They're trapped?" I was horrified.

"By choice," Gordo said. "It's safer for Joe as he is right now. It blocks out everything except for his mother."

I took a step toward Elizabeth, but Gordo grabbed my arm, holding me back.

"You have to listen," he said, "before—"

"Before?"

Elizabeth never took her eyes from me. They flashed orange. I couldn't see Joe and my head hurt.

"We have . . . we need something. Anything. A *thing* that keeps us holding onto our humanity." Gordo's grip loosened on my arm, but he didn't let me go completely. There was an almost electric quality to the touch and I wondered if it was the tattoos. Or him. Or whatever this was. "Magic takes a lot out of you. It can pull you places you never thought it could go. Dark corners that are better left alone."

"And wolves?"

"Wolves need it to remind them they're part human. Especially born wolves. It's easier for them to get lost in the animal. And they do, without something to tie them to the rational world."

I said, "Nothing about this is rational," and my voice was rough. I felt like I was tipping into something I couldn't come back from.

Gordo cut through the panic. "Joe will go feral, Ox. He'll go feral if he doesn't have a tether. Usually it's pack or family or an emotion like love and a sense of home. It can be anger and hatred, but at least it's *something*. He doesn't have it now. It won't happen today. Or tomorrow or maybe even a year from now. But if he can't be tied to his humanity, then one day he'll go feral and he'll never change back. And a wolf without a tether is dangerous. A . . . decision would have to be made."

A flash in the dark, a memory from before. About tethers. "Mark said . . ."

Gordo knew. He sighed. "Yeah. He did. You're my tether, Ox."

"When?"

"When you turned fifteen. When I gave you the shirts."

"I didn't feel any different."

You belong to us now.

"Yes, you did."

"Fuck," I whispered.

"It just happened," he pleaded. "I never meant to—"

"Can I be both?"

"Both?"

"To you and him."

"I don't . . . maybe. If anyone could, it'd be you."

"Why me? I'm nothing. I'm nobody."

He squeezed my arm. "You are greater than any of us, Ox. I know you don't see it. I know what you think. But you are more."

I was a man now, so I pushed away the burn in my eyes. "What do I need to do?"

"Are you sure?" Thomas said from behind me.

I only had eyes for Elizabeth. I could feel the wolves around me, but I never looked away from her.

"Yes." Because it was Joe.

"It'll be fast," Gordo said. "The ward will drop. You'll hear him.

He's been . . . loud. Don't let it frighten you. He'll catch your scent. Talk to him. Let him hear your voice. He doesn't . . . look like himself right now. Okay? But he's still Joe."

"Okay." My heart thundered in my chest.

This was not a dream.

"I won't let anything happen to you," Gordo said quietly.

"Okay."

"Ox. You have a choice."

Finally, I looked over at him. "And I've made it."

He held my gaze, eyes searching. I don't know if he found what he wanted, but eventually he nodded tightly. He brought up his left arm, palm toward the sky. All the tattoos on his arms had faded except for one, which was a deep and earthy green. It was two lines waving in sync with each other. He rubbed two fingers over them and muttered under his breath. The air turned static and my ears popped. The wolves around me growled and I looked back at Elizabeth.

The circle flared briefly and then went black. Dull and lifeless.

And then I heard it.

Low growling. Snarls. Small and angry.

I took a step toward Elizabeth. I held out my hand.

She pressed her nose against my palm and breathed in and out.

And then silence.

Hands stretched over Elizabeth from her other side. Black claws.

"Joe," I said quietly.

And he launched himself at me. Before I could move. Before I could think. There was a shout of warning, harsh growls. I was knocked off my feet, a heavy weight atop me. Claws dug into my shoulders, little pinpricks that burned. I saw flashes of teeth, eyes that flickered orange and red and blue and green. A nose was at my neck. My cheek. Inhaling me. Breathing me in.

He said, "*Ox*," and it was low and dark and angry.

He was caught partway between boy and wolf, like Thomas had been. But Thomas had been in control of his change.

Joe was not.

White hairs grew and receded along his arms and face. Fangs pierced his gums, then grew flat. There was a boy. Then a half wolf. Then a boy again. He groaned and said, "Ox, it hurts it hurts it—" and the rest was lost as his wolf came forward and words dissolved into spitting growls. His eyes flew through the shifting colors, and for a moment the colors combined into something like *violet* and *violence* and the claws on my chest pressed down harder. I winced at the pain and heard others around me and it sounded like they were about to tear him away from me and I couldn't let that happen. I couldn't let them take him away.

I said, "My dad left when I was twelve."

Everyone grew quiet.

The claws pulled away, only just.

"He drank too much. I told myself nothing was wrong, but there was. I think he used to hit my mom, but I don't know if I'll ever get the courage to ask her. She wore a dress to a picnic once and I think he tore it, and if I find out he did, if he hurt her and I didn't know, then I will make him suffer."

Joe whined, sounding pained.

"He put his suitcase by the door and he left. He said I was dumb and stupid and that people were going to give me shit. He told me he didn't want to regret me and so he had to leave. The thing is, I think he already did. I think he regretted every single part of his life. But he was right about some things. I was dumb and stupid because I thought he'd come back. I thought he'd come back one day smelling like he always did, of motor oil and Pabst and sweat, because that is the smell of my *father.*"

And it was. It had always been that way.

"But he didn't come back. And he won't. I know. But it's not because I did anything wrong. He was the one that was wrong. He left and we stayed and he was *wrong*. But I'm okay with that now. I'm okay with getting left behind because I have my mom. I have Gordo and the guys. And I have you. Joe, if I hadn't gotten left behind, I wouldn't have you, so you need to focus, okay? Because I can't have anything happen to you. I need you here with me, Joe, and I don't care if you're a boy or a wolf. Stuff like that don't matter to me. You're my friend, and I can't lose that. I will never regret you. Ever."

It was the most I'd ever spoken at one time. My mouth felt dry, my tongue thick. I ached all over, from everything. I heard my father's voice in my head, and he laughed at me. He said it wouldn't work. "You're gonna get shit," he said.

I hadn't known when Gordo had tethered himself to me. Not in a way that could be defined.

But I knew what it was now.

And I felt it. This warmth in my chest, up through my neck and arms. My face and legs. Like little flutters of sunlight through the leaves of a tree.

The wolves around me began to howl. Their song rolled over me, and I thought it would break me apart. I yelled along with them, melding my voice with theirs. I'm sure it was nothing like the song of a wolf, the measly cry of a human. But I gave it all I had because it was all I could give.

The howls died down.

The weight lifted from my chest.

I opened my eyes.

Above me stood a wolf. He was smaller than the others. Thinner. And he was pure white, not a single discoloration on his entire body. His ears twitched. His nostrils flared.

He looked down at me. His eyes were orange, bright, and beautiful. They flared briefly before they faded back to his normal blue, and I knew he was in there. I knew it was still the little boy who thought I smelled of pinecones and candy canes. Of epic and awesome. I tried not to think about how many things made more sense now, because it threatened to overwhelm me.

So instead, I said, "Hey, Joe."

And he tipped his head back and *sang*.

．　　．　　．

They ran through the clearing. Into the trees. Back out again. Chasing each other. Nipping at each other's heels.

Joe was gangly at first. Unsure. He tripped over his own feet. Sprawled face first into the ground. Got caught up in sights and sounds and smells.

He ran at me full speed. Feinted left when I braced myself. Yipped loudly as he flew by me. Turned back. Rubbed against my legs like a cat. Nose in my hand.

And then he was off again.

Thomas and Elizabeth stayed close by him. They'd growl at him softly if he started to get overexcited.

Mark sat next to me, almost as tall as I was. He chuffed quietly to himself while he watched Joe.

Carter and Kelly broke off into the woods. I could hear them crashing through the trees and underbrush. Stealthy predators, those.

And then it all hit me. It all crashed down upon my shoulders.

Reality shifted because it had to.

I inhaled sharply.

Mark whined softly at my side.

Gordo said, "Are you okay?" and I said, "Holy *shit*."

Gordo didn't laugh. I didn't expect him to.

"They're fucking *werewolves*!"

"Yes, Ox."

"You're a fucking *wizard*."

"I'm a witch," he said with a scowl.

"Why the fuck did you keep all of this from me!" I roared.

It wasn't meant to come out like that.

It was meant to be reasonable. Calm.

But I was scared and angry and confused and reality was shifting. Things made sense, so much more sense now, but they didn't. At all. The world was not full of monsters and magic. It was meant to be mundane and marred with little broken pieces of *fucking retard* and *you're gonna get shit, Ox.*

And it wasn't just meant for Gordo. No.

It was meant for all of them.

The wolves. The witch. The fucking tethers.

Don't make me regret you too, my father had said, and for some reason, all I could think about were the motes of dust in their (*her*) room, dancing in the sunlight while I touched the curved stitches that spelled out *Curtis, Curtis, Curtis.*

But that was then and this was now.

Because I was (*not*) twelve anymore.

I was (*not*) a man.

I was (*not*) pack. I was. I was. I was and the tethers. Holy God, the *tethers*, I could feel them *pulling* and—

Gordo was in front of me.

Suddenly I was *surrounded* by wolves. All of them.

They growled in unison as Gordo grabbed my arms. He ignored them.

"Ox," he said. "You need to breathe." He sounded hoarse.

"I'm *trying*." It came out high-pitched and broken. And I couldn't. I couldn't catch my breath. It was stuck somewhere between my throat and lungs. Little flashes of light danced across my vision, and my fingers felt numb.

One of the wolves whined at my side. I thought it was Joe, and wasn't that something? That I could already recognize him as a wolf even though an hour ago I didn't know such things existed?

Little things. Slotting into place.

Pack and the *touching* and the smells and the howls deep in the woods. The family nights where I wasn't allowed to follow that always came when the moon was white and round. The stone wolf in my hand. The way they moved. The way they spoke. The bad man. The bad man who took Joe. It had to be because of—

Joe whispered, *I'm going to be a leader one day*, and didn't I feel a fierce pride at that when he said it for the first time? Didn't I just *glow* with it even though I had no idea what it meant?

There were facts I was aware of.

Simple truths.

My name was Oxnard Matheson.

My mother was Maggie Callaway.

We lived in Green Creek, Oregon.

My father left when I was twelve.

I was not smart. I was dumb as an ox (*Ox*).

People were gonna give me shit.

I wanted nothing more than to have a friend.

Gordo was my father-brother-friend.

My mother liked to dance.

Tanner, Chris, and Rico were my friends. We belonged to each other.

The Bennetts were my friends (*pack pack pack pack*) and we had Sunday dinner because it was tradition.

Jessie was my girlfriend.

Joe was my—oh, Joe was *my*—

Those were my simple truths.

And reality shifted. Reality bended. Reality broke.

And here I stood in the middle of a moonlit field, my father-brother-friend with his tattoos that shifted more colors than I thought existed standing before me, shaking me, shouting, yelling, "*Ox, Ox, Ox, it's okay, Ox, it's okay don't be scared I've got you.*"

And here I stood in the middle of a moonlit field, surrounded by wolves (*PACK PACK PACK PACK*), and they pressed against me, and in my secret heart, through these little bonds that I hadn't known were there, I could hear whispers of songs and they were *singing* to me.

Elizabeth said, *hush, ChildSonCub, hush. there is nothing to fear.*

Thomas said, *Ox, Ox, Ox. i am your Alpha and you are a part of what makes us whole.*

Carter said, *don't be sad, FriendPackBrother, because we won't leave you.*

Kelly said, *i won't let anything happen to you. i will be by your side.*

Mark said, *there is no reason to be alone anymore. you will never be alone.*

And Joe. Joe sang the loudest of all.

He said, *you belong to me.*

MILES AND MILES / SUN BETWEEN US

Thomas said, "Do you want to become a wolf?"

It was the Sunday following the full moon. Thomas and I walked through the forest before dinner. Joe had tried to follow us, but Thomas ordered him back to the house, eyes flashing red, and I wondered why I'd never seen it before. How could I have missed what should have been so obvious to me? Joe had slunk back into the house, shooting one last quick glance at me.

He waited to ask until we were far enough away from the house that the others couldn't hear us. I had learned much about the wolves over the past few days. Heightened sense of smell. Of hearing. They could heal quickly. They could shift. Half shift. Full shift. Alphas and Betas and Omegas. Omegas were dark things. Scary things. Feral and without their tethers.

I learned more than I ever thought possible.

And we walked through the forest again. Just him and me. He touched the trees every now and then, like he always did. He breathed deeply. I asked him why.

"This is my territory," he said. "It belongs to me. It's been in my family for a very long time."

"Your pack."

He nodded. "Yes, Ox. My pack. Our pack."

And didn't that make me warm?

It did.

"These trees," he said. "This forest. It's filled with old magic. It's in my blood and it thrums and writhes within me."

"But you left," I said.

He sighed. "Sometimes, there are greater responsibilities than home. Sometimes, we have to do what is necessary before we can do what we wish. But every day that I was away, I felt this place. It sang to me and it ached and burned. Mark came back to check in because I couldn't. To make sure the place still stood."

"Why?"

He smiled at me. "Because I'm the Alpha. I don't know if I would have been able to leave again."

"How far does it go? Your territory."

"Miles and miles and miles. And I run them all, the ground beneath my feet and the air in my lungs. It's like nothing else, Ox."

I touched the nearest tree and tried to feel what he felt. My fingers scraped against the bark, and I closed my eyes. I laughed at myself quietly. I was ridiculous. I wasn't anything like them.

And he said, "Do you want to become a wolf?"

I opened my eyes because there *was* something there. There were these little bonds, like strings, that pulled in my head and my secret heart. I couldn't quite give them names yet, because they were so new, but it was close.

I could name Joe's, though. His was easy.

I said, "Do you want me to be a wolf?"

Thomas grinned at me, full and blinding. "So many layers," he murmured as we walked through the trees.

I wouldn't be like them, not completely. That much had already been explained to me. A human turned never was. There was a difference between being bitten and born. Instincts, for one. They'd had their whole lives. I'd be stumbling like a child.

"There would be differences," I said aloud.

"There would," he said.

"But I would be a Beta."

"Yes. One of mine. Eventually, one of Joe's."

"Why aren't Carter or Kelly going to be the next Alpha?"

He said, "They weren't born to be. Joe was. He will be an Alpha."

I didn't want to offend him, but I couldn't stop the words. "I would have something you wouldn't. If I turned."

"Oh? And what would that be?"

I touched the tree again. "I would remember what it was like to be human."

There was no anger from him. He put an arm around my shoulders and touched his cheek to my hair, rubbing once. Twice. A third time. They did that. I understood why now. I was part of them and they needed me to smell like I was. It was weird. And comforting. He pulled away. "You would," he said quietly. "And you would make a fine wolf."

"My mom," I said by way of excuse, trying to stall for time while everything reeled around me.

"It's up to you," he said.

"Is she pack?"

"In her own way."

"She would have to know."

"I trust you, Ox," he said, and I closed my eyes. The weight of his words were not lost on me. Not with his family's history.

"Would I lose myself?" I asked him. "The part of me that makes me *me*."

"No. I wouldn't let that happen. You would still be you. Just . . ."

"More?" I asked bitterly.

"Different," he said. "Ox. Ox. You will never need to be more. Of anything. You are perfect just the way you are. Humans are . . . special. Human pack members are revered. You will always be protected. You will always be loved."

A bee flew past my legs and I followed it with my eyes until it disappeared. "Then why ask?"

"Because you will always have a choice. We are defined by the choices we make. When you turn eighteen, should you want the bite, I will give it to you."

I looked at him. He was watching me closely. "I could run with you," I said shyly. "At the full moon."

He laughed. "You'll do that anyway. You might not be as fast, but we won't let you fall behind."

"Why didn't you tell me?"

His smile faded. "To protect you."

"From what?"

He said, "There are things far greater out there than you or I, Ox. Both good and bad. The world is bigger than you could possibly imagine. We're safe here. For now. But that might not always be the case. This is a place of power. And places such as this always attract attention."

"What's changed?"

"Joe."

I looked away. "Would you have told me if he . . . ?"

"Yes. One day."

And I left it at that. "It's probably dinnertime," I said. "It's tradition."

And his smile returned.

. . .

I wondered if Thomas had noticed I never answered his question. About becoming a wolf. I thought he did. I thought he knew everything.

. . .

"I keep you grounded," I said to Gordo not long after. We were alone in the shop, getting ready to close up for the day. It was almost time to go back to school and these quiet moments we had would become few and far between.

He didn't answer right away. I was okay with that.

I locked up the front doors and followed him out back, where he'd have his smoke and I'd pretend to have one too and we'd shoot the shit for another ten minutes like we always did before we went home.

He was sitting in his ragged lawn chair, twirling the lighter in his hands, cigarette behind his ear. He was watching a flock of birds flying by overhead.

"My father," he said.

I waited.

He cleared his throat. "My father," he tried again. "He was . . . not a very nice man."

I wanted to tell him that we had yet another thing in common, but the words died on my tongue.

"You don't know this world, Ox. Not yet. If you did, you would know my father's name. He was very powerful. He was strong and brave and people worshipped the ground he walked on. Hell, I did too. But he wasn't a nice man."

My father had been a great man. I'd thought him strong and brave, and I'd worshipped the ground he walked on. But he'd never been very nice.

Dumb as an Ox.

Because I was gonna get shit.

"Packs like the Bennetts—old packs with long histories—have a witch brought into their folds. It's meant to create peace and balance and add to the power of the Alpha. My father . . . he was Abel

Bennett's witch. Thomas's father. The Bennett pack was bigger then. Stronger. Revered and feared."

"What happened?" I asked quietly.

"He lost his tether," Gordo said. He chuckled bitterly.

"Your mother?"

"No. Another woman. She . . . it doesn't matter. She died. Were-wolf. My father killed many people after that."

I felt numb.

"I took his place," Gordo said. "I was twelve."

"Gordo—"

"I wasn't ready. For the responsibility. I made mistakes. My father disappeared. Fuck knows if he's even still alive. But I had a home. A place."

"Gordo?"

"What."

"I'm your tether."

"Yeah."

"Who was your tether before me?"

"It doesn't matter." He looked away.

But of course it did. "How long?"

"Jesus Christ."

"How long were you without a tether?"

I didn't think he'd answer. But then he said, "Years."

"You fucking asshole," I said hoarsely. "Why didn't you ask me?"

"I didn't think—"

"No shit you didn't think. You could have gotten hurt."

He lit his cigarette. Inhaled deeply. Blew out the smoke. "I had it under control."

"Fuck you and your control."

His eyes snapped to mine. "Just because you're in this now doesn't mean you know shit about it, Ox. Don't forget, I've had a *lifetime* of all of this. You're a fucking *child*."

I pulled myself to my full height. "A child who is part of the Bennett pack and tethered to you and Joe."

He watched me, a strange expression on his face. "Shit," he muttered. "Ox."

"Don't. Never again. You hear me? You don't keep shit from me. Ever again."

"Ox—"

"*Gordo.*"

"Jesus, kid. You're fucking scary sometimes. You know that, right? A bit of Alpha in you."

I said nothing. Just glared at him.

He sighed. "All right."

"Who was it?"

Smoke curled up around his face and he said, "Mark. Okay? It was Mark. I loved him. I loved him and he left and I stayed, and until I found you, I was lost in the dark. You brought me back, Ox. You brought me back and I can't lose you. I can't."

. . .

The others didn't know. Tanner. Rico. Chris.

Gordo said it was better that way.

Sometimes I didn't think even Gordo believed his own lies.

. . .

School started. My senior year.

The horn honked outside.

I opened the door.

Joe's smile was bright and blinding as he waved at me from the backseat.

He said, "Hey, Ox. Now I get to be like you guys. Time for school, yeah?"

. . .

Back in the woods after asking if I wanted to be a wolf, Thomas said, "Tethers are important, Ox. Especially when they're people. If it was an emotion, it'd have to be all-encompassing. And that usually only happens with rage and hate, and it turns and twists until the tether is black and burnt. When the tether is a pack, it's spread out among all members, and everyone carries the weight of the burden."

"And if it's just one person?" I asked. A breeze blew through my hair and I closed my eyes.

"If it's one person," Thomas said quietly, "then that person is treated as precious. But it'll become possessive. It's just the way it is. It's one of the most important things there is to a wolf."

"What's your tether?" I asked. As soon as the words came out of my mouth, I wanted to take them back. It felt like a deeply personal question that I had no right to ask.

But he said, "Pack. It's always been my pack. Not the individuals, per se, but the *idea* behind what pack means."

"Family," I said.

"Yes. And so much more. It can be harder when it's individuals."

"What if I'm tied to two people?"

He frowned. "We'll see, won't we?"

.   .   .

There's a third Bennett brother, the people in the hallway whispered. *He looks just like the others.*

Why are they still with Ox?

.   .   .

We needed a bigger lunch table.

Or maybe just a bigger bench.

I was surrounded by Bennetts. Kelly on my left. Joe on my right. Carter on the other side of him. They'd herded me to one side of the table, pressing in as close together as they could, Joe talking about this and that and everything he could even possibly think about.

Jessie looked amused, sitting across from us. I thought there was something else buried in that smile, too, but I couldn't figure out what it was.

I'm sure to anybody else in the cafeteria, it looked odd. The four of us and her.

I didn't care.

Joe talked and talked and talked. To me. To Carter. To Kelly.

Never to Jessie.

He gave me an apple slice.

I gave him some potato chips.

He said quietly, "I'm happy I'm here. With you."

I said, "Me too."

.   .   .

"Did you love him?" I asked Mark one fall afternoon.

"Who?"

"Gordo."

He said, "Don't," and walked away.

I didn't follow.

.   .   .

I made Gordo drop the wards around the house and the Bennetts came over for dinner at our house one Sunday.

At first, he refused. "It's not safe."

I said, "I belong to a pack of overprotective werewolves who live next door. I'm pretty sure I couldn't be safer."

"Christ," he muttered. "Remember when you didn't say much at all? Those were the good old days."

That hurt. More than I thought it would. I must not have been able to keep it from my face because he sighed and said, "Ox."

"Yeah?" I looked down at my shoes. I knew I didn't always say the best things or the smartest things, but I thought I'd been getting better. I was trying.

His hand curled around the back of my neck and there was a pulse of *something* between us. It wasn't as strong as it was with Joe or the pack, but it was there and it was *warm* and *kind* and it felt like *home*. "I'm sorry," he said quietly.

"I know," I said, trying to brush it off. "It's okay."

His fingers tightened. "No," he said. "It's not okay. No one should ever make you feel like shit. Especially me. It's unacceptable."

"I know."

"I'll be better, okay? I'm not the best, I know. But I'll do right by you. I swear."

"I know."

He squeezed my neck and dropped his hand. "I won't drop the wards," he said. "Not completely. I'll modify them, though. For Joe. Carter and Kelly."

"And the rest of the pack," I said.

He looked away. "Yeah, Ox. For the rest too."

.   .   .

We were having Sunday dinner for the first time at my house.

Mom was very nervous. She flitted about in the kitchen like a little bird.

I asked her why, and she said, "They're just so *fancy*. We're not *fancy* people, Ox."

"They don't care about stuff like that."

"I know."

"You look pretty," I said. And she did. She always did. Even when she was tired. Even when she was sad.

She laughed and said, "Hush, you." She swatted me with a dish towel and told me to make the salad while she checked on the lasagna.

Joe was the first through the door. His eyes darted around, taking in everything as quickly as he could. His chest heaved, breathing in as much as possible. His eyes were wide, almost blown out.

"Joe," Thomas said, coming up behind him. "Calm. Even breaths." I could hear the command in his voice, one that sent shivers along my skin. It was easier now to hear it for what it was. The Alpha. I wasn't a wolf, but I still wanted to bare my neck to him.

"It's a lot," Joe said quietly, trying to slow his breathing. "All at once."

I didn't understand, but I thought I wasn't meant to.

Elizabeth came in, followed by Carter, Kelly, and Mark. Mom chattered away, her nerves showing through in the up-and-down cadence of her voice. Either she didn't notice or chose not to question when the Bennetts touched almost everything in sight, dragging their hands along the couch. The dining room table. The chairs. The countertops. Carter and Kelly sprawled along chairs at the table, spreading themselves out as far as possible.

I knew what they were doing. They were making this place smell like them. Like pack.

Scents were important. They didn't want it to be just me and Mom. They needed to be mixed in too.

I hugged each of them in turn. Carter and Kelly rubbed their noses against my neck.

Joe took my hand. "Your room," he said. "I want to see your room."

He pulled me up the stairs without waiting for an answer. I didn't even need to tell him where to go. He held out his other hand and let his fingers drift along the walls, head darting from side to side. He growled low for a brief moment and his hand tightened in mine. I didn't ask what it was. I didn't know if I wanted to know.

But then we were in my room and he was all over. He didn't stand in one place for more than a second, and he touched everything he could get his hands on.

He muttered to himself, saying, "It's strong in here, so strong, strong, strong" and "I can cover it up, I can make it go away" and "Mine, mine, mine."

I let him. I let him do what he needed to do.

And then he stopped in front of my desk. Sucked in a sharp breath.

"Joe?" I asked, taking a step from the doorway.

"You kept it?"

"What?"

He didn't answer. I stepped up behind him. He was getting taller. The top of his head reached the middle of my chest. I felt of pang of something bittersweet. I didn't know why.

And then I saw what he was looking at.

The little wolf made of stone.

I was confused. "Yeah. Why wouldn't I?"

"Ox," he said in a choked voice. I looked down. His hands were curling into the desk, leaving little claw marks, scoring the wood. His eyes flashed orange and I said, "Hey." I put my hand on his shoulder and it was there again, that warmth, like it'd been with Gordo. But if Gordo had felt like a warm fire, then the pulse, the *pull* with Joe felt like the sun.

He sighed and the claws pulled back and away.

"I like your room," he said quietly. "It's just like I thought it would be. Cluttered and clean."

"Pinecones and candy canes?" I asked him.

He smiled. "And epic and awesome."

He touched the stone wolf once, just the tip of his finger to its head, and that sun between us burned so very, very bright.

A WOLF THING / WE'RE ALONE

They trained. The werewolves. The pack.

They moved in and out of the trees quickly and quietly.

They tracked me through the woods while I attempted to throw them off my trail.

Thomas said, "Attack," and their claws would come out and he would feint left and right and up and down.

I asked him once why we trained like we did.

"We have to be ready," he said.

"For what?"

He put a hand on my shoulder. "To protect what's ours."

"From what?"

"Anything that could take our pack or territory away." His eyes flashed red.

A chill went down my spine.

   .   .   .

I trained harder.

   .   .   .

"Merry Christmas, Ox." Joe grinned when I hugged him close, my chin on the top of his head.

   .   .   .

"You're different," Gordo said, taking a drag from his cigarette.

"Oh?"

"You move differently," he clarified.

"Maybe I'm just growing up."

"It's more . . . confidence. You hold yourself higher."

"It's a wolf thing."

"You're not a wolf."

"Close enough."

His eyes narrowed. "He did it, didn't he?"

"Who?"

"Thomas. He offered you the bite."

I heard Rico cackle loudly from back in the shop. Tanner and Chris yelled something in return. "Yeah," I said.

"Ox," he warned.

"My decision," I said. "He wouldn't do it until I turned eighteen, but it's still my decision."

"Just . . . fuck." Gordo was upset. "Just think of the consequences. You'll be hunted. For the rest of your life. There are things out there. Monsters and people who want nothing more than your head on a pike."

"Because I'd be a wolf?" I asked. "Or because I'm already part of a pack?"

"Shit," he muttered.

"Or maybe because I'm tethered to a witch?"

"I told you—"

"I'm not a kid anymore, Gordo."

His voice cracked when he said, "But you're all I have."

"Good," I said. "Then you know I'm never walking away from you. From this."

He closed his eyes and took a deep breath.

"You turned it down," I said, going off a hunch. "The bite. You said no."

His eyes opened slowly. "Easiest decision I've ever had to make."

We both knew that was a lie.

. . .

I didn't tell him that I'd decided to remain human.

For now.

. . .

Mom said, "Jessie came by the diner today."

I looked back down at my math homework. I didn't think I was doing it right.

"Said she hadn't really seen you for a few days."

"Been busy," I muttered. "Homework. Work." *Full moon with werewolves.*

"Priorities, Ox. They're good to have, but don't forget the good things."

Running with wolves was the greatest thing.

. . .

A dark pulse in the sun between Joe and me.

I snapped my head up from the desk in history class.

I was up and out the classroom door before I even knew I was moving.

I thought, *JoeSafeJoeFindJoe.*

Two other pulses, brief flares of light.

Carter and Kelly, and I thought, *pack.*

There was anger in the sun. It was contained, but it was going to break.

I knew, though I didn't know how.

Men's room. Hallway.

I pushed open the door.

Joe, pressed up against the wall. His bag at his feet, torn open. Pencils and papers across the floor.

Three guys around him. One held him against the wall, his forearm pressed against the neck. I recognized them vaguely through the descending red haze. Sophomores. Assholes.

Joe wasn't scared. At least not completely. I swore I could hear the quick but steady beat of his heart.

But he wasn't fighting back because he knew he was about to wolf out.

Then he saw me.

His eyes widened.

And the sun exploded.

I took the one that held him against the wall first. Grabbed him by the back of the neck and jerked him away. He said, "What—" and then he couldn't speak at all because he was on the floor, my knee on his chest, hands around his throat. His eyes went wide as I snarled and bared my teeth in his face.

The other two grabbed me by the shoulders and arms to try and pull me off, but I remembered my training and Thomas saying *keep calm and maintain control.*

I let them pull me up. I used the momentum and brought my knee into the stomach of the guy on my right and elbowed the guy on my left in the face. One bent over, struggling to breathe. The other cried out, a flash of crimson between his fingers. I stepped back, pushing Joe behind me. His hands fisted my shirt and he pressed his forehead to my back.

Carter and Kelly burst into the room, eyes flaring. They surveyed the room. Something settled in me when they looked satisfied with what they found. Not surprised. Satisfied. Like they knew I could handle this.

"So," Carter said. "Your names."

"Fuck you," the guy with the bloody nose said.

"Wrong answer," I said as Kelly moved toward him.

"Names!" Carter snapped.

Bloody nose said, "Henry."

The guy with hands on his stomach said, "Tyler."

The guy still on the floor said, "Go to hell."

Carter picked him up by his throat and held him up. His feet left the floor as he kicked.

Carter was close, but he was still in control. "Your. Name."

"Dex," the guy choked out.

"You got them?" Carter asked Kelly.

Kelly nodded as he breathed in. "Henry. Tyler. Dex. I got them." Their scents.

"If you *ever* come near my brother again, I'll kill you," Carter said. "Every one of you. And if I can't, Kelly will. And if *he* can't, God help you when Ox gets his hands on you." He threw Dex to the ground. Dex cried out as he landed on his side. Carter and Kelly stepped over him. The other two flinched away from them. They came and stood by my side, blocking Joe in. Kelly put a hand on my arm. Carter's shoulder pressed against mine.

Henry was the first to run. Then Tyler. Dex sneered, but it was a coward's sneer that stuttered and broke. He ran too.

I burned like the sun.

. . .

The principal looked at us. Me. My mom. All the Bennetts. "Five days' suspension," he said.

Carter, Kelly, and I said nothing, as we'd been instructed.

"Five days?" my mother said. "And the three that started this?"

"They are being dealt with," the principal said. I could see the thin film of sweat on his forehead.

"Are they?" Elizabeth said. "I should hope so. After they pinned my twelve-year-old son to the wall."

"And Ox broke a kid's nose!" the principal said. "He's lucky no charges are being filed against him."

"Yes," Elizabeth said. "Quite lucky. Though if there *had* been charges, I'm sure we could have found some of our own."

The principal wiped his brow.

"Mark?" Thomas said in a light tone.

"Yes?"

"How much money were we set to donate to the Green Creek school district this year?"

"Twenty-five thousand dollars."

"Ah. Thank you, Mark."

"You're most welcome."

"Now, Mr. Bennett," the principal said. "I'm sure we can—"

"I'm done speaking with you," Thomas said. "Your presence bothers me. Come along, everyone. It's time to leave."

. . .

Thomas and Elizabeth led me away from the others.

"You protected your own," Thomas said, eyes flashing red. "I am so very proud of you."

He was my Alpha and my skin thrummed with his words. I tilted my head back, baring my throat to him. He reached out and touched my neck gently.

Elizabeth held me close.

. . .

The suspension was lifted suddenly and without warning.

. . .

"I could handle myself," Joe grumbled as we walked down the dirt road.

"I know," I said.

"I could have taken them all down."

"I know."

"I'm not some little kid."

I said, "I know."

He scowled. "Say something else."

"I'm glad I could protect you," I said honestly. "And I always will."

He stared up at me with those big blue eyes. Then he blushed. It started at his throat and rose up through his face. He looked away. Kicked the dirt. I waited until he could make up his mind.

Eventually he grabbed my hand and we continued on down the road.

Another argument.

"They're my *family*," I snapped at her.

Jessie's face was flushed, her eyes bright. "I get that," she said. Her voice was hard. "Even if I don't fully understand their weird fascination with you."

"It's not weird."

"Ox," she said. "It's kind of weird. Like, are they some kind of cult or what?"

"Knock it off, Jessie. You don't get to talk about them like that. They've never had a single bad thing to say about you, so don't you talk about them that way."

"Except for Joe," she muttered.

"What?"

She looked up from her spot on my bed. "I said except for Joe. *He* doesn't like me."

I laughed. "That's not true."

"Ox. It is. Why can't you see it? Why are you so blind when it comes to him?"

"You leave him out of this," I said, my voice starting to rise.

She looked frustrated. "I'm just asking to be a part of your life, Ox. You blow me off. You keep things from me. I know something is going on. Why can't you trust me?"

I said, "I do," though it almost felt like a lie.

She smiled, but it didn't quite reach her eyes.

Just after Thanksgiving, Mom texted me, asking that I come straight home after work.

The house felt different when I walked in. It hit me in the chest. There was anger. Sadness. But relief. So much relief. It had to be a pack thing. I'd never felt the emotions in the house before. I wasn't a wolf, but I wasn't just human, either. I was something more.

It almost felt like seeing colors.

The anger was violet, heavy and cloying.

The sadness was a flickering blue. It vibrated along the edges of the violet.

The relief was green, and I wondered if that was what Elizabeth felt in her green phase. Relief.

Mom was at the table. Her face was dry, but her eyes were red-rimmed. She'd cried but it had passed, and I knew I wasn't completely normal anymore when I somehow knew exactly what she was going to say before she said it.

But I allowed her to say it anyway.

I owed it to her.

"Ox," she said, "I need you to listen, okay?" and so I said, "Yeah, sure," and put my hand over hers. Mine dwarfed hers completely, and I loved this tiny little woman.

"We have each other," she said.

"I know."

"We're strong."

"We are." I smiled.

"Your father died," she said. "He was drunk. Got behind the wheel. Went into a tree."

So I said, "Okay," even as my chest tightened.

"I'm here," she said. "I'm always going to be here."

We both chose to ignore the lie because no one could promise that.

"Where?" I asked.

"Nevada."

"Didn't get very far, did he."

"No," she said. "I don't suppose he did."

"Are you okay?" I asked, reaching out to brush my thumb over her cheek.

She nodded. Then shrugged. Her face stuttered a bit and she looked away.

I waited until she could go on.

"I loved him," she said finally. "For a long time."

"Me too." I still did. She might not anymore, but I still did.

"He was kind. For a while. A good man."

"Yeah."

"He loved you."

"Yeah."

"Just us now."

And I said, "No, it's not."

She looked back at me. "What do you mean?" A tear fell on her cheek.

"There's more," I said, and I was shaking.

She was worried. "Ox, what's wrong?"

"We're not alone. We have the Bennetts. Gordo. They're . . ."

"Ox?"

I took a deep breath and let it out slowly. I couldn't let her think we were alone. Not anymore. Not when we didn't have to be. "I'm going to show you something. You have to trust me. I will never let anything hurt you. I will always protect you. I will keep you safe."

She was crying now. "Ox—"

"Do you trust me?" I asked.

"Yes. Yeah. Yes. Of course." It was broken up with tiny little gasps.

"We never needed him. We survived."

"Did we? *Did we?*"

I took her by the hand, pulled her up. Wrapped my arms around her shoulders. Led her to the front door. It was cold outside, so I kept close. I was warmer than she was.

"Don't be afraid," I told her. "Don't ever be afraid."

She looked up at me, so many questions in her eyes.

So I looked up at the night sky, my head tilting back.

And I *sang*.

It wasn't as good as the wolves'. It never would be, because regardless of what I was, I was closer to human than anything else. Thomas had told me as much when he'd taught me deep in the woods. But it was strong, that howl, even when my voice cracked. I put everything I could into it. My violet anger. My blue sadness. My green relief, my fucking green relief that he was gone, gone, gone, and I never had to wonder about him again. There would be no more *what ifs*. There would be no more *whys*. There would be no more suffering, because we were *not* alone. My father had said I was gonna get shit, but fuck him. Goddamn him. I loved him so much.

I put it all in that song.

And even before the echo had died through the trees, there came an answering howl from the house at the end of the lane.

Joe.

And then another. Carter.

And Kelly. And Mark. And Elizabeth.

Thomas was the loudest of all. The call of the Alpha.

They heard my song and sang me one in return.

"Oh my God," my mother whispered and pressed closer against me.

There was a crash in the distance. The pounding of paws and claws on frost-covered leaves.

Violet was anger.

Blue was sadness.

Green was relief.

And through the trees came the flashes of orange. The flicker of red. The colors of familiarity and family and home.

I could hear them in me and they said, *we're here BrotherSonFriendLove. we're here and we are pack and yours and nothing will change that.*

My mother whimpered at my side, holding me tightly. She was trembling.

I said, "They would never hurt you."

She said, "How do you know?" She sounded rather breathless.

"Because we're pack." I pulled away from her, shushing her gently as she tried to hold me back. "It's okay," I said. "It's okay."

I never looked away from her. I walked backward down the porch steps, slow so I didn't slip on the ice. My breath fanned out around me in puffs of white. It was cold, but the moment I stepped foot on the frozen ground, I was surrounded by warmth. The wolves brushed up against me, yipping excitedly, nipping at my fingers and hands and arms. Joe jumped up on his hind legs, paws on my shoulders. He licked my face and I laughed and laughed.

Thomas sat back, waiting. Eventually, he gave a low growl. The others stopped moving around me and moved aside. When he rose to his feet, I heard my mother gasp.

His steps were slow and deliberate. He came up beside me and laid his head on my shoulder, wrapping his neck around mine, his nose running along my skin and hair. A rumble came from his chest, quiet and pleased. It was the first time I'd called them on my own. He was proud of me.

I was seven months away from being eighteen years old, but I still must not have been a man because I had to blink the tears away. "My father died," I whispered to him. Joe whined, but didn't come closer. "She thinks we're alone."

The rumble in his chest grew louder, and through the bonds that stretched between us all, I heard *hush no never alone here we're here don't cry SonPack don't cry never alone.*

I put my hands in his fur and held on tight. He allowed me the moments to grieve, because he knew all I needed were moments.

They passed, as these things often do.

He licked the tears from my cheeks, and I laughed quietly.

He put his forehead against mine, and I said, "Okay. I'm okay now. Thank you."

Thomas turned toward my mother. She let out a small, choked noise and took a step back, shivering.

I said, "It's okay."

She said, "This is a dream."

And I said, "No."

"Ox!" she cried. "What is this!"

Thomas stood in front of her, bowing his head. He pressed his nose against her forehead, and she said, "*Oh.*"

FIGHT FOR ME / FAMILY IS EVERYTHING

My mother said, "What a strange world we live in." And then she laughed.

And then she cried.

The pack huddled around her until the sun came up the next morning.

.   .   .

The days moved on.

.   .   .

"Mom knows," I said.

Gordo closed his eyes. I could feel the bond between us as he fought to control his anger. Violet with tinges of blue. Mixed in was gold, and I pushed at it until I realized it was jealousy. The sharp colors faded as he let out his breath.

"It's your pack," he said, face blank and voice indifferent.

My own violet pulsed. "Dad died."

Blue, blue, blue. "Ox. I'm so sorry."

And then his arms were around me and I was his tether, and I thought he might have been part of mine.

.   .   .

Shortly before my birthday, Jessie kissed me in my room. She pressed herself up against me until I took a step back, my legs hitting my bed.

I sat down.

She straddled my lap.

I laughed quietly and thought about the full moon that night. Mom was going to go with us for the first time, just to see.

Jessie said, "I think we should break up."

I said, "Okay."

Silence.

She pushed herself off of me and stood. "Ox." Her eyes narrowed. "What?"

"That's *it*? That's all you have to say?"

I was confused. "You said it!"

She rolled her eyes. "You're supposed to *fight* for me."

"Oh."

"Ox."

"What?"

"Do you want to fight for me?"

"Jessie," I said. "Why are you doing this?" I reached out for our bond, to see what her colors were, but then I remembered there wasn't any bond at all, and I felt a little sad.

She paced in front of me. "You're never here anymore."

"Here? I'm always here. This is my house. My room."

"No. *Here*. Like you-and-me here. *If* I get to see you. *If* you re-member to call me back. *If* you remember to text me. If, if, if, because you're always *distracted*. You're always *gone*. It's like you're fucking vacant and somewhere else and I don't deserve that, Ox. I don't."

She was right. She didn't. I told her so.

"Then *fix* it," she said.

And I said, "I can't." She heard what I meant.

I won't.

She took a step back away from me and I wondered what she saw when she looked at me. If I had changed. If I had become something different. Some days I still felt like the same old Ox. Other days I felt like howling a song to shake the trees.

"Why?" she asked.

"Look, Jessie," I said. My voice was even, but I felt my heart crack just a sliver. "I have . . . things. To do." I was never good with words, and they were failing me now. I struggled and latched onto the first thing that came to mind. "Priorities. I have priorities."

"And I'm not one of them," she said.

"No," I said, because that wasn't right. "You are." But that wasn't right either. It was an awful feeling. "Shit," I muttered.

"I love you, Ox," Jessie said. "Can't you see that?"

I could. And I loved her too. In my own way. "You're leaving," I said instead. "In a few months." Across the country for school.

"Yeah. I am. And we were going to *try*."

"Maybe we shouldn't."

She shook her head. "Why?"

"Because I can't give you what you need. And it's not fair."

"It's because of Joe, isn't it? It's because of that little shit—"

I stood. Quickly. I said, "*Don't.*"

Her eyes went wide. Her lip quivered. And she said, "I'm sorry. That's not . . . I don't know why I said that."

"This is between us," I said. "You leave him out of this."

Eventually, she left.

         •   •   •

"I can smell it," Joe said quietly. We sat on the porch and watched the sun. "You're sad."

I said, "Yeah," because I was.

"Do you want to talk about it?"

I shook my head. "Not yet."

He laid his head on my shoulder and said, "Okay."

Later, after the sun had set and the stars had come out in the sky, he said, "I won't ever leave you."

         •   •   •

Chris said, "You bastard. Jessie's heartbroken. Fuck you, Ox."

Gordo called him an asshole.

Tanner said love was hard.

Rico said I was a heartbreaker.

Chris didn't talk to me for three days.

On the fourth day, he came up to me, looking nervous.

I couldn't stand that, so I hugged him.

He hugged me back. He said, "I missed you. I'm an ass. You forgive me?"

I said, "Sure," and he grinned and bought me a sandwich at the diner.

He didn't say anything about Jessie. But neither did I.

         •   •   •

I turned eighteen. Thomas didn't ask if I wanted the bite. I didn't ask him to give it to me.

         •   •   •

Green Creek was small. Our graduating class only had thirty-four people in it. But you would have thought the crowd numbered in the thousands by the way we all yelled when Carter walked across the stage. He grinned and winked as he accepted his diploma.

Later, they said, "Oxnard Matheson," and the roar that followed knocked the breath from my chest. The Bennetts. My mom. Gordo and the guys. They screamed and howled. You would have thought I'd accomplished the greatest thing known to mankind.

I'll be honest. I wasn't expecting that. It hurt, but in a good way. Sometimes, pain can be good.

.   .   .

Carter said, "I won't be going far. Eugene's only a couple hours away."

"Won't be too bad," Kelly said.

"We'll see each other all the time," Joe said.

I said, "This fucking sucks."

"Yeah," they sighed.

We lay on the grass watching the stars above us. We were all angles and parallels, stretched out and touching in some way. Joe had his head on my chest, his legs stretching away from me. Carter's heavy legs were draped across mine. Kelly had his head on my shoulder.

I felt warm. And safe. And sad.

"It'll be okay," Carter said. "I promise."

"What if you don't come back?" Joe asked in a small voice. I rubbed my hands through his hair.

"I will," Carter said. "You're going to be my Alpha. Of course I'll come back for you. And for Kelly and Ox. We're a pack. One day, you'll lead us."

"But I don't know how," Joe said. "I don't think I'm going to be very good at it."

"You'll be the best," I told him. "The best Alpha who ever lived."

He preened and Carter and Kelly laughed.

They thought I was joking around. Silly old Ox.

But I believed that with all my heart.

.   .   .

Thomas took Joe into the forest sometimes. They stayed away for hours. I never asked what they talked about or what they did because I figured it was between the two of them. It was none of my business.

Until Thomas said otherwise.

He sent for me in the middle of summer. Carter showed up at the garage, eyes bright with something I couldn't quite place. He looked like live wires arced underneath his skin. If I didn't know any better, I would have thought he was losing control.

"Papi," Rico called out. "Lover boy is here. Take a break. Ten minutes should be enough to get off."

Chris and Tanner whistled and hollered at me as I rolled my eyes.

Gordo stood in the doorway to his office, arms across his chest, eyes tracking me as I walked through the garage. This was different, and he knew it too. He wasn't pack, but he could feel it. And the wolves never came here. The wards kept them out. Gordo was a dick, but I didn't know his story. Not completely. I tried not to blame him.

And there Carter stood, jittery, eyes flashing orange.

I asked, "Is everything okay?"

And he said, "The Alpha wants you tonight," in a voice filled with gravel, like his wolf was bursting out of his throat.

I wanted to ask *why* and question everything, but I knew better. This was a *message*.

I wrapped my arms around Carter instead and he whined at the back of his throat, his nose in the crook of my neck.

Eventually, he stopped trembling.

"Okay?" I whispered in his ear.

He nodded and pulled away. "I'll hang around," he said in his normal voice. "Give you a ride home."

I went back inside the garage. "What was that?" Gordo asked.

I said, "Pack business," and got back to work.

Carter didn't say much on the drive back home. Just little things about college and girls, and so I said something I'd been thinking for a long while, "This guy came into work. I thought he was attractive. I check out guys sometimes." It came out fast because that was the first time I'd said it aloud. It felt like relief. And terror.

Carter didn't say anything for a minute. And then he said, "Oh. Okay. Did you lick his balls?"

I laughed so hard that I thought I would die. Carter was laughing right along with me.

He said, "You know I don't give a shit, right? Like, of all the things in the world to freak out about, that's one of the least?"

I said, "Yeah, Carter. I know." My heart was pounding.

"Hey. Calm down, Ox."

Stupid werewolves. "I will."

"Am I the first you told?"

"Yeah."

He grinned. "I popped your gay cherry!" He frowned. "Wait."

"Oh my God."

"That's not what I meant."

"Oh my God."

"I popped your coming-out cherry." He grimaced as he stopped for a red light. "That didn't sound any better."

"Oh my God."

"Have you kissed a guy yet?"

I blushed. "No."

Before I could even react, he leaned over and planted a hard kiss on my lips, pulling away with a loud smack. "Now you have."

"Oh my God."

"You sound way too much like Joe."

"That was like kissing my brother," I said.

"Fuck you, Oxnard," he said with an easy grin. "You're lucky I'm straight. I would have hit that a long time ago." He sniffed the air and had the audacity to look offended. "Seriously? You're not aroused? At *all*?"

"My life," I groaned.

"I must be doing it wrong."

"That must be it."

"You still like girls?"

I shrugged. "Think so."

He punched me in the arm. "Greedy."

I laughed.

"It'll make things easier, though," he said, and I thought, *What?*

"What things?"

He shrugged. "The future. And all that comes with it."

And that was all he would say until we got to the house at the end of the lane. Thomas and Joe were waiting for us. "It'll be okay, Ox," Carter said before he went inside.

"Ox," Thomas said warmly. "Thank you for coming."

I smiled back a bit nervously. I knew he could smell it on me. Werewolves were like that. So he said, "There's nothing to be worried about," and I said, "Okay."

Joe took my hand and rubbed his forehead on my shoulder. He was getting tall. Almost thirteen years old and he was sprouting like a weed. I told him as much and he grinned blindingly at me.

Thomas walked into the woods without another word.

Joe tugged on my hand, and we followed.

I followed their example and didn't speak.

Eventually, we reached the clearing in the woods.

Joe dropped my hand and went to stand by his father. Without a word, they sat down on the grass, crossing their legs, facing each other.

Thomas said, "Joe, what does it mean to be an Alpha?"

"It means protecting others at all cost."

"Even at the expense of your life?"

"Yes. Pack is more important than anything else."

And man, did I want to step in and say something, but I kept my mouth shut. Thomas glanced at me briefly, a look of warning on his face, but he smiled quietly to let me know he understood.

"And why is the pack more important?"

"Because pack is family," Joe said. "And family is everything."

"Ox," Thomas said. "Sit with us."

And I did. I was unsure of my place here. Unsure of why I'd been invited along. Unsure of what to say. So I did what I did best and said nothing at all.

And neither did Thomas or Joe. They sat there, watching the leaves in the trees, hands trailing through the grass beneath, and everything was *green*. Green like the wings of the dragonfly I saw on the day Joe and I first met. Green like Elizabeth's phase when we first met. Green like Gordo's earth magic, sharp and pungent. Green like *relief*, like so much fucking *relief* that I was overwhelmed by it all.

I was. Because I was sitting next to an Alpha werewolf and a future Alpha werewolf and *I belonged* with them. To them. And they belonged to me.

The bonds were there. Between us. The bond between me and my Alpha. The bond between me and Joe.

We stayed there for hours and didn't say a word.

.   .   .

From that point on, I went with them more often than not. Sometimes we sat. Sometimes I watched as Thomas and Joe trained one on one, claws flying, fangs bared.

I asked Thomas again, "What is all this for?"

"What?"

"The fighting. The claws. The teeth. Training. All of it."

He said, "So when the time comes, we'll be able to protect our territory."

"From who?"

He shrugged. "Everyone."

"Thomas," I started. But then I stopped because I wasn't sure of what I wanted.

He waited, like he always did.

I want the bite.

I thought to say it. I really did. I opened my mouth to say just that, but I couldn't get the words out. I couldn't make it so.

He knew. Of course he knew. "I'll be here," he said. "If and when you're ready. If not me, then Joe."

"He's going to be great, you know," I said quietly. "Because of what you've taught him."

Thomas smiled. It was a rare thing, and it made me feel good to see it. "An Alpha is only as strong as his pack."

. . .

I asked him one day when Joe would become the Alpha.

He said it would be when the time was right.

I asked him what would happen to him then.

He said he would serve as his son's Beta.

I asked him what it would feel like to give up all that came with being an Alpha.

He said it would feel *green*.

I didn't ask him how he knew.

. . .

Sometimes Thomas sent just me and Joe out to the clearing.

Sometimes we talked.

Sometimes we didn't say anything at all.

He said it was for the bond between us.

. . .

Sometimes I thought they were keeping things from me.

It was just a feeling I had.

GROUND YOU WALK ON / THE FALLEN KING

She was in the kitchen singing along with her radio when I said, "Mom, can I talk to you?"

She looked over her shoulder as she stirred a saucepan on the stove. She smiled and said, "Hi, baby," and I almost turned and ran out of the room. I was eighteen years old, and I was scared of my *mother*.

She must have seen something on my face because she turned down the heat on the stove and turned. She reached out and touched my arm. "Okay?"

I shook my head. "Uh. Maybe? I think so. Possibly."

She waited.

I loved her. And she loved me. So I said, "I'm pretty sure I like girls."

She said, "Okay."

And so I said, "And guys." My palms were sweaty.

"Okay."

"Like . . . you know."

Her eyes widened slightly. "*Oh.* That's . . ." She squinted at me. "Equally?"

"What?"

"You like girls and guys. Equally? Or one more than the other?"

I shrugged. "Maybe the same? I can't say for sure because I've never done anything with a guy." I winced. "I really wish I hadn't said that."

She blushed. "Well. You're eighteen. You can . . . you know. Do. That. As an adult."

"Oh God," I groaned.

"No, no, it's okay!" She sounded nervous. "I just . . . You always hear that parents just *know* these things about their kids. I . . . didn't know." She frowned. "Does that make me a bad mom?"

"No! Er. No. Nope. You're . . . great. At. The mom thing."

She sighed. "Ox."

"Yeah?"

"I don't care about stuff like that."

"What stuff?"

"If you're gay or whatever."

"Bisexual," I said as if that would make it any better.

"Bisexual," she said. "Okay."

"This is awkward."

"Is it?"

"Isn't it?"

"You look scared," she said.

I looked down at the floor. "I didn't want to make you mad," I managed to get out.

And then her arms were around my waist and her head was against my chest. I put my forehead on her shoulder and hugged her back.

"I could never be mad at you for being who you are," she said quietly. "And I'm sorry if I ever made you think that."

"So. It's not. Weird? Or anything?"

She laughed. "Ox. You are a part of a pack of werewolves and you're asking me if something like this is weird?"

"You're pack too," I said quickly.

And she was. To an extent. Ever since that moment when Thomas had touched her head and she'd become aware of just how strange the world could be, she'd been pack. It had taken her weeks to accept what she'd seen, and maybe a little longer to believe it down to her bones. Kelly told me that for a long while she'd stunk of fear any time she'd come into contact with the Bennetts. I told him not to take it personally, and he'd just laughed and put his arm around my shoulders and said that of course they wouldn't.

She didn't come with us on full moons most times, but Thomas had insisted that she train like the rest of us when she could. At first, she was quiet and awkward. At first, she did little.

I don't know what changed. Maybe it was when Thomas took her on a walk through the forest and spoke with her about things I never asked about after. Maybe it was when Elizabeth took her to lunch and they drank peach wine and giggled like little girls. Maybe it was me and how she saw I needed this. Needed them.

I didn't know what caused the change. But one day, she came with her eyes flashing, her hair pulled back in a tight ponytail, and she managed to sweep my legs out from underneath me. I was dazed, looking up at the clouds through the trees, and she just *laughed*.

God, I loved that woman. More than anything.

Which is why I was so scared of disappointing her. With something so stupid as sex.

"Is there . . . you know." She looked up at me. "Anyone special?"

I shook my head. "Not since Jessie."

"Not a lot of pickings around here."

"Uh."

"You'll meet someone," she said, suddenly fierce. "You'll see. A girl or a boy and they'll worship the ground you walk on because you deserve to be treasured. And I'll be there to say I told you so because you've earned it. If anyone in this world has earned it, it's you."

. . .

Carter went to college. I found a rare weekend to go visit him. Kelly and Joe wanted to go, but they had homework and Elizabeth put her foot down.

Carter was okay with that.

He had a dorm room to himself.

He introduced me to a few people, but I forgot their names almost immediately because it'd been weeks since I'd seen my friend. He must have felt the same because he made the people leave and we lay on the floor, his head on my legs, and he said, "You smell like home."

We stayed there until the sun went down.

He took me to some club and got us in. I didn't know how. He said it was probably because we were bigger than everyone else.

The music was loud. The lights were flashing. I didn't know how he could stand it, given that all his senses were heightened. I could smell booze and sweat and the cloying sticky perfume of a woman who came out of nowhere and rubbed herself against me before she disappeared back into the crowd.

Carter just laughed.

He said, "Here," and handed me a glass of *something*.

I drank it. It was fruity and it burned.

He did too, but alcohol did nothing to wolves, unless they drank enough to kill a normal human. He'd told me once that he just liked the taste. He wondered what it'd be like to be drunk. I wondered what it'd be like to feel the pull of the moon.

I saw the glint of orange in his eyes.

It was hot in the club. Sticky and moist.

One moment I was laughing as two women came and sandwiched him on the dance floor, and the next there were pretty green eyes in front of me. Pale skin. A wicked smile with a hint of teeth.

He said, "What's your name?"

And I said, "Ox."

"Ox. That's unique."

I grinned because I felt good. "I guess. Who're you?" My limbs were loose. The bass crawled along my skin.

He said, "Eric," and, "You want to dance?"

"I'm not very good. I'm too big."

That wicked smile curved even farther. "That right?"

He pulled me by the hand and led me through the crowd. Carter caught my eye and asked a question that only I could hear and I shrugged and turned away.

Eric pressed himself against me, a long hot line of sweat and flesh. There was a roll of his hips against mine and I said, "*Wow.*" He laughed.

The song changed and I felt lips against my neck, a quick flick of a tongue.

Later, I was in a bathroom stall. Eric was on his knees. My dick was in his mouth, my head back against warm ceramic tile that shook with the beat of the music. My fingers were in his hair and everything was hot and wet. I grunted a warning and he backed away, jacking me until I came on the dirty floor. He stood up and kissed me while he jerked himself off. He sighed into my mouth. He tasted like stale beer and mint. He came on his hand. I felt raw.

"Thanks," he said, zipping up his pants. "That was great."

"Sure," I said, because I was unsure of what else to say. "You too."

And then he left.

I stood in the bathroom for a while, but it smelled of piss and my head hurt.

I couldn't find Carter and I tried to find that thread, that thing inside that said *BondPackBrother*, but I was overwhelmed by everything and so I said, "Carter, Carter, Carter," and for a moment nothing happened. And then he was in front of me, eyes narrowed, hands on my arms, looking me up and down, trying to find where I'd been injured.

His nostrils flared and he said, "Was it consensual?" and I blushed and looked away.

It took a moment, but I nodded.

His arm went around my shoulder and he chuckled near my ear, his forehead pressed against my hair. "You dog," he said.

"Says the werewolf."

He growled near my ear. "Was it good?"

"Shut up."

"Was it *awesome*?"

"Shut up, Carter."

"Did you *swoon*?"

"Oh, for fuck's sake."

"Look at you," he said. "Getting blowies in public. My little Ox is all grown up."

"Bigger than you," I muttered, and he just laughed and laughed.

He pulled me away. It wasn't until we got out onto the street that I saw the lipstick smeared across his lips. Across his neck. I told him he was a whore. He snarled, and I ran. He chased me, orange eyes flashing happily. He pretended to let me win.

We slept in the same bed, curled around each other because we were pack, and I knew he missed home.

I showered for a very long time before I left the next morning.

When I got back, Joe asked, "Have fun?"

And I said, "Sure, Joe," but it felt like a lie.

Nick happened a year later. He came in to Gordo's all dusty from the road. The clutch on his bike had blown out a few miles outside of Green Creek. He stayed for a week. I fucked him on the last three days he was in town. He left and I never saw him again.

Joe was fourteen and he didn't talk to me for three weeks after that. Said he was busy. Finals were coming up and he had to study.

"Sure," I said, trying not to worry at the strain in his voice. "You okay?"

"Yeah, Ox." He sighed into the phone. "I'm okay."

I almost believed him.

I had just turned twenty-two when monsters came to town.

For all Gordo's warnings about how big and scary the world could be, for all Thomas's notions of a territory protected, nothing had ever happened. No one came. Nothing attacked. I never asked questions about other packs or what else existed if werewolves were real. I lived in a bubble in a small town in the middle of the mountains and I thought that's where I'd always be.

Everything was good. Everything was fine.

Carter had just graduated and moved back to work with his father.

Kelly was taking online courses so he didn't have to leave the pack.

Joe was sixteen and still waited for me on the dirt road almost every day.

Gordo was thinking of opening another shop in the next town over.

Mom smiled when she ran with the wolves at night.

Jessie moved back to Green Creek and was a teacher at the school.

Tanner, Rico, and Chris took me out for beers, and we ate our weight in buffalo wings.

Mark was close to telling me about him and Gordo.

Elizabeth was painting in pinks and yellows.

Thomas smiled out to the trees, a king content with his domain.

I should have asked more questions. About what was out there. About what they could want. But I was naïve, and dangerously so.

I was walking toward the diner for lunch. I rubbed the grease from my fingernails. My hands were callused, signs of hard work. I marveled at how I had a place here. In Green Creek. My father had said I was gonna get shit, but he was dead and I had a place. Friends. Family. I had people. I was something. I was somebody.

It was a bright June day and I was alive and happy.

And then a woman said, "Well. Hello."

I stopped. Looked up.

She was wrong. Off. Dark. Beautiful with red hair and pale skin and a shark's smile on her face, all bite and teeth. She wore a pretty summer dress, blues and greens. She was barefoot, and I wondered if her feet burned on the cement from the sun.

"Hello," I said. There didn't seem to be anyone else on the sidewalk.

She took a step toward me. She cocked her head to the side and I thought, *Wrong. Wrong, wrong, wrong.* "My name is Marie," she said. "What's yours?"

"Ox."

"Ox," she breathed. "I do like that name." She was close enough to touch and I didn't know how that had happened.

"Thank you," I said. "That's very nice of you."

She closed her eyes and inhaled deeply. "You smell like . . ."

"Like?"

She opened her eyes. They flashed violet, like an Omega. "Human. Tell me, human. You play with wolves?" She took another step toward me.

I took an answering step back. In my head, Thomas was telling me to remember my training. To remember what he'd taught me. I didn't think it was really him, but I couldn't be sure. I knew Gordo had wards up all over town, so surely he would have known if another wolf had breached them.

"You should leave," I told her, "before—"

"Before?"

"You know why."

"Ox? What's going on?"

"Shit," I muttered. I looked over Marie's shoulder. Mom was hanging out the diner's door, watching me with concern on her face.

"Go back inside," I told her as Marie looked back at her and wiggled her fingers in an obscene wave. Her fingernails were painted blue.

"She smells like you," Marie said to me. "Did you know that? Like you and wood smoke and autumn leaves. And I know what she smells like now. Scent memory, Ox. It never leaves."

"Ox," Mom said.

"Inside," I snapped at her.

She went inside. I knew she'd be reaching for the phone.

Marie laughed. "Little human has some bite to him. Did the wolves teach you that?"

"This is the territory of the Bennett pack," I told her. "You don't belong here."

"Bennett," she said. "*Bennett*. Like that name means anything anymore. Let me tell you about the *Bennetts*."

"The fuck is this?"

Gordo was at my side. His face was twisted in anger. His arms were covered by his work shirt, but I knew the tattoos on his skin were starting to shift.

Marie hissed. "Witch."

"Wolf," he snarled back. "You got balls, lady, showing your face here. Thomas Bennett is on his way. What do you think he'll do when he sees you?"

A flicker of fear crossed her face before it disappeared. She smiled again, more fangs than not. "The fallen king? Coming out of hiding? Oh, glory be!"

"It's not hiding when you're in your own territory," I said.

"With humans in his pack," she said. "Low, even for him. Belly dragging across the dirt."

My hands curled into fists.

Marie grinned at me. "Aren't you just precious? I could gut you, you know. Right here. Before you could move. Your Alpha has been hidden away long enough. He's weaker now. Even I can feel it. I could take you and he could do nothing."

"Try," I said, and Gordo tensed.

But she didn't. She took a step back. Looked over her shoulder before turning back. She smiled a little and said, "Say hi to your mom for me, Ox," and then she was off, down the street until she disappeared.

.   .   .

They came two nights later.

They were feral. Four of them. Not a pack, as they had no Alpha, but somehow still working together.

They'd made a mistake, though. By showing themselves. Or, at least by Marie showing herself.

Thomas made Mom and me stay at the Bennett house in those days that followed Marie cornering me. I told him Gordo needed to be there too. Thomas didn't argue. Gordo did. I told him to shut the fuck up. I might have sounded slightly hysterical.

Mom went to work during the day. Carter and Kelly went with her.

Gordo and I went to work. He didn't let me out of his sight, even when we had to take a longer than normal lunch break so he could strengthen his wards.

Joe stayed home from school. I brought his homework, and he took it from me with steady hands.

Thomas and Mark holed themselves up in Thomas's office, whispering angrily into a phone, speaking to people I'd never heard of.

Elizabeth kept us calm, hands casually in our hair as she walked by.

On the second night, we sat down to dinner. Conversation was quiet. Silverware scraped against clay plates. Then Gordo took in a sharp breath and sighed. "They're coming," he said.

Alpha and Beta eyes shone around us.

We knew the plan. We'd trained for this.

I thought my hands would shake as I picked up a crowbar infused with silver, a gift from Gordo. They did not shake.

Thomas and Mark. Carter and Gordo. Out on the porch.

The rest of us stayed inside. Elizabeth and me in front. Kelly with Joe and my mother.

I saw them approach in the dark. Their violet eyes shone among the trees.

Thomas said, "This is Bennett territory. I will give you a chance to leave. I suggest you take it."

They laughed.

A man said, "Thomas Bennett. As I live and breathe."

Another man said, "And a witch no less. Smells like . . . Livingstone? Was that your *father*?"

Gordo Livingstone. His father, who'd lost his tether and hurt a great many people.

But Gordo didn't reply. It wasn't his place. The Alpha spoke for them all, even if Gordo wasn't pack.

Thomas said, "One chance."

The third man said, "The children will suffer. Especially little Joseph. I don't think it'll take much to break him." There was a nasty smile on his face, and I would have murdered him where he stood without a second thought if Elizabeth hadn't tightened her hold on my arm.

Thomas said, "You shouldn't have said that."

And Marie said, "You talk too much."

And then there were claws and fangs and desperate snarls. The wolves half-shifted and tore into each other. Thomas's eyes were fire-red and he seemed bigger than the others, so much bigger. I wondered why the Omegas thought they ever stood a chance.

Gordo went after the first man. His tattoos shone and shifted, and

I could smell the ozone around him, lightning-struck and crackling. The earth shifted beneath the Omega's feet, a sharp column of rock shooting up and knocking him into an old oak tree.

Carter took the second man, and they were all teeth and tearing skin. Carter roared angrily as the Omega sliced sharp lines down his back, and Kelly gave an answering snarl behind me, taking a step toward his brother before Joe grabbed his hand, eyes wide and frantic.

Mark raised the third man over his head and brought him down over his knee, and the crack of the Omega's back was sharp and wet. The Omega fell to the ground. His arms and legs skittered and seized.

Thomas took on Marie. Her red hair flew around her wolfed-out face. His red eyes tracked her every movement. He was grace. She was violence. Their claws hit and caused sparks to flare in the dark. He moved like liquid and smoke. She was staccato. She had already lost, but didn't know it yet. She would. Soon.

But.

We didn't know there was a fifth. Maybe the wolves should have known. Maybe they should have been able to sense him. Maybe the breaching of the wards should have tipped Gordo off. But there was blood and distraction, magic and breaking bone. Our family was fighting, and they might have been winning, but not without taking hits.

Senses were overloaded. Hackles were raised.

My mother was at the rear of us.

She said, "Ox."

So I turned.

An Omega had her. He held her against him, her back to his front. His arm circled around her, elbow against her breasts, hand and claws around her throat.

I said, "No."

The Omega said, "Call them off."

I said, "You'll regret this. Every day for the rest of your miserably short life."

He said, "I will kill her right now."

I said, "You will *regret* this."

The big bad wolf smiled. "Human," he spat.

My mom said, "*Ox*," and it was so soft and sweet and full of tears and I took a step toward her.

"Let her go."

The Omega said, "Call. Them. *Off.*"

And Joe. Joe. Sixteen-year-old Joe. Standing off to the side. Forgotten because the Omega had eyes on *me*, like he could sense that *I* had any power here. Like *I* had any control over the pack. Either he was mistaken or thought he knew something I didn't.

But Joe. Before I could take another step, he was moving, legs coiled, claws out. Jump-kicked off the wall. Launched himself up and over the Omega. Brought his claws down into the Omega's face. Eyes punctured and skin split. The Omega screamed. His hand around my mother's throat fell away.

Mom wasn't stupid. She had trained. She saw what was coming. She elbowed the Omega in the stomach. Brought the heel of her foot up into his balls. Ducked away.

Joe spun off him, dropping to the floor.

I took three steps.

The blind Omega growled, "There will always be *more.*"

I said, "You shouldn't have touched my mother," and swung the silver-infused crowbar like a bat. It smashed upside his head, skull cracking, blood flying. Skin burned and hair smoldered. The Omega grunted once and fell to the floor. His chest rose once, hitching, failing. Then it stopped.

The sounds of fighting fell away outside of the house.

I took a deep breath. I tasted copper on my tongue.

Mom said, "You okay?" She touched my arm.

I said, "Yeah. You?"

And she said, "Yeah. Better now."

I said, "Joe."

And he looked at me, eyes blown out, hands at his sides dripping blood onto the floor. I didn't stop to think. I didn't care. I stepped away from my mother and pulled him close. He fisted his hands in the back of my shirt, claws tearing lightly at my skin. I didn't care because it told me I wasn't dreaming and we were alive. His nose was in my neck because he was so tall now. So much bigger than the little boy I first found on the dirt road. He breathed me in and his heart beat against my chest, the blood of the werewolf I'd killed pooling at our feet.

.   .   .

Days later, I asked Gordo, "What else is out there?"

And he said, "Whatever you can think of."

As it turned out, I could think of many things.

. . .

Thomas led me through the trees and told me there were many packs, though not as many as there used to be. They killed each other. Humans hunted and killed them like it was their job. Like it was sport. Other monsters hunted and killed them.

"This was a fluke," he said. "Others know not to come here."

I didn't know who he was trying to convince, him or me. So I asked, "Why?"

"Because of what the Bennett name means."

"What does it mean?" I remembered Marie calling him a fallen king. Her body was nothing but ashes now, burned and spread across the forest.

"Respect," he said. "And the Omegas failed to understand that. They thought they could come into my territory. My home. And take from me. We spilled their blood because they didn't know their place."

"I killed him because he threatened my mom."

Thomas slid his hand to the back of my neck and squeezed gently. "You were very brave," he said quietly. "Protecting what's yours. You're going to do great things, and people will stand in awe of you."

"Thomas," I said.

He looked at me.

"Who are you?" Because there was something more that I didn't understand.

He said, "I am your Alpha."

And I accepted that for what it was.

LOW-SLUNG SHORTS /
YOU AND JOE

It was not a gradual thing.
Wait.
That was a lie.
I didn't *know* it was a gradual thing.
But it must have been. It *had* to have been.

Because it's the only thing that explained the cosmic explosion that was the feeling of *want* and *need* and *mine mine mine*. The force of it was ridiculous. It had to have been there. For a long time.

.   .   .

Joe turned seventeen in August. We threw a party as we always did. There was cake and presents and he smiled at me so widely.

He was seventeen that September when he started his senior year in high school. Kelly was at the beginning of his MBA. Carter worked with Mark and Thomas. Elizabeth did the things that made her happy. Gordo decided to wait on opening a second shop. Mom smiled more than she used to. I worked and breathed and lived. I had blood on my hands, but it was in service of the pack. I had nightmares about dead wolves with their heads bashed in. I woke up sweating, but every time I saw my mother's smile, the guilt eased just a little bit more.

Jessie kissed me one night in October. I kissed her back and then stopped. She smiled sadly at me and said she understood. I didn't tell her that I hadn't been with anybody since the night the Omegas came because I couldn't lose focus. I couldn't be distracted. And that I didn't feel that way about her anymore. So I just apologized and blushed and she shook her head and went home.

In November, Carter dated a girl named Audrey and she was sweet and pretty and laughed hoarsely. She liked to drink and dance and then one day she didn't come around anymore. Carter shrugged and said it wasn't meant to be. Just some fun.

Snow fell in December and I ran with the wolves through the powder, a winter moon shining out overhead, my breath trailing behind me as the pack howled their songs around me.

A man came to the Bennett house in January and talked for a long time with Thomas in his office. He was a tall man with shrewd eyes and he moved like a wolf. His name was Osmond, and as he left later that night, he stopped in front of me and said, "Human, eh? Well, I guess to each their own." His eyes flashed orange. And then he left and I seriously considered throwing my mug of tea at the back of his head.

In February, a young man followed Joe home from school. Joe looked bewildered but didn't make him leave. He was Joe's age and his name was Frankie and he was short and had black hair and these great big brown eyes that followed Joe everywhere. He was scared of me and this amused Joe greatly. I walked into Joe's room in the middle of the month to see Frankie lean forward and kiss Joe on the lips. Joe froze. I froze, but only for a moment before I stepped back out of the room and quietly closed the door. I smiled quietly to myself even as this strange twisting little thing curled in my stomach. I walked away and hoped he was happy. That little curl in my stomach never really went away, but I learned to ignore it.

It was March when he knocked on the door at three in the morning shouting, "Ox, Ox, *Ox*," and I panicked, grabbing the crowbar, telling my mother to stay in her room. She had a dagger already pulled out, and I stopped to tell her that she looked like a badass. She rolled her eyes and told me to go see what was wrong.

I opened the door and Joe said, "*Ox*."

He wasn't injured. There was no blood. Nothing was chasing him. He was okay. Physically. It didn't matter. I pulled him close and his hands were in my hair and he *shuddered* as he pressed against me.

"What happened?"

He said, "Frankie," and I wondered at the state of my head and heart when I began to plot the death of a seventeen-year-old boy who loved chunky peanut butter and cartoons. I told myself that if he'd hurt Joe, there wouldn't be pieces left to bury.

"What did he do?"

"Nothing," Joe said. "He did *nothing*."

"Then what's wrong?"

"You *asshole*," Joe shouted at me as he pulled away.

I said, "What?" because *what*?

"Look at me," he demanded.

And I did. Because I always did.

"What do you see?"

"Joe," I said. "I see you." Maybe a little rumpled. Maybe some bags under his eyes. Maybe he was a little pale, and if he wasn't a werewolf, I'd wonder if he was getting sick. But he *couldn't* so I didn't wonder at all.

"You *don't*," he cried. "You fucking *don't*." I'd never seen him so pissed.

"I don't . . . understand?" I asked him. Or told him.

"Gah!" he shouted at me, eyes flaring orange and red, and then he turned and left.

He apologized the next day. Said he was tired. I said, "Sure, Joe. Okay. No worries."

Then he held my hand and we walked down the dirt road like we always did.

It was April when Frankie stopped coming by the house. I wanted to ask Joe about it, but I could never find the words. Kelly said they'd broken up and I said, "Oh," even though what I thought in my head was *Good. Good. Good.*

It was May when everything exploded.

It was the strangest thing.

.   .   .

The days were hot and humid. The news said it was going to be the hottest summer in years. Heat wave, they said. Could go on for weeks and weeks.

It was almost my twenty-third birthday. I figured maybe it was time for me to move out of Mom's house, but the thought of not living next to the pack caused me to sweat, so I didn't push it too hard. Mom never complained. She liked me being there. And it meant I could keep her safe in case the monsters ever came again.

So from there, shortly before I'd been on the earth for twenty-three years, I went over to the Bennetts' for Sunday dinner. Elizabeth asked if I'd get some of the tomatoes out of the garden. She smiled at me and kissed me on the cheek.

Joe and Carter and Kelly were coming out of the woods, finishing up their run as I came back from the garden.

They were laughing and shoving each other the way brothers do. I loved all three of them.

Except.

Except.

Joe wore a pair of low-slung shorts. Just the smallest things. And that was it.

He was almost as big as I was now. We were eye level, or so close that it didn't matter, which put him a couple of inches over six feet.

There was a sheen of sweat over his torso. A spattering of wet blond hairs curling on his chest that looked to be cut out of granite. The soft definition of muscles on his stomach. A line of sweat that hit his happy trail and soaked into the waistband of his shorts.

He turned, saying something back to Carter, and I saw the dimples above his ass. The way his legs flexed and shifted as he hopped from one foot to the other.

He pointed wildly at something back in the woods and there was a blue vein that stuck out along his bicep and I wanted to trace it with my fingers because when had *that* happened?

And those hands. Those big fucking hands and I—

Joe had grown up.

And somehow, I hadn't really seen it until it was on full display. Right in front of me.

He must have seen me out of the corner of his eye. He turned and grinned at me, and it was Joe, but it was *Joe.*

So, naturally, that's when I walked into the side of the house. The tomatoes in my hands crushed against me. My head hit the wood siding and I thought, *Oh shit.*

I stepped back from the house. Bits of tomato fell onto the grass.

Dammit.

I felt my face flushing as I looked back at the Bennett brothers. They all stood there, watching me with concerned expressions on their faces.

"What the hell?" Carter asked. "You know there is a house right there? It's been there pretty much for forever."

"Uh," I said, my voice dropping lower. I couldn't even stop it. "Hey. Guys. What's up? Just . . . picking tomatoes." I crossed my arms over my chest and got tomato on them. I went to lean against the house, but I was farther away than I'd thought and fell into the dirt.

"What is even happening right now?" Kelly said.

Joe took a step toward me, and his *stomach* muscles were *flexing* and the low base heat of *want* roared through me and I remembered werewolves could *smell* it and I took a step back in absolute *horror.* "Hey," I said again, and my voice was breaking. I cleared my throat and tried again. "Hey. So. There's a. Thing. That I have to look at. In my house. Before dinner."

Now they were all looking at me weirdly. They couldn't smell my immoral raging lust yet. Or whatever it was. My *feelings.* That I couldn't be having.

Joe took another step toward me and he had *pecs.* He had a *chest* that was just . . . it was just very *nice* and it gave me *ideas* and I said, "Whoa there, cowboy," and kicked myself internally for such *bullshit.*

"What's at your house?" Joe asked, and that motherfucker started *sniffing* the air.

"Ox," Carter said. "Your heartbeat is going *crazy.*"

Stupid fucking werewolves. And Joe was standing *right there.* With *muscles.*

"To change!" I shouted, and all three took a step back. I lowered my voice. "I have to . . . change. My shirt." I pointed at it. "Tomatoes and houses don't mix. Ha-ha-ha."

"I still have no idea what is happening," Kelly said.

So I said, "I'll be right back," and turned the opposite way, trying to stop myself from running.

"Uh, Ox?"

I stopped. "Yeah, Joe?"

"Your house is the other way."

"So it is." But instead of walking past them so they could smell me, I walked the long way around the house. When I came into view again, they were standing in the same spot, watching me.

I went inside and locked the door.

"What happened to your shirt?" Mom asked.

"Tomatoes," I said.

"You look flushed," she said. "Your face is bright red."

"It's hot out."

"Ox. Did something happen?"

"Nope. Not a single thing."

"You're breathing really heavily."

"It's a thing I do. Big guy, you know? Need big breaths."

"Yeah," Mom said. "I don't think that's a thing."

"I need to change my shirt." I refused to look her in the eye.

"You want me to wait for you?"

I shook my head. "No. No. That's . . . fine." I wanted her to leave so I could punch something.

She waited until I'd stepped away from the door before pushing past me. She frowned when she tried to turn the knob. "Did you lock this?"

I smiled. I probably looked crazy. "Force of habit."

"Uh-huh." She went out and closed the door behind her.

I punched the wall. It hurt like a bitch.

He was only seventeen. That was wrong.

Except he was almost eighteen.

Which . . . okay.

But.

It was *Joe*.

And back and forth and back and forth.

My phone went off. A text message.

Joe.

Where r u???

I looked at the clock. I'd been sitting in front of the door for twenty minutes already.

"Shit," I muttered.

I couldn't *not* go to dinner. It was tradition. And if I begged off sick, someone (*JoeJoeJoe*) would come and check on me.

So I had to go.

I couldn't do anything about my heartbeat. They'd hear that regardless. I'd think of something.

But the smell.

I ran up the stairs and tore off my shirt, grabbing another from the drawer. I pulled it on as I went into the bathroom. I found an old bottle of cologne I never wore anymore because the wolves didn't like it. *It blocks you out,* Joe had told me once. *Most of you, anyway.*

I sprayed myself at least six times.

I texted back:

on my way

It took me another twenty minutes to convince myself to walk back to the house at the end of the lane.

Finally, I told myself to man up because I was almost *twenty-three fucking years old* and I'd fought *monsters* (once) and I'd trained with *wolves* (many times). And it was just *Joe.*

Who apparently I wanted to do stuff to. With. Around.

That did nothing to calm my heart rate.

It felt like I was walking to my death with every step I took to cross the way to the Bennett house.

I could hear them all out back. Probably getting ready to eat. Laughter. Talking. Shouting.

And then the conversation just *died.*

Even before I could get around the side of the house.

"Is that *Ox?*" I heard Mark ask. He sounded worried.

There was a crash and multiple pairs of feet running.

They rounded the corner and just *stopped.*

"Where is it?" Mark demanded.

"Are we under attack?" Thomas asked, ready to wolf out. His eyes went red.

"Ox?" Carter asked. "Dude. Seriously. Your heart, man. You sound terrified."

"Hey, guys," I said. I learned early on that you shouldn't run from a wolf when they were about to shift. Sets off instincts. I wanted to run so bad.

Because *Joe* was standing at the front. He'd changed. White shorts. Green shirt that hid *nothing.* He was barefoot too. And his feet were sexy as all hell.

"Uh," I said. "Hey, guys."

"Why do I feel like this is a thing I should be getting," Kelly said.

Joe's nose wrinkled. "What's that smell?"

So, of course, all the Bennett men started sniffing the air. It wasn't funny. At all.

Carter took a step toward me. "Dude. Ox. What the hell. What did you bathe in?"

"Nothing," I said, sounding defensive, even as I took a step back. "I don't know what you're talking about."

"Ox," Joe said with a frown. "Are you okay?"

And I couldn't even *look* at him when I said, "I'm fine. Everything's fine."

"That . . . was a lie," Kelly said.

Joe took a step toward me. I took another step back.

"Did something happen today?" Thomas asked.

I wanted to say, *I may have started picturing your underage son naked*, but I didn't know if that was something someone could say to an Alpha werewolf.

So I said, "Nothing happened. I just wanted to . . . smell. Different?"

The Bennett men stared at me. I stared sort of over their shoulders.

Joe said, "Ox."

"Yeah," I said, looking at a tree.

"Hey."

"What?"

"Look at me."

Jesus fucking Christ. I looked at him.

Even I could see the worry on his face. His stupid handsome face. I felt myself blush.

"Maybe we should—" Mark started, but then Carter said, "Oh, no *way*," and so *I* loudly said, "Carter, can I talk to you for a moment? Now? Please? Right now?"

Carter gave me the biggest shit-eating grin even as Joe glanced between us, eyes narrowing. "What did you do?" he asked his brother.

"Absolutely nothing," Carter said, sounding rather delighted about *something*. "And it's *amazing*."

"Carter," I barked. "Now!"

Before the others could protest, Carter moved forward and gripped my arm, dragging me toward the forest. "This won't take long," he called cheerfully over his shoulder to the others.

"*What* won't?" I heard Joe ask.

"Oh, I'm sure you'll find out soon enough," Mark said, and oh my God, I was *doomed*.

.   .   .

Since werewolves were impatient as all hell, Carter only dragged me far enough until he knew we were out of earshot before he stopped, dropped my arm, turned to look at me, and said, "You got a boner over my little brother."

I had to at least try. "I have no idea what you're talking about."

Carter said, "You drenched yourself in the worst-smelling thing you could find so you could cover up the smell of your *boner*."

"Stop saying *boner!*"

He waggled his eyebrows at me.

I glared at him.

He said, "It's about time."

And so I said, "*What?*"

He squinted at me. "You and Joe."

"What *about* me and Joe?"

"Seriously. That's what you're going with."

It was either that or have a panic attack. "Yes," I said. "That's what I'm going with."

"It's okay," he said. "You're allowed to have a boner for my seventeen-year-old brother."

I groaned, burying my face in my hands. "You're making this so much worse."

He snorted. "I highly doubt that. If you think it's awkward for you, think about how *I* feel right now."

"You keep saying *boner!*"

"Yeah," he said easily. "I'm having such a good time right now."

"Carter!"

"Why are you freaking out about this?"

"Why are you *not?*"

"Is it about the whole werewolf thing?"

"What? No. I don't care that he's a—"

"And it's not that he's a guy. You've fucked men before."

"What the hell? Just going to throw that out there, are you?"

"Is it that he's seventeen?" Carter asked. "Dad won't care. Well. He probably won't care *too* much."

I stared at him in horror. "What are you even *talking* about?"

"Ox," he said slowly, as if speaking to a child. "It's Joe, man. What did you think was going to happen?"

"I don't . . . I just . . . he was wearing those *shorts* and—"

Carter grimaced. "Okay, smelling it was one thing, but *hearing* about it is one step too far. That's my little brother."

I let out a slightly strangled noise.

"Ox, you know this was always going to happen, right?"

That stopped me cold. "What?"

"The wolf."

"I told you, I don't *care* that he's a wolf—"

But Carter was already shaking his head. "Not that. The stone wolf. The one he gave you for your birthday."

"What about it?"

Carter sighed. "Man, this isn't going to go over well."

Which did nothing to make things better. I told him as much.

"Look," he said. "When wolves are born, their Alpha gives them a wolf carved from stone. Sometimes they do it themselves. Sometimes they have others do it. But each natural wolf is given one. I don't know when it started, and honestly, it's some archaic bullshit, but whatever. It's tradition, and you know how Dad is with tradition."

I nodded, because I did.

"It's a wolf's most treasured possession," Carter continued. "Something to be protected and revered. Or so we're taught."

"Then why did he give it to me?"

Carter smiled quietly at me. "Because that's what you're supposed to do with it."

"I don't—"

"When we're old enough, we're told that one day, we'll find someone. Someone that feels good to our wolf. Someone that makes our heart race. Someone that completes us. Tethers us. Makes us human."

Gooseflesh prickled along my skin.

The birds sang in the trees.

The leaves swayed on the branches.

It felt green here. So very green.

"When we find that person," Carter said, "when we find that one person that makes us forget everything bad that's ever happened to us, well . . . That's what the wolf is for. It's a gift, Ox. A promise."

"A promise of what?" I croaked out.

He shrugged. "It can mean many things. Friendship. Family. Trust." He closed his eyes and listened to the sound of the forest. "Or more."

"More?"

"Love. Faith. Devotion."

"He . . ."

"Yeah, man. He did."

"He was *ten*."

Carter opened his eyes. "And he spoke to you after not speaking for over a year. We all knew. Even then."

I felt a weird sense of betrayal at that. "Yet another thing to keep from me?" I asked, unable to stop the bitterness in my voice.

Carter shook his head. "You were sixteen, Ox. And you didn't know about werewolves."

"But when I did—"

"Jessie," Carter said.

And so many things clicked into place. "Holy shit," I breathed. "That's why—"

"That and you were kind of a dick about it."

I glared at him.

He shrugged.

"I'm not going to do anything about it," I said. "He's young. He's going to college. He's going to have a *life*. He's my friend, and that's—"

Carter snorted. "Yeah, good luck with that, Oxnard. Trust me. When Joe catches wind about this—and he *will*—you aren't going to stand a chance."

"He won't," I said, determined. "And you won't say a goddamn thing."

He grinned at me.

. . .

Carter made me go back home and shower, saying that my stench was overwhelming and there was no way I could eat with them, smelling like I did.

I punched him as hard as I could.

He just laughed at me.

I tried to drag it out as long as I could, thinking of absolutely everything *but* Joe.

The shower lasted four minutes.

I was dressed and walking back toward the Bennett house ten minutes later.

I could hear them all, including my mother, in the backyard. Elizabeth was laughing. Carter was yelling at Kelly. My mother was talking with Mark.

Before I could round the corner of the house, I felt a hand on my shoulder.

I didn't even need to turn to know who it was.

But I did anyway.

Joe stood behind me, eyes concerned, fingers trailing down my arm, gripping my elbow lightly. We were standing so close to each other, inches apart. I could feel the heat of him, his knees bumping mine.

"Hey," he said.

"Hi," I managed to say back.

"You okay?"

"Yeah," I said. "Fine. Everything's fine."

"Uh-huh. Want to try that again?"

"I have no idea what you're talking about."

"Ox," he said in that tone of voice that we both knew could get me to do *anything* he asked of me, and now that I was aware of what exactly that could entail, I could barely breathe.

"The wolf," I blurted out.

"What? What wolf?"

I scowled. "The one you gave me."

From this close, I could see the faint flush spreading up his neck. But his eyes never left mine. "What about it?"

"I just . . . I'm . . . thank you? For it. I guess."

"You're welcome? Why are you . . . wait. What did you and Carter talk about?"

"Um. Nothing?"

"Really. That's what you're going with."

"Nothing," I insisted.

"You're acting weird."

"*You're* acting weird."

He rolled his eyes. "The smell thing, the going off with Carter in the woods, bringing up the wolf out of nowhere. Don't even get me started on walking into the side of the house when we came back from . . ."

He trailed off, and I *knew* that expression on his face. I *knew* what that meant. *That* was the look he got when his mind started racing into overdrive, putting all the little bits and pieces together.

"We should probably go eat," I said hastily. "We don't want to keep everyone waiting. It's very rude."

His eyes widened.

Well, fuck.

"Ox," he said, a hint of his wolf poking through, eyes flashing. "Anything you'd like to tell me?"

"No," I said quickly. "Absolutely not."

"You sure about that?" he asked, his grip on my elbow tightening.

I just barely managed to pull my arm free. "I'm hungry," I said, voice rough. "We should—"

"Sure," he said. "Let's go."

I blinked.

He smiled at me.

My heart stuttered a bit.

The smile widened.

No one commented as we rounded the corner, though I was sure every single one of them aside from my mother had heard the entire conversation. Carter winked at me. Kelly looked rather pleased. Mark smiled his secret smile. Elizabeth watched me fondly. Mom just looked confused.

Thomas, though. Thomas looked more at ease than I'd ever seen him before.

Joe crowded into my side, sitting down next to me, not leaving any room between us.

The meal was an exercise in torture.

He leaned in often when talking to me, breath on my neck, whispering in my ear.

He touched my arm, my hand, my thigh.

He had a straw in his soda. He never used straws. *Never.* But he had one now, pulled from somewhere, eyelashes fluttering up at me as he *sucked*, cheeks hollowing.

I dropped my fork. It clattered loudly onto my plate.

"Joe," Thomas sighed. "Really?"

"Oops," Joe said. "Sorry." He didn't sound sorry at all.

Kelly said, "Oh man, this makes so much more sense now. And is much more gross."

"I made pie for dessert," Elizabeth said, coming back to the table. "Whip-cream topping."

I groaned.

Joe looked delighted.

Even more so when he ran a finger through the cream, licking it from his skin, never taking his eyes off of me.

Carter and Kelly had matching looks of disgust and horror on their faces.

"Stop it," I hissed at him.

Joe cocked his head at me before leaning in and saying in a low voice, "Oh, Ox. I'm just getting started."

AND A BOW TIE / ANYTHING FOR YOU

I should have known he wasn't going to drop it.

He let me have three days to worry over it. To fret over every little detail of every interaction we'd ever had.

Things made sense now. Jessie. The men I'd slept with. The way he'd disappear from my life for days after them.

And Frankie. Frankie had been his attempt at . . . what? A normal life? Something that wasn't me?

I didn't like Frankie, I discovered. At all.

Three days. He let me have three days.

Three days of him smiling at me.

Three days of trying to figure out the hidden meaning of every text he sent me.

Monday and Tuesday, he was waiting for me on the dirt road as I walked home from work.

He said, "Hey, Ox."

I blushed.

We walked home together, me trying to find the words to say *this can't happen* and *you deserve so much better than me* and *you were only ten, how could you do that, you were only* ten *years old,* but unable to speak them aloud.

His hand often brushed mine and I thought to take it every now and then.

The third day, he wasn't on the road.

I wanted to feel relieved.

Instead, I was disappointed.

Until I got home.

Mom had had the day off, the first in a long while.

So, of course, she was home when I got there.

And so was Joe.

Sitting at our kitchen table.

Wearing dress pants, a dress shirt.

And a bow tie.

Which, unbeknownst to me, turned out to be one of my greatest weaknesses.

I walked into the kitchen door at the sight of that.

"Huh," Mom said. "Things are starting to make sense now."

I rubbed my sore nose as I scowled at the both of them. "What's going on?"

"Joe asked if he could speak with me," Mom said.

"I brought her flowers!" Joe blurted out, sounding breathless and nervous.

"And he brought me flowers," Mom agreed, tilting her head toward the vase sitting on the table, filled with irises, her favorite. How he'd found that out, I'd never know.

"Why are you bringing her flowers?" I asked.

"Because Mom said it was nice to do and would get her on my good side when I asked her if it'd be okay that I kept you for the rest of my life," Joe explained. Then his eyes widened. "Shit. That wasn't supposed to come out like that."

"Oh my God," I said faintly.

"You want to keep him for how long now?" Mom asked, squinting at Joe.

"Uhh," Joe said. "Crap. This isn't going like I wanted it to. I had everything I needed to say planned out. Hold on." He reached down and pulled a notecard from his pocket. It was rumpled, the corner ripped. He stared down at it, mouth moving silently as he read whatever the hell he'd written on it. A drop of sweat trickled down his forehead.

This had to be a dream.

"Joe, maybe we should—" I tried.

But he looked up at my mom, a determined set to his jaw. "Hi, Ms. Callaway," he said. "These flowers are for you."

I groaned.

"Thank you, Joe," Mom said, lips twitching. "Is what I said ten minutes ago when you gave them to me and then sat there staring at me while waiting for Ox to get home."

"Right," he said. "You're welcome. Speaking of Ox, I've come to talk to you about him."

"You're wearing a bow tie," I said unnecessarily.

He glanced over at me. "Mom said I had to dress up for this."

I heard a low snort of laughter coming through the open window above the sink.

And I *knew*.

I stalked over to the window and looked outside.

There, sitting spread out on the grass, were the rest of the Bennetts.

Goddamn *fucking* werewolves.

"Hello, Ox," Elizabeth said without a hint of shame. "Lovely day, isn't it?"

"I will deal with all of you later," I said.

"Ooh," Carter said. "I actually just got chills from that."

"We're just here for support," Kelly said. "And to laugh at how embarrassing Joe is."

"I heard that!" Joe shouted from behind me.

I banged my head on the windowsill.

"Maggie," Joe said. Then, "May I call you Maggie?"

"Sure." My mother sounded like she was *enjoying* this. The *traitor*. "You can call me Maggie."

"Good," Joe said, obviously relieved. "Do you know Ox over there?"

"I've heard of him," Mom said.

"Okay." Joe glanced down at his card before looking back up at my mother. "There comes a time in every werewolf's life when he is of age to make certain decisions about his future."

I wondered whether, if I threw something at him, it'd distract him enough for me to drag him out of the kitchen. I glanced over my shoulder out the window. Carter waved at me. Like an asshole.

"My future," Joe said, "is Ox."

Ah God, that made me ache.

"Is that so?" Mom asked. "How do you figure?"

"He's really nice," Joe said seriously. "And smells good. And he makes me happy. And I want to do nothing more than put my mouth on him."

"Ah well," Thomas said. "We tried."

"He's our little snowflake," Elizabeth told him.

"You want to *what*?" I asked Joe incredulously.

He winced. "I didn't mean to say it like that." He was sweating much more heavily now as he looked back at my mother. "I want to court your son."

"What does that mean?" she asked.

"It means I want to provide for him to prove my worth," Joe said. "And then, once he agrees to be mine, I'll mount him and then bite him and everyone will see that we belong to each other."

I was wheezing something awful.

"Joe," Elizabeth called in from the window. "Maybe not talk about that part just yet. Or ever."

"Right," Joe said, pulling on his bow tie like it was too tight. "Forget I said that part."

"I don't know if I *can*," Mom said, looking between me and Joe.

"*Mounting?*" I managed to say. "Of all the things you could have gone with, you went with *mounting*?"

"I'm nervous!" Joe cried. "It's not my fault! That was the only thing I could think of!"

"*You have it written down,*" I hissed at him.

"I mean," Mom said, "you just threw it out there like it was nothing."

I ignored the sounds of choked laughter coming from behind me.

"Okay," Joe said. "Let's try this again. Hi, Maggie. How are you? These flowers are for you. I think your son is the greatest thing in the world."

Everyone fell quiet.

"Do you?" Mom asked.

He nodded. "I do. There's a lot you don't . . . know. About me. Things were . . . hard. For a while. Sometimes, they still are. But Ox, he just . . . I have nightmares. About bad men. About monsters. And he makes them go away."

I tried to swallow past the lump in my throat.

"And I've been waiting," Joe said. "For him to look at me like I looked at him. And he finally did. *He finally did.* And I'm going to do everything I can to make sure it stays like that. Because I want him for always."

"You're seventeen," she said. "How can you possibly know what you want being so young?"

"I'm a wolf," he said. "It's not the same. We're . . . wired differently."

"And if he says no?"

Joe paled. "Then, uh. I guess. I will. Be okay? With that?"

"Would you?"

He nodded, hands clenched into fists at his side. "Maybe not. But I would respect it. Because Ox is my best friend above all else. And I would have him any way I could."

"Hmm," my mother said. Then, "Ox? What do you think?"

Everyone held their breath.

And I . . . what?

Stared, maybe. My skin felt too tight.

Like it would split.

Like it would split and then I'd wake up because it was just a dream. All of it was just a dream.

And so I said, "*Why*?" because that was the one thing I couldn't quite figure out. The one thing I couldn't get. My daddy was dead but he'd said I was gonna get *shit*, and this wasn't *shit*. This was terrifying; this was *opportunity*. This was *responsibility*, and it wasn't shit. It wasn't shit at all.

"Why what?" Joe asked. He sounded confused.

"Why me?"

Now he scowled. "Why not?"

"You're going to be Alpha one day." And he'd be a great one.

"And?"

I looked down at my hands. "That's important."

"I know."

"I'm not . . ."

"You're not what?"

"You know. Anything."

Then he was in front of me and he was *pissed*. He practically *vibrated* with it. "Shut up," he said. "Just shut *up*."

I said, "Joe—" but he cut me off with, "You don't get to say that. You don't get to even *think* something like that."

"You're *seventeen*—"

He was snarling now, and I knew if I looked up at him, his wolf would be fighting through. "So? You think I don't know what I'm doing? You think that because I'm *only seventeen* I don't know what I'm talking about? I haven't been a kid for a very long time, Ox. That was taken away from me the first time he made me scream into the phone so my mom could hear it as he broke my fingers. I haven't been a kid since he *ripped* it from me and made me into something else. I know what this is. I know what I'm doing. Yes, I'm *seventeen* years old, but I knew the day I met you that I would do *anything* for you. I would do *anything* to make you happy because no one had ever smelled like you did. It was candy canes and pinecones. It was epic and awesome. And it was *home*. You smelled like my *home*, Ox. I'd forgotten what that was like, okay? I'd forgotten that because *he* took it away from me and I couldn't find it again until I found you. So don't you sit there and say I'm *only* seventeen. My father gave Mom his wolf when *he* was seventeen. It's not a matter of *age*, Ox. It's when you know."

My voice was hoarse when I said, "But I'm not—"

"Shut *up!*" he cried. "You know what? No. You don't get to decide what you're worth because you obviously don't know. You don't get to decide that anymore because you have no fucking idea that you're worth *everything*. What do you think this is? A joke? A decision I made just for the hell of it? It's not. It's not destiny, Ox. You're not *bound* by this. Not yet. There's a choice. There is *always* a choice. My wolf chose you. *I* chose you. And if you don't choose me, then that's *your* choice and I will walk out of here knowing you got to choose your own path. But I swear to God, if you choose me, I will make sure that you know the weight of your worth every day for the rest of our lives because that's what this is. I am going to be a fucking *Alpha* one day, and there is no one I'd rather have by my side than you. It's you, Ox. For me, it's always been you."

So I said, "Okay, Joe." I looked up at him. His wolf was close to the surface.

And he said, "Okay?"

I said, "Okay. Okay. I don't know if I see the things you do."

"I know."

"And I don't know if I'll be good enough."

"*I* know you will," he said, eyes flashing orange.

"But I promised you. I said it will always be you and me."

His face stuttered a bit, and he said, "You did. You promised me. You *promised*."

I said, "I'm not much. I don't have a lot. Sometimes I feel dumb and I say stupid things. My dad left, and I make mistakes all the time. I didn't go to college, and I come home with grease under my fingernails and on my pants. I don't have many friends. But I made a promise to you, and even though I wish you'd find someone better, I keep my promises. So, yeah, Joe. Okay? Just yeah."

I must not have been a man yet because my eyes burned a bit. Mom was crying at the table and I could hear Elizabeth sniffling outside the window, but there was Joe in front of me. He was the little boy who had found me on the dirt road the day I turned sixteen. The little boy who had become a man and stood before me a few days before I turned twenty-three. He thought I was worth something. I wanted to believe him.

So he pressed his forehead against mine and breathed me in and there was that sun, okay? That sun between us, that bond that burned and burned and burned because he'd given it to me. Because he'd chosen me.

And I got to choose him back.

WHAT LIFE IS / I NEED YOU

So mates were a thing.

And I learned that I still didn't know jack shit about werewolves.

. . .

I said, "I feel like this is something I should have been told."

Thomas looked at me as we walked through the trees. "Is it?"

"Yes."

"Ah."

"Elizabeth is your mate."

"For lack of a better word, yes. We can call it that. But she is so much more to me."

"How did you know?"

He laughed. "Because every time I saw her, I wanted nothing more than to make sure she never left my sight again."

I understood that. Completely.

"You knew," I said. "About Joe and me."

"Yes."

"That's why . . ." I stopped.

He waited.

"When you train him. You bring me out."

"Yes."

"Because of what I am. To him."

"Yes."

"Mate."

"If you want to call it that. It's very romanticized, but I suppose that's as close as we'll get."

"What am I?"

He looked surprised. "You're Ox."

And I said, "To him. What is Elizabeth to you?"

"Layers," he said with a chuckle. "So many layers. She is mine and I would do anything for her. She makes me stronger because of that. An Alpha needs it more than any other. I wouldn't be without her."

"And that's what I'll be to Joe?"

"Maybe," he said. "Or more. You're different, Ox. I don't think even I know how different. It will be truly a sight to behold. And I, for one, can't wait to see it."

"See what?"

"Your everything," he said.

The sun disappeared behind a cloud overhead. "Why did you let him?"

"Let him?"

"Give me his wolf."

"Because he chose to."

I frowned. "You could have stopped him."

"I suppose."

"Carter said you tried to."

"Because we didn't know you."

"But you let him anyway. Why?"

Thomas touched my shoulder. "Because Joe of all people should have been allowed to make a choice. After all he'd been through. And for the first time since we'd gotten him back, he had a choice. He chose to speak to you. He chose to bring you back to the house. He chose to hold your hand. That's what life is, Ox. Choices. The choices we make shape what we'll become. For a long time, Joe's choices were taken from him. And then they were ruled by fear. But you came along and he made his own choice. So yes. I could have stopped him. I could have told him to wait. I could have told him no. But I didn't because he chose. He chose you, Ox."

"Who was it?"

Thomas looked away.

I said, "I need to know."

"Why?"

"Because if I'm choosing this, I'm choosing all of it."

His name was Richard Collins. He'd been an Alpha until it had been stripped from him. He'd raped and murdered members of his own pack. Fed humans to the more feral of them. He was a monster and he did not care. They tore the Alpha from his body, but he escaped before they could do anything more.

Thomas and Richard had been friends when they were children. Here. In this territory. They were pack and they loved each other very much. As brothers.

Human hunters had come one day.

Thomas and his father had been away.

They'd tortured Richard's mother and father in front of him. Many others too.

Flesh had charred and the air had filled with ash.

Much of the Bennett pack was gone.

Richard had gone away then.

No one knew how he'd become an Alpha. Magic, maybe. Murder. Sacrifice.

He was cruel and he took life and hope away, until he was caught.

But then he slipped through their grasp.

Thomas had been asked to come back east and help the other packs find him.

To stop him.

They searched for years and years and years. Moving all over the country.

Thomas hadn't thought there was any hope for his old friend, but he hadn't allowed that to stop him.

They were in Maine when he got the call.

Joe was gone. Taken from the front yard in their little house by the sea.

They couldn't find him. Couldn't track him. The scent was gone, like it'd never been there.

They looked for three days.

On the third day, the phone rang.

Richard said, "Thomas. Thomas, Thomas, Thomas."

And Thomas said, "You son of a bitch."

Richard said, "You weren't there. You did nothing to stop them. They screamed for you to help them. *I* screamed for you. For your father. *But you weren't there.*"

Thomas begged, "My son. Richard, my son. Please."

And Richard Collins said, "*No.*"

He called a couple of times a week and Joe *shrieked*. He made Joe *shriek* and Thomas thought he was losing his mind.

It took eight weeks to find him. A mixture of scents and sheer luck led them to a cabin in the middle of the woods so much closer than they thought it'd be. But they did find him, battered and alone.

He was not the same. He was a wolf, but wolves did not shift until puberty. He healed, but it was slow.

And he would not speak.

Once I could be sure my voice would work, I asked, "What did he want?"

"To inflict pain," Thomas said. "As much of it as possible."

And I asked the question I'd asked him once before. "Is he dead?"

And Thomas said, "No. He will spend the rest of his days rotting away in a cell formed by magic. The magic won't allow him to shift. For all intents and purposes, it has taken his wolf away from him."

My hands curled at my sides. "Why didn't you kill him?"

He watched me with sad eyes. "Because revenge is the lesson taught by animals. Because it's more difficult to show mercy. I showed him mercy because he'd never shown my family the same."

And for a moment, I hated Thomas. I thought he was weak. A coward. And he knew that. He must have known every thought that ran through my head at that moment.

He waited.

It passed because I knew him. But I had to be honest.

I said, "I don't know if I'd have been able to do the same."

"No," he said, not unkindly. "I don't expect you would have."

And we walked on through the forest.

.   .   .

Mom asked, "Is this what you really want?"

I said, "Yes."

"He's seventeen, Ox."

"And nothing will happen until he turns eighteen." I didn't want to talk about that part with her anymore. It buzzed along my skin until I felt flushed and hot. It was too much. The thought of touching. Of *being* touched.

She looked out the window to the summer sun. "What happens if it doesn't work out?"

And I didn't want to think about that. I didn't want to think about that at all, so I said, "It's about chances. That's how everything is."

.   .   .

"We're friends first," Joe whispered in my ear. "You're my best friend, Ox, and I promise that will never change. We'll just be . . . more."

"Will I have to become a wolf?" I asked Thomas. "To be with Joe?"

"No," Thomas said. "You don't."

"I've thought about it," I said quietly.

"Have you?"

"Yeah."

He waited.

"I don't have to be?" I insisted.

"No," he said again. "You're wonderful just as you are."

I wondered if this was what it felt like to have a father who loved you enough to stay despite all your faults.

Elizabeth said, "There is no one else I would have picked for him. Ox, you will do wondrous things together. He will be a leader, and as an Alpha, he will put the pack above all else. But remember that you'll always be his heart and soul."

Mark said, "I knew. From the very first day, I knew that you were made for something great. I am proud to call you my friend and pack."

Carter said, "I hope you're ready for werewolf stamina. Like, for real. You're going to be sore. For *days*."

Kelly said, "I really wish I hadn't heard Carter say that. I need to pour bleach on my brain. For *days*."

I dreamt of wolves and a bloodred moon. They sang to me and I took their songs and made them my own. I ran with them on four legs and my heart thundered in my chest. I could see and smell and hear everything and it was all green, green, green and Beta orange and Alpha red. The colors fit against the song and we *sang* because we were *pack pack pack*.

"Uh, Ox?" Mom called as I got ready for work. The sky was starting to lighten outside.

"Yeah?"

"I think it's started."

"What?" I tucked in my shirt as I walked down the stairs.

She was on the porch, the front door standing open. I came up behind her.

She said, "At least he kept it off the porch like I asked."

A fat rabbit lay on the grass, throat shredded, eyes wide and sightless. Blood pooled underneath it, tacky and dark. Flies buzzed around it, landing on stiff paws.

"I'm not eating that" was the first thing I said.

Mom elbowed me in the stomach. "He might be listening!" she hissed at me.

"I mean. Uh. Wow. That looks so good!" I was almost shouting.

"Subtle, Ox."

"A werewolf is courting me with a dead rabbit. There's nothing subtle here."

"Couldn't have been flowers," she muttered as she slid on her rubber boots by the door.

"He gave you flowers," I reminded her as she stepped down the porch.

"I meant for you," she said. She bent over and grabbed the rabbit by the ears, pulling it up off the ground. It came up with a low crackle, grass stuck to the underside. "Courting. I swear."

"Why are you *touching* it?" I said, sounding horrified.

"We can't *leave* it here," she said. "He'll be offended."

"I'll be honest. I'm already offended."

"Quick," she said as she walked by me into the house. "Look up rabbit recipes on the Internet before you go to work."

"You're dripping on the floor!"

"It's just a dead rabbit, Ox. You sound hysterical."

"I sound *hygienic*."

I wasn't very good with Internet stuff, so I googled "what to do when your future werewolf mate/boyfriend/best friend courts you and brings you a dead rabbit."

First, there was a lot of porn.

Then I found a recipe for Maltese rabbit stew.

It was delicious.

The stew, not the porn.

The porn was weird.

·   ·   ·

Gordo said, "So. You just got a basket of, like, eighty mini muffins delivered to you."

I said, "Mini muffins?" and I looked up from a tire rotation I was doing on a 2012 Ford Escape.

"Uh. Yeah. Like, eighty of them."

"That's a lot of muffins."

"Lynda from the bakery brought them over. Well, actually, her son did because the basket was too heavy for her to carry."

I sighed.

Gordo narrowed his eyes. "Dreamy sigh," he accused.

He followed me into his office.

Sure enough, there was a basket of mini muffins. The biggest basket I'd ever seen.

I knew what this was.

It didn't count as hunting. Not that I was complaining. I didn't think Gordo would appreciate dead animals at the shop.

There was a note in an envelope.

It said, *Shut up. This totally counts as hunting.*

I sighed again.

"Ox," Gordo said.

I said, "So. Mates are a thing, huh?"

And he said, "*Ox.*"

. . .

"You're just a *child!*" he shouted at me later after the others had gone home. It'd been building all day.

I said, "I'm twenty-three years old, Gordo. I haven't been a child in a very long time."

He narrowed his eyes. "Do you even know what this means? What you've agreed to? This is for *life*. When the wolf attaches, it is for *life*."

"I know." Thomas had told me. I might have had a minor meltdown, but that was yesterday. Today was different.

"And you still agreed? Are you out of your fucking mind?"

"Funny," I said. "I thought this was *my* life. Not yours."

He started to pace in front of me. "How the fuck am I supposed to protect you if you keep doing these things to yourself?"

"I can protect myself. I don't need you or anyone else to do that for me."

"Bullshit. You know I need—" He cut himself off with a growl.

"You need me. I know."

"That's not what I was going to say." He slammed his palm against the desk.

"Gordo."

"Fuck off, Ox."

"He's going to be the Alpha one day."

"I don't care."

I pushed on anyway. "He's going to need a witch."

He reeled like I'd struck him. "Don't. Don't you dare."

"What the hell happened to you?" I demanded. "Why do you hate them so much?"

He laughed bitterly. "It doesn't matter anymore."

"It does if you're always going to be like this. Look, I know you're worried about me. That's what you do. But you have to trust me. I already have enough doubts as it is. I can't have them from you too. I need you, man. To have my back."

He pounced on those words, of course. "Doubts? Then why are you even doing this?"

I said, "Not about him. About me. What if I'm not good enough for him? What if I can't be what he's going to need?"

He stopped his pacing and his shoulders sagged. "Ox, you can't think like that."

I snorted. "Yeah? It's actually pretty easy to."

"Your father did this to you," he said with a scowl. "I should have kicked his ass when I had the chance."

I looked up in surprise.

"I don't like this," Gordo said. "At all. But I'm going to say it anyway, okay? Anyone should count their lucky stars if they got to call you their own. I am not giving you my approval because it doesn't matter to you anyway. Nothing I can say matters at this point." His voice cracked. "But he had better treat you like you hung the moon or I will tear him from this earth."

I reached out and squeezed his shoulder, trying to stop my knees from buckling. Of course everything he said to me mattered. How could he think otherwise? I said, "Gordo. Gordo. His wolf. He gave me his wolf. The stone wolf."

Gordo smiled sadly. "I figured he did. When he came to see you?"

I shook my head. "The day after I met him. When he was ten. I didn't know what it meant. They said I had a choice."

And there it was. That look on his face. That *fear*.

He said, "Even then?"

I said, "Even then," and of course, "Gordo. *Gordo*," because a realization struck me and I was so fucking *blind*.

"Yeah, Ox."

"Did . . . ?" I almost stopped. But then, "Mark did. Didn't he? Gave you his wolf."

The tattoos on his arms flared briefly as he hung his head.

I rubbed my hand through his hair. It was getting long. I needed to remind him to get it cut. He'd forget so many things if I didn't tell him.

He said, "Yeah. Yes." He coughed. "He did. And I gave it back."

. . . .

We were running under the full moon.

The wolves surrounded me as the trees whipped by.

They whined and yipped and lived and laughed.

Joe kept crowding me closer and closer. He was almost as big as Mark now. When he became the Alpha, he'd be the size of Thomas.

We came to our clearing. The others spread out ahead, chasing each other. Nipping at paws and tails.

Joe didn't leave my side.

He told me once that when the wolf took over, all human rationality left. He could understand and he could remember, but it was on a baser level, all animal and instinct.

He was still Joe, but he was a wolf.

Who apparently decided I didn't smell enough like him.

He rubbed his torso over my legs and thighs.

He pressed his head and snout against my chest and neck, dragging his nose across my skin.

Carter and Kelly approached, wanting to play.

Joe growled at them, a rumble that came out as a warning. *Stay away*, it said.

They cocked their heads at him and lay down flat.

He turned back to me and *whuffed* in my ear and neck.

Carter and Kelly scooted forward slowly.

Joe ignored them because he'd found something interesting to sniff behind my ear.

They inched closer.

Joe touched his nose to my forehead.

They scooted closer.

Joe turned to glare at them.

Carter yawned, as if bored.

Kelly put his head on his paws.

Joe turned back to me.

"You're being dumb," I told him.

He bared his teeth at me, shiny and sharp.

I batted him across the snout.

I said, "I'm not scared of you."

Carter and Kelly sprang forward, rubbing up against me on either side.

Joe snarled at the both of them, eyes flashing.

They just laughed at him.

Later, they hunted.

I lay on my back, watching the moon overhead.

The air was warm and I was happy.

.   .   .

He killed a doe and dragged it out of the woods to lay before me.

Its tongue hung out of its mouth, eyes wide and unseeing.

I said, "Seriously?"

He preened, muzzle caked with blood and grime.

"Seriously," I sighed.

.   .   .

He said, "When I found you, I thought you were the entire world."

He said, "I gave you my wolf because it was made for you."

He said, "When Jessie came, it broke my heart."

He said, "I tried to like her. I promise. And I do. I did."

He said, "But I hated her. I hated her so much."

He said, "When you broke up, I ran into the forest and howled at the moon."

He said, "And then I smelled men on you."

He said, "I smelled them on you and I had to stop myself from tearing you apart."

He said, "I wanted to tell you to wait."

He said, "I wanted to tell you that you needed to wait for me."

He said, "But I couldn't. Because it wasn't fair to you."

He said, "And then Frankie came and I . . . I don't know. I never thought . . ."

He said, "You confuse me. You aggravate me. You're amazing and beautiful, and sometimes, I want to put my teeth in you just to watch you bleed. I want to know what you taste like. I want to leave my marks on your skin. I want to cover you until all you smell like is me. I don't want anyone to touch you ever again. I want you. Every part of you. I want to tell you to break the bond with Gordo because it burns that you are tethered to someone besides me. I want to tell you I can be a good person. I want you to know that I'm not. I want to turn you. I want you to be a wolf so we can run in the trees. I want you to stay human so you never lose that part of yourself. If something were to happen to you, if you were about to die, I would turn you because I can never lose you. I can never let you leave me. I can't let anything take you from me."

He said, "Richard told me things. Terrible things."

.   .   .

My breath caught in my chest. My hand froze in his hair.

Stars shone overhead. The grass felt cool at my back. Joe's head was heavy on my stomach. I looked down at him. His eyes glittered back up at me, dark and more feral than I'd ever seen them.

I could have said, "Hush. We don't need to talk about him."

I could have said, "It doesn't matter anymore. He can't touch you."

I could have said, "I'll find him and kill him for you. Tell me where he is."

What I said was, "Did he?"

I didn't know if that was the right thing to say.

Joe let out a shuddery breath. "Yeah."

"Okay."

"Ox."

"Yeah?" I managed to say through the rage and murder in my heart.

"It's okay."

Of course he could smell it. I wonder what scent anger had. I thought it probably burned.

So I said, "Okay."

"You need to know. Before."

"Before?"

He turned his head slightly and rubbed his nose against my side, along a rib. "So you know. Everything."

"You're not broken."

He said, "You don't know that."

I said, "I do. You're alive. If you can take another breath, if you can take another step, then you're not broken. Battered, maybe. Bruised. Cracked. But never broken."

He said, "Richard told me that my family didn't want me anymore, that they'd given me to him and wanted me to bleed."

I had to stop myself from howling a song of despair.

He said, "Richard said that it was my fault that it was happening. That if only I'd been a better son, if only I'd been a better boy, none of this would have happened. He said that they hated me because I wasn't the Alpha they wanted. That I was too small. That I wasn't a good wolf. That I didn't deserve to be Alpha because I would cause the pack to break apart and everyone would die. And it would be my burden to carry."

He sighed. "I don't know if I can explain it, really. That feeling inside. The Alpha. I'm not one yet, but it's close. It bubbles just below the surface. There are times when all I can think of is marking you so everyone knows who you belong to. To carve my name into your skin so you never forget me. To hide my family away so no one can ever hurt them. I have to protect what's mine. Richard tried to take that away from me, and I think it made it worse. I don't think he knew that he was making it worse."

I said, "It's not bad," though I wasn't sure if that was exactly right.

His eyes flashed at me in the dark, orange with flecks of red. His voice was a growl when he said, "I want your blood on my tongue. I want to break you open and crawl inside of you. I am a monster because of the things I could do to you that you wouldn't be able to stop me from doing." He looked away and took a calming breath. Another. And then another. When he spoke again, his voice was quieter. "Dad knows this. Mom does too. It's why I go with him. To the middle of the woods. To learn control. For myself. For them. For you. Because he broke something in me. He made me this way. He made me want to be a monster, and I don't always think I can stop it."

I brushed a strand of hair off his forehead. "I'm not scared of you. I never have been."

"Maybe you should be."

"Joe." A hint of annoyance edged my voice.

"I would kill for you," he said harshly. "If anyone tried to hurt you, I would kill them."

I said, "I know," and I said, "because I would do the same for you."

He laughed, and it was tinged with wolf, all snap and snarls. "I see him sometimes. When I close my eyes."

"I know."

"I don't know if that'll ever go away."

"I know that too."

"And you still said yes?"

I said, "Yes," and moved my hand in his hair again.

He sighed.

We watched the stars.

They were so much bigger than we could ever hope to be.

Someone told me once that the light we see from them is hundreds of thousands of years old. That the star could already be dead and we'd never know it because it still looked alive. I thought that was a terrible thing. That the stars could lie.

I said, "Are you scared?"

"Yes," he said immediately. Then, "Of what?"

"Becoming the Alpha."

"Maybe. Sometimes. I think I'll do good, you know? And then I think that I won't."

"You'll do good."

"Yeah?"

"I'll help." Because I would.

He was quiet for a while. "I didn't think we'd get here."

That hurt to hear. For the both of us. "I'm sorry."

He shook his head. "Don't be. You have a choice. You're human."

I said, "And you? Do you have a choice?"

He said, "It's you. I would always choose you. I don't care if it's a biological imperative. I don't care if it's some destiny. I don't care if you were made specifically for me. It doesn't matter. Because I would choose you regardless."

I thought of kissing him then. I thought on it quite a bit.

But I didn't. I should have.

Instead, I said, "You're not a monster," and touched his cheek. His ears. His lips. "You're not. I promise you. I swear to you. You're not."

And he said, "Ox. Ox. *Ox*." And he shook and broke and I crumbled right along with him.

I think we both cried a little then.

Because we weren't yet men.

GET YOU A BEAR / HURT YOU

Sometimes I drove home in the old truck Gordo had bought me. Most times I walked home because I knew Joe would be there.

I could count on it. It didn't need any explanation. It just was.

So of course he was there, days later. Standing in the shadow of an old elm tree, the sunlight filtering through the leaves and dancing on his arms and neck. He'd been small, before. That first day. The runt of the pack. The little tornado.

But not anymore. Part of it was genetics. Part of it was him becoming an Alpha. He'd grown into himself, and I know he heard the moment my heart tripped all over itself, because he smiled at it like it pleased him.

"Hey, Joe."

"Hi. Hi, Ox."

I stopped in front of him, unsure. It'd only been a week since this . . . thing. This *thing* had started. This . . . *thing* between us.

"Hi," I said lamely, words drying up on my tongue.

We stared at each other.

It was *stupid*.

So I said, "This is weird," and at the same time, Joe said, "I want to take you on a date."

I choked on my tongue. And coughed. And finally said, "Yeah. Sure. Okay. Yeah. Sounds great. When? Now? We could go now."

His eyes went wide. "Right now?"

I said, "No! No. I didn't mean. You know. We could."

"Oh. Well. Maybe? We could . . . go. Someplace."

"Are you going to bring me more dead animals or mini muffins?" I blurted out. Then cringed. "You . . . ah. Don't have to." I didn't even get to *have* any mini muffins because the guys at the shop had eaten them all. Except for Gordo. Gordo had just glared at them.

He looked at me strangely. "Do you *want* more animals? I can go hunt right now! I'll get you another deer. Or a bear. I'll get you a bear!"

Then he started taking off his clothes, so I said, "You're getting *naked*?" Because of all the *skin*.

His shirt was already off when he said, "What?"

I grasped onto the only thing that made sense. "You're seventeen!"

"Not for too much longer," he said and his voice was *deep*. Because he was *leering*.

Instead of focusing on that, I said, "I don't need a bear."

"Deer?" he asked.

I shook my head because the idea of him dragging a dead deer out of the forest and leaving it on the front lawn made me queasy.

"You should put your shirt back on," I said.

He squinted at me. "Why?"

"Because of . . . you know. All of *that*." I waved my hand at his entire being.

Then he grinned. And it was *evil*. "All of this?" He flexed his chest. *Unfairly*.

I managed to say, "Yes. To all of that."

He took a step toward me. "We could . . . ah. You know." He waggled his eyebrows at me and I thought, *Fuck*.

I took a step back. "Or we could wait until you're eighteen."

Then he glared. There was a bit of wolf in it. "That's not how this works."

"Yeah, because you know how this works. With all the courting you've done."

"I can't wait until I'm Alpha so I can tell you what to do all the time."

"I'm going to tell your dad you only want to be Alpha so you can get in my pants."

He groaned. "Don't talk about my dad while I'm trying to seduce you."

"Stop talking," I begged him. "Please."

And then, of course, Carter and Kelly appeared, on their run.

They stopped and stared at us.

We stared back. I felt guilty. Because their underage brother was shirtless and it probably smelled like a whorehouse where we stood.

Kelly said, "This is awkward."

I said, "Nothing happened!"

Carter said, "Oh my God, it stinks like *sex*."

Joe said, "I'm going to kill him a bear."

There was more staring.

Kelly said, "I am so uncomfortable right now."

I said, "Put your clothes back on."

Carter said, "It's like I'm drowning in pheromones and boners."

Joe said, "Or maybe a deer."

All the staring.

Kelly said, "I hope you both know you've ruined life for me."

I said, "Your *shirt*, Joe. Put on your *shirt*."

And then, just because he was a *dick*, Carter said, "It's a good thing I popped Ox's gay kissing cherry like *years* ago. You're *welcome*."

Joe roared and Carter *laughed* and took off, Joe's shirt falling to the ground and his shorts tearing as he shifted into his wolf. They took off through the trees, Joe snarling and howling in anger.

Kelly and I stood on the dirt road.

"So," I said.

"Yeah," Kelly said.

"Is he really going to kill a bear?"

Kelly snorted. "Probably. Now that you've made out with Carter."

"I didn't *make out* with Carter!"

"But you kissed him?"

"He kissed *me*."

"I really don't see the difference."

"He's straight."

Kelly arched an eyebrow at me. "I don't know if werewolves identify as anything but fluid."

"But . . . he said . . . he *told* me—"

Kelly rolled his eyes.

"I don't know *anything* about werewolves," I muttered.

Kelly huffed as he heard Joe's angry roar echo through the forest. "Pretty sure we're listening to fratricide," he said.

"I don't know what that is."

Kelly said, "Joe's gonna kill Carter."

"Seriously?"

Kelly shrugged. "Probably. It certainly sounds like he wants to."

"You don't seem too worried about that."

"Eh," Kelly said. "What can you do? I haven't had sex with either a guy *or* a girl yet."

"Uh. Thank you for sharing?"

"Thought about it," he said.

"Okay."

"Seems like a lot of work," he said with a frown as some wolf got thrown into a tree by the sound of it.

"It is," I assured him.

"I made out with a guy, though," he said.

"What? When?"

"At this . . . *thing*. I don't even know. Then there was this girl. I don't know if that counted, though. She just . . . put her tongue on my face. Like, near my nose."

"Okay?"

"Is it bad to be twenty-one and not have had sex?"

"Uh . . . no? Why are you asking me?"

He stared at me. "You're the future mate of the future Alpha. You have to answer questions like this."

"I do?"

"Yeah. It's, like, your job."

"Oh. No one told me."

"What did you think you'd be doing?"

"Honestly? I'm not really sure. This was all kind of . . . sudden."

"When you got a boner for Joe?" he asked sympathetically.

"Oh my God."

"So you have to give advice and stuff. Help the pack when we have problems. It's what Mom does. It's what she did too. When the pack was bigger."

"I'm not your mom."

He dismissed that with a wave of his hand. "Might as well be." His mouth twitched. "Or something like it. Dad?"

"I will make sure you never get laid."

He shrugged. "I'm sure it'll happen when I'm ready."

I nodded. "And not a day before. Don't let anyone pressure you into anything."

He grinned. "Thanks, Dad."

I took a breath to stop from punching his face. He would have healed from it while I walked away with a broken hand anyway. "Okay. I'm not very good at talking. Or advice. Or much else." Because if he needed it, if they needed me, then I'd do what I could.

"You do okay."

I smiled at him. "Yeah?"

"Except for the part where you made out with Carter before Joe has ever gotten to tap that."

Wolves snarled somewhere in the forest. I said, "That's just swell."

.   .   .

"Joe's taking me out on a date," I told Mom, because I told her everything now. It seemed easier that way.

She said, "Oh? Where?"

I shrugged. "I don't know. He might kill me a bear."

She nodded. "Sounds about right. Well . . . have fun with that. I have to get to the diner. Don't sleep with him yet."

I almost fell over. "Uh. Okay?"

She sighed. "You want to, though."

"Jesus Christ, Mom—"

"Do you need me to pick you up some condoms? I think I have a coupon."

I banged my head on the kitchen table. "Please leave. Please."

So she kissed me on the forehead and went to work.

.   .   .

We went on a date.

It was awkward.

Not because of us.

Well. Not *just* because of us.

He knocked on the door.

I opened it before he'd even finished.

He said, "These are for you." He handed me more mini muffins. And then he grumbled, "I couldn't find any bears."

I said, "That's okay." Because I didn't honestly know what I would have done with a bear carcass.

He rubbed the back of his head. "Sorry."

"So, mini muffins?"

He grinned brilliantly. "Mini muffins."

"I am okay with that."

"You look hot," he blurted out. Then he frowned. "I mean, you look very nice. I am going to keep this classy. Mom told me to keep it classy."

I glanced down. I was wearing jeans and a red button-up shirt.

"Thanks?" I asked him. But I meant to *tell* him that, so I said, "Thanks." And then, "You look very nice too." Though my traitorous mouth almost said *fuckable* instead of *nice*. "I like your . . . pants."

"My pants," he said.

Gray slacks. Wool, maybe?

I stared at them.

And he said, "Really? Just what do you like about them? Maybe how they'd look on your floor?" His eyes widened. "Whoa. That sounded classier in my head."

How had he moved that much closer without me noticing?

I could feel his breath on my cheek.

"We," I said. "Uh. We should. Go?"

He said, "We could stay," and his lips scraped against my cheek.

So I said, "Thanks for the muffins," and stepped away.

He glared at me. "I can smell it, you know."

And I said, "That's not normal."

He rolled his eyes and dragged me to Elizabeth's car.

It was expensive. With so many buttons. I pressed one and my seat vibrated and I said, "Ooh."

We also went to the only fancy place in Green Creek. And by "fancy" I mean it was the only place that had tablecloths and folded napkins.

So of course Frankie was the waiter.

He said, "Hi, Joe!" with a big smile. He glanced at me. And grimaced. "And Ox." It came out more stilted.

"I didn't know," Joe told me, eyes wide.

I said, "That's okay." Because it *was*. I didn't *care*. Just because *Frankie* had gotten there first didn't meant *anything* to me. "Hi, Frankie. It's nice to see you again."

Frankie ignored me and said, "So, how have you been? Haven't seen you this summer. Excited about senior year?"

Joe said, "Things are good. I've been—"

And so I said, "I'd like a lemonade, and what are the specials?"

Frankie glared at me, and I thought Joe was about to laugh his stupid head off.

Frankie told us the specials. Sarcastically. And then turned back to Joe and said, "Sorry about that. You were saying?"

And Joe said, "Maybe give us some time to decide?"

Frankie said, "Are you sure?"

I said, "Yes."

And so Frankie left.

Joe said, "That was *awesome*."

I scowled at the menu. I didn't know what half the things on it were. I just wanted a hamburger.

"You were *jealous*," Joe crowed.

"No, I wasn't."

He kicked me under the table.

I ignored it because I'd just found hamburgers on the menu.

Joe said, "Ox."

I stared at the menu.

"Ox. Ox. *Ox*."

I said, "What!"

"So jealous," he whispered.

Frankie brought back the lemonade. It spilled on the table when he set it down. He said, "Oops," and set Joe's water down carefully. And then he just stood there.

I said, "More time."

Frankie looked at Joe.

Joe said, "*Ox*," and he was *amused*.

And a woman behind me said, "Ox?"

Joe growled low in his chest. Frankie arched an eyebrow at him.

I turned. Jessie was being seated at a table behind us with a woman I didn't recognize. I said, "Hi, Jessie."

Frankie said, "So, Joe. I was thinking."

Joe said, "Well, *hey*, Jessie."

She looked over my shoulder. "Hey, Joe. It's nice to see you." There was a small smile on her face like she knew something I didn't. She said, "Out on the town?" and I *knew*.

I said, "Yeah," but kept my face and tone blank.

Frankie said, "Joe, I was thinking. There's this—"

Joe said, "So, Jessie. I think I might have your class next semester."

I said, "Oh no."

Jessie said, "Is that right?"

Frankie said, "Yeah, me too," and everyone but me ignored him. I tried to make him leave by willpower alone. It didn't work.

"Should be exciting," she said. "We'll be reading some great books. Some cool projects going on. You can't call me Jessie in class, though. You'll need to call me—"

Joe said, "Is that right? I can hardly wait." He didn't sound like he meant that at all.

I said to Frankie, "We aren't ready to order yet," because he wasn't getting the message.

The woman Jessie was with said, "Ox? Oh, isn't that your . . . ?" She trailed off, having the decency to blush.

"Yes," Jessie said. "That's Ox."

"He's so . . . big," the woman said as if I wasn't sitting right there. "Look at his hands."

Everyone looked at my hands. I hid them in my lap.

Jessie grinned and said, "You know what they say about a man with big hands—"

"We're on a date," Joe said quite loudly.

Frankie said, "You're what? But he's so *old*."

Jessie said, "You're what? But he's so *young*."

Joe and I said, "Hey," at the same time, sounding equally offended.

"He's only twenty-three," Joe said.

I said, "He's almost eighteen." And God, that argument sounded awful.

Frankie said, "I knew it. The whole time." He looked pissed.

Jessie said, "I totally called this." She looked amused and hurt. It was a weird combination.

I said, "You what?"

Joe said, "No. Frankie. It's not like that. Okay, it was, but that's not it."

Frankie said, "Oh, please. You only talked about Ox every second of every day."

Jessie said, "It was always Joe, Joe, Joe."

"Don't you have other tables to wait on?" I asked Frankie.

"We *are* best friends," Joe said to Jessie.

"No," Frankie said. "Slow night."

"Oh, I was always aware of that," Jessie said. "Even when we were dating—"

Joe pressed his foot against mine as he growled. I pressed back. I saw a flicker of orange in his eyes.

I said, "Joe."

He looked at me.

I said, "Stay with me."

He said, "It's too loud."

I took his hand. It curled into mine. I felt the pinpricks of claws.

I said, "Joe."

He said, "I need."

I said, "Okay."

Frankie said, "Joe, I—"

"Walk away," I said. "Now."

Jessie said, "Is he okay?"

I said, "He will be. Please, just go back to your dinner."

Frankie walked away.

Jessie turned around.

I only had eyes for Joe. Always Joe.

His nostrils flared. He said, "You're bleeding."

I said, "It doesn't hurt. You would never hurt me."

Joe said, "Ox," and I said, "Let's go."

So we left.

.   .   .

We walked through the woods.

He took my hand in his and held it up to his face.

The skin was slightly swollen. A little red. Little flakes of dried blood littered my palm.

I stopped and waited for him to finish whatever he was doing.

He said, "I told you."

"What?"

"Remember?"

"Yes, but what?"

"That I wanted to see your blood. That I wanted to taste it."

I said, "Yes, but you'd never hurt me to do so."

"How do you know?" And there was the flash of those Halloween eyes.

"Because I know you."

And he stepped closer.

"I can hurt you," he said.

"I know."

"I have claws. And teeth." His chest bumped mine.

"I know. You won't scare me away, Joe."

His gaze faltered. "I'm not—"

"Either that or you're testing me."

"Ox."

I said, "No. You wanted this. You gave me your wolf. You came after me."

"It's not—"

"It's not going to work."

And there was fear there. Real fear. "What won't?" he croaked.

"Scaring me away. I know what I'm in for. I would have run a long time ago if I couldn't handle it. My daddy told me I was gonna get shit all my life. And fuck if I didn't believe him. But now I don't. Not anymore. So don't give me your shit. I won't take it. I won't ever take it."

His breath on my face.

This was Joe. And I was Ox.

His nose touched mine.

My hands found his waist. He shuddered under the touch.

He rumbled deep in his chest.

He said, "Mine."

My cheek scraped against his.

The wolf growled, "*Mine.*" It was a great and terrible thing.

So I said, "Yeah, Joe. Yeah. Yes."

And turned to kiss him.

But before our lips could brush together, a howl rose up, echoing through the trees. Birds took flight. The forest shook with it.

It was Thomas. Of that I had no doubt. Because I knew my Alpha.

But it was a song filled with such rage and despair that I staggered back, the pack bond bursting in my head and heart with red and blue.

And violet. So much violet that I was all but *buried* in it.

Joe's eyes flared to life, and he sang out his response. I could hear the fear in it. Pure, cold fear. The song itself was Alpha red and Beta orange. And blue. So blue.

It died in the trees around us.

Everything was quiet as I struggled to breathe.

He said, "We have to hurry," and his eyes blazed.

So we did.

And everything changed yet again.

WORD OF WARNING / IT'S A RIGHT

There were men at the Bennett house.

Men I'd never seen before.

They stood in front of the house next to black SUVs.

They heard us coming, and for a moment their eyes glowed orange in the dark, and I wondered if Joe and I could take them. We were outnumbered but we weren't weak. Thomas had seen to that.

It wasn't necessary. Thomas came out onto the porch and growled low. The men stood down.

Another man came out from behind him.

Osmond. The man who'd come in the winter.

He said, "Be still. All of you."

The men next to the SUVs turned away from Joe and me, eyes scanning the forest behind us.

Osmond said, "Where is your witch?"

Thomas said, "He'll be here," and I wondered what Gordo would have thought about that. Being called Thomas's witch.

"What happened?" Joe demanded.

"Go inside," Thomas said. "The pack is waiting."

Joe looked like he was gathering steam to argue, but Thomas's eyes flashed red and Joe said nothing. He stalked by his father and went into the house.

I moved to follow.

Thomas touched my shoulder and I paused.

"I'm sorry," he said.

"For what?"

"I know you were on your date."

I shrugged. "This is important?"

He said, "Yes."

I said, "Then it's okay."

Thomas sighed. "Joe is very lucky."

Osmond said, "Date? With *Joe*? Thomas, he's a *human* and—"

Thomas had him pinned against the wall before I could even think to react. The Betas behind us growled out in response, but they came no farther. They may have had some loyalty to Osmond, but they knew their place.

Regardless, I moved until I stood with my back to Thomas, glaring at the wolves in front of me. I wouldn't leave my Alpha unprotected.

"Word of warning," Thomas said, voice even and cold. I glanced back at him over my shoulder. "You do not get to come into my territory, into my *home*, and pass judgment on things you know nothing about. My son has chosen. It doesn't concern you. Speciesism has no place in Green Creek or in my pack."

"But he's to be the *Alpha*. What do you think—" He was cut off when Thomas half shifted, fangs descending, muscles expanding.

"It. Doesn't. Concern. *You*," Thomas said.

Osmond nodded.

"Apologize to Ox."

Orange eyes.

Thomas growled, "*Now*."

"I meant no offense," Osmond said stiffly, glancing at me. "My apologies, Ox."

I said nothing as I turned away from the wolves below us.

Thomas stepped away and Osmond slumped against the house. The Betas in the yard did nothing.

Thomas said, "Ox, join them inside if you would." He never took his eyes off Osmond.

I touched his arm. "Are you sure? I could stay and help you."

He smiled quietly. "I'll just be a moment, Ox."

I went inside.

The others were in the living room. Mark was standing, looking out the window, face pinched.

Elizabeth was speaking quietly to Joe, but I couldn't hear what they were saying.

Carter and Kelly stood up as soon as I entered and crowded around me. They were both rumbling low in their chests and I could feel it vibrating into me. I didn't know if it was for my benefit or theirs.

"All right?" Kelly asked me.

"Yeah. What's going on?"

Carter said, "No idea. Osmond and his bitches came and they went into Dad's office. Five minutes later, Dad's storming out, breaking the door off its hinges and howling for you and Joe to come home."

I said, "Mom. Where's my mom?"

"Gordo," Kelly said. "He's getting her from work."

"It's bad?" Because they would know better than me.

They looked away.

Thomas came in. He ignored the rest of us and went to Joe and Elizabeth. I heard Joe say, "What happened?" but Thomas hushed him gently and told him to wait.

Osmond followed and he pointedly avoided my eyes.

It was only minutes later that a car approached outside. Osmond tensed, but Thomas said, "The witch and Ox's mother."

There was some growling outside, but I heard Gordo say, "Oh, shut the fuck up before I burn your furry asses."

Mom's eyes were wide as she walked through the door. She sought me out and took my hand. I told her I didn't know what was happening.

Gordo came in a moment later and stiffened slightly. "Osmond," he said.

"Livingstone," Osmond said, sounding just as formal.

"This isn't going to be good, is it?"

Osmond sighed. "It never is, Gordo. I'm sorry it's come to this. The—"

"Ox," Thomas said.

I looked over at him as Osmond fell silent.

"Do you remember what I said? About tethers?"

He'd said many things about tethers. I told him as much.

He said, "They pull. In times of great uncertainty. They'll pull. Like you've never felt them pull before. You'll need to hold on as tightly as you can. Do you understand?"

"Thomas," Gordo said with a scowl. "What the hell happened?"

Thomas ignored him. He only had eyes for me. "Do you understand?"

I said, "Yeah. Yes." Because I did. Or I thought I did. I could feel the tension rising in the room and there were little flickers on my skin. In my head. My chest. Pulling me toward Joe. Toward Gordo. I touched these little strings that tied us together and sent back a wave of *calm* and *peace* and *it's okay we're fine we're all just fine because we're pack pack pack*, even if Gordo wasn't. Not really. But he was tied to me. And I was tied to them.

"Tether?" Osmond asked. "Who?"

"Mine," Joe said, eyes burning orange.

Gordo said, "And mine." The raven on his arm glowed briefly and looked ready to take flight.

Osmond looked at me, head tilted. "Just who are you?"

"I'm Ox," I said. "Just Ox. That's all."

For some reason, he didn't look like he believed me. It was the strangest thing.

Thomas said, "Richard Collins has escaped," and the air was sucked out of the room.

I almost said, "Who?" but then I remembered and the anger that bloomed through me felt like I'd been set on fire. It was a terrible rage, and for the first time in my life, I thought about the effect murder would have on a soul. Surely it would chip away at it piece by piece until there was nothing left but charred ruins, smoke curling in the air, and the taste of ash on a tongue.

But it was murder I thought of. Consequences be damned.

If Richard had shown his face right then, I would have murdered him without remorse.

If he'd put his hands up in surrender, I would still have taken his life without a second thought.

If he'd begged for forgiveness, I would have spilled his blood without hesitation.

I was almost consumed by it because it was *Joe* and it was *unfair* and wasn't he mine now? Wasn't he mine to protect and cherish?

He was, but the bond between us wasn't complete. He had claimed me, but he hadn't marked me.

And it was *unfair*. Because we were supposed to have time. To do it the way he wanted to. The way *we* wanted to.

There was a hand on my shoulder. My mother. There was a hand on the back of my neck and it was Gordo. He wasn't pack. He wasn't. By his own choice. But it was close. I was his tether, and I was learning how it might just be possible that the reverse was true.

I said, "*How?*" because Thomas had said he was in a cage. Of *magic*. Of something I didn't understand because I didn't know how magic worked, but his wolf was supposed to be *contained*. I wondered just how stupid I was for believing everything I was told without question.

And then Gordo said, "No, no, no," and I *knew*. Because Gordo knew, and it pushed along the tether, all violet and blue and there was *black* in it. Because *black* was fear. Black was terror.

A cage for a man to contain his wolf made of magic.

It seemed only fair that such a cage could *only* be broken by magic.

Osmond said, "We think it was your father, Gordo. We think Robert Livingstone found a path back to magic and broke the wards that held Richard Collins."

.   .   .

I made a choice. Though all my instincts were screaming *JoeJoeJoe*, he was surrounded by the pack and Gordo had nothing.

He walked out the door. I followed.

The wolves in the yard moved out of our way and I said, "Gordo."

His tattoos flashed angrily and started to shift. He kept walking.

I said, "Stop."

He ignored me and reached for his car door.

With all that I had, I growled, "Gordo. I said *stop*." It rolled out of me like a storm through a valley, dark and electric.

Gordo stopped.

The wolves around me whimpered and lowered their eyes.

I heard Osmond come out on the porch behind us muttering, "What the hell?"

"You don't understand, Ox," Gordo said. His voice was harsh.

"I know."

"You don't know what he did."

"And you don't know if this was even him."

His hands curled into fists at his sides. "Magic has a signature, Ox. It's like a fingerprint."

"But you said his was taken from him. How'd he get it back?"

Gordo shook his head. "I don't know. There are . . . ways. But. It's dark. It's fucking dark magic and I can't even begin to think of what this means." He reached for the car door.

"You can't leave."

He sighed. "Ox, I'm no good here. I'm not pack. I have to find out—"

"I don't care. I don't care what you think of the pack or any other bullshit. You're staying here and we're working together on this. Nothing else matters. I need you, man. You know that. I can't do this by myself."

He said, "You're not alone. The pack is with you."

So I said, "And who's there for you? You're *my pack*," knowing I was laying on the guilt, but I didn't care. I didn't know what this meant. I didn't know who these people were, aside from the horror stories.

"Goddammit," he muttered. "You fucking suck, Ox."

"Yeah."

We waited there. In the dark.

Then, "Ox, what if it's him?" And it was said in a small voice. A choked voice. I'd never heard him sound like that before in all the years I'd known him.

I took a step forward and put my hand on his shoulder. He was shaking.

I thought of all the things I could say. And all the things I couldn't because of what I didn't know.

I said, "You're not alone."

He shuddered at that. I didn't know if it was a good thing or bad.

"Do you remember? How it was when Dad left?"

He nodded.

"I was scared."

"Ox—"

"But you helped me to not be scared anymore."

"Yeah?"

And so I said, "And now it's my turn to do it for you."

He turned so fast that I was almost knocked down. But then Gordo had his arms around me and I felt the magic in him, the swirls of shapes and colors, and I searched for the green, the relief. It was there, buried deep in the violets and blues and reds and oranges.

       .   .   .

Back in the house, I said, "Joe."

He said, "Ox," and took me by the hand. He led me away from the others. I knew they could still hear if they chose to. But I knew Thomas wouldn't allow it.

We found a dark corner of the house, away from prying eyes. Away from any light.

His eyes glittered in the dark.

He said, "I won't let anything happen to you."

I said, "I know."

He said, "He's going to come."

I said, "I know."

Joe sighed. "He wants to be an Alpha."

"Thomas."

"Or me. To get to Dad. He tried it once. He could try it again."

"Why? Why you? Why Thomas?"

Joe said, "There are things, Ox. I swear . . . I just. There are things you don't know. I never . . ."

I tried to keep my anger in check. I did. He didn't deserve it. Not after everything that'd happened.

But knowing I was kept in the dark, that Joe had . . .

I didn't want to get angry.

I said, "Oh?"

Joe looked upset. "It's not like that."

"It sounds pretty clear what it's like."

"Ox."

"I'm part of your pack."

"Yes."

"And I'm your mate."

He said, "*Yes.*"

"But you've kept things from me."

And Joe said, "Not by choice."

"There's always a choice," I said, throwing his words back at him.

He whined low in his throat. "It's not—"

"What is he? Thomas, I mean."

"I would never lie to you." Joe sounded like he was begging.

I put my hand on the back of his neck and brought our foreheads together. His bright eyes were on mine, never looking away.

I said, "I know," because I did. I told myself I did.

Joe rubbed his nose against mine and said, "He was the highest-ranking Alpha out of all of us. He was the leader. In charge of all the wolves. He stepped down when I was taken. And for years there have been interim figureheads. But it's the Bennett bloodline. It's a birthright. And it is supposed to be mine."

They let him go after what happened to Joe. He told them, for the sake of his family, he needed to go, and maybe one day, Joe would be ready.

They didn't want to, of course. Osmond and the men like him in positions of power. There were councils. And organizations. Meetings of werewolves. Alpha gatherings.

They went on even though Thomas did not.

He turned away in order to save his son.

And then he just never went back.

No wonder Osmond freaked about me being human. Being courted by Joe.

Joe was meant to be the next great leader.

Just like he told me he would be when he was a kid.

I should have tried harder.

I should have asked more questions.

But when the fantastic reveals itself in front of you, it's easy to go blind to all the rest.

THE BEAST / FIRE AND STEEL

They took her on the second day, as dusk fell.

We were prepared. We were. We were.

We *were*.

I've told myself that over and over again every day since.

We *were*.

I swear to God. On everything I have.

We *were*.

But not enough. It was never enough. It *could never have been* enough.

Mom said, "I need to go to the house. Pick up some clothes. A uniform for work tomorrow."

I said, "I'll go with you."

She said, "Stay here. It's just down the road. You're busy as it is."

And I was. I was training. With Thomas. Joe. The others. Osmond watched me closely. I felt like I had something to prove to him. Knowing what I was. My position. Within the pack.

With Joe.

I said, "You can't go alone."

Osmond said, "I'll send two of mine along with her."

And I said, "Okay."

Okay.

I said *okay*. Like it was nothing. Like it was absolutely *nothing* at all.

Elizabeth and Mark were inside. Carter and Kelly were clawing and slicing at each other to my right. Gordo was checking the wards around town. Osmond was watching us move back and forth, but his eyes kept coming to me. I was something he couldn't figure out. He was cautious. Curious. Ever since the tone in my voice had caused his Betas to tremble.

We didn't talk about it. Or, at least, I never heard him talk about it.

I was distracted.

I said, "*Okay*."

"You need anything?" she asked me, like it was nothing. Like it was *nothing*.

I shook my head. Wiped the sweat from my brow. Feinted left when Joe came at me. Spun once. Knocked my fist into the back of his neck. Sent him stumbling.

I said, "Nah. I'm good." Because I was. I was fine. I was okay. The unknown was coming toward us, a monster capable of horrendous things, but I was with my family. The sun was shining overhead. There were a few clouds in the sky. I could hear birds. Could smell the trees and grass. It was green. It was all so fucking green that even the violet edges of it were distant because we were *pack*. We were stronger than anything that could come at us, and if Richard Collins showed his face, it'd be the last thing he ever did. If Robert Livingstone came smelling of ozone and lightning, we would rip the magic from his skin and he would be nothing more. This was a promise. Because of Joe. Because of what he was. To his pack. To the people like Osmond. To me.

I was focused.

I didn't ask the questions I should have.

Why Gordo's father would be with Richard Collins.

What they wanted.

What they were after.

(Who the weakest link was. Who would be the easiest to take out first. Who could be torn away. Who was kind and beautiful and not deserving of such a fucking cowardly act, a monstrous thing that—)

Mom said, "I'll be right back."

And Joe came at me again.

Thomas watched with careful eyes.

Carter and Kelly snarled and snapped.

Osmond pointed at two of his Betas and they followed my mother.

They were big guys.

I thought nothing of it.

We were safe here. On Bennett land. In Bennett territory. With a witch's wards and a forest filled with old magic that I would never understand. I didn't need to, though.

Because my Alpha did.

And he would protect us.

I knew something was wrong twenty minutes later.

Mom was pack. She was.

But it wasn't the same as it was with me.

I was tied to the Bennetts.

The bonds between us were strong. When the moon was full, I could hear them whispering in my head.

But that had passed.

It was a new moon.

And she didn't have the bonds we had.

She was tied to them because of me.

The wolves were within me.

She flitted along the edges, bright little bursts of light.

But I knew.

It was small at first. Just this little pull somewhere in the back of my head.

Thomas was watching Carter and Kelly and Joe.

I took a drink of water. It was cold and sweet and that little pull itched.

I said, "Hey."

I said, "How long?"

I said, "How long have they been gone?"

Osmond frowned and said, "Twenty minutes. Thereabouts."

I pulled out my phone. Sent a text.

whats taking so long

And waited.

I started to sweat.

And then a response: *Just finishing up. Can you come help me real quick?*

And I said, *sure.*

"Be right back," I told Osmond. "She needs some help."

He said, "Ox."

I looked at him.

"Never mind," he said after hesitating.

I went through the house.

Elizabeth and Mark were in the kitchen. They smiled at me as I passed them. It was pinched on the both of them, but they were trying.

"Okay, Ox?" she asked.

"Yeah. Mom needs some help real quick at the house."

Mark said, "Hang on, I'll go with you."

I shook my head. "No need. I don't think it'll take long."

"Ox—"

I laughed. "It's okay. I promise."

"Just . . . be quick. Okay?"

"Yeah."

And I *was* quick. I moved across the lawn toward my house. I kept my eyes and ears open because it was what I'd been taught. The wards were up, sure. I was surrounded by wolves. I was in a pack. I was big and strong. My father had said I was gonna get shit, but he was dead and buried and I was alive. I was important to someone. To many someones. I had friends. I had a family. Maybe I was gonna get shit, but it'd be met with fang and claw.

I moved with purpose.

I was aware.

Nothing was wrong.

Nothing felt off.

I was human, but I'd grown into my instincts.

It was fine. It was all fine.

But I still played it safe.

I went through the side door into the kitchen.

As soon as I closed the door behind me, it felt like a wet blanket had fallen over me.

Muted. Dark.

The air smelled sharp, almost like smoke.

The pack bonds were there, but they were grayed and dull. Muffled.

"Mom?"

And a man said, "Hello."

He was leaning against the counter near the sink. He was a tall man. A slender man. Thinning brown hair. Little wrinkles, pronounced around his eyes. A sharp, angular nose above even teeth. Tan skin without a single mark that I could see. He smiled at me and it was a *kind* smile. Full of laughter. Amusement.

He was *pleased*.

He said, "Ox, isn't it?"

I took a cautious step because of the *wrong wrong wrong*. "Where's my mom?"

He cocked his head, the smile fading slightly. "That was rude," he said. "I asked you a question."

I said nothing.

He sighed. "Ox."

She kept the good silver in a cabinet on the other side of the kitchen. I could—

He said, "I've certainly heard stories about *you*. The human who runs with wolves. The man in a wolf pack. Tell me, Oxnard. Do you feel the pull of the wolf within you? Does it claw at the human tissue surrounding your human bones?"

"Where is she?" That heavy feeling wouldn't leave and I wondered if this was what magic felt like when you were engulfed by it. If Gordo felt like this all the time.

He frowned. "I asked you a question."

"I'm not a wolf."

"I know *that*. I'm aware of *that*. That's not what I asked."

"No. I don't feel it."

The man said, "That was a lie. Why would you lie to me, Ox?"

"I'm sorry. Please. Where is she?"

"They can't hear you, you know."

"Who?"

"Your pack. They don't know that anything is . . . amiss. It's powerful. The spell."

"Tell me."

"Do you know who I am?" he asked. His eyes were bright and green until they were consumed by orange. But it wasn't the Halloween orange I was used to, vibrant and alive. No, this orange was rotting.

"No."

"That was another lie. Ox. Have they taught you *nothing*?"

I said, "Don't do this."

He laughed. "Do what?"

"Hurt her."

"Ah. Well. Of course. You can stop that, Ox. If you wanted to."

"How?"

"It's simple, really. Give me Joe and Thomas Bennett and I will give you your mother. You will call them and ask for them to come over here. I don't care what you have to say to get them here. Just those two and those two alone. If I even *suspect* you're trying to tip them off, I will paint the *walls* with her blood."

"You can't—"

He said, "That's where you're wrong. Because I *can* do it. And even more, I *am* doing it. This is happening, Ox. As we speak. As you breathe. Standing there with your little rabbit heart."

"You *can't*—"

"Ox. Ox. You can't argue with me. Not on this. I am a *beast*. I was made to be this way by the might and folly of men and I stopped denying what I am a long time ago. I will take what is rightfully mine and all will be well."

"You don't have to do this," and my voice *cracked*.

He said, "You have a choice to make, Oxnard. Hurry. You have a minute to decide."

I took a step toward him, my hands in fists at my sides. My head hurt and I could only think *MOM* and *JOE* and *THOMAS* and there was so much *anger*. So much *rage* that this man, this deceptively simple-looking man could come into *my* house and try to take everything from me. Everything I had. Everything I'd built.

I said, "Richard Collins."

He grinned. Bowed his head. Extended his hands in a neat little flourish. "At your service."

His rotted eyes flashed again.

I said, "I'll kill you. For everything you've done."

His smile widened. His teeth were more wolf than man. "I can see why Thomas likes you. Human or not, you've got a little somethin' somethin', am I right? Forty-five seconds, Ox."

I said, "Don't do this. Take me. Leave them alone. I'll go with you."

His smile faded. "So quick to sacrifice yourself?"

"Just take me." Another step forward. "I'll go quietly. Wherever you want."

"You'll kill me, you'll go with me, which is it? You're confusing the situation, Ox. How fickle the will of men."

I struggled to take a breath.

"Thirty seconds, Oxnard. And I have no use for a human aside from getting me what I want. You just won't do."

And another step and there she was. I could see her. In the living room. There were other men with her. Omegas, all of them. Their eyes were violet-bright, and my mother . . . oh God, my *mother* was on her knees, facing me. Gag in her mouth. Tears on her cheeks. She saw me and her eyes widened and she leaned toward me, and one of the Omegas grabbed her hair, snapping her neck back and—

"Kill you," I said hoarsely. "All of you. Every one of you. I swear it. I swear on all I have."

They laughed.

Osmond's Betas were kneeling on either side of her, blood spilling from wounds that hadn't closed. Wouldn't close.

"Fifteen seconds," Richard said.

I said, "I don't have my phone I don't have it I don't have it I swear I don't," and I couldn't *breathe* because this was *MOM* and *JOE* and *THOMAS* and he was making me *choose*, he was making me *decide* between them.

He said, "Kill the Betas," and before I could even take another step, two Omegas stepped forward and grabbed the heads of the kneeling wolves. A quick snap of the wrists and there was a crack and pop of bone and tissue and they fell to the floor, legs jerking and hands shifting to claws. Their heads had been twisted so far around that the skin had torn and blood spilled. There would be no coming back from that. No healing. The Omegas stood above them and waited for them to die. It didn't take long.

"I'm serious, Ox," Richard said quietly. "There are things I need. Things that must be done before I can leave here. I will do anything to take what's mine, what's owed to me. Can't you see that? Ox, she's *scared*. This is your *mother*. You're not mated to Joe. Not yet. You can find another. There will be a nice boy or girl for you down the road, but you can never have another *mother*, Ox. She's your only one. Please don't make me hurt her. I would feel so *bad* about that. I would. I really would."

And I knew that. I did. I did. She was my one and only. The only one I'd ever have.

"I'll go back and get them," I said. "I promise. I'll get them and bring them back."

Richard sighed. "Ox. Ox. Ox. That's not how this goes." He sounded so disappointed. He walked toward my mother.

I looked at her, and I was seven again. Or six. Or five and I was looking at my mommy, asking her what I should do, begging for her to tell me just *what the fuck I should do* because it was all *violet* and *blue* and all I could see was *red*.

And my mother looked back at me. With those dark eyes. She was no longer crying. Her face was wet, as were her eyes, but tears no longer fell. There was fire and steel buried in a cold resolve and she just *looked* at me and I knew. I knew what she was doing.

She was being brave and stupid and I hated her.

I hated her for it.

Because she was making the choice for me.

She was saying good-bye.

I said, "No. No, no, no." And took a step toward her.

The Omegas snarled.

Richard was a few steps away.

And her eyes flickered behind me to the door I'd come in. The door she was telling me to leave through when she moved.

"Mom."

She nodded.

Richard said, "This is touching. Last chance, Ox."

I croaked, "*Mom.*"

She smiled around the gag. A bright and shining smile that was the most awful thing I'd ever seen.

And then she *moved*.

It was grace. It was beauty. Fluid, like water and smoke. She coiled down and then rose up quicker than I'd ever seen her move before. Her head snapped back, smashing into the Omega behind her. His nose broke as he cried out and I took a stumbling step backward because if I *moved* quick enough, if I stepped out of the house and out of the magic that choked me, then I could call for my pack and they would save us, save *her*, and we would never have to be alone again.

Except Richard's hand curved into black claws.

His raised his arm in the air.

I remembered the night of my sixteenth birthday, when we'd danced in the kitchen.

The way she had smiled at me.

The soap bubble on my ear.

How she had *laughed*.

And as I pushed through the door to sing my family home, the hand of the beast came down across her throat.

The floor was wet, after. Around her.

The sound she made was wet.

Her eyes were wet. Her lips.

And her throat. Her throat.

Her throat.

And she started to fall and I pushed the door open and the magic *held* and it *pulled* and I screamed out my song of loss and horror and *pushed* through it.

When I came out on the other side, there was a hole in my chest where a bond had broken, and I knew. I knew, I knew, I knew.

And I sang then. I crawled on my hands and knees and *sang*.

I sang a song for my mother, heart-shattered and soul-deep.

They knew. My pack. As soon as my song hit their ears, they knew. Their answering howls were rage and fury and despair.

And I crawled toward them, calling back, begging for them to take away this pain. Begging for this to be a dream. A nightmare. But I had read that there was no actual pain in dreams. I remembered that through the haze of magic and darkness. I remembered that. And this couldn't be a dream, then, because all I could feel was pain. It rolled over my whole body until I was gagging with it.

Joe reached me first as a wolf, shreds of clothes he hadn't bothered to discard hanging off him. He pressed up against me and shuddered along with me, whining deeply as he rubbed his nose over me. He shifted and growled, "Ox, Ox. Please. Please, just look at me. Please. Where is it? Why do you smell like blood? Did he hurt you? Please don't be hurt. Please tell me what's wrong. You can't be hurt. You just can't. You can't ever be hurt." And his hands ran over me, trying to find any injury.

Wolves flew by us, toward the house.

The sun was setting behind the mountains.

Joe took my face in his hands and kissed my forehead, my cheeks, my chin.

He said, "I'm sorry. I'm sorry. I'm sorry." Like it was his fault. Like *he* had done this.

And for a moment, an awesomely terrible moment, I thought he had. I thought all of them had. The Bennetts. Because if they'd never come back, if I'd never met them, never heard them speak or seen their secrets unfold before me, my mom would still be with me. We'd be sadder. We'd be quieter. We'd be lonelier.

But we would *be*.

And the moment passed.

It passed because I had been given a choice. Between her and them.

And I'd chosen.

The air was warm and birds were singing and Joe's hands were smooth, but I felt *none* of it. I heard *none* of it.

There were no tears on my face.

I didn't cry because my father had told me men didn't cry.

I pushed Joe's hands off me and stood.

Thomas stepped out of my house. He had shifted from his wolf. He gripped the porch railing and closed his eyes. Osmond came out from behind him. I could hear the others moving inside the house.

I said, "Where is he?"

And Thomas said, "He's gone into the woods."

"Can you track him?"

Thomas took a step toward me. "Ox, I'm—"

"Can you track him?" I repeated.

Osmond said, "Yes. But it's what he wants. How many?"

"Five or six," I said. "Omegas, all."

Osmond closed his eyes. "They're gathering behind him. He's leading them. There'll be others. He's trying to become the Alpha to the Omegas."

Elizabeth came out, her face ashen. She was still clothed, so she must not have shifted. She pushed past Osmond and Thomas and reached for me even before she'd reached the bottom of the stairs. Her arms came around me and held me close. Mine stayed at my sides.

She said, "Ox."

I said, "We find him. Tonight." I didn't look away from Thomas.

She said, "Oh, Ox," and there was a hitch in her breath.

"He won't run," Osmond said. "This was planned."

And Thomas said, "Call Gordo. We need to move soon."

·   ·   ·

I sat on the porch, crowbar in hand.

The pack curled around me. Joe wouldn't leave my side.

I had never felt this cold before.

It was full dark when Gordo returned.

He got out of the car and said, "Ox."

I stood.

He said, "I'm sorry."

I said, "For what?"

"What happened. I've . . . made some calls. She'll be taken care of."

"What does that mean?"

"I won't let anything happen to her."

It was too late for that. "That's good."

He took a step toward me. "I can take you away from here. Away from all of this."

And the wolves growled around me.

I ignored them. "And go where?" I asked.

"Anywhere you want. We can leave Green Creek and never look back."

Joe stood and moved around in front of me. "Back off," he snarled, and I knew his eyes were orange.

"Joseph," Thomas said, his Alpha voice rolling through us. "Stand down."

Joe looked like he'd been struck. He said, "Ox. You can't."

Gordo said, "He can. He can do anything he wants."

"Can I?" I asked.

"Yes," Gordo said. "Anything."

I turned to Thomas. "Can I?"

"Yes, Ox," he said quietly.

"Good," I said. "I want to hunt down Richard Collins and kill him."

No one spoke.

Then, "Ox," Gordo said, sounding like he was choking. He took another step toward me.

My hand tightened on my crowbar.

"This isn't what she'd want," he said.

And I said, "Don't you tell me what my mother wanted." My voice shook. I didn't know if it was with sadness or rage. "Don't you dare." Because she was still lying in our house in a puddle of her own blood and he didn't get to say anything about her. Elizabeth had told me she'd covered her with a blanket and I'd wanted to say thank you, but instead I said nothing because of how *inconsequential* it was. A fucking *blanket*.

"Please," Gordo said. "Let me take you away from here. Away from all of this."

"I don't run from things," I said as coldly as I could. "I'm not you."

And he took a step back, eyes going wide.

A hand on my shoulder. I thought it would be Joe. Or Thomas. Or Elizabeth.

But it wasn't.

It tightened with the barest hint of claws as Mark said, "Stop, Ox. I know it hurts. I know it burns like nothing you've ever felt before. But *stop*. This isn't his fault. Don't say something that you won't be able to take back."

I ground my teeth as I bit back words I knew would hurt. That was the danger with knowing and loving others. You always knew things about them to throw back in their faces.

I was capable of doing that. Most people are.

But it came down to a choice.

So I swallowed down the hurt *(it's his fault it's your fault it's all of you because you brought this here you made this happen why couldn't you just leave us alone why did joe have to give me his wolf i hate you all of you)* and asked, "Will you help me?"

Gordo said, "Ox. This is . . . this isn't the end, okay? I promise. It seems like it. It feels like it. But it's not the end. I swear to you."

And then Osmond said, "Gordo, you should know. There was a . . . dampening. On the Matheson house. A powerful one. It didn't just mute the bonds. It made it so that no one outside the house could sense any distress in them."

Gordo said, "My father. The wards to the north. They were modified. And I never felt them change. He's the only one that could have done it. It felt like him. But different."

"Could you change them back?" Osmond asked.

Gordo nodded. "I'm better than I used to be. He doesn't know that. He might have seen how complex they were at first, but he won't know just how deep they go. It was like an infection on the surface. I healed them."

Osmond's wolves appeared out of the dark. "North," one said. "They went northwest."

"How many?"

"Ten or so. Maybe more. Maybe less."

Osmond looked to Thomas. "What's northwest of here?"

"A clearing," Thomas said. "One we use often. He knows of it. We played there as children. It's a sacred place for my family."

"He's spiraling," Osmond said quietly. "Coming into your territory. Knowing the magic that's here in this forest. It's *old*, Thomas. And on the far side of a full moon? He can't possibly think he'll win."

"He's probably heard the stories of the fallen king," Thomas said. His voice was bitter and dark. It was the first time I'd ever heard him sound like that. "He no doubt thinks me weak. That all he has to do is divide and conquer. He started with the humans because all he knows of humans is how easily they can break. He didn't expect to find the strength in them."

His words were proud, but I felt nothing from them. I couldn't.

He looked at me and said, "If I asked you to trust me and stay here, would you do it?"

"No."

"Ox."

I said, "That's not fair."

Red curled into his eyes. I felt the pull of it, the need to submit blooming deep within me. "I could make you," he said. "You know I could."

"You wouldn't, though."

"Oh? And why wouldn't I? I am your Alpha. You do as I say."

"That's not who you are. And I trust you to remember that. But I'm not staying here. Where you go, I go."

He looked sad. "Sometimes we go places where others cannot follow."

"He took her from me." My voice shook.

Thomas said, "I know."

He stepped forward then. Stepped forward until he was standing in front of me. He put his hand on my neck and pulled me to him, my face at his throat. A soothing rumble rose up from his chest and he whispered, "I am so sorry this has happened to you. I wish I could take away all of the pain you feel. But I wouldn't, even if I could, because that pain shows you you're alive. That you're breathing. That you can take another step. And where you go, I will go too. We will finish this and then our pack will help put your mother to rest. You are not alone, Ox, and you never will be."

The crowbar fell to the ground as I gripped him tightly.

I still didn't cry.

ALPHA

They waited for us in the clearing. The stars were bright overhead, and the violet Omega eyes shone in the dark. I counted fifteen shadowy figures. All wolves. Omegas weren't supposed to group like this. It was almost like they were pack. They didn't have an Alpha, not yet, so they couldn't be Betas. But they seemed united somehow.

Richard said, "Thomas."

And Thomas said, "You shouldn't have come here."

Richard laughed. "You knew this would happen one day." He glanced over at me before looking back at Thomas. "Humans, Thomas. Really? Still? Have you learned nothing from the past? You should be thanking me for taking care of the problem for you."

I was not an Alpha, but layers of red fell over my eyes and all I could think of was *death* and *murder* and *blood*.

Thomas said, "That's always been your problem, Richard. You underestimate the value of those you deem beneath you. Just because you can't appreciate their value doesn't mean it isn't there."

Richard's eyes flashed. "Your idolatry was amusing thirty years ago. It's since lost its meaning."

Gordo's voice was low when he asked, "Where is he?"

Richard smiled. "Who?"

"You know who."

"Ah. But I just want to hear you say it."

It was a game to him. All of this was.

"My father."

Richard said, "Yes. Him. He had . . . other matters to attend to. He sends his regards. I'm sure you'll see him soon." He scanned over the rest of us until he stopped on Joe. "Well, *you've* certainly grown up. Hello, Joseph. It's lovely to see you again."

And that was enough. That was it. No more. He could speak to me as he wanted. He could say shit to Thomas. And Gordo. They could take it. They could. But this man had killed my mother and now he was talking to Joe and I was done.

But apparently so were Carter and Kelly because they *flew* forward as I snarled, their claws extended, their teeth bared.

I followed because they were my brothers.

I followed because of my mother.

I followed because of Joe.

The bonds were there. Between us all.

We were pack. We were outnumbered, but we were still pack.

I raised my crowbar and smashed it down on a clawed arm that swiped at me. Bone cracked before the claws tore at my stomach. The Omega screamed as his skin burned away at the touch of silver. He started to shift to his wolf, but I spun low on my heels, launching myself up halfway through, arcing the crowbar up in a golf swing. The shock of the impact shook through my hands as the Omega's jaw broke. Shards of teeth and blood sprayed from his mouth and splattered over his face as he rocked back. The curve of the crowbar slid through the skin on the underside of his jaw and hooked behind the ridge of his teeth. I jerked my arms as hard as I could and tore his jawbone from his skull.

A line of fire etched down my back. I grunted and stumbled away. Somewhere off to my right, Joe roared in anger, either at the Omega that had come up from behind me or at something else, I didn't know.

I turned on the Omega behind me. She had blood on her face. She sneered at me and reminded me of Marie.

She said, "Your mother will start to rot soon. Decompose and fill with gas. How she'll *bloat*."

And I knew what she was doing. Thomas had taught me that. Rage and anger caused surges in power and strength at the cost of precision. It was easy to sink into the red sheen because it was all-encompassing. But it made you sloppy.

She was baiting me.

And it was close.

Because she was talking about my *mother*.

Maggie Callaway had never hurt anyone. She'd been given shit all her life, and all she wanted was to be happy. She'd never asked for much. She hadn't *needed* much. She'd had me. Eventually, she'd had the pack too.

And she'd been taken from us.

From me.

It was close, though, because the Omega was *right*. I could feel it pulling me under. Blood trickled down my back, and the pain was bright and awesome and *it was so close*. But then there was a *ping* through the bonds of the pack. A pulse. It hit me and I took it in and it said *home* and *trust* and *sorrow* and *love*.

And part of it was missing. Because *she* was gone.

It was acid on my skin.

Ice in my veins.

I said, "You shouldn't have come here."

And I was *clear*. I was *precise*. I took a step forward and her claws came toward my face, coated with my blood. She was fast. I side-stepped her, feinting left but going right. I brought the crowbar around in a flat arc behind her, the curved point slamming into the back of her head.

She grunted, low and guttural. Took a breath. Let out a choked sound.

I crouched and slid my right shoulder under the crowbar. It held tight in her head as I grabbed it with both hands. I gritted my teeth together and pulled myself to my full height. The Omega fell against my back as I jerked the crowbar forward. The momentum caused her to flip up and over my back, feet going skyward, landing flat on her face in front of me. She twitched along the ground as I tore the crowbar loose. I raised it above my head to bring it down again and again and again.

I was hit from the right side. The force of it knocked me off my feet and into a tree, shoulder first, my head rapping against wood. There were stars and lights flashing. I fell to the ground and thought, *get up get up get up*, but nothing happened. It was easier to stay down.

There were snarls and angry roars around me.

My vision wouldn't clear.

I closed my eyes again.

I thought of many things.

Like Joe.

And my mother.

How dark it was.

How much my back hurt.

How much my head hurt.

How much my heart hurt.

"Ox!" a voice cried out above me.

I meant to tell whoever it was that I was okay.

Instead, I said, "G'way."

The voice said, "I need you."

And it was *Joe*. It was *Joe* who knelt beside me. *Joe* whose claws stretched against my skin. *Joe* who said my name again and again telling me to *move*, to *open my eyes*, to *be okay, just be okay*.

Part of me had been taken away. Crushed and destroyed when blood hit the floor.

Part of me had burned up and become nothing but smoke and ash and charred remains.

But part of me still held together.

The part that belonged to Joe. To Gordo. To my pack.

I opened my eyes. My vision blurred. I blinked once. Twice. A third time.

He was there above me. With his orange eyes. His sharpened fangs. Half-shifted and worried.

I reached up and touched his face.

He closed his eyes and leaned into the touch.

I said, "We have to finish this."

He opened his eyes and said, "It's almost over."

He pulled me up, and it *was* almost over.

But not in the way I'd hoped.

We were too spread out. I couldn't see Carter or Kelly, but I could hear them snarling somewhere in the trees, their anger evident. The bond between us was stretched tight and thin, pulsing in dull rage.

I thought I saw a flash of Elizabeth, full wolf and graceful, eyes bright and teeth bared, but then she was gone, Omegas crawling after her.

Mark was crumpled on the ground, breathing shallowly. Gordo stood in front of him, tattoos glowing, blood dribbling down from a gash on his forehead. A group of Omegas surrounded them. Gordo grinned. His teeth were bloody. He said, "Yeah. Come on. *Come on.*"

And then there was Thomas. The Alpha.

I said, "No," because he was bleeding from every inch of exposed skin, half-shifted, eyes red and claws dripping. Dead Omegas were strewn about his feet, gore spilling into the grass of the clearing.

He was breathing heavily, chest rising and falling. His right arm hung uselessly at his side, a knob of bone poking out of his forearm, his healing not yet kicked in. His shoulders were hunched and his fangs extended, and still more Omegas came. They poured out from the trees and I didn't know how there could be so many. How so many Omegas could be in Green Creek without us knowing. Without *Thomas* knowing, because this was his land, this was his *home*, and I didn't *understand*.

They swarmed on him and he roared.

The trees shook in the forest.

The stars were bright overhead.

And then we were betrayed.

Joe growled deep and low in his throat, muscles twitching, ready to launch himself toward his father. To help him. To save him.

Osmond said, "Hey," and as we turned, startled, he backhanded Joe across the face.

The force of the hit knocked us both off our feet. Joe flew into a tree, crying out as his back snapped viciously, falling and writhing on the ground.

I lay on the ground, stunned, watching the stars in the sky above. I thought of my mother and, for a moment, forgot that she lay covered in a blanket in our house, her blood cooling underneath.

I said, "My head hurts, Mom," but the stars didn't say anything back.

Then the stars were blocked out.

Osmond looked down at me, head cocked.

I said, "You did this."

He said, "There really wasn't any other choice."

He raised his foot above my face. I wondered if it hurt to have your skull smashed in.

Richard Collins said, "Leave the human alone, Osmond. I'm not finished with him yet."

Osmond drew his foot away but didn't move from my side.

I turned my head. The grass felt cool on my cheek. Joe was lying feet away on the ground. His skin was sweat-slick, face twisted in a grimace of pain. His hands were fisted at his sides.

I said, "Joe," or tried to at least. It came out broken and weak. He didn't hear me. Or, if he did, he was in too much pain to do anything about it.

I couldn't see Gordo anymore, and I wondered if he was alive.

I turned my head the other way. It took more effort than I thought it would.

The Omegas had overtaken Thomas and had forced him down. He knelt before Richard Collins, and just the sight of it, just the mere *thought* of Thomas on his knees for *anyone* was enough to cause my blood to boil.

"You know," Richard said, "I expected more from the great Thomas Bennett. I'm a little . . . disappointed."

Blood poured from Thomas's mouth as he shrugged. "Expectations can be a bitch," he croaked. "Trust me when I say that I'm just as disappointed in you."

Richard nodded. "I'd forgotten what it sounded like when Joe's bones broke. The wet snap of it. His back, I think."

Thomas growled deep in his throat, but even I could see his strength was ebbing. Too many wounds, not enough time to heal. He was an Alpha, but he wasn't immortal. He struggled against the Omegas, but they held him tightly.

Richard said, "Before you die, I want you to know. I blame you. For everything. My family. My father. All of it. Every last part of it. Your parents. Your pack. Witches and wolves. I lay all of their deaths at your feet, and I am going to take your life because of it. I will become the Alpha, and I will *rape* your territory into submission. This old magic will be mine, Thomas. As will your wife. And sons. You are a false God, unworthy of what you've been given."

I was not a wolf. I was a human who was part of a wolf pack. I couldn't move like they could, not really. I couldn't heal like they could. I couldn't fight like they could. I did not have claws or fangs or eyes that glowed. I was Ox, that was all.

But they were mine.

These people had come into my home and had taken from me. They'd given me *shit*, just like my father had said they would. People were going to give me *shit* because I was Oxnard Matheson, because I was a stupid fucker who couldn't even protect his own family.

But no more.

No more.

I pulled on the pack bonds. I pulled on them as hard as I could.

Osmond was distracted by Richard's words. My fingers found the crowbar in the grass.

I remembered what Thomas had taught me. My father had said I was going to get shit all my life, but he wasn't my real father. Not anymore. My father had helped to make me, but it was Thomas who'd shaped me into what I was.

I thought we were going to die. All of us. But I was going to take as many of them with us as I could.

Osmond wasn't expecting me to rise up. He wasn't expecting me to sweep my leg out into the back of his knees, knocking his feet out from under him.

I was moving before he even hit the ground.

Somewhere in the trees, a wolf sang, and I felt the song burn within me, the bonds saying *OxMateBrotherSonFriend*, and I moved quicker than I ever had in my life.

I was not a wolf.

But my God, did I give the impression of one.

Richard started to turn as I came up behind him. His Omegas barely had a chance to react.

The crowbar stabbed through his back much more easily than I thought it would. Flesh parted and the crowbar scraped against bone. Blood spurted out over my hands and face and I *pushed*.

Richard screamed as he shifted, claws coming up and over his shoulders, reaching for the crowbar, reaching for *me*, trying to slice and cut and mark.

I pushed the crowbar in farther, hoping I'd manage to skewer the bastard's heart. Hoping that it was enough, because Thomas was *gushing* blood now, and I didn't know how much longer he'd last and—

Richard's claws fell onto my shoulder and *squeezed*. They punctured my skin and he pulled me around, my blood-slick hands slipping from the crowbar.

He brought me around in front of him, and even though I must have outweighed him by a good fifty pounds, he grabbed me by the neck and lifted me off my feet.

His orange eyes were bright, his breath hot on my face.

He said through a mouthful of lengthening teeth, "Little human. How I admire you."

A pulse off to my right, lighting up the forest around us.

It was Gordo, and the ground was shifting underneath us, a dull rumble that turned into something much louder. Green light shot along the ground, the earth groaning as Gordo called its magic to him. I saw symbols flash beneath my feet, arcane lines that formed stars and crescent moons, ravens that flew underneath me, trailing green sparks in their wake. The earth *burst* apart underneath us and Richard *snarled* in my ear, teeth snapping, biting, and—

He was knocked off his feet as the ground broke beneath him, cracking and rolling. Everything was *green*, flashes of light that boiled my blood and *sang* to something deep within me.

Richard grunted as he fell away from me, and in the chaos and confusion, I heard the screams of the wolves. I didn't know if they were mine or the others'. I fell to my knees, the pain glassy and bright, stomach twisting with vertigo.

A wet hand grabbed my arm and *pulled*.

I followed blindly.

We were deep in the trees before I could focus.

Thomas led me away, away, away.

"We have to go back," I croaked out, but I didn't try to get away.

He said, "Trust me."

And how could I not?

I ached everywhere. My back was torn to shreds.

He said, "You must listen to me." His breath rattled in his chest, a wet sound.

The stars were bright above.

The trees swayed.

He said, "You will be needed now. More than ever. The weight of the Alpha can be a dreadful burden, and whoever carries the weight of it on their shoulders must be able to stand strong and true."

"No," I said. "No, no. You—"

"Ox."

The wind rippled through the leaves.

There was an ache in my head and heart.

"They will *need* you," Thomas said. And then he stumbled, going down to one knee, grip tightening on my arm. He groaned quietly, head hanging down as blood dripped from his mouth. I pulled my arm from his grasp. I reached down under his arms, latching my hands in front of his chest. He was substantial and coughed harshly as I lifted him up, my back screaming with the strain.

The sounds of the earth splitting apart continued from behind us, but they were distant.

We continued on.

He said, "All of them."

"What?"

"The pack. They will need—"

"Why?" I asked.

Thomas took a deep breath and turned his face toward the sky. I wondered if he could feel the moon, even though it was hidden. "I knew you were different," he said. "When I first saw you. Even if it hadn't been for Joe, I would have known." His eyes flashed red again and again. It called to something in me, and I thought my blood was boiling underneath my skin.

"If I'm anything," I said, "it's because of you."

He said, "Oh, Ox. I only showed you what you already had inside."

I pushed on the pack bonds, but they were lost in a haze of pain and Gordo's magic.

He said, "You must listen to me."

I grunted as he stumbled again. Somehow I was able to hold him upright.

"You will—" He coughed, body shaking. Then, "The tether will be the most important thing. Those ties that bind you to each other. It'll have to be you. For all of them. It's a terrible thing I must ask of you, especially in light of all you've lost. But it can only be you."

"I'm not—"

"You *are*," he said fiercely. "You are *more* than you think. Ox. The power of the Alpha passes to the one who takes it. If it can't be me and it can't be Joe, then it needs to be you. He's not here and I am *asking* this of you."

"What?"

"Richard can't have this," Thomas said, lips shiny with blood. "He *can't*. The things he would do with it . . . no. And I can't hold on. Not like this. Not for very much longer. I can't heal, not from this. I'm slipping."

"No," I said. "*No.* You *can't*—"

"I need you to become a wolf," Thomas said. "I need you to do this for me."

It was too much. This . . . everything he was asking of me. I still hadn't yet made a decision if I was going to take the bite before all this happened. And now? Now he was saying—

"You want me to be the Alpha." My voice sounded small.

"Yes."

I couldn't find the words.

Thomas said, "I believe in you, Ox. I always have. You are my son just as much as the others are. I will always be—"

"There you are," Richard Collins said from behind us.

Thomas snarled, forcing me behind him with strength I didn't think he'd be capable of. I tripped over my own feet, falling to my knees. Thomas towered over me, but he only had eyes for the other wolf.

Richard didn't look much better. Someone had removed my crowbar from his back. His skin was soaked with blood. His rotting eyes shone darkly, claws extended, teeth sharp and flashing in the starlight.

He said, "You had to know it would always come to this, Thomas. There was no other way that this could end."

"Only because this is what you chose," Thomas said quietly. "We were friends once. Brothers."

"If you were my *brother*," Richard snapped, "you wouldn't have let them die. And even if they still had, you would have done *everything* you could have to make sure the ones responsible suffered. The humans should have *suffered* for what they brought upon our pack. And instead, you embraced them."

"They were a few," Thomas said. "A select *few.* What *possible* outcome do you think this will have?"

Richard's claws extended farther. "I will become the Alpha," he said. "And then I will make them pay. For everything. The humans will bow to me and I will *end* them."

He launched himself at Thomas, shifting in midair, clothes shredding into tatters, hair sprouting. Before I could even shout a warning, there was a snap of bone and muscle and wolf met wolf among the trees, fangs snapping, paws scrabbling for purchase.

Thomas was the bigger of the two, but even shifted, the blood still flowed, matting his fur. Richard was vicious in his assault, and I was knocked back as they rolled toward me, teeth buried in each other, broken growls falling from their mouths.

I looked around for something, *anything*, any kind of weapon I could use to stop this. To stop Richard before he could make things worse. I came upon a rock just smaller than my hand. I grabbed it without a second thought because this was my *Alpha*. This was *Thomas* and I couldn't let him go.

He'd taught me about myself. Who I could be.

Alpha meant father.

(You are my son.)

It meant safety.

It meant home.

I didn't make a noise as I rose to my feet. I didn't hesitate as I moved toward the white wolf fighting against the brown one. I didn't think twice as I tracked their movements, waiting, waiting for that right moment.

It came quicker than I would have hoped.

Richard knocked Thomas back.

Thomas crashed into a tree with a deep whine.

He slid to the ground, eyes unfocused.

Richard stood above him.

His lips pulled back over his teeth.

A low rumble started in his throat, and I saw his muscles coiling as he prepared to attack.

It took only seconds, really.

One moment he was standing above Thomas and the next I was bringing the rock down on the back of his head. There was a sharp *crack* that I hoped at the very least meant a split skull. The wolf yelped, and for a moment, I felt a sick thrill. That we'd won. That I'd taken him down. That he would fall to the ground and would never rise again.

I saw the swell of blood on the top of his head. It spilled down between his eyes and onto his snout, dripping to where his lips curled.

But he did not fall.

He turned to me.

Thomas tried to push himself up but collapsed back onto his paws.

I took a step back.

The great and terrible beast took an answering step forward.

"Come on, you fucker," I said hoarsely. I tightened my grip on the rock because it was all I had.

I thought of Joe. And my mother.

I felt bad. I'd left one behind for the other. And now I was doing it again.

But at least he'd be safe if I could take Richard down with me.

And that was the only thing that mattered.

I wouldn't let him take Joe.

Not again.

Richard's ears flattened to the back of his head, and even though it seemed impossible, I could have sworn the wolf was smiling.

Like he *knew* he'd won.

I remembered what I'd been taught.

It was all I could do. And as long as I remembered, maybe Joe would be okay. And Thomas. The others. And one day, they would look back and remember me for the things I'd done since the day we'd met rather than the last thing I did.

.   .   .

There was a day Thomas and I had been walking through the woods. He'd made Joe stay behind. Joe wasn't too happy about that, but Thomas had just flashed his eyes in that way he did and Joe had stopped complaining. Mostly.

We didn't talk for the longest time. It felt good to be silent with someone, not needing the weight of conversation. Thomas knew that about me. He knew that sometimes I couldn't find the words to say what I wanted, so I just said nothing at all. He didn't think I was stupid. Not like others had before him.

There was a moment, brief and bright, when I thought of my father. I still wasn't quite sure what wolves could pick up by heartbeat and scent, if sadness had a taste to it, or if anxiousness felt heavy.

My father wouldn't have understood this. The wolves. The pack. My place with them. He wouldn't have understood any of it.

Not really.

He would have given me shit for it.

Tried to take it away.

My father hadn't been a good man.

I knew that now.

He'd spoken in indifference and callousness.

In rage and violence.

But I'd loved him anyway, because I was his son.

And he was my father.

I wondered what that said about me, that I could love someone like him.

Despite his everything.

It wasn't the first time I'd told myself it was better that he was gone.

But maybe it was the first time that I'd believed it completely.

That hit me hard.

That I'd ever thought it was good that someone was dead was beyond me, because I wasn't that person.

I didn't speak in indifference. In callousness.

In rage and violence.

My heart stuttered in my chest.

I took a breath, sharp, like a soundless gasp.

Thomas wrapped his big hand around the back of my neck and squeezed, leaving it there as we walked. He didn't speak. He was. He was just.

There.

My heartbeat slowed.

My breaths returned to normal.

My feet didn't drag.

We walked on.

Strangely enough, I spoke first. Later, of course. Much later. I thought maybe he'd been waiting for me to speak.

I said, "How do you always know?"

Thomas didn't even act surprised at the question. "You're mine," he said simply. "I'll always know."

"Because you're the Alpha?"

"That too," he said, his eyes never leaving mine.

And I heard all the things he'd left unsaid.

·　　·　　·

The beast came for me, there in the darkened woods.

My Alpha lay quietly underneath an old oak tree whose branches rattled in the wind. His chest rose shallowly and held. It fell and took forever to rise again.

Richard crouched.

I narrowed my eyes.

I said, "You should have stayed out of my territory."

Richard leapt.

His claws reached for me.

His jaw opened wide.

I brought the rock up and—

A flash of white, crossing in front of me.

Richard yowled as he was thrown to the side.

A wolf stood in front of me, hackles raised, head crouched low to the ground, teeth bared in a furious snarl at Richard, who was pulling himself back to his feet.

Joe.

Joe was here.

Joe was all right.

This wasn't a dream, because my back ached something fierce.

I reached out and curled my fingers in the fur on his neck.

I felt the rumble deep within him.

It sang to me.

Richard flashed rotted eyes as he glared at Joe, moving slowly around us.

Joe moved with him, always staying between us. I could feel the anger in him, the rage and the anguish. I tried to reach for the others, the strings that connected us all, to make sure none of our pack had been lost, but everything was jumbled. My head hurt and I couldn't focus on anything but the green relief of having Joe here, of knowing that he was okay. That he wasn't still lying beneath a tree, back snapped and writhing.

We could do this. We could—

Richard ran at us without making a sound. Joe tensed beneath my hand, readying himself for the impact. I dug my heels into the earth and fought every instinct that told me to run, because I was *not* a coward, and I was going to fucking *stand with my mate*—

Lights shot up around us, rising from the earth, the ground beneath our feet groaning as it shifted. Richard collided with the light and was thrown back as if electrified, eyes rolling up into the back of his head as he landed at the base of an oak. He twitched, legs skittering on the ground, digging through the dirt.

"Ox," a voice said from behind me.

I turned.

Gordo stood there, leaning against a tree, panting. His face was sweat-slick and pale. He cradled his left arm against his chest. His clothes were torn. He was bleeding in more places than he wasn't.

And the tattoos on his arms were the brightest I'd ever seen.

"How did you—"

"It's the territory," he said, voice thin and weak. "It belongs to the Bennetts. It always has. It doesn't like intruders. The earth, it ... I can hear it. It talks to me. I can keep him out. For now. But I can't hold it, Ox. Not forever. Whatever has to happen needs to happen now."

I reached out and touched the light (barrier?) that surrounded us, separating us from Richard. It felt solid under my fingers, and warm, and there was that thread that connected me to Gordo, one that I'd always felt faintly before. It was never as solid as the others, because even though we were tethered together, he wasn't pack.

But now it was bright. And strong.

"What has to happen?" I asked, not sure if I wanted the answer.

Gordo said, "*Ox.*"

And I knew.

Then a voice spoke softly.

It said, "Dad?"

I looked over.

Joe had shifted to human again and was kneeling next to his father. There was a deep, dark bruise stretching the length of his back where he'd struck the tree. Even as I watched, the edges were fading as it healed. I didn't know if it was because he was who he was that he'd survived that impact. If Carter or Kelly could have done the same.

His father was stretched out before him, still a wolf. His eyes were open and watching his son. He whined quietly in the back of his throat. His tail thumped once. Twice.

Joe said, "You gotta get up."

Thomas stretched his neck until his nose touched Joe's hand.

"They're okay," he said, like he could hear his father's question. And for all I knew, he could. "They're taking care of the rest. But they need you. Okay? You gotta get up." His voice broke at the end.

Thomas sighed, a great and heaving thing. Like his fears were slipping away.

From behind us, a wolf howled, a song of fury.

I whirled around.

Richard Collins stood, and he was angry. He was snapping his jaw and started hurling himself at the barrier. His eyes were darker than they'd been before, like he was lost to the wolf, all feral and rage. Every time he slammed into the green, the light pulsed outward, like a ripple in water. And it only made him angrier.

"Thomas," Gordo choked out. "You have to do this. *Now*. I can't—"

Thomas began to shift, slower than I'd ever seen it. By the grimace on his wolfish face and the way his body tensed, it was a painful shift. Bones that were broken before were still broken. Cuts were wide and bled freely without any sign of stopping.

Joe moaned above his father, hands shaking as he reached out. He hesitated as if unsure where to touch him.

Richard screamed and continued his assault.

Joe said, *"Dad."*

Thomas Bennett smiled up at him. His mouth was red and blood dribbled down his cheek. His eyes were clear.

He said, "I'm glad you're okay."

"We have to get up," Joe begged. "We have to get up and go. Mom's waiting for you."

"You're going to be fine," Thomas said. "It'll hurt. For a while. But you'll be *fine*."

Joe shook his head. He grabbed his father's hand and held it in his own. "I can't do this," he said. "I'm not ready." He sounded so impossibly young.

"You are," Thomas said. "You have been. It's what we've been working toward. You've—"

There was a loud groan of bone and muscle. Then, Richard said, "I can save him, Joe. I can save him. You just need to give me what I want. I can help you. And him."

Richard stood, nude and bloodied, eyes on Joe but unable to take a step forward because of Gordo's magic.

"Don't," Thomas said, eyes never leaving his son. "Don't listen. It's not—"

"You don't need it," Richard said. "I can take this all away. Your father will be *fine*. I will be the Alpha, and I promise you that all of this will seem like a dream. You can go home, and you'll never see me again."

I didn't need to be a wolf to know he was lying.

And for all he was worth, for all he'd been through, for all the horror he'd seen, Joe hesitated.

I saw it. It was small, but it was there.

Thomas saw it too.

But so did Richard.

And he *smiled*.

So I took a step forward and said, "Joe."

Joe looked up at me, Halloween eyes bright and wet.

"He makes promises," I said, "that he won't be able to keep."

Joe bit his lip. "But—"

"He's *human*," Richard said, voice dripping with disdain. "Even if he is *pack*. He doesn't understand. He'll *never* understand what you are. What you're supposed to become. His kind are the reason any of this is happening at all. They betray you, Joe. They will always betray you."

"I promised you," I said, taking another step. "That it would always be you and me. That I would take care of you. That I would never lie to you."

Tears tracked down his face.

"They can *only* lie!" Richard roared, smashing his fists against the barrier. "It's all they are *capable* of!"

"Hurry up, Ox," Gordo bit out through gritted teeth.

"You trusted me with your wolf before you even knew me," I said. "Back when I thought I was nothing. But you showed me. You *trusted* me. And I'm asking you to do it again."

His eyes were wide. His breath hitched in his chest.

He tore his gaze away from me and looked back down at his father.

"This isn't the end," Thomas whispered to him, voice barely able to be heard above Richard's shouts. "You'll see. I am so proud of you and what you have become. What you *will* become."

"I can't do this alone," Joe wept. "I *can't*—"

"And you won't have to," Thomas said. "Because an Alpha is nothing without his pack. And your pack will always be with you."

"Ox!" Gordo cried in warning, and I looked over. He'd fallen to his knees, sweating heavily, chest rising and falling rapidly.

Richard howled in triumph.

"Joe," I said. "You have to—"

Joe's claws were out before I could finish, black and sharp. The barrier flickered as he brought them down to his father's chest, above his heart, fingers spread to five sharp points.

Voice trembling, Joe said, "Do you remember? That day in the woods. We chased the squirrels. And you told me you were happy I was your son."

Thomas smiled his quiet smile. "I love you too."

Joe pierced his father's chest.

The world was a large and scary place. That's what Gordo had taught me. That anything I could think of was probably out there. There were questions I didn't ask because I was scared of the answers I would get. There were questions I hadn't thought to ask but whose answers were kept secret from me anyway.

And then there were questions I wasn't even prepared to understand. Why did my father leave? Why did Joe choose me? What was my place in all of this?

How would Joe become the Alpha?

He knew. He knew, because he didn't hesitate. Not at this. Not when his mind was made up. I wondered when Thomas had told him. Or if it was instinct. Something simply known from the past to the future.

His claws went into his father's skin, pressing down until his palm was flat against Thomas's chest. Richard screamed his fury, and at first nothing happened. I thought maybe something had gone wrong. Truth was, I didn't know *what* to expect, transferring the power of an Alpha from one to another.

I still didn't know jack shit about werewolves.

It started with a tingle along my skin.

Like a whisper in my ear.

Joe didn't move.

Thomas didn't move.

But then my skin was *crawling*. There was a surge in my head and heart, and I wondered if this was what it felt like to be struck by lightning. The pack bonds were *bursting* in my chest and I could feel them all, every single one of them, and there was a poignant relief, so *greengreengreen* because they were *alive, all of them*, but it *hurt* because Carter's was strong and Mark's, and Elizabeth's and Kelly's and Gordo's (because he was there *too*, for the first time like *pack* and I could taste his magic at the back of my tongue, ozone-tinged and bitter).

And *Joe*. Joe's was the brightest out of all of them, the strongest, and there was such *power* there that I could barely breathe.

And Thomas.

Thomas's was there too.

But his was faded. The thread was thin.

Weaker than it had any right to be.

Like it was barely hanging on.

The barrier snapped back into place.

Thomas opened his eyes. They flashed orange and dull.

He sighed in such green relief.

He said, "Ox. A wolf is only as strong as its tether."

His eyes closed.

He exhaled.

His chest did not rise again.

The thread snapped and disappeared.

Joe said, "*Dad.*"

Hair sprouted along his cheeks. His face began to stretch into his half shift. His lips curled. His teeth lengthened into spikes. He tilted his head back and *sang* the song of the Alpha, eyes wide and burning red.

OPEN WOUNDS / THE WAY HOME

Richard was gone.
Osmond was gone.
Robert Livingstone had never appeared.
Most of the Omegas were dead.
Those that lived had fled.
But, of course, I wouldn't even think about that until later.

.   .   .

They knew.

The others.

Even before they found us under the oak trees, they knew.

They would have felt the moment he'd died just like I had. Probably even more so, given that I was still human.

It was Carter and Kelly who burst from the trees first, running on four legs, high-pitched whines pouring from them. They skittered to a stop once they saw us: Thomas still against the grass. Joe on his knees, head bowed over his father, claws at his sides. Gordo leaning against a tree, face in his hands, tattoos glowing brightly.

And myself, numb for my mother, now a body under a blanket.

For Thomas, body still warm, blood still leaking.

Carter unfroze first, coming over and running his nose up Joe's arm. His neck. His hair. He breathed in and out in short little bursts, taking in the scent of his new Alpha. His coat was matted with blood, and he favored his right front leg, but he kept pressing against his brother.

Kelly finally moved toward them, his eyes wide, mouth open as he let out little yips, like soft barks over and over again. He left Carter and Joe alone and collapsed at his father's feet, nosing against his toes. His calves. Eventually, he laid his head on his father's legs and trembled.

Mark came then. In human form. While the other wolves were nude, he wore tattered pants, frayed and ripped and spattered with grime and gore. Open wounds were healing slowly, and he had a nasty-looking bite on his right shoulder where it looked like a large chunk had been torn away. He took a stuttering step toward Thomas and the others but stopped, hands curling into fists at his side. Instead, he went to Gordo first, whispering something I couldn't quite make out. Gordo didn't look up, but he shook his head. Mark's eyes darted around the tree line, eyes hard and jaw set.

And then she came.

She moved slowly, whether from grief or injury, I couldn't tell. A shattered heart can be heavier than a broken limb. She was a wolf, which I selfishly was thankful for. A wolf's face can only move so much like a human's. The sorrow etched on her face as a wolf was nothing compared to what it would have been had she been human.

I didn't think I would have been able to take it.

I was cold.

My teeth were starting to chatter.

Carter had stopped rubbing up against Joe and was now nudging his father, making sounds in the back of his throat as if begging for his father to get up.

Kelly whined against his legs, trying to bury himself in his father's scent.

Joe breathed heavily, nostrils flaring, hands leaking blood from where his claws had cut into his palms.

Mark stood watch.

Gordo slumped against the tree, head on his knees, tattoos moving wildly. The raven flew up one arm and disappeared into the sleeve of his shirt. It appeared on his neck, wings spreading up to his ear.

And Elizabeth.

She didn't move toward her husband. Or her children. Or her brother-in-law.

She came to me. Slowly. Stiffly.

She pressed her nose into my hand. My fingers curled near her ear. I felt it flick against my skin.

She pushed harder.

I looked down.

I was wrong about being thankful she was a wolf because of the lack of humanity.

Because her eyes were the most human of all.

And they were stricken.

I broke the silence.

I choked out, "I'm so sorry," because I should have done more to protect him. And maybe if I hadn't let him drag me away, he would have been fine. If he hadn't put himself between Richard and me, Elizabeth wouldn't have lost her mate.

She took my hand gently in her mouth, her teeth dimpling my skin. For a split second, I thought she would bite down. I thought she would spill my blood for allowing this to happen. And I would have let her, too.

Instead, she tugged on my hand, pulling me toward the others.

I didn't understand.

But I went anyway.

She didn't let go.

And she didn't look away from me.

She backed up slowly, step by step, eyes never leaving mine.

I focused on her because it was getting harder to breathe.

The sounds were getting to me. I could hear Gordo moaning, low and broken. I could hear Kelly's *whuffing* sound as he shuddered against his father. I could hear what could only be considered sobs coming from Carter.

Joe, though.

Joe wasn't making any sounds.

At least out loud.

But I could feel him.

His horror.

His anguish.

His fury.

And it was louder than the rest.

I was overwhelmed by it.

Consumed by it.

But Elizabeth didn't let me go.

And I knew what she was trying to do.

She whispered, *PackSonLove.*

She whispered, *you belong to us.*

She whispered, *we belong to you.*

She whispered, *i feel your pain. i feel your grief. we have lost. i have lost. but so have you.*

She whispered, *please do not blame us. please do not hate us.*

She whispered, *she should not have been taken from you. and he should not have been taken from us.*

I let her pull me. I let her words flow over me through the threads. Through the bonds. The others heard her too. They heard what she spoke. Even Gordo, who raised his head in surprise, staring at Elizabeth as she tugged me closer. Somehow, he'd become part of this. Of us.

She reached her sons and her husband, her back legs bumping into Kelly, who didn't open his eyes. She tightened her bite just slightly before she let go of my hand.

I heard the telltale signs of a shift, and Mark made his way over. Elizabeth sat near her husband's head, leaning down and licking away the blood from his face. Mark sat next to her, his wolf large and imposing, the biggest of all of them.

At least for now.

Because even though he'd been dead only a short time, Thomas looked smaller than he'd ever been in life. I didn't know if it was death or the fact that he'd died a Beta, but he was diminished now. Less substantial.

Joe didn't look different, aside from the way his eyes looked as if they were filled with blood.

But he *felt* different.

There was something radiating off him, something larger than he'd ever been before. I didn't understand what it meant to be an Alpha. I didn't understand what it meant to be wolf. To be connected to the territory like he was now.

I wanted to touch him.

But I couldn't raise my arm.

He hadn't yet moved away from his father.

Carter and Kelly lifted themselves up from Thomas. They stayed shifted and moved until they sat as Mark did, looming over Thomas. Mark sat at his left side. Carter and Kelly sat near his feet.

Elizabeth pulled away from her husband's face and sat near his head, her leg pressed against his cheek.

Joe stayed at his right side.

They were deliberately placed around him based on their positions in the pack.

They waited.

I didn't know for what.

Until they all looked at me.

Except for Joe.

I thought about running away.

Disappearing into the trees.

Finding my mother's body and lying next to her. I would close my eyes and sleep, and when I awoke this would all have been a dream. Even though there was pain, even though I could feel *everything*, this would be a dream because it couldn't be real.

But there was blackness in my head.

There was murder in my heart.

And it felt real.

I couldn't move.

The wolves waited.

Somewhere, a killdeer called out from the trees. An odd bird, it was. Singing at night.

I thought the whole forest could be holding its breath.

From behind me, Gordo said, "They're waiting for you."

I didn't turn to look at him. I couldn't. Not while the wolves were watching me.

"You're part of them," he said. "You're part of this."

That little voice, that mean little voice whispered in my ear again, saying I never really had a choice in the matter. That if they'd just stayed away, none of this would have happened. And I wouldn't be feeling as guilty as I was.

And my mother would be in the kitchen. Popping soap bubbles on my ear.

Carter whined at me, soft and low, ears drooping.

Because he could probably feel what I was thinking. Maybe not in so many words or specifics, but he would get the gist of it.

They all would.

So I swallowed it down and let it slide down my throat. It burned.

I felt Gordo's hand on my shoulder.

Out of the corner of my eye, his tattoos pulsed and writhed.

"You feel it too," I said.

He sighed. It was the only answer I needed.

I shrugged off his hand.

Took a step forward. And then another. And then another.

Until I'd taken my place. Next to Joe.

I knelt down beside him. My shoulder bumped his. He was stiff, unmoving. He stared down at his father, bloodred eyes glowing in the dark.

Something settled when I took my place next to him.

It wasn't much, especially not in the face of all that had happened.

But it was there.

Because he was my Alpha now.

And I was his mate.

. . . .

"Why do you howl?" I'd asked Thomas.

He'd dug his bare toes into the dirt and grass and leaned his back against a tree. The sun had been shining overhead.

He'd said, "In the wild, wolves call to each other. It can be meant as a warning for others encroaching on a territory. It can be a rallying cry, to bring the pack together. It's used in a hunt, to show location. And sometimes, they howl together to show happiness. To make them seem like a bigger group than they are. It's called a group howl, and it's a beautiful thing to hear."

"And that's why you do it?"

He closed his eyes and smiled. He was amused by me. I was enraptured by him. "I think we do it just because we like to hear the sounds of our own songs. Narcissistic creatures, we are." The smile faded slightly. "Though sometimes, the songs are meant to sing a pack member home. It's easy to get lost, Ox, because the world is a wide and scary place. And every now and then, you just have to be reminded of the way home."

We didn't speak for a long time after that.

. . . .

I wasn't a wolf.

I didn't think I'd ever be. Not by choice.

But two members of my pack were *lost*.

I tilted my head back.

My eyes stung.

The stars blurred above me.

I said, "Ah God."

It came out rough.

I cleared my throat as it tried to close.

I thought of my mother.

I thought of Thomas.

They were lost to me now.

I needed to sing them home.

And so I did.

It was a broken sound, cracked and splintered. It wasn't very loud, and it grated against my ears. But I put everything I could into it even as I realized I maybe wasn't quite the man I thought I was as my cheeks became wet, my breath hitching in my chest.

My howl died away quickly.

I took another breath.

Mark howled with me, his voice melodic and heartbroken.

Carter and Kelly harmonized along with us, mixing in with our song.

Elizabeth picked up the song as we breathed in, her howl high and long. The song changed because of her, because of what she'd lost, and the wolves took her song and made it their own, their voices inlaid with hers, octaves above and below.

I felt Gordo on the periphery. I felt his hesitation. His awe. His sadness. He didn't howl, but his magic sang for him. It was in the earth below us. In the trees around us. He didn't howl, but then he didn't have to. We felt it, just the same.

Joe shifted next to me.

It was smoother than any shift I'd seen him do before.

One moment he was a sad boy, lost and bloody, and then he was a wolf, bright white in the darkness. He was already bigger than he'd been before tonight, his paws maybe twice their original size. Where he'd come up to my waist before, he would now probably be up to my chest if I'd been standing. He wasn't as thick as his father had been. He was bigger, yes, but still wiry. I thought that would change with time as he got older.

The others let their songs echo and fade into the forest as they waited.

Joe looked at each of us in turn. His eyes lingered on me the longest.

His song was deeper than it'd ever been before. I felt every single emotion (*hurt pain love oh God why why why*) he put into it and it was all I could do to keep from flying apart.

There in the forest, under a new moon and stars that lied, we sang our pack home.

.   .   .

Things moved quickly after that.

The next three days were a whirlwind, the Bennett house filling with people I'd never seen before. They went with Joe and Mark and Elizabeth and Gordo into Thomas's office and disappeared for hours, wolves all. They whispered quietly to each other, the ones I didn't know. They eyed me as Carter and Kelly lay curled around me, still shifted, whining piteously as their feet kicked in whatever dreams they had. I didn't let these strangers intimidate me. I stared right back.

I got only bits and pieces.

Richard had gone underground.

Robert Livingstone hadn't been found.

Osmond, though.

Osmond had been a surprise. No one had expected him to switch sides. He too was gone.

It rankled them, the wolves. To know now that they'd had a traitor in their midst. Especially one as high up as Osmond. I didn't blame them. But I certainly didn't trust anyone I didn't know in the Bennett house. I got the impression they were having a hard time trusting each other.

Elizabeth wouldn't let me go back to my house. She said it wasn't right. Not now. Maybe not for a long time. I stayed in Joe's room. In his bed.

But Joe was never there.

They said it was a burglary gone wrong. That my mom had come home and interrupted someone at the house. I had an alibi, of course. I was with the Bennetts. The Bennetts, who everyone respected. Who everyone was in awe of. The town might not have understood them, but they understood the way they looked. The wealth they had. The things they'd done for the town.

The coroner said it looked as if my mother's throat had been slit with a serrated knife of some kind.

I told the police we didn't have anything of the sort.

It must have come from the intruder.

And where is Thomas? the police asked.

Away on business, Elizabeth said. *Out of the country. Will be for months.*

Later it would be said that Thomas died of a heart attack overseas.

But for now, he was just gone.

When will he be back? the police asked.

Hopefully soon, Elizabeth said.

Somehow, her voice remained even.

Outsiders couldn't see the cracks.

But I could.

.   .   .

My mother was buried on a Tuesday.

There was nothing special about Tuesdays, but it was the first day we were able to lay her to rest.

The town mourned her along with us.

With me.

The preacher said placating things about God and the mysteries of His plan. We might not understand why these things happen. All we can do is hope to know that things happen for a reason.

The sun was shining when she was lowered into the ground.

The pack never left my side.

Joe held my hand through it all, but we never spoke.

Tanner, Chris, and Rico were there. They pushed everyone out of their way and didn't even bother trying to shake my hand. The three of them wrapped themselves around me and held on for dear life. There was a little flare of *something* from them that I felt crawl along my skin, but it was lost under the weight of what I faced.

Jessie was there too. She waited until she could stand in front of me. She whispered something I didn't remember. Her lips pressed against my cheek, lingering and sweet.

Joe watched as Jessie squeezed my hand.

He looked away as she left.

Later, after I'd stood in line and let people cry on me and shake my hand and tell me how sorry they were, I stood above the hole in the ground where my mother lay. It wouldn't be filled in until every-one left.

The pack stood away, among the trees. Waiting.

It wasn't fair. None of this was.

I said, "I'm so sorry," and thought about the day we'd lain on our backs, her in her pretty dress with the blue bows, and watched the clouds go by.

.   .   .

Thomas was burned on a Tuesday night.

There was nothing special about Tuesdays, but we'd already buried my mother that afternoon, and it was better to have it all said and done.

Those same people that had filled the house in the days that followed Richard's attack now filled the forest. Some were in human form, but most had shifted into wolves. My pack had all shifted, aside from Gordo and myself. But we walked with them, Elizabeth and me on either side of Joe. The others brought up the rear. I curled my hand on Joe's back and held on for all that I was worth.

No one spoke about God and His infinite plans. In fact, it was near silent as we watched Thomas's body atop the pyre constructed in the clearing in the woods. The wolves gathered around me. My wolves. Everyone else kept their distance.

It was Gordo that started the fire.

As he approached the pyre, I wondered if Thomas had felt him as part of the pack before he'd taken his last breath. If he'd felt the witch come back at last. We hadn't spoken about it. About what it meant. About what would happen now. I hadn't even tried. There was a small resentment that they'd kept me out of that office, those secret meetings, but I pushed it away.

He placed both hands on the pyre.

His tattoos came to life.

He bowed his head.

There was a lick of fire underneath his fingers.

It caught the wood and the fire spread.

I stood there and watched Thomas burn.

Joe led them, after.

It's called a chorus howl, Thomas whispered to me. *The harmonies allow any tricksters to think the group is bigger than it is.*

And they did. They sounded like they were in their hundreds rather than dozens.

Gordo had muffled the territory so no one in Green Creek would know. His magic was useful when he wasn't trying to deny his place.

Still, I wondered if people in town could hear it. Or, at the very least, feel the passing of leadership from one king to another. They lived in the territory, after all.

I felt it. I felt all of it.

The fire was hot against my face.

The songs howled around me, and they were as loud as I'd ever heard them.

They hollowed me out. Made my skin brittle and tight. I was a shell compared to what I'd been only days before. I didn't know what to fill the space with. I didn't know if there was anything *to* fill the space with.

The fire died down, eventually. Until it was nothing but ember and ash.

It'd be spread later throughout the territory.

But for now, the strange wolves left.

Our pack remained.

We inhaled the smoke and it filled our lungs until we coughed it away.

Gordo left then. Hands in his pockets, head lowered.

Mark was next. He headed away from the Bennett house, deeper into the woods. We wouldn't see him again for two days.

Carter and Kelly left with their mother, one on either side of her, holding her upright as she stumbled, legs weak.

It was just Joe and me then.

He sat on his haunches, watching the last lick of flame, the last burst of sparks.

I sat beside him, leaning against his side.

He huffed out a breath as he towered over me.

I pressed against him harder.

He snorted, eyes flashing.

The heat from the pyre began to fade away.

And still we stayed.

Night birds cried.

An owl called.

I said, "I'm here."

Joe scratched the grass with a giant paw.

I said, "Whenever you're ready."

His ears twitched.

"We'll figure this out."

He whined in the back of his throat.

"We have to."

He bent his head down, running his nose along my cheek. My neck. Behind my ear, huffing his scent onto me like he hadn't done since he'd become the Alpha.

I loved it.

And him.

But I couldn't say it. The words stuck in my throat.

So I hoped he felt it in my scent. Because that was all I could give.

It should have stopped there. That should have been the end of this terrible day.

It wasn't.

Other words found their way from my throat, saying the very last things I should have said.

But I was buried then. In anger. In grief.

So I wasn't thinking about what *could* happen.

Just what I wanted.

I said, "He took from us."

I said, "He took part of our pack away."

I said, "He hurt us."

I choked, "He took my *mom*."

Joe began to growl.

I said, "He's gone."

I said, "We have to find him."

I said, "We can't let this happen to anyone else."

I said, "We can't let this happen again."

I said, "We have to protect the others."

I said, "And we have to make him pay."

And that was it. Later, I would realize that was it.

That was the moment we began to say good-bye.

INTO THE BONES / LOSING YOU

I still didn't see it coming.
Maybe I should have.
But I didn't.

. . .

They left us. After a while.
The strange wolves. The ones I didn't know.
They left, going back to wherever they'd came from.
But not before they held their secret meeting once more.
I couldn't even find it in me to ask questions.
To give two shits about who they were.
I stared at the closed door.
And walked away.

. . .

They left and all was quiet.

Carter and Kelly spent hours upon hours in the woods, restlessly moving through the trees. If they didn't come home at night, I'd find them in the clearing, lying flat on their stomachs near a section of burnt grass, tails thumping to a beat only they could hear.

Elizabeth would disappear for long stretches of time. I never followed her. I never found out where she went.

Mark stayed on the porch, scanning the tree line. I knew what he was looking for, but I didn't think it would happen. Richard was gone.

And he would stay gone because of Gordo. Gordo, who spent the days that followed shoring up the wards he'd placed around Green Creek. Now that he was pack again, he could access areas of his magic that had been blocked to him before. I could feel the pull of it every time he did something different, that strange sensation that felt like walking down the stairs and missing the bottom step.

Joe stayed in his father's office.

I tried to keep all of them together.

I lay with Carter and Kelly on the grass. Under the stars.

When Elizabeth was in the house, I made sure she ate.

I stood on the porch next to Mark, running my fingers through his fur, watching.

I followed Gordo around, watching as he muttered under his breath, keeping an eye out to make sure no one in Green Creek saw the way the tattoos moved along his arms. He said it wasn't necessary. That no one would find out. I went anyway.

Joe barely spoke to me, even when he was human and even when I was at his side.

I didn't understand what he was going through. I didn't understand what Thomas had given him. I didn't understand what it meant to be the Alpha. All I could do was hope that I could be enough as his tether.

Of course, any courting he'd been doing before had stopped.

I didn't mind. I knew there were other things he had to focus on. More important things.

.   .   .

One day I went to work, just to do something different.

Gordo wasn't there. He was with Joe, talking about things I wasn't supposed to hear.

I might have glared at both of them. They'd stared back with blank faces.

I might also have slammed the door on my way out of the house.

I wasn't proud of that.

So without any better idea of where to go, I went to the shop.

I stayed off the main street. I didn't want anyone to stop me. To try and talk to me. To offer condolences. I was sick of condolences.

It probably didn't help that I was pissed at Joe and Gordo, even though I tried very hard not to be. But they'd never kept anything from me. Not since I'd found out about witches and wolves. For the most part, anyway.

But when I saw the shop for the first time in days, some of that anger lessened. It dampened the sadness. I thought maybe this was going to be an escape. At least for a little while.

I walked into the shop. The bell on the door to the waiting room rang overhead. It caused my heart to ache a little, but in a good way.

"I'll be right out!" a voice called from back in the shop.

I knew that voice.

My throat closed. Just a little.

"Welcome to Gordo's," Rico said, coming into the waiting room. He was running a rag over his hands, trying to remove the oil under his fingernails. There was the sweet scent of coconut oil on the rag, which Rico swore by. The rest of us used soap and water. Rico said there was no accounting for taste. "How can I help—"

Then he stopped. And stared.

"Hey," I said. "Hi. Hi, Rico."

"Hi." He snorted and shook his head. "Hi, he says. Hi, like he's some little—Get your ass over here, Ox."

I got my ass over there.

The hug was good. Really good.

"It's good to see you," he whispered, arms around me tight.

I just nodded into his neck.

Then he dragged me back into the shop.

There were a couple of cars up on the lifts.

The radio was blaring Tanner's country music, something about a man and how all his exes lived in Texas, but he hung his hat in Tennessee.

Tanner himself was under the hood of a 2012 Toyota Corolla. It looked like he was replacing the timing belt, singing along with the radio.

Chris was running a diagnostic check on a truck, squinting at the computer screen, even though his glasses were sitting on top of his head. He'd said he hated how he looked in them.

I took in a deep breath with the smell of grease and grime and metal and rubber. It was the same when I'd been a kid, coming in with my daddy, Gordo offering to buy me a pop from the machine.

It was just missing the man himself.

But that was okay. He was busy now.

"Look what the *gato* dragged in," Rico said.

They looked up.

I waved awkwardly.

They were on me before I could even take a step back.

They laughed. They held me. They rubbed their fingers over my head. Through my hair. Their arms went around my shoulders. They pressed their foreheads to mine. They told me I was a sight for sore eyes. That they'd missed me. That they were going to work me to the bone when I was ready.

I couldn't find the words to say what I wanted. Sometimes, when your heart gets so full, it takes away your voice and all you can do is hold on for dear life.

.   .   .

I walked home at dusk.

There was no one waiting for me on the dirt road.

I'd expected that.

But it still stung.

The fading sun shone through the trees.

I ran my hand through the tall grass that grew along the road.

I wondered where I was going.

What I was doing.

How long it would take before I could breathe freely again without this weight on my chest.

How long it would take before my pack wasn't so fractured anymore.

How long before Joe would talk to me again.

To any of us, really.

I wondered many things.

I stopped in front of my house.

My house. Not the one at the end of the lane.

I stared up at it.

I told myself to keep walking.

To go to the Bennetts'. To stay there like I'd been doing for the past week.

I needed to check on them. To make sure they were okay. To make sure they had eaten something, at the very least. I couldn't let the wolves go hungry.

So imagine my surprise when I found myself at my own front door, my hand hovering above the knob. I told myself to walk away.

I put my hand on the doorknob and twisted.

It didn't move.

I didn't understand.

And then I realized it was *locked*, and we *never* locked the door. Not even after my father left, because *we had no reason to*. We lived in the country. The house at the end of the lane had been vacant, and then it had been inhabited by wolves. There had been no *crime*, there had been no *monsters* to come out of the forest at night.

Not before.

It was change and my hand shook with it.

I didn't have my keys. I didn't know where they were. I never needed—

We'll put it here, my mother whispered. *In case you ever need it.*

The spare.

She'd put a spare key under the porch, hidden underneath a rock. She'd shown me one day when I was nine. Maybe ten.

I was down the porch and reaching under it before I had another thought.

I couldn't find the rock. Dead leaves and spiders, yes, but not the *fucking rock*—

My knuckles rapped against stone.

I pulled it out of the way. It fit in my hand the same way the one in the forest had. The one I'd struck Richard with. It—

There was no key.

I took a breath.

Shook my head.

Looked again.

It was there. Just a little bit in the dirt. A potato bug lay curled against it, shell shiny and gray.

I took the key and realized the last person to touch it had been my mom.

Dad had never used it. He'd never needed it. If he came home late, stumbling out of his truck, lost in a fog of beer, the door had always been open.

I'd never used it. I came home from school. From work. From the library. From a walk in the woods where I'd felt Thomas's territory humming through my veins.

She'd been the last one to touch this key.

I remembered the day I'd held my own work shirt for the first time, my name embroidered in careful stitches.

I remembered the first time I'd held Joe's hand, the little tornado who said I smelled of pinecones and candy canes. Of epic and awesome.

This felt just as important.

I climbed the steps again to the house.

I put the key into the lock.

The tumblers clicked.

I twisted the key.

I pressed my forehead against the wooden door and breathed.

The light was fading behind me. Shadows were stretching.

I took the key from the lock and put it in my pocket to keep it safe.

I turned the doorknob and opened the door. It creaked on its hinges.

The shadows were deeper in the house. I took a step and was *assaulted* with the smells of home, of furniture polish and Pine-Sol. Of spring flowers and autumn leaves. Of sugar and spices. It smelled *warm*, but it was there, wasn't it? That odor of greasy pennies, undercurrent to the smell of *home*. Because this *wasn't* a dream. I could feel the pain in my chest so surely that I *knew*.

I closed the door behind me.

It was dark in the house.

I was going into the kitchen. Or upstairs. To her room. Or my room. I needed new clothes. I'd been wearing Carter's for the last week, and even though I smelled like *pack*, I needed to smell like *me*. It was a plan. A good one. I'd go upstairs and get a change of clothes, a *few* changes, and then I'd—

I was in the living room.

I was told how it would be.

One of the strange wolves had told me.

He'd said, "I'm sorry. We tried. We tried to clean it as much as we could, but the . . . it soaked. Into the wood on the floors. It—"

It was there. A dark stain, the edges of which were ragged. It had been scrubbed. It had been power washed. It had been *scraped*. But they couldn't get it all.

My mother's blood had soaked into the bones of the house.

But that was only fair. Because she was part of it. This was *her* home and she had *died*—

I was out on the front lawn, on my hands and knees, retching into the grass. The bile splashed hotly against my hand, near my thumb. I croaked out a wet moan, a string of saliva hanging from my bottom lip.

In some distant thought, I felt a *ping* of fear.

There was a roar, much deeper than I'd ever heard it before.

That *ping* became a *clamoring*.

I heard the breath of a large animal.

The sounds of great paws upon the earth.

He was there as I retched again.

There was the snap and creak of bone and muscle and then Joe was before me, hands frantic, rubbing down my back and arms as he said, "*Ox.*"

"Joe," I groaned, spitting away the bitterness in my mouth. "It's fine, it's fine, it's *fine*—"

"I could feel it," he said, voice cracking. "Through everything. In the house it's hard to see because *everyone* feels the same way. It's over *everyone*. But then you weren't there and I couldn't remember where you were and I *felt* it. It was like being stung on every part of me. I could always feel it before, but nothing like this. There has never been *anything* like this. Like *you*."

"I don't—"

"This must have been what he felt like. My dad. *All the time.* Because you're mine—my pack. It's . . . *Ox*. It's so big, I don't know what to *do* with it."

And it was weird, hearing him like that again after a week of near silence. Because he sounded like he did when he was a kid, just a kid who hadn't spoken in fifteen months and who had climbed me like a tree to demand to know what that smell was. It righted me, barely, but somehow.

He was quiet as I rocked back on my feet and tried to catch my breath. His hand was in mine, not caring that it was sweating and bile-slick.

He said, "Why did you go in there?"

I looked up at the sky. Night was overtaking day. It was orange and red and violet and black, stretching above us. I saw the first hints of stars. The first slight curve of the moon.

"I had to," I said. "I found the key and I had to."

"You can't go in there alone."

"It's my *house*."

Joe's eyes flashed. "I am your Alpha."

And there was a tremor that rolled through me at the redness in his eyes, a need to bare my neck and *obey*, a whisper that grew into a storm. It yanked at the thread that connected us until I was *shudder-ing* with it, until I had to grind my teeth together just to fight it back. I closed my eyes and waited for it to be over.

It didn't last long. Because Joe pulled it back.

He said, "Oh fuck. I'm sorry. I'm *so sorry.*" His eyes were wide and he looked so impossibly young.

"Don't do that to me," I said hoarsely. "Ever again."

"Ox, I—We—I didn't mean it. Okay? I swear to you, I didn't mean it."

He squeezed my hand so hard I thought my bones would break.

"I know," I said. Because I did. That wasn't who he was. None of this was who we were. Everything was so fucked. "I know."

He looked miserable, this seventeen-year-old kid who now had everything resting on his shoulders. But there was anger in him too, low and pulsing, and I didn't know how to stop it. Mostly because it resembled my own.

He said, "You can't go back in there. Not by yourself. Not until we—"

"You can't fix this," I said as kindly as I could. "Not now."

He flinched away, but I held onto his hand.

"Ox, I—"

"I didn't mean it like you think."

"You . . . you don't know what you mean."

"Maybe. I don't know. Everything is weird right now."

"I know."

"But we'll fix this."

"I know."

"We will," I insisted.

He looked away. "We need to talk, Ox. I've . . . made a decision. About this. About everything. I need you to . . . We just have to talk, okay?"

And I felt cold.

⋆　　⋆　　⋆

We stood in Thomas's office. All of us in the pack. It was the first time the wolves had all been human at the same time since the night Richard came. The fact that we all stood together was not lost on me, especially since Gordo was with us too.

Gordo, who apparently had a place in the pack now. Something had happened the night Thomas died, something that bound him to the Alpha, just like the rest of us. I didn't know if it was his magic, the changing of the Alpha, or a combination of both. Gordo wouldn't talk about it. In fact, none of them would talk about it.

I thought there was a very real chance they all knew what this was about except for me.

Elizabeth looked pale and wan, an afghan wrapped around her shoulders.

Carter and Kelly were frowning, standing side by side near Joe.

Mark was looking out the window, arms across his chest.

Gordo leaned against the far wall, staring down at his hands.

Joe sat behind his father's desk. He looked like a child playing grown-up.

And there was me. In-the-dark me.

No one was talking.

So I said, "What did you do?"

All gazes snapped to me, but I only had eyes for Joe.

He sighed. "We're leaving."

"What? When?"

"Tomorrow."

"You know I can't leave yet," I said. "I have to meet with Mom's lawyer in two weeks to go over her will. There's the house and—"

"Not you, Ox," Joe said quietly.

I froze.

"And not Mom. Or Mark."

My skin buzzed.

He waited.

"So it's you," I said slowly, not quite sure I understood. "And Carter. Kelly."

"And Gordo."

"And Gordo," I repeated flatly. "Where are you going?"

"To do what's right," he said, his eyes never leaving mine. There was something building here, something between the two of us, and it wasn't good. None of it was good.

"Nothing about this is right," I said. "Why didn't you tell me about this?"

"I'm telling you now."

"Because *that's* the right—Where are you going?"

"After Richard."

I should have expected that.

I hadn't.

It hit me like a hammer to the chest.

"Why?" I choked out.

"Because he took from us," Joe said, hands curling into fists. "He took from us, all of us. From me. From *you*. You *told* me that we needed to—"

"I was *angry*," I cried at him. "People say things when they're *angry*."

"Well I still am! And you should be too. Ox, he—"

"And what do you think you're going to do?" I asked him. "What do you think could possibly happen here?"

"I am going to hunt him down," Joe said, claws popping. "And I am going to kill him for everything he's taken from me."

"You can't divide the pack," I said, sounding rather desperate. "Not now. Joe, you are the goddamn *Alpha*. They need you here. All of them. *Together*. Do you really think they'd agree to—"

"I already told them days ago." He winced. Then, "Shit."

The buzzing intensified. "You did what."

I looked at each of them in turn.

Carter and Kelly were staring at the floor.

Mark and Elizabeth met my gaze. Elizabeth's eyes were dull and muted. Mark looked harder than I'd ever seen him before.

And Gordo. He—

"Ox—" Gordo started.

"No," I snapped. "I'll deal with you later."

He sighed.

I looked back at Joe. He looked stricken but resolute.

"That's it, then."

"Yes."

"You're just going to go after him."

"Yes."

"You're going to hunt him down."

"*Yes*."

"And leave the rest of us here to . . . what? Wait for you? To hope that he doesn't kill you? To hope he doesn't come back here where you've left us unprotected? Is that what an Alpha does?" I didn't mean to say that last part. It just came out. And I saw the hurt on Joe's face before he carefully slid his face into a blank expression. He'd never done that to me before. Hidden himself away. We were open with each other. Always. Until this last week, when he'd apparently kept secret far more than I thought he was capable of.

He said, "I don't expect you to understand, Ox. Not completely. This is something I have to do."

"It's not. You don't *have* to do *shit*. You really think this is what Thomas would have wanted? Do you really think this is what he wanted for you? He wouldn't have—"

Joe's eyes flashed red. When he spoke, it was through a hint of fangs. "He was *my* father, not yours. You don't get to—"

"Joseph," Elizabeth said, her voice a whip crack of warning.

But the damage was already done.

I took a step back, suddenly unsure about everything. My place here with the pack. With Joe. It was funny how just a few words could make me question everything.

Joe made a wounded noise, broken and soft. "Ox," he said. "I didn't mean that."

And I knew that. Or at least I thought I did.

But it still hurt more than anything. Especially coming from him. My father still haunted me, even though he was bones in the ground.

And for the first time, I felt my own mask slipping into place, forcing back the hurt. The anger. The sheer terror at the idea of Joe leaving. I wasn't scared for us, those that he was leaving behind. I was scared for him.

And they'd all decided this. Without me.

The human in the pack.

"How long?" I asked, voice short and clipped.

The wolves looked anxious. Gordo frowned.

"Ox," Joe said, voice soft.

"No," I said. "You want to do this? Fine. You want to make decisions without including me? Go ahead. Obviously things aren't the way I thought they were. But since you're capable of making these decisions, you can answer the goddamn question. How. *Long*?"

The blank look was gone from his face. Now he looked like a scared little boy, not the Alpha of the Bennett pack. Most every single part of me was screaming to go to him. To hold him close and never let him out of my sight again. To make this *right* somehow, because I thought that was supposed to be my job.

But I didn't.

"As long as it takes," he said quietly.

"And the rest of us?"

"You'll stay here."

"And if he comes back? Or anyone comes? Omegas looking for territory. People like Marie. Or whatever else is out there that none of you have told me about."

"There will be . . . protections in place," Gordo said. I didn't look back at him, never taking my eyes off Joe.

"Like there were when your father came," I said. Low blow again, but necessary.

"I'm better prepared this time," Gordo said, "now that I know. Richard won't be able to return to Green Creek. Or my father. Or Osmond."

"But others can."

"They won't," Joe said, sounding less confident than he should, especially if he was trying to sound convincing.

The mask slipped. "How could you know that? You won't even be here."

Joe flinched.

"Just so I understand," I said. "My mother died. Your father died. You took his place. And your first act as Alpha is to divide your pack so you can have revenge."

Joe's eyes bled red again. "You're right," he said coolly. "I *am* the Alpha. And I will do what I think is right. You may not agree with me, Ox, but you will respect my decision because *I* made it."

"That's not how that works," I said, even though a large part of me was demanding I bare my throat in deference. "Just because you're who you are now doesn't mean I'll blindly follow you. Your father understood that. I don't think you do."

His claws gouged the wood on the desk as he growled deeply.

Carter and Kelly whimpered, eyes darting between us.

Elizabeth was pale.

Even Mark looked worried.

Gordo, well. Fuck him.

"What if he hurts someone else?" Joe asked, as he regained control.

"What if he tries to take away someone else's family? Do you think I could let myself live with that? He *hurts* people, Ox. And he does it because he *can*. I can't let that happen anymore."

"Then we all go," I said. "If you're going, then you take the rest of us."

He shook his head. "No. Absolutely not."

"Why?"

"Because I don't want to risk my mom. And we can't leave the territory unprotected."

I bit back the need to point out that they'd left Green Creek for years and nothing had happened. "Fine," I said. "Then Carter can stay. Or Kelly. Mark is already here. But I'm going with you."

"No," Joe said.

"Why not?"

"Because I said so."

"That's not good enough."

"Really?" Joe said, sounding furious. "You want to know why, Ox? Because I just lost my father and I am *broken* because of it. Losing him *hurts* more than anything I've ever felt before. But losing you? Ox, if anything happened to you, it would *kill* me. There is no point for me if you're not here. So no. You're not going. You're going to stay here because I love you more than anything in this goddamn world and I don't fucking *care* if you're pissed. I don't *care* if you hate me because of it. As long as I know you're safe, then that's all that matters. That's *why*, you bastard."

I wanted nothing more than to tell him the same.

But I pushed. Because this wasn't right. "You can't use your feelings for me to keep me here, Joe. That's not how this works. I'm not going to stand aside just so you can—"

"*I don't care!*" he roared, slamming his fist down onto his father's desk. The surface cracked, the wood splitting. "You're my *tether*, Ox. And you're *Gordo's*. What do you think would happen if we lost you?"

"You're an asshole," I said. "Jesus Christ, Joe."

"The decision has been made."

"Obviously. I don't even know why I'm here, then, or why we're talking. Seeing as how you'll do what you want anyway. You want to leave? Fine. Go. I won't stand in your way. Not anymore."

"Ox—"

"You've made up your mind?"

He nodded and looked away.

"Good," I said. "Now deal with the consequences."

And I turned and left.

BEFORE YOU GO / BITTERSWEET

It was Gordo who found me first.

I was near our clearing, lying on my back, staring up at the stars through the canopy of trees. From where I lay, I could see the ground where Thomas's pyre had been, the earth scorched. I couldn't bring myself to go any closer.

I didn't even need to look up to see who it was. I wondered when I'd started knowing the pack through bonds alone. I thought most of the others were around but hanging back. All of them except for Joe. He wasn't in the woods.

"When we were out," I said dully, eyes tracing over Canis Major. "When you were resetting the wards. You knew already, didn't you?"

He hesitated. Then, "Yes."

"And he told you not to tell me."

"Yes, but I agreed with him."

I snorted. "Of course you did."

Gordo sighed, and I saw him out of the corner of my eye, moving in the dark off to my right. "He's not wrong, Ox."

"Are you saying that because he's right? Or because you think something is going to happen to me?"

Gordo didn't answer. His silence spoke volumes.

"I can take care of myself."

"I know," he said.

"That's shit, Gordo."

"Yeah." He sat down next to me, knees up against his chest.

"And you're going along with it."

"Someone has to make sure he doesn't kill himself."

"And that someone is you. Because you're pack."

"Looks like."

"By choice?"

"I think so."

"There have to be others looking for him. For them. Because of what Thomas used to be. They won't just let this go."

"They won't," Gordo agreed. "But they won't be looking the same way we will either."

"How?"

His tattoos flared. I turned away.

"You mean to kill."

He sighed.

"You're okay with that?"

"Nothing about this is okay, Ox. But Joe's right. We can't let this happen to anyone else. Richard wanted Thomas, but how long before he goes after another pack just to become an Alpha? How long before he amasses another following, bigger than the one before? The trail is already growing cold. We have to finish this while we still can. For everyone. This is revenge, pure and simple, but it's coming from the right place."

"You honestly believe that."

"Maybe. Joe does. That's enough for me."

We were quiet for a little while, each of us lost in our own thoughts. Then, "I'll bring him back, Ox."

Everything hurt.

"Can you trust me to do that?"

I didn't want to, but if there was anyone who could, it'd be Gordo. I told him as much.

"Good," he said, reaching his leg out and bumping his boot against my hip.

"You should talk to him," I said. "Before you go."

"Joe?" he asked, sounding confused.

"Mark."

"Ox—"

"What if you don't come back? Do you really want him to think you don't care? Because that's fucked up, man. You know me. But sometimes, I think you forget that I know you just as well. Maybe even more."

"Well, shit."

"Yeah."

"When did you get so smart?"

"Had nothing to do with you, that's for damn sure."

"Then you're going to have to do the same."

I frowned. "What?"

"Talk to Joe before we go. You can't leave it like that, Ox."

"I could," I said. "Very easily."

"You won't."

"How you figure?"

Gordo shrugged. "You love him."

"He kept this from me."

"He knew how you'd react."

"That doesn't make it right."

"I didn't say it did."

I glared at him. "You should have told me."

He sighed. "Probably. Little late for that now. I'd forgotten how it's different being in a pack. There's free will, but it's blended in with the wolves. He's the Alpha. I have to listen to him."

"Do you trust him?"

"Do you?"

I shook my head. "Not to take care of himself."

Gordo patted my hand. "Good thing I'll be there, then. And yeah, I think I do. He's young. But then so was I when all this started. We have that much in common at least."

"Is it enough?"

"We'll see."

We were quiet for a time. Then, just because I could, I said, "So essentially, you're now the witch for a seventeen-year-old Alpha. Good job on that one."

He snorted and shoved me hard. "Get the fuck outta here with that."

"Dick."

"Bitch."

He laughed.

And maybe I did too. Just a little bit.

.   .   .

He left.

I waited for the wolves because I knew they'd come.

Carter and Kelly appeared first, ears flattened on their skulls, tails drooping between their legs. They lay down far enough away that I could only just make them out in the dark, but close enough that I could hear their little pleading whines, the little huffs of air.

When I didn't scold them or send them away, they moved closer. And waited.

Closer. And waited.

It didn't take long before they were lying pressed up against me on either side, heads resting on my chest, watching me with big eyes. Their ears twitched, listening to the sounds of the forest, but they didn't look away.

"I'm mad at both of you."

Kelly whined and pressed his nose against my chin.

"You're both jerks."

Carter huffed and put his paw on my hand.

"You need to take care of each other," I told them. "And him. And if it looks bad, if it looks like the fight is too big, you take him and you come running. I don't care if he's the Alpha. Fight it. Fight him. You drag his ass if you have to. You get me?"

They flashed their orange eyes at me.

I heard them whispering in my head.

They said things like *brother* and *love* and *please don't be mad at us please don't hate us please don't leave us,* and I didn't have it in me to correct them.

I wasn't leaving them.

They were leaving me.

Carter was dozing.

Kelly's tongue was lolling out of his mouth as I scratched his ears.

Mark and Elizabeth came then. Elizabeth was a wolf. Mark was not.

He walked next to her, nude, shoulders hunched slightly.

I felt Elizabeth, but it wasn't like Carter or Kelly. It was waves of pain and grief. It was a terrible sadness. She wasn't green. There was no relief in her. She was deep in her blue phase now, and I didn't know if she'd come out of it.

She lay at my feet and closed her eyes.

It didn't take her long to sleep.

Mark sat next to me.

He said, "She's going to stay like that, I think. For a while."

"As a wolf?"

"Yes."

"Why?"

He said, "It's easier to process things. We can remember most everything when we're wolves, but it's different. It's baser. Complexities are harder to understand. We deal in broad strokes. We can see the shapes of things. It's harder to be more specific. It's her way of coping. The sadness of a wolf isn't the same as the sadness of a human. Mostly."

I understood what he was saying. And I thought maybe that sounded like cheating. "I'm not a wolf," I said.

"No," he said.

"And my heart is breaking."

"Yes."

"I can't shift it away."

"It's not any easier to deal with, Ox. It just makes it easier to understand."

"I don't think I understand many things," I admitted.

He said, "Neither do I" and "We'll need you, you know" and "You're very important to us."

"Why?"

"Why are you important? Or why will we need you?"

"Yes."

"We hurt, Ox," he said. "Just like you. We may not understand your pain, but we feel it just the same. Everyone hurts differently. And when a pack member passes, especially when it's the Alpha, there is this great hole that opens up like a chasm and we're *desperate* to fill it. To make it disappear. Or at the very least to forget about it. Just for a little while. Whether it is to hide away in the forest at night—"

"Or to find the one that caused it in the first place," I said.

He smiled quietly. "I told him not to, you know. Joe. I told him he was making a mistake."

"Did he listen?"

"I'd like to think he did."

"Not well enough."

"It can be hard to hear what you don't want to when you're desperate and all you know is anger."

"But it's easier when we're with each other. That's what pack is supposed to be."

Mark nodded. "Which is why we'll both need you. And I hope you'll need us. Because we're here too, Ox. I promise you. We won't leave you behind."

I wanted to believe him.

. . .

I left them in the woods.

Mark shifted and curled around Elizabeth. Carter and Kelly whimpered as I moved but found solace with the rest of their pack. They knew where I was going. They thought they were going to give us the privacy we needed.

But they didn't know what I was going to ask for.

Because I'd made up my mind.

My mother whispered, *I'll do right by you.*

Thomas whispered, *You protected your own. I am so very proud of you.*

I thought maybe they walked with me through the forest, but I wasn't sure. I didn't know if I could tell the difference between memories and ghosts.

The threads between us were gone.

But my mother's hand brushed against my ear, and I felt Thomas squeeze my shoulder.

I wasn't dreaming because I hurt.

Joe was still in the office, sitting in his father's chair, a faraway look in his eyes as he stared off into nothing. It was hard to believe that only a week had gone by since we went on our first date, that flare of bright and awkward hope that had been bursting in my stomach. It was hard to think about how he'd sat at our kitchen table, wearing his bow tie, talking to my mother like he could believe nothing else in the world but what he was asking for. Like I was something he could be proud of.

He didn't look at me. But he knew I was there.

I tried to find the right words to say what it was I felt.

I said, "I want you to give me the bite."

And Joe said, "No."

The room was quiet after that for a long time.

Finally, I said, "It's my choice, Joe."

"I know," he said, looking at me, eyes clearing even as I watched.

"And I'm the one making this choice."

"I know."

"I want this."

"Do you?"

"Yes."

"You didn't before. Yesterday. Last week."

"Things were different yesterday. And last week. And all those years ago when Thomas offered it to me to begin with."

"When?"

I blinked. "When what."

He looked tired. "When did my dad offer you the bite?"

"He told me I could take it when I turned eighteen."

"He did?"

"You sound surprised."

Joe rubbed a hand over his face. "I am. I mean—I knew he must have done it. At some point. I just didn't know when."

"He didn't tell you?"

"Why would he have? It wasn't about me."

"Wasn't it, though?"

"I don't see how—"

"It was. Joe, all of this is about you. That's what I am. That's *all* I am now." Because I didn't think I was anyone's son anymore. I didn't know if someone could be considered an orphan at the age of twenty-three. But if they could, then that's what I was.

"But you didn't."

"No."

"Why?"

For a moment, I didn't know how to answer. But then I remembered something Thomas had told me once. "I didn't have to be something different to be in your pack. To belong with all of you. Thomas said I was good enough just as I was. And I think I needed to see that before I became something different."

"And have you?" he asked.

I scowled at him. "That's not the point."

"I'm not going to bite you, Ox."

"That's it, then? Because you said so, that's the way it's going to be?"

"I *am* the Al—"

"That doesn't work with me," I retorted. "You should know that better than anyone. I don't give a damn what color your eyes are. You're *Joe*, okay? So don't you dare try to pull that bullshit on me."

"I'm leaving."

Now I was just getting pissed off. "Even more reason for me to take the bite. So I can do what I can while you're off doing whatever the fuck you're going to be doing."

"Ox. We're leaving tomorrow."

Was he *trying* to hurt me more? "I know."

He shook his head. "I can't leave a newly bitten wolf, especially one of my own. If you ever take the bite, you'll need your Alpha near to help you through your first full moon. I can't do that for you if I'll be gone. You saw how bad it was for me when I first changed. And my father was already there."

"All the more reason to take me with you."

His nostrils flared, and I swore for a moment that I saw his lip tremble. "You know I can't."

"Fuck your *can't*," I growled at him. "You're doing everything possible to make sure this goes *exactly* the way you want it to. And since when do we keep secrets from each other? Anything else you aren't telling me? Anything else you all decided for me? Please, Joe. Tell me. Tell me how things should be for me from now on. Tell me what to do."

"I don't expect you to understand—"

"Because I *don't*. It sucks, Joe. It fucking sucks. My *mom* is gone. Your *dad* is gone. And now you're trying to take away yourself too? What the fuck do you think you're doing to me?"

His eyes were wet, cheeks flushed. "It's not all *about* you—"

"He killed my mother!" I bellowed at him. *"That fucking makes it about me!"*

He was crying now. Joe was crying and I hated it. Oh God, how I *loathed* it. To see him with tears on his face, to see him be the seventeen-year-old kid I knew he was, the kid who was supposed to be happy and going on dates. The kid who deserved everything good after the hell he'd gone through at the hands of a monster. The kid who shouldn't have had to worry about being the Alpha yet, or carrying the weight of a pack on his shoulders. He was just a *kid*, for Christ's sake.

And I wasn't helping. I was hurting him because *I* hurt. Because *I* was a little bit dead inside.

"You can't leave," I said, voice broken. "You can't leave me, Joe."

"You think I *want* to?" he cried. "You think I *want* this? Ox, I never want to be away from you. I never want to be apart from you. I never want to be anywhere that you aren't. You are *everything* to me. When I saw you, when y-you were with my d-d-*dad* and that *man*, I was never so scared in my *life*. Okay? Do you get that? He *took* me. He *hurt* me. For *weeks*. But the worst moment of my life was when I thought he was going to hurt *you*. So you will fucking stay here! You'll fucking d-*do* what I say, because I *can't* lose you. Ox, I *can't*. Not you. Not you too."

He was sobbing by the time he'd finished. Joe, the Alpha were-wolf, was *weeping* at the thought of something happening to me.

I could take many things.

I wasn't weak.

I was strong, most of the time.

The pack had made me that way.

But the sight of Joe like this . . . I just.

I just couldn't anymore.

I was on the other side of the desk even before I thought about it.

I gathered him up as best I could, and he fit against me so right, it was like he was a little tornado again, and I was just some big dumb Ox who didn't know what it meant to belong to someone.

I felt the power in him, yes.

I felt the pull of him, oh yes.

But he was just Joe.

And I was just Ox.

And maybe my father was wrong when he said that men didn't cry. Sure, people gave me shit just like he said, but I knew I was a man. And I cried right along with Joe. Because everything was falling apart and I didn't know how to stop it.

. . . .

We lay in his bed on our sides toward each other, knees knocking together, faces inches apart. The room was dark. His eyes were bright and his breath on my face was warm. I didn't know what time it was but knew it had to be late. And I also knew that if I fell asleep, Joe would be gone by the time I woke.

I had to fight it.

For as long as I could.

Because I couldn't bear the thought of waking alone.

He watched me, and I felt the pulse of *something* between us, whatever fledgling bond that was there. Not the bond of an Alpha to his pack but the bond between mates. I wanted to hold onto that thread as long as I possibly could, because the thought of it being gone when I woke terrified me.

He reached up and traced his fingers over my eyebrows. My cheeks. My nose. My lips. I pressed a gentle kiss against his fingertips. He sighed and his eyes fluttered shut.

"This sucks."

"Yeah," I said. Because it did.

He opened his eyes. "It wasn't supposed to be this way."

"I know."

"You have to help her, Ox."

I knew who he meant. "I will."

His breath hitched in his chest. "You *have* to. She's my *mom*."

"I know."

He gripped my hand and held it between us. There were hints of red in his eyes, notes that had never been there before.

He said, "I meant it. What I said."

"When?" I asked, trying to take him all in, trying to catalog every single detail of him that I could, for those moments I knew would come. When I couldn't sleep because he was gone.

"When I said I loved you."

My traitorous heart stumbled in my chest. "Yeah. I know, Joe."

"Because I do."

"Yeah."

"I just . . . needed you to know that. Before."

"Okay, Joe. Hey, I love you too. You know I do. I have for a long time."

"Yeah, Ox. I know." He let out a shaky breath. "This isn't fair. We should have had more time."

I said, "It's okay," even though it wasn't. Part of me wanted to point out that this was his choice. His doing. But I didn't have the strength to fight with him anymore. Not now. Not like this. "We're here now."

"You can't forget me," he said fiercely, squeezing my hand until my bones ached. "No matter what happens. You can't ever forget me."

"Yeah, Joe. I know. I couldn't even if I tried. I don't want to try. You'll see. You do what you have to do, then you'll come back and everything will be right as rain. It'll be over before you know it. Weeks, even. Days. I promise. Okay?"

"And then we'll be mates, right?"

"Sure, Joe."

"Forever."

"Yeah." But even that didn't sound long enough.

"Ox?"

"Yeah?"

His eyes searched mine. Then, "Can I kiss you?"

It was said so shyly, so hesitantly, that I ached with it. "You want to?" I asked quietly.

He nodded once, a little jerk of his head.

"I guess that's all right," I said.

"I'm not your first."

"No."

"And you're not mine."

"No," I said, jaw tense.

"But you're the only one that matters. So, it's like it's the first. For the both of us."

I kissed him then. I couldn't not after that.

He gave a grunt of surprise when our lips touched, a little exhalation of air that was almost like a sigh. It was chaste, barely there. His lips were slightly parted and his eyes were open and on me, and I thought maybe they were endless. He brushed his nose against mine and tightened his fingers around my own. I reached up and cupped his cheek, fingers over his ear and holding him in place.

He flared within me, bursting and warm.

It was bittersweet, strong and heady.

I pulled away first.

He shuddered and pressed his forehead to mine.

He said, "I will come back for you."

I believed he would try.

.   .   .

I fought it. For as long as I could.

But everything caught up to me. Thomas. My mother. Joe becoming the Alpha. The funerals. The fire. Joe's decision.

Everything.

I tried to stay awake.

I screamed at myself that he'd be gone the moment my eyes closed.

He whispered, "Sleep, Ox."

I whispered back, "But you'll be gone."

The smile he gave me curved sadly. "The sooner I leave, the sooner I can come home."

My eyes drooped. I forced them open again.

"I'll miss you," I said. "Every day."

He looked away, but not before I saw the shine in his eyes.

I fought it. With everything I had.

But my body fought back.

Eventually, my eyes closed and I couldn't open them again.

I felt his hands in my hair.

I felt his lips on my forehead.

And as I fell into the dark, I heard him say one last thing.

He said, "I will come back to you."

And then I was gone.

. . .

When I dreamed, I dreamed of him.

We walked through the forest, the moon full overhead.

He held my hand, and his eyes were red.

In the shadows beyond the trees came the sound of great paws upon the earth.

The wolves circled around us, but we weren't afraid.

Because they were ours.

Joe said, "It'll be okay."

And I *smiled*.

. . .

I woke slowly.

I didn't know where I was.

In that moment before I came fully awake, nothing hurt because nothing was wrong.

My mother was still alive.

Thomas was still alive.

There was a weight against me, like I was surrounded.

In my muddled mind, I thought I'd fallen asleep at the Bennett house, surrounded by pack. I remembered a fatly shining moon and thought we'd spent the night running in the woods.

I'd have to call Gordo, I knew. He always worried after full moons. He didn't like waiting until I walked into the shop later in the day. He needed to know.

I couldn't remember if my mom had come out the night before. So I'd have to call her too.

Joe and I would have breakfast. Maybe our feet would tangle together under the table. And maybe I'd work up the courage to hold his hand. Carter and Kelly would probably make fun of us for it after hearing the way our heartbeats went out of control, but that was okay. Elizabeth would scold them and Mark would smile his secret smile and Thomas would just look content as he watched us from his place at the head of the table. And when I caught his eye, he'd flash his red, red eyes at me and wink, and I would *know* what it meant to have a father again, I would *know*—

The fog started to clear.

The pain started.

It was a sliver at first. An irritant, just underneath my skin. I picked at it. I worried at it.

It only made things worse.

I took in a great, gasping breath.

I was awake.

They were gone.

Mom. Thomas.

Carter and Kelly.

Gordo.

And Joe.

I opened my eyes.

Two wolves lay curled up against me.

Elizabeth and Mark.

They breathed deeply, lost in sleep.

I envied them.

Because the pain came rolling over me, glassy and sharp.

I pushed outward, trying to find the others. Trying to feel them. The bonds. The threads between us.

But there was nothing.

I pushed again.

Nothing. It was like we were cut off.

The loss was so great that, for a moment, I couldn't breathe. I tried to fist my hands at my sides, but my left hand wouldn't close around the object it held.

I looked down.

In my hand was a wolf statue. Made of stone.

I watched it for a long time.

I knew what it meant. Who'd placed it there.

Eventually I nodded.

I said, "Okay, Joe. Okay."

And began to wait.

THE FIRST YEAR / PINPRICKS OF LIGHT

The first year was the hardest.

Because we didn't know there was going to be a first year.

"You text me," I'd told him as we'd lain in the bed. I could still taste him on my lips and I wanted nothing more than to kiss him again. "Every couple of days. So I know."

"I won't tell you where we are," he said. "Because I know what you would do."

I scowled at him. "Fine. But you text me. You understand?"

He did.

I miss you, the first text said, three days after they'd gone.

I stared at it for hours.

"She left everything to you," the attorney said as I sat across from him in his office. Elizabeth and Mark were close by, hiding in the woods. "The house. The accounts. And eventually, there will be a life insurance payout, but those things take time. It should be enough to pay off the mortgage and then some when it comes, though. She wanted to make sure you were taken care of should something happen to her. You're set, Ox. For now. I'll get everything ready for you to sign to make it as easy as possible. You just focus on healing. Lord knows you've earned it."

I nodded and looked out the window, thinking about soap bubbles on my ear.

Carter and Kelly are fighting, a text said. I told them to stop. They didn't. So I went Alpha on them. They aren't fighting anymore.

"What the fuck is this supposed to mean?" Chris said, glaring down at a letter Gordo had left for them at the shop.

I have to be gone for a while. Tanner, you're in charge of the shop. Make sure you send the earnings to the accountant. He'll handle the taxes. Ox has access to all the bank stuff, personal and shop-related. Anything you need, you go through him. If you need to hire someone to pick up the slack, do it, but don't hire some fuckup. We've worked too hard to get where we are. Chris and Rico, handle the day-to-day ops. I don't know how long this is going to take, but just in case, you need to watch each other's back. Ox is going to need you.

Rico and Tanner were crowded into Gordo's office. Chris's hands shook as he held the letter, voice growing tighter and tighter with every word he read.

You'll have to deflect, Gordo had told me in the woods. *They'll push you, Ox. For answers. You need to hold off as long as possible. They're my brothers. I never wanted them involved in our world. But I don't know how much longer that can last. Not now. I'm sorry to put this on you. I never wanted this for you. For them.*

They all looked up at me.

"Did you know about this?" Tanner asked.

"Yeah," I said, heartsore and tired. I wasn't sleeping because of the nightmares.

"That asshole," Rico growled. "How the fuck could he leave you like this? After everything?"

"Where did he go?" Chris asked, dropping the letter back onto the desk.

They all looked at me expectantly.

And I resented them then. Gordo and Joe. Because of the position they'd put me in. My back was against a wall and I didn't know how to answer the question without bullshit.

Joe had left.

Gordo had gone with him.

They'd forced my hand.

And maybe I was already tired of carrying this burden alone.

So I said, "What do you know about werewolves?"

. . .

I thought we had something, he said in his text. I thought we'd found what we needed outside of Calgary. But it was just a dead end. A fucking dead end. Ox, it hurts.

I thought about calling him.

But he'd asked me not to. He needed to focus, he'd said.

There was no green here.

.   .   .

"*Dios mío*," Rico breathed, watching as Mark shifted in front of them, once a man and now a wolf.

"Should I be scared?" Tanner asked, voice high-pitched. "Because I feel like I should be scared. Okay. I'm scared." He squeaked loudly when Elizabeth came out of the house and sat on the porch, watching them with her head cocked, tail thumping lightly against the wooden slats.

"Far fucking *out*," Chris whispered. "This is like some Lon Chaney fucking shit!"

They all looked at me and waited.

"What?" I asked.

"You do it now," Rico said.

"Like, just *do* it," Tanner said.

"Show me your *American Werewolf in London*," Chris said.

"Jesus fucking Christ," I muttered. "I'm not a wolf."

They were very disappointed in that.

.   .   .

A text came in the middle of the night.

It said, Please tell me you're all right.

im all right

Bad dream

about what

He didn't reply.

.   .   .

"Gordo's a witch," Tanner repeated.

"Shut the fuck up," Chris said.

"I *knew* that motherfucker was up to something," Rico said. "He sacrifices chickens at midnight and bathes in their blood, doesn't he?"

We all stared at him.

"What?" Rico said. "It could happen. It's a thing. I know my shit. I've *seen* stuff, man. Like *things*. *Mi abuela* used to slaughter chickens all the time. It was very hardcore."

"That actually explains a lot," Chris said. "Because of all his weirdness."

"Like how his tattoos always seemed to be in different places," Tanner said.

"Or how when we all moved here, he always went around our houses, rubbing the walls and muttering things," Rico said.

"Or how he didn't think it was funny when I wanted to put up witch Halloween decorations at the shop," Chris said. "*Because they were funny.*"

"Or how he had daddy issues and never explained why," Tanner said. "I always thought his dad was just a jerk. I didn't know he was an *evil* jerk."

"There were really a lot of clues," Rico said. "I'm slightly disappointed in us."

"We aren't very self-aware," Chris said with a frown.

"Holy shit!" Tanner said. "He can do *magic*."

I sighed and gave in. "He has shiny arms."

"Shiny arms?" Rico said. "Like . . . what?"

"His arms. They glow when he does magic."

"Shiny arms," Tanner said. "That's . . . amazing."

"Magic," Chris said. "I . . . don't know what to do with that."

"And what about you?" Rico demanded. "How do you fit in with all of this?"

That led to tethers and mates.

"Like destiny and bullshit?"

"Oh my god, Ox, your life is like those shitty sparkly vampire movies. That I've never seen and don't like at all, shut up."

"Oh man. That explains the whole Jessie thing. She never stood a chance in the face of sparkly vampire destiny or whatever it is."

I put my face in my hands.

The conversation went on for another three hours after that.

At the end, it was Tanner who spoke.

He said, "Your mom was very brave."

And then he hugged me.

I held on for dear life.

Eventually, Rico and Chris came over too and I was surrounded.

. . .

A text came from Gordo.

Joe's fine. Ran into some trouble. He's sleeping it off. He didn't want you to worry.

I didn't sleep much that night.

. . .

They started coming to the house, Rico and Tanner and Chris. At first it was just every few days, and only for a little bit at a time. They were slightly wary at first, jumping at every little thing. Laughing too loudly. They would talk to Mark. They would watch Elizabeth. They would ask questions, always asking questions.

Soon, though, they came almost every day. We ate dinner together. The second full moon after the others left, Rico, Tanner, and Chris were there. They were nervous. I told them not to be. I didn't understand what was happening, but I was starting to see them differently. Mark just smiled his secret smile when I asked, though it was a shade less bright than it used to be. Elizabeth was always a wolf, so I could never ask her, though I talked to her like I normally would. For some reason, she seemed to like the sound of my voice. I didn't know if she could understand me, especially since she'd been a wolf for so long. Mark said it would be harder for her to come back the longer she stayed, but that she'd do it when she was ready. He trusted her and said I should too.

Mark and Elizabeth ran through the trees under the light of the moon. They didn't sing, though. None of us did. We couldn't seem to find the songs within us to show how we felt.

. . .

How are they? he asked.

okay, I wrote back. your mom hasn't shifted yet. I didn't tell him about my friends knowing about them now, because I didn't want it to get back to Gordo. Not yet, at least.

I waited for him to write back.

It was days before he responded again.

. . .

Mark put an obituary in the newspaper announcing Thomas's death, revealing no details. He asked for privacy. Condolences were sent. And flowers. So many flowers. They were red and orange. Violet and blue. There was so much green.

Elizabeth touched each one of them with her nose, inhaling deeply.

Sometimes, it felt like I couldn't breathe.

.   .   .

"We'll have burners," Joe had whispered to me as we lay side by side. "Cell phones that can't be traced. We'll trade them out every now and then. But I promise you I'll keep in touch."

"I don't understand," I'd admitted.

"I know," he'd said, tracing his fingers over my cheek. "I know."

.   .   .

"Are you ever going to change back?" I asked Elizabeth.

She licked my hand before she turned and walked into the forest.

I waited for a long time until she came back.

.   .   .

No words from him, this time.

Just a picture. The full moon.

I stared at it, running my thumb over it, like I could tell where he was just by looking at it.

I couldn't, though.

.   .   .

Five weeks after they left, and two days after the full moon, there was a knock at the door.

I had just gotten home from work (and home being the Bennett house because I could still see the stain on the floor at the old house). I sat at the kitchen table, back sore and fingers stained black. Elizabeth came in and lay at my feet, her snout resting on my boot, eyes closed and breathing deeply. Mark moved in the kitchen, watching over a pot on the stove. Whatever he was making smelled spicy and my stomach rumbled at the aroma. I was hungry.

The moment before the knock came, both Elizabeth and Mark stiffened.

Then, three taps on the front door.

It wasn't Rico or Chris or Tanner. I'd just left them at the shop not an hour ago. And they didn't knock anymore. They just came in, bringing in dust and laughter and grease. They weren't like the others had been. And I thought maybe that was a good thing.

So I knew it wasn't them. And while Gordo had said that no one could approach the Bennett house who harbored ill will, given his wards, we still snapped to attention.

Elizabeth was up and moving toward the door even before the knocks had died away.

Mark half shifted and went to the window, scanning the backyard to make sure we weren't being surrounded.

I grabbed my crowbar.

The threads between us burst brightly.

And there were other threads.

Newer threads.

They were weak. Faint.

But they were there. I didn't see where they led, but they pulsed gently.

The knocks came again.

I approached the door.

Elizabeth growled quietly, coiled and ready to attack.

Mark moved off to my side, out of sight of anyone on the other side of the door.

I put my hand on the doorknob.

Took a breath.

And opened.

We were not attacked.

A man I'd never seen before stood there.

He wasn't much older than I was. He was shorter, too, and leaner. His dark eyes crinkled as he squinted up at me, framed by chunky black glasses. His skin was pale and his hair was black, cut almost militarily short. He wore jeans and dusty boots, like he'd been on the road for a while. He was a Beta, and an attractive one at that, but I could tell he knew that.

He arched an eyebrow at me as Elizabeth growled louder.

"Wolf," I said.

"Ox," he replied. He grinned and white teeth flashed. "I come in peace and bring tidings of great joy. My name is Robbie Fontaine. You may have known my predecessor, Osmond."

Elizabeth snarled at him. I heard Mark growling somewhere off to my right.

Robbie winced. "Yeah, probably not the best idea to mention that name. That's my bad. Won't happen again. Well, I can't actually promise that. I'll probably say some shit I don't mean. For that, I'm sorry. I'm still sort of new at this."

"At what?" I couldn't help but ask.

"Being in the position that I'm in."

"And what position is that?"

He cocked his head at me, assessing. "Why," he said, "I'm here to protect you."

I snorted. "Protect."

That smile came back. "Indeed. I need to see your Alpha."

. . .

Robbie Fontaine came from the east.

There was a new Alpha in place. For now. Her name was Michelle Hughes. She'd risen to Thomas's old position, governing over all packs in the United States.

Including mine.

"She's a good woman," Mark said. "Good head on her shoulders. She'll do the right thing. We're okay there. She'll be good, for the next few years."

Until Joe comes back was left unsaid.

We sat in the living room, Robbie across from us on the sofa, while we were on the couch, Mark pressed against one side of me and Elizabeth against the other. I thought maybe this would be enough for her to shift back, but she didn't.

"She sends her condolences," Robbie said. "She would have come herself, but there are . . . pressing matters, as I'm sure you understand."

Mark nodded. It was all very diplomatic.

"Where's Joe?" Robbie asked. "He's not here." He knew that, though. He knew that the moment he entered the house. Probably even before. I didn't want to think why Elizabeth and Mark hadn't heard him approach.

I waited for Mark to speak. He didn't.

I was surprised to find him looking at me. Obviously waiting.

Robbie didn't miss that little exchange.

I looked back at him. "He's not here," I repeated slowly.

"Ox, is it?" he asked me.

I nodded.

"I've heard things about you."

"Oh?"

"Good things. They talk about you. The wolves. They say you're a human, but that you're just as strong as us. Trust me when I say it's hard to impress them. But you've done that."

"I didn't do anything," I said.

"Maybe," Robbie said. "Or maybe you just don't understand exactly what you've done. It's really rather remarkable."

I said, "I don't know you."

"No," Robbie agreed.

"I knew Osmond. A little."

Robbie frowned. "It was a surprise. To all of us."

"Was it?" I asked.

"Yes."

"A surprise."

"Yes."

"Your surprise ended in my mother's death. In my Alpha's death."

Robbie blanched. "I'm not—"

"I don't know you. I didn't know you were coming. You're a surprise. And I don't like surprises."

"I'm not here to hurt you," Robbie said. "Or take anything away from you."

"Osmond would have said the same thing," I said.

Robbie looked at Elizabeth. Then at Mark. They both remained silent at my sides.

I waited.

He dragged his gaze back to me. "Curious," he said.

"What?"

"You. You're not what I expected."

My father's voice whispered in my head, saying people were always gonna give me shit. "I get that a lot."

"Do you?"

"Why are you here?"

He blinked several times, as if coming out of a fog. "Osmond was Thomas's liaison to the interim Alpha when one was necessary. I've assumed his position."

"Thomas is gone."

"He is," Robbie said. "But Joe is not. And the Bennett line is very strong. Where is he?"

"Do you know who I am?" I asked, leaning forward.

"Oxnard Matheson," he said promptly, looking a little surprised to be giving the answer.

"Did Osmond tell you? Or his other wolves? What I am. To Joe."

His eyes flickered down to my open work shirt, his gaze crawling along my neck. "The human mated to an Alpha," he said. "But you haven't mated. Not yet."

"We will."

Robbie grinned. It was a nice smile, though I didn't trust it. "Romantic," he said.

"How many wolves are looking for Richard Collins?" I asked.

He flinched. It was a small thing, and I didn't know if it was because of the question or the change in conversation, but it was there. I noticed these little things now.

He said, "Many."

"And how many is that?"

The smile slid from his face, and I thought his eyes flashed orange. "Seven teams," he said. "Made up of four wolves each. A coven is also involved. Because of Livingstone."

"And Osmond?"

"He'll be found."

"It's been six weeks."

"These things take time. Where is your Alpha? I need to pay my respects. And there are others. Brothers, I'm told. And the Livingstone heir."

"You were told."

"I am very good at what I do," he said.

I snorted. "Obviously. If they sent you."

We were quiet. The grandfather clock in the hallway ticked the seconds by.

It was a waiting game.

I didn't look away.

Funnily enough, Robbie did, after a while.

He averted his eyes down and to the left. His head bowed slightly. I didn't understand because it was something I'd seen others do to Thomas. It was a sign of—

"He's gone, isn't he?" Robbie said.

I didn't speak.

Robbie sighed. "Shit."

Three little pinpricks burst along the faint threads in the pack bonds.

Elizabeth and Mark sighed on either side of me, soft and low.

They were coming, and I closed my eyes, wondering when this had happened. When they'd become like mine. Like ours. I could track them, almost. They'd be here in a few minutes. They were traveling fast.

"He went after him?" Robbie asked. "After Richard."

"He did what he thought he had to," I said.

"He's the Alpha," Robbie said, sounding slightly horrified, "and he *left* the territory? And the pack?"

I stared at him. The little pinpricks of light were brighter now.

"Why didn't you stop him?" Robbie demanded. "He has a *place* here. And a goddamn *future* to think of."

"You really think that someone can tell an Alpha what to do?" Mark asked. "Especially a new Alpha?"

"It's not *right*—"

A loud truck approached the house at the end of the lane.

Robbie narrowed his eyes and moved toward the window.

The rest of us didn't move. Because somehow, we knew.

"Humans," Robbie said. "Three of them. They don't have guns. Though I think one guy is carrying a hammer, for some reason. We need to act—"

"Sit down," I said lightly.

Robbie looked startled.

I thought, for a moment, he wouldn't.

He did, though. He didn't look away from me.

Tanner, Chris, and Rico burst through the door, eyes wide and frantic. Rico, of course, held a hammer high above his head, wielding it like he was about to crush some skulls.

"Where's the thing we need to kill?" Tanner growled, eyes darting around the room.

"I know karate," Chris said. "I took it for three months when I was ten."

"I have a hammer," Rico said.

"Jesus Christ," I muttered. But I thought, they were ours. I glanced at Mark. "You felt them?"

He was looking at them with something akin to awe. "But they're all *human*."

"Hey," I said, punching his arm. "So am I."

"That's different." He shook his head. "You were here because of

Joe. That wasn't a surprise. They're here because of *you*. And everything we feel is because of *you*."

Before I could even process what *that* meant, Elizabeth hopped down from the couch and approached the others. She pressed her nose into their hands, each in turn, one after the other.

I was reminded of the sound my mother made the night she'd found out the truth. The little sound of *oh*, shocked and breathy, when Thomas had touched her for the first time.

I knew what Elizabeth was doing.

She was acknowledging them.

Because somehow, in the short weeks since our world had gone to hell, Tanner, Chris, and Rico had become part of our pack.

And I didn't know how.

.   .   .

The texts were getting more sporadic. Sometimes they came in the middle of the night. Sometimes a whole week would go by. I carried my phone everywhere, waiting.

Once, I sent a message first.

things are changing. i don't know what to do

At three in the morning, he replied.

I know.

I pulled up the covers in his bed over my head and waited until sunrise.

.   .   .

Robbie stayed.

We didn't want him in the Bennett house because there was no trust there. He didn't want to be too far away. There were a couple of motels in Green Creek, but people would ask questions if he stayed too long. Mark thought he was all right. I asked if he'd known him from before. Mark shook his head. He'd made some calls and verified Robbie was who he said he was, and Gordo's wards had let him through to begin with. And since I trusted Mark, trusted Gordo, I told Robbie he could stay at the old house.

The old house, because that's how I thought of it.

I didn't think I'd ever live there again. At least not for a long time.

Because there were nights I woke up and felt the heavy magic holding me down, cutting me off from the pack.

There were nights when I didn't know if I was dreaming or if I was awake, and my mother would be standing at the edge of my bed, tears drying on her face, her eyes *steeling* right in front of me, and she would tell me to *run*, to *run away from*—

Those were the nights I missed Joe the most.

I had never been one for nightmares.

Not really.

But now?

Now they were all I had.

I remembered how Joe had been when he'd woken screaming for me.

I didn't scream when I snapped my eyes open, though I wanted to.

I muffled it down, lodging it in my throat as sweat dripped down my neck.

It was easier that way.

So I couldn't go back to the house. Not while the floor was stained. Not while the look on her face was still fresh in my head. The wet sound she'd made when she'd fallen.

Robbie didn't ask, and he didn't say anything the day after his first night in the house. The only thing I asked of him was that he stayed in my room and left my mom's room alone. He had no business in there. And I didn't want him getting his scent on anything. The door was shut and would stay that way until I could open it and breathe her in.

"Sure, Ox," he said. "I can do that." Then, "She wanted you to know, too, that she's sorry for what you lost. Especially for one so young. She . . . understands loss. In her own way."

"Who?" I asked, confused.

"The Alpha."

My eyes widened a little at that. "She knows who I am?"

His lips twitched. "Yes, Ox. Many people know who you are."

"Oh," I said, because I didn't know what to do with that.

So I did nothing at all.

.   .   .

Two weeks went by without an update.

I thought I could understand what it felt to lose one's mind slowly.

I imagined all possible things. Capture. Torture. Death. I thought I would know if something was wrong. I thought I would feel it if anything happened to them. But the reality was that, the longer they were gone, the greater the distance, the less I felt. I didn't think I'd know if any of them were hurt. If Joe was hurt.

Because I could feel the others that had stayed in Green Creek more than I could feel him.

Stronger than I'd ever felt any of them before.

Elizabeth was *blue*, she was so damn *blue*, and I knew she needed to howl her sorrow at the moon, but she kept her song inside and let it fester instead.

Mark was strong and sturdy, as always, but I knew about the photo he kept in his desk drawer. The photo he didn't think anyone knew about. The one where he and Gordo were Joe's age, and their arms were around each other's shoulders, grinning. Gordo was smiling at the camera, looking younger than I'd ever seen him. Mark, though. Mark only had eyes for Gordo.

I never asked if they'd talked before Gordo and the others had left.

I hoped Gordo had done the right thing.

But I never had the courage to find out.

Tanner, Chris, and Rico were there too, getting stronger every day. It was a slow process, but they were *bonding* like the rest of us.

Still. Four months in and I thought maybe we were barely holding ourselves together.

Maybe that's why those two weeks I didn't hear from Joe hurt more than it should have.

Maybe that's why I was angry when he finally texted. From a new number, the old phones obviously tossed out.

The message was short.

We're okay.

And I lost it.

I dialed the number.

It rang a few times, then fell off into an automated message, saying the voicemail wasn't set up.

I called again.

And again.

And again.

It was the fifth or the sixth time when the call connected.

He didn't say anything.

"You fucking asshole," I snarled into the phone. "You *don't* get to do that to me! You hear me? You *don't*. Do you even fucking *care* about us? Do you? If you do, if even a part of you cares about me—about *us*—then you need to ask yourself if this is worth it. If what you're doing is *worth* it. Your family needs you. I fucking need you."

He didn't speak.

But I knew he was there, because I could hear the way his breath caught in his throat.

"You asshole," I muttered, suddenly very, very tired. "You goddamn bastard."

We stayed on the phone for an hour, just listening to each other breathe.

When I opened my eyes again, it was morning and my phone had died.

.   .   .

It was six months after they left that I realized something had to give.

We couldn't keep going on as we were.

Joe was texting more regularly, maybe once every few days, but the updates were as vague as always, and the longer it was taking, the less hope I had of when I would see them again.

Robbie, as it turned out, knew less than we did. Or so he said. He seemed as frustrated as the rest of us with the lack of information. Every now and then I'd stumble across him on a hushed phone call, and while I couldn't hear what was said, the expression on his face was enough. The teams of wolves out searching for Richard, for Robert, for Osmond were coming back empty. No one knew where to look. No one knew if he was in hiding or if he was building up Omegas. Every registered Alpha was put on notice. But Mark told me that for every three or four registered Alphas, there was one that *wasn't* known.

Richard could try and track down those unknowns.

If they didn't know he was coming, they wouldn't stand a chance. Especially not with Robert Livingstone at his side.

There were rumors that Richard Collins was in Texas. Or Maine. Or Mexico. Someone had seen Robert Livingstone in Germany. Osmond was in Anchorage.

None of it ever panned out.

Michelle Hughes wasn't pleased that Joe and the others were gone.

None of them were, the faceless higher-ups that knew who I was. Robbie seemed to be filled with a mixture of glee and terror as he told us this, that the teams out searching were also instructed that, if they came across Joe, they were to apprehend him and bring him back east.

They never found Joe.

.   .   .

But at home, things needed to change. Elizabeth still hadn't shifted back and I was worried the day would come when she wouldn't be able to anymore.

Mark was getting quieter and quieter. He spoke only when spoken to, and then it was only a few words before lapsing back into silence.

Tanner, Chris, and Rico didn't know what to do. They were pack, but they didn't understand what that meant. After the initial burst of *newness*, of the joining of their threads to ours, the excitement wore off. Elizabeth didn't run on the full moons. Mark was just as inclined to disappear.

I walked through the woods, sunlight filtering through the trees.

It's going to break soon, Thomas said, walking at my side.

"I know," I said, even though he wasn't really there.

Something needs to change, my mother said, running her hands along the bark of a Douglas fir.

"I know," I said, even though she was buried in the ground six miles away.

They were right, these ghosts. These memories. These few things I had left.

An Alpha isn't decided by the color of his eyes, Thomas said as I picked up a pinecone from the forest floor.

Do you remember when he left? Mom asked. *You stood in the kitchen and told me you were going to be the man now. Your face was wet but you said you were going to be the man. I worried. About us. About this. About you. But I believed you too.*

And she had.

Both of them had.

I found myself in front of the house.

The old house.

It looked as it always had.

I stood there for a long time.

Eventually, there was a nudge at my hand.

I looked down.

Elizabeth watched me with knowing eyes.

I said, "We have to change. This isn't working. Not anymore."

She whined.

"I know it hurts," I said. "I know it's easier for you like this now. But we can't do this. Not anymore."

She nudged my hand again.

I looked back up at the house.

She waited until I was ready to speak again.

She was good like that.

I said, "I need to go inside."

I said, "I want you to come with me."

I said, "And when we come back out, I'll want to hear your voice."

I said, "Because it's time. For both of us."

She followed me into the house.

.   .   .

Robbie had somehow removed the stain from the wood where she'd died.

It looked like it always had.

In my room, things were mostly the same.

I trailed my fingers along my bookshelf.

I pulled out the Buick shop manual she'd given me on my birthday a long time ago.

Inside was a card.

> *What do you call a lost wolf?*
> *A where-wolf!*
> *This year will be better.*
>
> *Love, Mom*

I didn't know if I was dreaming or awake.

I put it back and wondered if I had soap bubbles on my ear.

Elizabeth watched and waited, never leaving my side.

I cried. Just a little. A few tears that I wiped away with the back of my hand.

I stood outside her door, hand on the doorknob.

I had to gather all my courage. I'd faced down Omegas. Osmond. Richard.

But this was harder.

Finally, *finally*, I opened the door.

It smelled like her. But then I knew it would.

It was faded, but it was there.

Motes of dust caught the sun.

It was like before, after my father.

When I left the room, the door remained opened.

. . . .

"I meant what I said," I told her. "We leave here, I hear your voice."

She looked from me to the front door, then back to me.

"It's hard," I said. "And it will be for a long time. But that's why we have each other. Why we have a pack. We need to start remembering that again."

I held out the quilted blanket for her to take, to cover her nudity should she choose to. I wasn't going to push any harder than I already had, because I was worried it'd be too much.

She stared at my offering for a long time.

I thought maybe I'd failed.

But then she reached out carefully and took the quilt between her teeth. I let it slip between my fingers.

She dragged it along the floor and around the corner.

I heard the shift of bone and muscle. It sounded painful after so long.

There was a sigh.

I waited.

There was a shuffle of feet.

Elizabeth Bennett stepped around the corner, eyes tired but more human than they'd been in a long time. Her lightly colored hair fell along her shoulders, the quilt clutched tightly around her.

When she spoke, her voice was dry and raspy.

It was a wonderful thing.

She said, "I don't mind being lonely when my heart tells me you are lonely too. Do you remember?"

"Dinah Shore," I said. "You were dancing. You were in your green phase."

"That song," she said. "I told you it's about staying behind. When others go to war."

I played my part. "Staying behind or getting left behind?"

"Ox," she cried, *"there is a difference."*

· · ·

she shifted back
   You did it, didn't you?
   no she wanted it
   You did it, Ox. Trust me on that.
   you need to come back
   joe
   are you there
   JOE

· · ·

Sometimes she smiled. Sometimes she looked very far away.

Mark had hugged her when we'd come back to the house the day she'd shifted back. They hadn't really spoken, just clung to each other for what seemed like hours.

She didn't cry.

Mark did, though.

He'd said, "I'm sorry. I'm so sorry."

Not for the first time, I thought everything my father had told me had been bullshit.

Robbie was in awe of her.

"Don't you know who she is?" he'd hissed at me.

I did. "She's Elizabeth."

"She's a *legend*."

Tanner, Chris, and Rico fumbled through their introductions, blushing furiously as she kissed each of them on the cheek, lingering and sweet.

I made fun of them for that later. They blushed again.

I didn't know if she tried to call Joe or Carter or Kelly. I didn't know if they felt her better than I ever could. I told her what I knew, how long it'd been, the vague responses I got.

She'd nodded, looked off into the distance, and said, "We should do dinner on Sunday."

So we did.

Because it was tradition.

Elizabeth stood in the kitchen, sashaying to a song playing low on the old radio. I didn't think it was Dinah Shore. I thought maybe that would hit too close to home right now.

Mark and Tanner were on the grill outside, even though it was cold. Rico and Chris were setting the table.

Robbie looked unsure as he stood along the edge of the kitchen, near the doorway.

"Ox," Elizabeth said. "Did you finish dicing the onions?"

I said, "Yes," and handed her the bowl. Because we were pretending that everything was all right.

"Thank you," she said, and she smiled. It was a shadow of what it used to be, but it was there. She was stronger than I'd given her credit for. I wouldn't make that mistake again.

She stirred in the onions and said, "Robbie, is it?"

"Um," Robbie said. "Yes?"

"Are you sure? You don't sound sure."

"Yes," he said. "I'm sure."

He still didn't sound very sure.

"Robbie what?"

"Fontaine."

"Fontaine," she said, glancing at him briefly before looking back at the stove. "Ah. Your mother was Beatrice."

"You knew my mother?" he asked, sounding shocked.

"We went to school together. I was sorry to hear of her passing."

He shrugged awkwardly. "It was a long time ago."

"Still. She was a smart woman. Very kind. We weren't as close as I would have liked to have been. Different paths."

"Yeah," he said hoarsely.

"Do you have a pack?" she asked.

I heard the weight of her words, even if he didn't.

Robbie shrugged again. "Sometimes? Nothing permanent. Given my job, I tend to float around a lot. Any bonds I form are usually temporary."

"Temporary? That can't feel good."

"It is what it is, I guess." He looked uncomfortable. Nervous. I remembered feeling that way around her at the beginning.

"But you're here."

"Because I was told to be." His eyes widened. His next words were hasty. Rushed. "Not that I wouldn't want to be here or anything."

"Of course," she said smoothly. "Someone has to report back our every move to Michelle."

He blushed furiously. "Not *every* move."

"Oh?"

"I haven't told her about . . . you know."

"About?"

"How you're back."

"Why not?"

He looked at me for some reason instead of answering her right away, eyes darting over my face. Elizabeth caught it and chuckled quietly.

"It just didn't seem right," he finally said, looking back at her.

"Interesting," she said. "Be a dear and get the vinegar from the pantry?"

I watched as he was invited into her space. He seemed just as surprised as I was. But he moved quickly and without hesitation.

"He fits," she said as I arched an eyebrow at her.

"Does he?"

"You don't feel it?"

"I don't know." Because I didn't know *what* I felt anymore.

"What an odd creature you are, Ox," she said. "I've always thought so. It's such a wonderful thing."

I looked away.

. . .

We left Thomas's seat at the head of the table empty.

Because it was now Joe's.

I moved to take my seat, but Mark shook his head and pointed to where Elizabeth usually sat, at the end opposite the Alpha.

Elizabeth didn't even try to sit there, moving instead to my old seat as she spoke softly with Rico. There was no hesitation. She didn't even look at me.

I didn't understand what was happening, not completely.

Sure, I had the basic *idea* of it.

I was the mate of the Alpha.

I had a place in the pack, higher than it'd been before.

But I wasn't a wolf.

We hadn't yet mated.

And Joe wasn't here.

The food was served.

Everyone waited. So I did too.

Until I realized they were waiting for me.

I looked at each of them in turn.

They held my gaze steadily.

I knew I should say something. But I'd never been very good with words.

I needed to try, though. For them. Because they needed it. And I think I did too.

I said, "We're pack. It's time for us to start acting like one again."

And even though we weren't whole (and the thought that we ever would be was a hope that I didn't dare believe, not yet), and even though the absence of those we loved throbbed like a rotted tooth, I took the first bite.

The rest followed suit.

It wouldn't be until later that I realized that had never happened before. That even when Thomas had been missing at dinner, we'd never waited for Elizabeth to eat first before we did. It was only done for an Alpha.

.   .   .

At the end of the first year, I received a message in the middle of the night.

I didn't see it until morning.

I'm sorry, it said.

I didn't understand.

about what

A response came almost immediately.

Failed message delivery. The number you are trying to reach has been disconnected or is no longer in service.

A cold chill crawled up my spine.

I called the number.

It rang once.

An automated message.

Disconnected.

No longer in service.

It was okay, I told myself. It was okay because these were burners. The phones. They'd just gotten a new one. Joe had forgotten to get me the new number. Like he always did.

I just had to wait.

I set my phone down, pulled Joe's comforter up onto my chest. It didn't smell like him. Nothing did in his room. Not anymore.

But that was okay.

Because I just had to wait.

THE SECOND YEAR / SONG OF WAR

It was partway through the second year that the Omegas came.
They weren't prepared for us.

· · ·

Jessie said, "Hey, Ox."

We were at the garage. Tanner, Chris, Rico, and me. Robbie was
there too, having decided he was bored enough that he wanted to
learn his way around. It was slow going because he was absolutely
terrible when it came to cars, so much so that I barely trusted him to
do an oil change by himself.

But he tried.

I learned a lot about him. He was a year younger than I was. His
mom had been killed in a turf war between rival packs when he
was just a kid. His father lived in Detroit, a human he saw only
every now and then, given that he didn't want anything to do with
pack life after the death of Robbie's mother. But they were two separate people, and their paths had no real reason to cross. It saddened him, sometimes, but he didn't want to do anything about
it. He didn't have a mate. He'd had a boyfriend once, a long time
ago, and a girlfriend later, but he wasn't focused on that. He had a
job to do.

He confused me. It wasn't a good thing.

"Why are you still here?" I'd asked him.

He'd just shrugged and looked away. "I'm told to be."

I didn't believe him. Not anymore. Not when I'd overheard him
on the phone, talking with those faceless people in the east, saying
he didn't want to be replaced, that he was *fine* out here with us, that
he *wanted* to stay. Nothing had happened since he'd been here and he
wanted to make sure it stayed that way.

He made it sound as if it was just a job when he spoke to us.

He was lying, but I didn't think it was a bad thing.

Still, there was only so much a person could do to watch over us
before boredom set in.

So he came to the shop.

He didn't need to be paid much, given he was already making an unknown amount just for being in Green Creek.

We just made sure to keep it off the books.

It was good, though, having someone else to talk to.

I could feel it building, just like it had with Tanner, Chris, and Rico. The need to bind him to us. To make him a part of who we were. It didn't happen right away, because he'd come in a stranger at a time when trust wasn't given out very easily. I'd known the guys from the shop for years. They were my friends.

He wasn't.

Not at first.

But he was becoming . . . something.

I knew we all felt it. But we never talked about it.

So he was there too when Jessie came. She didn't sound surprised to see me. I hadn't seen her for any length of time since the funeral, when her hand had been on mine. We saw each other in passing, maybe in traffic or at the grocery store, but I was rarely ever alone anymore. There was always someone from the pack with me.

There wasn't time for her.

Not that there had been before, either.

It was one of the reasons we'd ended up the way we had.

But even if it hadn't been that, it would have been Joe. Eventually, everything would have led to Joe. I was thankful, for the most part, that we'd parted when we had. It made things easier.

So when she said, "Hey, Ox," I was able to smile at her. I remembered the little flutter in my heart and stomach that I used to get at the sight of her, especially that day she'd come into the shop the first time, mother dead, following her brother to a small town in the middle of nowhere. It seemed like that belonged to somebody else's life.

"Hey, Jessie," I said, and she stepped over, not really caring that my hands were dirty when she pulled me into a hug.

I ignored the warning growl that came from behind me. I figured it was too low for Jessie to hear it, but even if she had, she wouldn't have understood the territorial growl of a wolf. Robbie didn't know Jessie, and Robbie was closer to us then than he'd ever been before. Not quite pack, but I didn't think it'd be too much longer. If he wanted. If we all did.

"It's good to see you," she said, pulling back.

To make things easier, I stepped away. I remembered how Carter, Kelly, and Joe had acted at her familiarity. I didn't want there to be any trouble.

I glanced over my shoulder and shot a glare at Robbie, who had the decency to look sheepish—and confused, like he didn't know why he'd growled in the first place.

"You too," I said when I turned back to Jessie. "What brings you in?"

"Lunch with Chris," she said, holding up a fast-food bag. "Figured I'd stop by. Haven't been here in a while. The place is looking good."

"Thanks," I said. "Chris is on the phone in the office. He'll be out in a little while. Rico and Tanner are picking up some parts."

She nodded, glancing over my shoulder. "Don't think we've met," she said to Robbie. "I'm Jessie. Chris's sister."

"Hi," Robbie said. And that was it.

I barely stopped myself from rolling my eyes. Fucking werewolves.

"Hi," Jessie said, not even bothering to hide her smile. She looked back at me. "He'll fit right in here."

I didn't know if that was an insult or not, so I just nodded.

"How have you been?" she asked.

I shrugged. "Okay." I knew what she was really asking, the part she was leaving off, the how have you been *since your mother died*. That was fine, though. She didn't pity me. And I didn't want her to.

Something in her eyes softened. "That's good," she said. "I know that it was . . . sudden."

There was a flare of pain in my chest, a swelling black thing at just how *sudden* it was. It was dark and oily, with little thoughts of *it was the fault of the werewolves* and *if they'd told me what was going on, I could have saved her* and *they kept secrets from me like it was nothing and look how everything happened*. These were the thoughts I had sometimes when I was by myself in bed, unable to sleep, the clock slipping past three in the morning.

She didn't know that, though. Otherwise, she wouldn't have followed it up with "And how's Joe? I know he went to a private school for his last year. He has to be getting ready for college, right?"

That was the cover we'd given. The grief at the death of his father had been too much for him to stay in Green Creek. He wanted out. So he went back to Maine. Carter and Kelly went out of state, vaguely east. No one seemed to question anything about Gordo. Not really.

In reality, we didn't know where they were. No one had heard from any of them since they'd apparently cut off all communication. Carter, Kelly, and Gordo had ditched their phones too.

Robbie had said no one back east knew anything more. No one had seen them. No one had heard from them.

Elizabeth said all things happened for a reason. That we needed to trust that they knew what they were doing.

Mark was quiet on the matter.

I thought it was bullshit. I'd never felt anger toward Joe before, not really, not something that could plant roots into my skin and bones and grow into something else. But it was happening now. I thought maybe the growth was poisonous, because there were times when I told myself he'd abandoned us, that he'd only been thinking about himself and his selfish desire for revenge. That it was unfair, to me, to his brothers, to the rest of his pack. That he was putting himself in harm's way for *nothing*. And apparently we'd been too much of a distraction to maintain contact with us.

That's what I told myself.

True or not, I didn't think it mattered.

"Yeah," I said. "College, and all that." It almost sounded believable.

She squinted at me. "You guys still . . . ?"

I shrugged. I didn't know how to answer that. Were we still . . . *what*?

Those were the other little thoughts I had. The ones that said I was nothing to him. That he hadn't just left *us*, he'd left *me*. That other things mattered more than I did. That he was just a kid and didn't know what he wanted.

Sure, my father was wrong most of the time, but he'd said I was gonna get shit.

And Joe was giving me shit.

"Huh," Jessie said. "I always thought it was kind of a done deal."

"Things change," I said, forcing a smile. "We'll see what happens when he comes back."

If he comes back at all, that little voice said.

She reached out and took my hand in hers, squeezing my fingers gently. "He'll come back," she said, like she knew what I was thinking. And maybe she did. There was a time when we'd known each other well. "You know that, Ox."

Robbie growled again, fits and starts, like a motor trying to catch.

"Yeah," I said. Because it was easier to agree than to argue with her about things she didn't understand.

"We should get together sometime," she said. "If you're free."

"I think I can—"

"We have that thing, Ox," Robbie said.

"What thing?" I asked, trying to find my last bit of patience.

"That thing," he insisted, "that will take up a lot of your time."

"I don't know what you're—"

"You won't be free. For a while."

"Is he a Bennett?" Jessie asked, sounding amused. "Because he sounds like a Bennett."

"He's a Fontaine," I said with a frown. I didn't understand what she meant.

"Sure," she said. "Anyway, call if you get a chance. The phone number's the same."

I nodded and she turned toward the office, where Chris was just getting off the phone.

I turned on Robbie. "What was that?"

"Nothing," Robbie said. "I mean, I don't know what you're talking about."

"Robbie."

"Ox. Let's finish this oil change."

"We were fixing the alternator."

"Huh." He looked down at the car. "That makes more sense than what I thought we were doing."

"She's a friend."

He scowled. "You didn't hear her heartbeat. Or *smell* her."

"Oh God, I hate werewolves," I muttered.

"She stunk like arousal."

"You shouldn't go around *smelling* people."

"I can't help it! Tell *her* to not go around smelling like she wanted to hop on your dick!"

"Who wants to hop on dicks?" Rico asked as he and Tanner walked over.

"No one," I said quickly.

"That girl," Robbie said. "Jessie."

I sighed.

"That's Ox's ex-girlfriend," Tanner said.

"From high school," Rico added helpfully. "Because those are the relationships that last forever."

Robbie looked slightly horrified. "You *dated* her?"

I put my face in my hands.

"But you're mated to the *Alpha*!"

That stopped me cold. I dropped my hands. I glared at Robbie and said, "I'm not mated to *anyone*. If I was, you can sure as shit bet he'd be here and—"

The others stared at me as I cut myself off. This wasn't the time for that. Not now. Maybe not ever.

"Ox," Rico said gently, like he was approaching a cornered animal. "You know he'd—"

So I said, "Don't."

He didn't.

I muttered something about going to lunch and left them standing there.

· · ·

They came four days later.

During those four days, I got more pissed off. I had *problems*, and I couldn't think of a single way to be rid of them.

Because werewolves were my problem.

Packs were my problem.

Maybe I just wanted a normal life, away from everything that shouldn't exist.

Maybe I wanted to leave all of this behind and find a place where wolves didn't know my name.

Thomas had told me once that the longer a human was in a pack, the stronger the scent of pack would be on them until it was a part of them, ingrained into everything that they were.

Any wolf would know I belonged to others, no matter how much I scrubbed my skin.

And it grated on me.

I stayed away from the others as much as I could. I worked later, not leaving the shop until well past midnight. The guys at the shop tried to push me, but I snapped at them to leave me alone.

Mark and Elizabeth didn't push.

I didn't want them to, but I was confused as to why I thought they should.

I should have known Elizabeth would wait until she thought I was ready. Sometimes, I thought she knew me better than I knew myself.

I rubbed my hand over my face as I walked down the dirt road toward the house at the end of the lane. It was probably foolish of me to be out in the dead of night alone, but I had faith in Gordo's wards, even if I was losing faith in the man himself.

I was tired. Of a lot of things.

I sensed Elizabeth before I actually saw or heard her. I didn't think this happened to most humans in wolf packs, but I didn't know any others to ask. And the thought of asking questions these days was exhausting. Especially on top of everything else.

I said, "I know you're there," and expected her to walk out from the trees as a wolf.

Instead, she said, "Of course you do. I wouldn't have thought anything less."

She melted out of the shadows, moving with an inhuman grace. She wore a loose pair of sweats and an old sweatshirt of Thomas's, the sleeves falling over her hands. Her eyes flared briefly in the dark, that Halloween orange that reminded me so of her son. There was an ache in my chest at the very thought of him.

And she knew. Because that's just something she could do.

She said, "Ah. I wondered if that was it."

"I wish you wouldn't do that," I grumbled.

She laughed quietly. "I can't not. It's who I am."

"Lurking in the forest in the middle of the night is who you are?"

"I don't *lurk*." She sounded moderately offended.

"You kind of do," I said. "It's part of your whole . . . thing."

"I like you," she said seriously. "Very much."

I couldn't have stopped the smile on my face even if I'd tried. "I know. I like you too."

I started walking toward the house at the end of the lane.

She fell into step beside me.

"You've been avoiding us," she said.

"I've been busy," I said.

"Ah," she said. "At the shop."

"Yeah."

"Must have been big."

"What?"

"The influx of people to Green Creek who all needed their cars worked on at the same time."

I glared at her.

She smiled serenely back at me.

"Dozens of them," I said.

"You're upset."

I stopped walking and fisted my hands at my sides.

"It's okay to be upset," she said.

"I'm not *upset*," I growled at her.

"Of course not," she said. "You're only avoiding your pack, and when you *do* see us, it's like you despise us. Not upset at all."

"I don't *despise* anyone," I said.

"That certainly can't be true. There are many people out there to despise."

"Elizabeth—"

"We don't blame you."

I blinked. "For *what*?"

"Blaming us."

I took a step back. "I don't—"

"It's okay if you did. Or do. I don't know that I wouldn't if I was in your position. It's certainly a proper place to rest your grievances."

I hung my head.

"After all," she continued, "if you'd never heard of wolves, none of this would have happened. If we hadn't come back to Green Creek, you never would have met us and your mother would be sleeping in her bed. Or, rather, I hope she would have been, because you can never really know what might happen. Life can be funny that way."

"Why are you telling me this?" I asked.

"Because someone has to," she said. "And since Joe's not here, I need to be the one to do it."

My anger flared, a bright and burning thing. She felt it, if her eyes widening slightly meant anything.

She said, "He didn't want to leave you, Ox."

I laughed bitterly. "Really. Because he sure as hell left pretty damn quick for someone who didn't want to leave."

"He didn't—"

"Don't tell me he didn't have a *choice*," I snapped at her. "Because he *did*. He could have *chosen* us. He could have *chosen* . . ." I didn't want to finish that thought, because it would have made it all the more real.

But Elizabeth knew. "He *did* choose you, Ox," she said, ignoring the anger in my voice. "Or have you forgotten that? He gave his wolf to no one else. Only you. It's only ever been you."

"A lot of good that does us now. He's only God knows where with Carter and Kelly. With *Gordo*. Fuck, we don't even know if he's *alive*. If any of them are."

"They are."

I stared at her. "You know this."

"Yes."

"Because . . ."

"Because I am their mother. And I am a wolf. I would know if they were gone, sure as I knew when it happened to Thomas."

My throat felt dry. "I can't feel them. Not like before."

She reached out and grazed her fingers along my arm. I didn't know if I wanted her touching me or not, but she drew her hand away before I could step back. "I don't expect you can," she said. "You're not a wolf. Even if you are more than you used to be, it's not the same."

"Have you talked to him?" My heart thudded in my chest.

"No," she said sadly. "I haven't. Any of them. If I had, you would know. Ox, I understand why he did what he did, even if I don't agree with it. It's a terrible thing to lose a parent. As you very well know. And I don't mean to minimize anything of yours, but Joe lost his father *and* his Alpha. And then had to assume the role he'd been preparing for much earlier than he thought he'd have to."

"It's not about what's right," I told her. "It's about revenge. Did you even try and stop him?"

She looked as if I'd slapped her, and that was the only answer I needed.

"Look, it's—"

"What would you have done?" she asked. "If you'd had the chance to make things right and ignored it, only to find out your inaction caused others to suffer?"

She didn't sound like she was judging me, merely curious. "I would have put the pack first," I told her honestly. "Even though I was angry, and even though I wanted nothing more than to see Richard Collins dead, I would have kept the pack together. To keep them safe. To keep them whole. And once we were all back on even ground, we would have made a decision. Together. That's what Thomas taught me. He said that above all else, pack comes first."

She smiled a wobbly little smile. "He loved you," she said. "Thomas did. Very much. As do the rest of us. Joe, above all others. I don't know if you understand this, Oxnard, but we need you. More than you could possibly know."

My eyes burned and I wanted nothing more than for her words to be true. "But what about what *I* need?" I asked her.

"You need us just as much as we need you."

"I need him."

"I know."

"They need to come back."

"I know."

"Will they?"

She touched my arm briefly. "When they can."

It wasn't good enough, but I knew it was all she could give.

She said, "Let's go—"

My phone rang.

It was shockingly loud in the quiet forest.

"Sorry," I muttered. And for a brief moment, my heart tripped all over itself because I *knew* this was it. This was going to be *Joe*, and he'd say he was *sorry*, that he never meant to be gone this long, that he was coming home, that he'd never leave my side again and everything would be *fine*.

I fumbled with the phone. The screen was bright in the dark, blurring my eyes, and I couldn't *see*, I couldn't—

"Hello?" I croaked out. "Joe, it's—"

"Ox?" a tearful voice said. "Ox. They . . . hurt me, Ox."

Not Joe.

"Jessie?" I asked, confused and angry and hurt all at once. Because it wasn't Joe, it wasn't Joe, *it wasn't Joe*—

"Ox," she said. She was crying. "Their *eyes*. They're *glowing*—"

"Where are you?" I bit out, hand tightening on the phone.

And then she screamed.

"*Jessie!*"

The scream fell away.

Another voice came through the phone.

It said, "Hello, Ox." It sounded like it spoke through a mouthful of very sharp teeth.

"Who is this?" I snarled into the phone.

"I found a friend of yours. She smelled like you. A little bit. Maybe like a memory from long ago. Trying to travel back inside your little . . . wards."

"I swear to God, I'll fucking kill you if you touch a hair on her head."

"Oh no," the voice growled. "I suppose you'll have to kill me, then. Because of her blood. It tastes so good."

"What do you want?"

"Better. Thank you. It's simple, really. I want you, Ox. The remains of your pack. He will be so . . . pleased. With me. He will *love* me . . . for taking away everything he could not."

"You don't know who you're—"

"Ox," the wolf snarled, because it couldn't have been anything but a wolf. I'd been around them long enough to recognize the sounds they made. The anger they could have. "I don't think you're *listening*."

Jessie screamed again, her voice cracking in the middle, bright and shivery with pain. "Don't," I pleaded into the phone. Because this was my fault. He was doing this to her because of *me*. "Don't hurt her. Not any more. What do you want?"

"Come to me," the wolf said. "Outside these . . . *sticky* things. These *burns*. These goddamn *wards*. Step outside them. And we'll see . . . what we'll see."

"Where?" I said through gritted teeth.

"The bridge. I'm told there is only one. You have twenty minutes, Oxnard. I'm afraid I really must insist on that. Twenty minutes. Or her blood will be on *your* hands."

The wolf clicked off.

My hands were shaking as they fell to my sides.

"You heard?" I asked.

"Everything," she said, eyes flaring orange in the dark.

"They don't know, do they."

"No. They think we're fractured."

"Good," I snarled. "Because they've fucked up."

She half shifted, claws popping and fangs descending. Hair rippled along her cheeks and brow.

And for the first time since she'd howled a song of mourning at the death of her Alpha, Elizabeth Bennett tilted her head back and *sang*.

Only this time, it was a song of war.

.   .   .

We *were* fractured.

Parts of us were gone. Our pack wasn't whole. That much was true.

But we made up for it. We filled those spaces with temporary things to hold us together while we still could.

"What's the point of all this?" Rico had asked, sweat dripping down his face as he trained in the woods with the others..

I'd remembered what Thomas had told me. About pack. And protecting one's territory. "It's just in case," I'd told Rico. Tanner and Chris were within earshot, panting out little sharp bursts of air. Mark was half-shifted. Elizabeth was full wolf. Their eyes flashed at me.

"In case of what?"

"Anything. Go again."

And they did. Again.

And again.

And again.

.   .   .

It was an oddity, where the wolf had wanted us to meet. An old covered wooden bridge outside of Green Creek. It was supposed to be quaint, even though the paint was peeling and the wood was cracked. People from the city came up in the fall to take pictures of it when the leaves changed. It stretched over a creek bed that trickled with cold water from higher up the mountains.

It meant, though, that it was out of the way, so nobody from town would get hurt.

We didn't bother with a car. Mark met us in the trees, already shifted, eyes bright in the dark, tail twitching. Elizabeth disrobed while Tanner called my phone, having heard her song. "Is this real?" he asked.

"Yes," I said through gritted teeth. "They have Jessie."

"Fuck. Chris, he'll—"

"Get them. Meet at the shop. I'll tell him."

"Ox—"

"Move," I snapped. "*Now*."

He grunted and disconnected.

I turned back to the others.

Robbie was there now too, a gray wolf with black striping along his face. He was smaller than Mark and Elizabeth, and leaner, but his teeth were sharp and his paws were big. That thin thread that somehow stretched between us and him pulsed gently, and I could feel the *packpackpack* riding along each little wave. We hadn't quite acknowledged it, none of us had, because betrayal ran deep. He wasn't Osmond, but he was still part of where Osmond had come from.

But Robbie had been here. He'd trained with us. He'd eaten with us at our table. I didn't think it'd be too much longer before whatever obstacle there was between us fell away.

I wondered if Joe could feel them.

I wondered if he even cared.

They followed me through the trees, running in the dark by my side. I didn't need to look where I was headed. I knew this place, these woods, this forest. I knew every inch of it. Thomas had taught me that. He'd shown me that a territory was a home and this was my home. I knew where to jump. Where to duck. I didn't think of *how* or *why*. It just was.

We were careful when we got to Green Creek, keeping in the shadows. It was late, very late, and the streets were empty, but there were already rumors of wolves in the woods, and we didn't need anyone in town thinking they walked along the streets.

The shop was dark, but I could feel them toward the back.

Their voices cut off as we rounded the corner. They looked at me as the wolves went and rubbed up against them.

Tanner tossed me my crowbar, careful to not let it touch Robbie, who had pressed his side against Tanner's leg.

I caught it as Chris said, "We heard it. The howl. It was like . . ."

"In your head?"

They all nodded, looking relieved.

"You get used to it," I said. "Mostly."

"What happened?" Rico asked.

"Chris," I said. "I need you to listen to me."

He frowned. "What . . . what happened?"

"Omegas," I said. "Outside the wards."

"They can't get in, right?" Rico asked. "Why are we—"

"They have Jessie," I said, not taking my eyes off of Chris.

He paled. "What?" he whispered.

"They made her call me."

He took a step forward, stiff and radiating anger. "She's alive?" he demanded.

"Yes." And I thought she still would be. They needed leverage. We had nine minutes. Maybe ten. "I heard her voice."

"What did she say?"

She'd screamed, but I didn't need him to know that. "That they had her, and that their eyes were glowing."

"Fuck," Rico muttered.

"They took her," Chris said to me.

"Yes."

"And we're going to get her back."

"*Yes.*"

"Ox," he said, and I put my hands on his shoulders, pressing my forehead to his. "She's all I have. She's not . . . She's my sister, Ox. They can't *do* this to her."

"We'll get her," I promised him. "We'll bring her back, and they will regret the day they took her from us."

He exhaled heavily and his shoulders trembled underneath my hands. But I could *feel* the moment he pushed it aside, the way he tensed and hardened. The way his eyes grew dark. The way he bared his teeth.

"They think," I said, raising my voice so the others could hear, "that we're nothing. That they can come here and *take* what they want. That we're *broken.*"

The wolves growled and gnashed their teeth.

"We're going to show them just how wrong they are."

And maybe, just maybe, for the briefest of moments, I could understand Joe and the choices he'd made.

· · ·

I felt Gordo's wards before anything else. They stopped ten yards before the covered bridge. We weren't trapped. We could leave Green

Creek anytime we wanted to. This wasn't about keeping us in. It was about keeping out all others who intended to do the pack harm. And if anything was strong enough to push through, supposedly we'd know. Gordo had said he didn't think anyone could get by them, not even his father, but they were mixed into the pack bonds, a sort of alarm system.

They hummed just under my skin the closer we got. It felt like I was warm and vibrating, and Gordo's magic whispered little songs in its own way. It was tied to us, maybe more to Joe, but they were gone and the wards remained. I spared a thought for him, then pushed it away. I didn't have time for memories. Not now.

He had stretched them far around Green Creek, deep into the woods. They didn't cover the entirety of the territory belonging to the Bennetts, but enough that we were safe.

There were wolves standing in front of the bridge outside the wards.

I approached first while the others kept out of sight. I knew the wards were messing with the Omegas' senses, so it didn't seem likely that they'd know how many others were with me. Maybe they were even stupid enough to think I'd come alone.

Violet eyes watched me. I counted ten pairs tracking my every step.

I didn't see Jessie. I'd forgotten, briefly, that I couldn't feel her like the others. I remembered that day in my room when she and I had ended and I'd tried to do the same. She wasn't pack. I couldn't feel her like that.

I stopped just before the wards. Somewhere off to my right, Gordo had burned a rune into one of the trees. The invisible line before me thrummed. I took a breath. It stank of ozone.

"You come alone, human?" a familiar voice growled from in front of the bridge.

The wolf from the phone.

I said, "What is your name?" I could only make out his Omega eyes.

He said, "Where are the others? The remains of what you once were."

"I asked you a question."

The Omegas around him laughed as he stepped forward. He was still mostly hidden by the shadows, but I'd gotten used to the dark.

The wolf didn't look that much older than I was. His beard was patchy, his hair pulled back and tied off with a leather strap. His fangs had dropped and were dimpling the skin of his bottom lip. I thought maybe he was smiling.

"You," he said, voice filled with gravel, "asked *me* a question."

The wolves laughed again.

"Your name," I said.

"Humans don't get to *ask* anything," he growled. "You are the *scum* beneath our feet. The fallen king made a mockery of the wolf pack. And look where that got him. Filled with holes, his blood spilled upon his own ground."

Easy, I told myself. *Easy.*

Because there was a very real chance I was about to launch myself at him, not giving a shit about how many there were of them.

He's goading you, Thomas whispered. *He doesn't understand what you have become.*

I didn't understand either. I didn't know what I was. Not anymore.

I didn't think most humans felt like I did, even if they'd belonged to a pack.

Thomas had said I didn't need to be a wolf. That I didn't *need* to be more than I already was. He hadn't been wanting that for me. He'd offered me a gift not because he'd wanted me to change, but because he'd wanted me to be more connected to him. To the others.

Even though I sometimes heard his voice, even though I sometimes walked with him and my mother, they weren't there. These were just memories, pieces of them I'd stored away that clawed their way out of me when I least expected it.

I wondered if he'd known what I would become.

I'd never get to ask him.

But even back then, before, he'd watched me. I'd catch him, every now and then. Like he was expecting something from me.

I said, "I will ask you one more time."

"Human," the wolf spat at me.

I brought the crowbar up and rested it on my shoulder. The metal scraped against my ear. The pack bonds were electrified. Mark and Elizabeth. Tanner. Chris and Rico. And Robbie too, his quiet pulse becoming more like a beacon. He was here now. With us. I thought Joe would be proud.

Maybe he'd even tell me that one day.

If he ever came back.

If I ever forgave him.

I said, "What. Is. Your. Name?"

"Come out here," the wolf said. "Beyond the stickies." He cocked his head at me, his elongated ears flicking back and forth.

"Here's what's going to happen," I said, tired of him. Tired of all of this. "You're going to give me the girl. Once I see what kind of condition she's in, I'll make a decision as to whether you walk away from here or crawl." I tilted my head, my gaze staying on him. "Or how deep in the ground I bury you."

The wolves didn't laugh at that.

I saw two or three of them take a step back. Them, I would spare. If I could.

The wolf in front of me paused. "You," he said, "are a conundrum. Why is it you are the way you are?"

"Because of my father," I said, thinking of Thomas.

He watched me for a moment. Then he raised his voice and said, "Bring the girl."

It couldn't be that easy.

From the shadows of the interior of the bridge, two figures emerged from the darkness. One stuttered with every step it took. The other dragged the first harshly.

Jessie.

She was walking on her own, but I could hear the low hitches of her breath. She was limping, barely putting any weight down on her right foot. Her eyes were wide and her cheeks were wet. But her mouth was set in a thin line, her jaw tensed. She was scared, yes, but she was *pissed*. That was good. Anger was a better motivator than fear. It also probably meant the wolves were underestimating her. Just like they were underestimating me. My pack.

She saw me and her voice was raw when she said, "*Ox.*"

"It's okay," I said. "Just look at me. It'll be okay."

"It really won't," the wolf said as he took Jessie by the arm. She struggled against him, but his grip was iron tight. "Tell me, Ox. Do you think that little crowbar of yours would do anything to prevent me from ripping out her throat right in front of you? Do you think you could stop me before I stop her heart?"

"Another wolf said something like that to me once," I said quietly.

"Before Richard Collins. This wolf held my mother almost the exact way you're holding her. I bashed his head in. He died a very painful death."

"History doesn't repeat itself."

I shrugged. "It can."

"Not for your mother," the wolf said with a nasty smile. "Tell me, Ox. You saved her the first time. Why not the second?"

Easy, Thomas whispered.

"What do you want?" I asked, barely containing my rage.

His eyes flared violet. "Simple," he said. "You. Since your Alpha has . . . *abandoned* you all, he will need an incentive to come back out of hiding. You will provide that incentive. We will be rewarded. *He* will put us above all others when we give you and your Alpha to him."

"And if I don't?"

"The girl," he said. "She'll die. The rest of this town will die. What remains of your pack *will die.*"

I snorted. "The wards will hold. You can't touch them. The pack. Or this town."

"Ox, what the hell is this?" Jessie asked, voice high and quavering.

"For how long?" the wolf asked. "Mistakes will be made. You can only stay in there for so long. I can stay out here forever. And anytime a person leaves this place, I will be there to kill them. One by one."

"You should have told me your name," I said. "That's all I asked for."

He narrowed his eyes. "You don't know who you're—"

"I gave you the option," I said, finally letting my anger show. My voice deepened and I felt *something* surging along the pack bonds. "To let this go. To walk away. Or even crawl. Now, I don't know if any of that is an option."

BrotherPackLoveSonFriend

They were there. All of them.

Those of us that remained.

Because regardless of those that were missing, we *were* a pack. We lived as one. We ate together as one.

We trained as one.

Ever since that day when Elizabeth had shifted back, things had been different. Since Tanner and Chris. Since Rico and Robbie. They'd come when we were alone and made us something more again. Maybe not whole, but we were held together. There were doubts, yes, mostly mine, because of the things I couldn't let go. The anger of betrayal. The loss of my family. The fractured pieces Joe and the others had left behind.

But we weren't down. Not completely.

I had my pack.

And my pack had me.

"In a minute," I told the Omegas, "there's going to be yelling. Probably some screaming. Things are going to get confusing. Blood will be spilled. I want you to remember something for me when that happens. All I wanted to know was your name."

There were ten of them.

There were seven of us.

But they didn't know that.

The wolf holding Jessie took a step forward.

They came then. To my side.

The wolves first. Teeth bared and snarling at the intruders who dared to come into our territory, who dared to try this again.

Elizabeth and Mark stood to my right. Robbie came to my left. They brushed against me, coiled muscle and bristling hair.

The others followed. Tanner and Rico stood next to Robbie. Both held guns loaded with silver bullets, something Gordo had made sure I'd always saved in case of an emergency. A year ago, Rico had never even *held* a gun before. Now he was the better shot of the two.

Chris came to stand between Elizabeth and Mark. He flexed his wrists and spring-loaded knives infused with silver shot out from his sleeves. He'd made them himself with materials and tools from the shop. Said he'd found the schematics online. He rocked his head back and forth, neck popping loudly in the silence.

"What is this—" the wolf started.

But that was as far as he got.

Even before he'd finished the hard end to the first word, we were moving. No sound was made aside from our feet in the dirt. I didn't even think they were aware of what was happening until it was almost too late for them.

Jessie saw us coming and didn't wait to be rescued. She brought her right foot up at an angle, her thigh pressing up against her stomach. Then, just as quickly, she stomped her foot down into the wolf's knee, knocking his sideways, the bones cracking wetly as they broke.

I didn't even give him a chance to register the pain before I brought the crowbar up in a golf swing upside his head, knocking him back. Blood and teeth flew into the air as he landed on his back, leg out at an odd angle.

The wolves snarled around us as they attacked each other, teeth and claws biting and tearing. I grabbed Jessie and dragged her away from the fight. I felt the wards rush over me as we passed through them. "You stay here," I snapped at her. "Don't come one step closer. They can't get to you here."

"Ox—"

But I didn't stay to listen to her. I turned and ran back through the wards, directly toward the wolves snarling and growling in front of me.

An Omega, half-shifted, eyes crazed with rage, bellowed and headed straight for me, claws outstretched as it leapt. I slid to my knees into the dirt, sliding swiftly even as my pants tore, rocks digging into my skin. I lay back as low as I could go as I slid toward the wolf. It flew over me, its teeth snapping near my neck, claws trailing along my skin. I brought up the tip of the crowbar and shoved it upward. The wolf's skin bubbled and smoked as the silver cut into it. Bones cracked in his rib cage as I thrust it up as hard as I could, his momentum carrying him over me, splitting him from his chest down to his stomach. He landed awkwardly on his shoulder, crashing into the ground and rolling away. He didn't move when he stopped facedown, blood pooling beneath him in the dirt.

Behind me, gunfire erupted.

I turned back toward the sound.

Elizabeth had her teeth sunk into the neck of a wolf below her. The wolf was on its back, legs kicking feebly as she tore into it.

Mark was bigger than any of the other wolves, almost by half. He took down two of them even before I could move, teeth soaked with blood.

These Omegas were far less coordinated than the ones that had come before. I didn't think Richard Collins had sent them. They fought against us, but they didn't fight together. They moved independently of each other. They weren't bonded.

Robbie yelped as an Omega clawed his back. He twisted and snapped his teeth over his shoulder, trying to bite at the Omega's legs. I didn't wait for him to reach them. I ran full speed toward them both, knocking the Omega off Robbie's back. We hit the ground, the Omega scrabbling above me, teeth near my throat.

Before I could throw it off, Chris was there. He punched the wolf in the back of the neck, knife shooting forward from his wrist and into the spinal cord. The wolf convulsed on top of me, legs skittering and scraping against my skin. Chris jerked his arm back, the wolf's head rising with his arm until the blade slipped free. Chris was moving again even before I pushed the dead wolf off me.

Tanner and Rico were moving in tandem, standing back to back, arms extended, firing at any wolf that came near them. They kept moving in a slow circle, firing in short, even bursts. When one reloaded, the other moved to cover him.

One wolf slunk in low from the side, trying to remain undetected as it stalked toward them both. Its teeth were bared and it crouched, ready to jump.

"Two o'clock!" I shouted at them.

Tanner ducked immediately as Rico whirled around, arm sweeping over him, moving until the wolf fell within the gun's sight. He fired once, the bullet catching the wolf in the throat. The wolf fell back, and I knew that the bullet was breaking apart internally, the silver spreading in the bloodstream, poisoning the Omega, slowing its healing enough that it wouldn't survive.

The sounds died down around us.

I took a deep breath and let it out slowly.

Rico and Tanner lowered their guns.

Chris was already running toward Jessie, who stood behind the wards looking shell-shocked.

Pain flared briefly in my arm. There was a gash near my shoulder, not deep, but long. A tooth or a claw had caught me at some point. I probably needed stitches or it would scar. I didn't think it mattered one way or another. Scars showed what I'd been through. That I was still alive. It was bleeding sluggishly. It'd be fine. For now.

Mark was standing near Robbie, growling at three Omegas who hadn't shifted during the fight. They were near the bridge, the fear evident on their faces. I didn't know if they were here by choice or if they'd been forced. Thomas had told me once that Omegas were lost, mostly. On their way to being feral. Marie certainly had been. I didn't know if they'd be able to find their way back or not.

Elizabeth was standing over the wolf that had been doing the talking. He was still conscious, his body burning from the silver. I knew he'd heal, eventually. If I let him.

There were six dead wolves lying on the ground. The gunfire would be noticed soon. We didn't have much time.

"Rico," I said.

"On it," he said. He pulled out his phone and dialed 911 as he started to walk away. "Yes, hello? I think I hear gunfire. Has anyone called that in? It sounds like it's coming from out near the south end of town, so hunters? Maybe in the woods?"

Which was in the opposite direction.

I walked over to Elizabeth. She was growling low in her throat, a consistent rumble as the wolf below her bled and choked.

I ran my hand down her back as I knelt beside her. She pressed into the touch but didn't look away.

"Gah," the wolf said, a bubble of blood bursting from his mouth. A thin red mist dotted his cheeks and forehead. "*Gah.*"

"You should have told me your name," I said quietly. "But that wasn't your first mistake. I wouldn't even say coming here was your first mistake. Do you know what was?"

"*Gah. Gah. Gah—*"

I said, "Your first mistake was underestimating me. My pack. I may be human, but I run with wolves."

I stood and moved toward the other Omegas.

Mark and Robbie had herded them up against the wall of the bridge. They cowered as I approached.

Mark and Robbie parted briefly to allow me to step between them. They crowded my sides immediately, pressing their warmth against me.

"You didn't shift," I said to the Omegas. "Why?"

There was fear in their eyes as they watched me. None of them spoke.

I took another step toward them.

They whimpered.

And then bared their throats at me.

I stopped.

Because that shouldn't have happened. That was only for—

I wasn't—

I *couldn't* be—

Something in my scent or the beat of my racing heart must have given me away, because suddenly Mark was there, Robbie was there, Elizabeth was there, and all three were touching me, running their noses over my legs and arms. Rico and Tanner and Chris were there too, somewhere. I could feel them in my mind, bright and loud. Robbie's thread was stronger than it'd ever been before, and it pulsed with *friend* and *home* and *packpackpack*.

I could barely breathe.

"You will take them from here," I managed to say. "Your wolves. You will not leave a single trace. You will go back to where you came from. If you see Richard Collins, you will tell him what happened here today. And if I ever see your faces again, I will not let you walk away."

They were moving then. The Omegas rushed toward the dirt roadway, gathering up dead wolves. The wolf that had been the only one to speak was slowly pulling himself to his feet. His jaw was obviously broken and stuck out at a sharp angle. He was bleeding profusely from the mouth. He took a staggering step toward us. His eyes were filled with hate as he glared at me.

I said nothing as he stumbled by, following the other Omegas across the bridge. I could hear sirens in the distance, far away and getting fainter. They weren't coming toward us. At least not yet.

I stared into the shadows on the bridge for a very long time.

Movement occurred around me. Rico and Tanner picking up shell casings. Chris kicking up the dirt and covering the blood that had been spilled. Jessie muttering, demanding answers, wondering who those people were, what the hell had happened, were those *wolves*, oh my god, Chris, *what* is *all of this*?

Robbie and Mark were somewhere off to my left, sniffing along the ground. I knew they were tracking scents to make sure no other Omegas or anything else lay in secret waiting until our backs were turned.

It was Elizabeth who approached me.

She moved around me until she was in front of me. She sat down, head high, regal and proud. She waited until I could no longer ignore her gaze. I looked at her. She flashed her eyes at me. There was a pull in me at the sight, one much stronger than I'd ever felt before.

"I can't be," I told her.

She didn't move.

"You know I can't be. I'm not a wolf." I didn't know who I was trying to convince.

There was a brush along her thread. It said *silly boy* and *it doesn't matter* and *pack it's what is right for pack* and one other word I didn't want to hear. One other word that shouldn't be possible. One other word that felt like I was betraying Joe.

"I don't want it."

She huffed and looked stern.

"I mean it. I can't. I *can't*—" Then another thought struck me and caused goose bumps to prickle along my arms. "Did you know?"

She cocked her head at me. It wasn't an answer.

"Did *he* know?" I demanded.

Not Joe.

But she knew who I meant. I could feel the gentle wave of sadness run through her.

"Answer me!" Because the thought that they had known since the beginning, since that very first day when they'd stood on the porch of the house at the end of the lane, was all I could think about. It wasn't true, it *couldn't* be true, but *what if*? What if all of this had been to get to *this* moment, *this* fucking realization? Did anyone have a choice in this? Did Joe?

Did I?

Mark came over then, sitting next to her. He pressed his nose against her ear before looking back at me with an identical expression on his face.

Robbie came too, but he was moving slower, as if unsure of himself. His shoulders were lowered, his ears pressed to his skull. His tail was curled between his legs. He looked spooked, as if he thought he'd be rejected if he moved any quicker. He kept his eyes averted as he sat next to Elizabeth.

"What the fuck is going on?" I heard Jessie ask from behind me.

"They're recognizing him," Chris said quietly, and it was another blow to whatever wall I'd hastily constructed in the face of this damning recognition. If *they* felt it, then—

"As what?"

"Why?" I asked as a last resort. My voice cracked and I could do nothing to stop it. "I am not *anything*. I am not *anyone*. You shouldn't be doing this. This isn't what was supposed to happen! It's supposed to be *him*. He's going to come back, okay? He's going to come back and you need to—"

There was the telltale sign of a shift, the creak and groan of bone and muscle. The wolf took human shape.

But her eyes remained the same.

She said, "*Ox.*"

"So . . . this is a thing," Jessie said faintly. "Mrs. Bennett is naked and this is a thing."

We ignored her.

I waited for Elizabeth to speak again, because I had nothing left to say.

I didn't have to wait long.

She said, "Sometimes, it's not about being able to shift. Some of us are already born with a wolf in our heart. The color of your eyes doesn't matter. The fact that you are human does not matter. What matters is that you have taken your place like you were meant to."

"I didn't ask for this," I told her desperately.

"I know," she said softly. "But you are what we need."

"My father . . ."

Her eyes hardened. "Your father didn't understand the value of who you are. Of who your mother was. I've seen you in his shadow. I know the words he spoke to you. But you don't belong to him. The moment my son found you on the road, you belonged to us."

"Did you know? Even then? Did Thomas know? Is that why you did all of this? Is that why Joe . . ." *gave me his wolf?* But I couldn't get the words out. Because the thought of Joe being forced into something that he didn't have a choice over, that he didn't even *want*, made me cold.

She knew, though. She always did. "No," she said quietly. "We knew you were a remarkable young man, Ox. Kind and caring. We knew that from the very start. And that you'd make a wonderful addition to our pack. But the rest? This? Ox, *this* is something we never thought would happen. You can plan for life, but life *always* has plans of its own. If Thomas hadn't died, if your mother hadn't died, if Richard

Collins hadn't escaped or even focused on our family to begin with. If, Ox. It's always about the *if.*" Her eyes flared orange and I felt the *pull* like I'd never felt it before. "But it's not *if* now. Now it's something else."

Mark tipped his head back, baring his throat.

Robbie did the same, tail thumping nervously.

Elizabeth tilted her head to the side, the long column of skin muted in the starlight.

She said it then.

The one word.

And I hoped that Joe could forgive me.

Because as much as I wanted to fight this, I didn't think I had the strength.

Not anymore.

"Alpha."

THE THIRD YEAR /
MYSTICAL MOON CONNECTION

I t was in the third year that Robbie moved into the main house, shortly after being recognized as part of the Bennett pack. His superiors didn't seem surprised. A gruff man came to the house, wearing a wrinkled suit and a skinny tie. His eyes widened briefly when I entered the room, able to sense something about me I still didn't quite understand.

He was blunt and to the point. There had been no sign of Richard Collins, no tangible proof of him for well over a year. The teams that had been searching for him since he'd fled Green Creek were coming back with nothing. There weren't even rumors of him anymore.

The same was said of Joe and the others. We hadn't heard anything from them, though Elizabeth kept insisting that they were alive, that she would *know* if something happened to them, to her sons. I didn't have the heart to disagree with her, though I lay awake at night imagining a hundred different things that could have happened to them. That they'd found Richard and he'd killed them, becoming an Alpha. That even though they were alive, they were never coming back. That I'd never see Carter again. Or Kelly. Or Gordo.

And Joe, of course. Because he was on my mind more than the others.

The gruff man told us that they'd continue the search, but it seemed halfhearted. They spoke as if Michelle Hughes was going to be long term, as if she would be finally taking Thomas's place as the head Alpha permanently. "We'll give it time," he said, sipping black coffee. "But we can't wait forever."

He asked to speak to me privately. I glanced at Elizabeth, who nodded before agreeing. She pointed toward Thomas's old office, and I hesitated only briefly. The others left the house. Tanner, Rico, and Chris were at the shop.

The gruff man waited until he was sure the others were out of earshot before closing the door to the office. I sat behind the desk, more intimidated than I'd expected to be. I tried to push it down, but I think he knew.

Then, "She's curious about you."

I didn't expect that. "Who?"

"Alpha Hughes."

"Why?"

He snorted. "Because you're human, and somehow you've become an Alpha. Of the Bennett pack, no less."

"Joe's the Alpha of the Bennett pack," I said. I was just temporary. I'd accepted my new status more than I had before, but it was still a work in progress. One that I hoped would be over very, very soon.

"Joe's not here."

"He will be." And I wondered if the gruff man heard the traitorous thump of my heart.

"How did you do it?" he asked. "She'll want to know. Not because you've done anything wrong or because she'll want to take anything from you."

I narrowed my eyes. "Why go there first?"

He shrugged. "Because you did. And I don't blame you. Neither does she. This pack has been put through . . . a lot. Which is an understatement. You don't hand out trust easily."

You meaning the pack. He spoke to me as if we were one out of respect. "There aren't many people *to* trust."

"Alpha Hughes—"

"Is someone I've never met," I said sharply. "So I can't be expected to trust her."

"That hasn't stopped her from wondering about you."

"Keeping tabs."

"Robbie," he said.

"Robbie," I agreed.

"Would you believe me if I told you that his updates have gotten exceedingly vague as time has gone by?"

I would, because they had. I nodded slowly, wondering if I was going to have to fight this gruff man for one of my pack. Because Robbie wasn't his. He didn't belong to Alpha Hughes. He belonged to me. Here. With the pack.

"She understands."

"Does she?" I asked.

"Probably more than you know. I can't say you don't have the instincts we do, because I don't know what you are. But a wolf knows when he fits. When he finds a home. There's a pull. In his head and chest. It starts off small at first. But it grows, if allowed. And you've allowed it."

"You can't take him back," I said bluntly. "I won't let you."

He eyed me for a moment. Then, "I wouldn't ask that of him. Or you."

"He's mine now." And something primal in me took great joy from the thought.

"We know. It's not exactly ideal, but—"

"Better than Osmond."

The gruff man flinched at that. "Fair."

"*Fair*? I think that might be an understatement."

"Osmond was . . . unforeseen."

"Osmond was a mistake. I think even Thomas knew that. Before it happened."

"No one could have seen that coming."

"Maybe you weren't looking hard enough. Do you even know how it happened? When? Was he turned, or did he always belong to Richard Collins?"

The gruff man rubbed a hand over his face. "Those are questions we hope to ask him if he's found."

"*When* he's found."

"For someone who doesn't *trust* what I'm saying, you're putting an awful lot of faith in our teams."

"I'm not talking about your teams," I said coolly.

"He'll work for us, Robbie will," the gruff man said. "We ask that you keep us informed of any . . . changes."

"Changes."

"To your pack. Normally, when a pack adds members, there's a vetting process. To avoid any chance of letting someone in who has other interests at heart."

I blinked. "Was I vetted?"

"Partly. Mostly it was the word of Thomas. People usually didn't say no to him, even after he stepped down. He was . . . persuasive."

That didn't sit right. "You want control."

"We want to be safe," he countered. "There aren't as many of us as there used to be. Things change. Attitudes change. If things kept going as they were, there'd be mostly bitten and not born. When a species is dying, everything must be done to preserve those that remain. This isn't about control. It's about survival."

"Richard Collins doesn't give two shits about that."

"Richard Collins is a psychopath."

"Fine," I said. "Robbie can still report to you. But if you push him for things he shouldn't be discussing, if you attempt to go behind my back—"

"Threats aren't necessary," the gruff man assured me. "Though I would be lying if I said you're not gonna get shit about this."

I froze, but it was a small thing.

The gruff man caught it, though. He arched an eyebrow at me.

I cleared my throat. "How?"

"Others aren't going to take kindly to a human Alpha. There is barely tolerance for bitten Alphas. But you? You're *human*. Some will see it as a slap in the face. Others will think you're lying."

"Do you?"

He shook his head slowly. "Maybe before I got here. Maybe I'd heard the stories about you before, the human in the wolf pack. And maybe I didn't necessarily believe everything I'd heard. Thomas always said how revered they should be, even after humans had tried to exterminate us. And yet he hid you from us. Not you specifically, no. We knew about you. But the fact that you were going to be mated to the future Alpha? He kept that from us. No one knew until Osmond came. We were . . . concerned."

"Concerned enough to send a traitor and a handful of Betas without knowing who their loyalties were with."

"We didn't know he was—"

"No," I said. "I get that. But it doesn't seem like any of you know much about anything."

"Be that as it may," the gruff man said, "there will be pushback on this. On you. *I'm* convinced, because I'm here. In your territory. I can feel the way you've bonded with it, with your pack. But others won't see that."

"That's not my problem. I'm not looking for tolerance. I just want everyone to leave my pack alone."

"You should have chosen a different pack, then," he said dryly. "Being a Bennett almost ensures you won't be left alone. If this goes on much longer, you'll need to register. All Alphas must register with the head Alpha. It helps us keep track of the wolf population. To make sure Alphas aren't building packs without our guidance."

"If what goes on?"

"You. This. If Joe doesn't return."

"I can't make new wolves," I reminded him. "I'm still human."

He watched me for a long time. It was unnerving how little he needed to blink. "That doesn't mean you won't draw them to you. You don't need to bite them to make them yours. Robbie. The other humans. You can *grow* without ever having to be a wolf yourself."

"You sound like I'm someone to be feared."

"We don't know what you are," the gruff man said. "And there is always fear in the unknown."

"He will."

"What?"

"Joe. He'll come back."

"You have faith in him." He sounded surprised.

And so I said, "Always."

.   .   .   .

It was enough of the truth that the gruff man didn't catch it.

Because I *did* have faith in Joe.

But I thought maybe it was waning as the days went on.

.   .   .   .

Robbie waited nervously as the gruff man left, standing just beyond earshot. As soon as the car disappeared down the dirt road, he practically ran to my side. I could hear the others in the forest, the yips of Mark and Elizabeth, the laughter and shouts of Tanner and Chris and Rico.

"Well?" he demanded, wringing his hands, eyes darting to mine and then away.

"Well?" I teased.

"Ox!"

I rolled my eyes. "You can stay. You'll still work for Alpha Hughes, but you can—"

"She's not my Alpha," he interrupted in a rush, eyes wide. "She isn't—She *can't* be my Alpha. Not like . . . okay. She just *can't*."

"Why?" I asked, curious. "I know you weren't really a part of her pack. Or any pack, really. But you work for her. Why wouldn't you be part of hers?"

"It never fit," he said. "*I* never fit. Not with them. Even when other packs took me in after my mom died, it . . . it never felt *right*. They kept me safe. They kept me fed and clothed, they helped me through my grief, but I just . . . couldn't. They asked me to stay. And I couldn't. So when I came of age, I floated. I bounced around. And then Alpha Hughes asked me to do a job, and when *she* asks, you just do it. No questions asked. And I came here and *did* my job and it was *fine*, Ox, it was *good*. And even though you didn't trust me for a long time, none of you did, I still felt more myself here than I'd felt since . . . I don't even know." By the time he was finished, his cheeks were flushed and his eyes were wide and flickering orange. He sounded breathless, like he was afraid I was going to reject him where he stood.

"Robbie," I said, oddly touched. "You're going—"

"Because *you're* my Alpha," he blurted out. "You're the only one I want to be my Alpha. Not anyone else. My wolf just . . . You're it, okay?"

So I said, "Okay, Robbie. Hey, it's okay. You're staying. With us. With me."

He gaped at me. "Are you serious?"

I nodded.

The smile on his face was wide and blinding.

And even though I still felt a bit like a child playing dress-up, there was a pride there I didn't know what to do with, even as I knew I didn't want to let it go.

. . .

She stayed away for a while, Jessie did.

Not that I could blame her.

I'd been only sixteen when I'd found out the truth, still young and naïve enough to believe in impossible things.

She wasn't sixteen. She was in her twenties. Which meant she was cynical.

But I didn't blame her. I couldn't. She'd witnessed something most people wouldn't have known what to do with. Wouldn't have known how to process. She'd been taken and beaten, held hostage in a fight she had nothing to do with.

She'd been coming home from a night out with friends two towns over. They'd gone to a late dinner. Had a couple of drinks, but not so much she couldn't drive after.

She'd been coming back when she'd seen another car stopped on the side of the road, a woman standing in the darkness by herself next to it. The emergency flashers blinking yellow.

She'd stopped. Because it had been the right thing to do. The woman was alone. And even though Green Creek was *safe*, Jessie said she wouldn't have been able to forgive herself if she hadn't stopped and later heard that it *hadn't* been safe.

The woman had smiled at her. She'd said her car had broken down. And to top it all off, her cell phone was dead, could Jessie just *believe* her luck?

It'd happened swiftly. One moment she'd been walking toward the woman, and the next she'd been *surrounded* by people whose eyes glowed violet.

They'd hit her.

They'd made her bleed.

They hadn't touched her, not . . . that way.

But her personal sense of self had still been violated.

She'd distanced herself from Chris. I'd rarely seen her as it was, but I knew she and Chris were close. The anger he'd felt after that night at the Omegas was stronger than I'd ever seen in him before. He threw himself into the training that followed, working until his muscles quivered and he dripped with sweat. I told him to stop, to take a break, to walk away if he needed to. To ignore the pack and focus on Jessie if that's what he thought was right.

He looked at me, stricken. "Are you telling me to leave?" he'd asked, voice small.

I hadn't known the extent of my reach over them. Over the pack. I didn't understand, not really, up until that moment. Because if I'd told him to leave, he would have. He would have left us and cared for his sister and stayed away from the pack because I'd *told* him to do so. And it would have hurt him, and me, in the process.

It was selfish. I should have told him to leave.

I didn't.

I said, "No. No, I don't want you to leave."

He relaxed and let out a long, slow breath.

*   *   *

She did come back, though. During the summer.

The bell over the front door of the shop rang out.

I ignored it, focusing instead on the radiator fan I was trying to install. Robbie was at the front desk. For everyone's sake, we'd agreed it'd be safer if he was kept away from any and all tools, as he had a tendency to hurt himself and others if he came within a few feet of anything sharp. He answered the phones now. Dealt with the customers. Scheduled the appointments. People who came to the shop loved him, and he loved talking to them. It made life easier for all of us.

Until that day when I heard shrill, raised voices.

"I don't care what the *fuck* you are, you will let me back there because I have something I need to say to them!"

"Look, lady—"

"It's Jessie, you asshole."

"*Jessie*, you can't just—"

"Oh, for fuck's sake, get the fuck out of my way."

Chris sighed from the next auto bay over. "This isn't going to go well. Knowing her, it's been building up all this time."

"Better you than me," Tanner snorted.

"Actually, she's probably gonna scream at *alfa* over here," Rico said.

"What did *I* do?" I said with a groan.

"*Jefe*, what *didn't* you do."

"Son of a bitch," I muttered, setting the fan down. Then, in the same low voice, "Robbie, just let her back here."

Robbie cut off mid-retort at the front of the office. I heard the door that led from the reception to the shop slam open.

"Ox!" Jessie bellowed.

"This is going to be loud," Chris said.

"Should we leave?" Tanner asked.

"Nah," Rico said. "I want to watch what happens."

"As your Alpha, I command you to save me," I told them.

They just stared at me. Useless fucking pack.

Jessie was on a warpath, hair pulled back in a severe ponytail, face flushed, eyes bright. Robbie trailed warily after her, tense like he didn't know if he should attack her if she got too close. I shook my

head once at him, and he scowled over her shoulder at me before he
went to stand with the others.

Jessie stopped right in front of me, mouth in a thin line. She still
had that little freckle that I used to kiss. I don't know why I focused
on that.

She said, "You're a fucking sack of shit."

I sighed.

She said, "You *knew* about this? This whole *time*?"

"Jessie," I said evenly. "Hi. Welcome to Gordo's."

She stared at me. She was pissed. I didn't blame her. Not really.

I was an Alpha, but she could be scary, so I said, "Chris has known
about this for a while now too."

"*Hey!*" Chris yelped. "Why are you throwing *me* under the bus?"

Jessie narrowed her eyes. "Oh, don't you worry," she said. "He's
going to get his. I can promise you that."

"You suck, Ox," Chris muttered. "Worst Alpha ever."

Robbie growled at him.

"But *you*," she said, poking me hard in the chest. "*This* is all *your*
fault."

"How is this *my* fault?" I asked, somewhat offended.

"Werewolves!" she shouted at me.

"Yes," I said. "It's also been six months since you found out about
them. Why are you doing this now?"

She blinked at me. "I needed time to *process*."

"Okay," I said. "And now you've processed."

"Werewolves," she repeated.

"Werewolves," I agreed.

"You knew. This whole time."

"Not the *whole* time."

"Yeah," Rico said. "It was only *almost* the whole time."

Jessie poked me in the chest again as I glared at Rico. He just
winked at me.

"Are you one of them?" she demanded.

"No," I said slowly.

"So you're human."

"No," I said, even slower.

"What the hell does *that* mean?"

"It means that I'm not quite—"

"Are you going to bite me?" she asked.

"You didn't mind it when we used to—"

"Not the time, Ox!"

"Right," I said hastily. "I'm still not very good at jokes. Or figuring out when is the best time to tell them."

"You can't bite me!"

"I'm not going to! I'm not a were—"

"You're *something*."

I was getting a headache. "Not something that can change you."

"You changed my brother. He told me. He told me he can *feel* you. That he's part of you and your . . . *pack*." She spat that last word like it was curse.

And yeah, she had me there.

Shit.

She poked me a third time. "You will tell me *everything*."

"Right now?" I asked, trying not to whine. I was the goddamn *Alpha*. Why was she telling me what to do?

"Right. *Now*."

Goddammit.

So I did.

It took a few hours. I may have stumbled on a few parts (and glossed over others, because even though it had been two years, the deaths of Thomas and my mother were still sharp enough to cut), but I tried to leave out as little as possible. I felt I owed it to her, for all the shit I'd put her through since I'd known her. To give her credit, she rarely interrupted, and only when she didn't understand something and needed it explained further. The longer I talked (more than I'd ever talked before), the quieter she got.

At the end, she stared at me for a long while. My throat was sore, so I didn't say anything back, waiting for her to decide whatever she was going to do.

Finally, she said, "And all of that truly happened."

"Yes."

"You didn't say much about him."

I played dumb. "Who?"

She knew, but she said "Joe" anyway.

I tried to swallow down the bitterness that rose like bile. "There isn't much to say."

She rolled her eyes. "Aside from the fact that he's your mate and imprinted on you like you're some creepy-ass *Twilight* fan fiction?"

I shrugged. "I don't know what most of that means."

"I do," Rico said, "and I'll admit that's not something I'm very proud of right now."

"You have a mystical moon destiny with Joe," Jessie said, sounding exasperated.

I squinted at her. "A what?"

"Your *thing*. With *Joe*."

"It's not—"

She sighed. "God, I am so glad I got out of that when I did."

"It wasn't destiny," I said, ignoring the little jab. "It was a choice. He chose me."

"And you chose him back. After you found out what it meant."

I had, but a lot of good that was doing me. So I said nothing.

"Explains a lot," she said.

"Does it?"

She looked at me as if I was an idiot.

"What?"

She said, "Ox, Joe *hated* me."

"He didn't hate you." Disliked strongly, maybe. But hate? I didn't think Joe was capable of hate. Not even for Richard Collins. Not back then. Now, though? I didn't know about now. I didn't know him anymore to say what he was now.

"You're stupid," she said seriously. "This whole thing is stupid."

"Kind of," I agreed.

"Agreeing with me isn't going to get you off the hook," she warned me.

"I know." Well, I hadn't known, but I did now. So maybe I wouldn't have to agree with her as much.

"That explains why you've been moping for the last couple of years."

"I haven't been *moping*—"

"Kind of moping," Rico said. "Maybe not all of the time."

"But most of the time," Tanner said.

"He stares off into the distance sometimes," Chris added helpfully. "With his quiet strength. And his angst."

"I hate all of you," I said very seriously.

"*I* didn't say anything," Robbie said.

"He was never at college," Jessie said. "So that's another lie you told me. Told *everyone*."

"It wasn't supposed to be a *lie*—"

"Why haven't you gone looking for him?"

Like that hadn't crossed my mind before. "I wouldn't even know where to start. And I promised him I'd stay here. Look after the others. The pack."

"You wouldn't be able to find him by your mystical moon connection?"

"My mystical—Jesus. Stop calling it that!"

"He gave you a wolf made of stone that essentially promised him to you forever," she said flatly. "If that's not a mystical moon connection, then I don't know what is."

"Sort of what it is," Robbie said, wincing as I glared at him. "Sorry, Ox."

"So you're just going to sit here and do nothing," she said, sounding strangely disappointed.

"I'm not *not* doing nothing."

"Your English is so good," Rico said.

"You're not finding him!"

"He made his choice," I snapped.

"And you're just going to let it happen?"

"It's already *been* happening. Just because you're finding out about all of this *now* doesn't mean the rest of us haven't been dealing with it for *years*."

"I don't understand why you haven't done anything about it. About *him*."

"What could I have done?" I asked, voice harsh. "There were obviously things that were more important than others."

For the first time since she'd walked into the shop, Jessie's face softened. It was close to pity, and I didn't want that from her.

"Look, it's—"

"Ox, I don't know that anything was more important than you."

She reached over and squeezed my hand. "Maybe you didn't see it, but I did. The way he looked at you." Her smile was sad. "You were everything to him. And I don't think that's changed."

"You can't know that." I pulled my hand away. She frowned at me. "We don't even know if he's still—" I cut myself off and shook my head. "It doesn't matter. He's not here. *They're* not here. We are. And I have a job to do. Something that I never thought I'd have to do, but there it is. So yes, werewolves are real. Yes, apparently I am the . . . Alpha. Or something close to it. And I'm sorry you were hurt because of this. But I will make sure that doesn't happen again."

"How?" she asked. "You can't promise anything like that."

"No," I said. "But I can do my best. And it'd make things easier if you were one of us."

"I don't want to be bitten," she said quickly. "That's not—"

"—even a possibility right now," I said. "But if you agree, if you become part of this, you'll naturally start to defer to me. I don't even understand how it works, but it'll happen."

"Why don't we just see how this goes?" Jessie said, but I could already see her agreeing, whether she knew it yet or not.

· · ·

It didn't take her long to decide.

Not that I expected it to.

Elizabeth took her into the forest a week later, warning us not to follow as she needed to talk to Jessie alone, woman to woman. Jessie looked slightly uncomfortable at the thought, but mostly intrigued, so I let it go. Elizabeth wouldn't hurt her.

They came back four hours later, flushed and bright and happy. Jessie was laughing and Elizabeth was smiling, the lines around her eyes and mouth less pronounced.

"She'll do just fine," Elizabeth said to me, trailing her fingers along my shoulders as she passed me by.

And that was that.

· · ·

Others came that year.

After the Omegas had taken Jessie, it'd been quiet, though we'd been prepared. Robbie did his part and kept in touch with those above him. The gruff man. Alpha Hughes every now and then, though I think that was getting less and less frequent given that he was my Beta now. She never asked to speak to me. I never asked to speak to her. I didn't know how much longer she'd let this go on. Sometimes at night, I'd lie awake and wonder if she'd come and try to take them away from me, because I wasn't really what they needed.

She didn't, though, even though every day I waited for the other shoe to drop.

They still looked for Richard Collins, and Osmond, and Robert Livingstone. They never found them.

And I think they were still looking for Joe too, because he was an Alpha that had fallen off the grid. It wasn't so much about bringing him home as much as it was about keeping tabs on him.

Robbie assured me he didn't relay pack business to anyone who wasn't pack.

I believed him because I trusted him.

He wouldn't lie to me. Not about that.

I was sure.

But others came again.

Jessie, who had always been a strong woman, refused to be the damsel in distress ever again. She threw herself into the training with the others, soon surpassing the other humans. The look on her brother's face the first time she swept his feet out from under him with a well-timed swing of a wooden sparring staff was proud and shocked and slightly angry all at the same time. She'd stood above him, grinning, the staff resting against her shoulder, a light sheen of sweat on her forehead.

"Who's next?" she'd asked as Rico and Tanner tried to leave quietly without getting noticed.

They were noticed.

Ten minutes later, they were both in the dirt, Jessie crowing above them.

So when others came, we were ready.

But they weren't Omegas.

The first was just a man.

And he brought news of Joe.

· · ·

I was at the shop late, drawing up invoices for the past month. Chris normally took care of this, but I'd let him off the hook as he'd had a date with a girl from the next town over. It was casual, he'd assured me. At least for now. I didn't want to think about what would happen if it became more than that. Jessie assured me that it was fine, that she was nice and sweet, and to stop worrying about things that hadn't happened yet.

It didn't work that way, but it was a nice thought.

I was contemplating packing up and finishing the rest of the invoices the next day. There were already three threatening texts on my phone, one from Mark, the other two from Elizabeth, telling me that if I didn't get home within the hour, they'd be coming for me. They weren't idle threats, so I decided to head out.

Just as I switched off the light, there was a knock at the front door of the shop, a sharp rap against the glass.

I paused.

Whoever it was, they weren't one of mine.

It was after nine. It probably wasn't someone looking for an oil change.

I picked up my phone and hesitated just a moment. But it was better to be safe than sorry. I pulled up our group message and sent a single word.

standby

I got responses from everyone within twenty seconds. Even Chris. I was pleased, even as I felt the bonds between us all flare. I pushed as much *CalmPeaceLovePack* back as I could, hoping it'd be enough.

Because it was nothing.

Well. It was probably nothing.

The knock came again.

Whoever it was seemed persistent.

Gordo's wards were still up.

I had faith in them even if I didn't have faith in the man who'd cast them.

Not really. Not anymore.

But Gordo had told me that even though he was strong, and even though he was sure of what he could do, magic wasn't infallible. It wasn't the be-all and end-all.

Something had to give one day, he'd told me.

But I didn't have to worry about that. Because he'd be back by then. That's what he'd told me.

And I had believed him.

I had my crowbar. I never went anywhere without it now. It was an extension of me, and I kept it close at all times. An Alpha kept his pack safe. The crowbar was one of the ways I knew how to do that. I picked it up from where it leaned against my desk, its weight familiar. I didn't think of the violence anymore, of how easy it would be for me to kill whoever it was that came for what was mine. If I did, I was sure my hands would shake, sure I would hesitate. I didn't have time for that. Not anymore.

I moved through the darkened shop. Even the sign for Gordo's was dark, turned off when the shop had closed. The light from the office couldn't be seen from the front of the shop, so whoever it was had no way of knowing someone was there.

Unless they'd been watching.

I narrowed my eyes, letting them adjust to the darkness.

The knocking came again, soft, polite raps against the glass. The door didn't shudder. The knocking wasn't angry. Just insistent.

I pushed through the door from the shop to the reception area, moving slowly.

There was the outline of a person standing at the front door, back-lit by the hardware store sign across the street that Harvey always forgot to set on the timer. Whoever it was didn't seem to have anything in their hands, but I knew that didn't mean anything. Weapons could be hidden in sleeves. Fangs could descend. Gordo had told me that whatever I could think of was out there, and even after all this time, I could still think of many, many things.

I switched on the lights.

It was a man. An older man, face scruffy with gray and white stubble, dark eyes blinking against the sudden burst of fluorescence. He frowned a little as he watched me, head cocked. Then he smiled, teeth big and crooked. He knocked on the glass again.

"We're closed," I said, raising my voice.

The smiled widened. "I'm not here about my truck, Ox."

I kept my face blank. "How do you know my name?"

"Everyone knows your name," he said through the glass. "You're not exactly unknown around these parts. All I had to do was ask. The folks at the diner are really partial to you."

"Why were you asking about me?"

"Open the door. It's best we talk face to face."

"Yeah, I don't think that's going to happen."

The smile slid off his face. "I could just break the glass."

"Then you'd be committing a crime."

He snorted. "Call the police. Have me arrested. Then you won't get to hear what I have to say."

"Why should I care about anything you have to say?"

"Because of your wolves."

I tensed, alert. Angry. It was a threat, I thought. It *felt* like a threat.

"My wolves," I said. "I don't know what you mean by that."

He rolled his eyes. "That's what you're going with? I've heard you're not as stupid as you look, Oxnard. Don't start now."

"Who are you?"

"David King," he said with a tiny little bow. "At your service."

"I don't know you."

"No," he agreed. "But I know you."

And maybe I was getting tired of people saying that to me. "You're not a wolf."

"Human as they come. Which, apparently, is more than I could say for you."

"And you come here," I said, baring my teeth, "into *my* territory?"

"Your territory," he said, sounding amused. "How fascinating. I wonder how that works. You haven't taken the bite. There's been no one here to bite you."

I said, "You should know my pack is ready. In case."

"In case?" he asked. "In case of *what*?"

"Anything."

"You would kill me?"

"If I needed to. If you threatened me and mine."

"You're not like the others."

"Others?"

"Wolves."

"I'm not a wolf."

"No," he said. "But close. Closer than any human should have a right to be. How do you do that?"

"What do you want?"

"I came to deliver a message."

"Deliver it."

He blinked. "That's it?"

I said nothing.

He sighed. "I thought this would be more dramatic, honestly."

"Sorry to disappoint."

"In that, yes. But you? Never. A human Alpha. Never heard of such a thing. I can see why he was so desperate for me to come here."

I was tired of his games. "Who?" I growled and felt a surge of satisfaction when his eyes widened slightly.

"Joe," he said. "Joe Bennett sent me."

Things went fuzzy, like that old TV my daddy used to fuck around with, twisting the rabbit ears until he got a picture that popped and scrolled. I was static and snow and blood rushing through veins.

"Joe," I croaked out.

"Got your attention, have I?" David said and smiled again. "Good."

Yes. He did have my attention.

It was not a thing he should have wanted.

He didn't have time to react when I rushed the door, curling my right arm into my chest, breaking through the glass with my shoulder. I grunted as the glass shattered around us, sharp stings prickling along my skin. David let out a low cry and tried to stumble back, arms pinwheeling. I crashed into him, knocking both of us off our feet. He landed on his back on the sidewalk, glass crunching underneath him. I pushed myself up before he could counter, straddling his stomach, pressing the crowbar up and under his jaw, the sharp tip digging into the soft skin.

"One push," I said, "and this goes into your brain."

"Impressive," he wheezed. He stopped struggling. There was a thin cut from the glass along his right cheek, blood dribbling down toward his ear. "I . . . didn't expect that. I should have. But I didn't."

"Where is he?"

"Jesus Christ, how much do you weigh? I can't *breathe*—"

"Last chance," I snarled at him.

"I don't know where he is!"

"You're *lying*!"

"I'm not! I swear to Christ. I'm not here to hurt you or your pack. I'm trying to *help* you, you overgrown—"

"Is he alive?"

"What?"

"*Is he alive?*"

"Yes! Yes. Last time I saw him, yes."

"When?"

"Three months ago."

"Where?"

"Alaska."

"Who was with him?"

"His brothers. A witch. I didn't ask their names!"

I pressed harder. Blood welled around the tip of the crowbar. "What did you do to them?"

"Nothing. *Nothing.* They saved me. Jesus Christ, they *saved me.*"

"From. *What?*"

"Richard Collins!"

And I *paused.*

He wasn't lying. I didn't know how I knew, but I *did.* This man *wasn't* lying.

And he was the closest thing I'd had to Joe in almost three years. "What did he say?" I asked, voice hoarse. "A message. You said you had a message."

"If you would just *get off of me—*"

"Tell me what it is!" I roared in his face, spittle flying.

"He said . . . he said *not yet.* He said for me to tell you *not yet.* He said you'd know what it meant."

Not yet.

That fucking bastard.

"Anything else?" I asked coldly.

"No. No, just Oxnard Matheson. Green Creek, Oregon. Not yet. Not yet. Not yet."

.   .   .

David King had been a hunter of wolves years before. He'd been raised in the King clan, his father and grandfather before him doing the same work. He'd been raised to kill anything with sharp teeth. But after his first kill at the age of seventeen, after he'd seen the light in a female Beta's eyes die as she choked on her own blood *because of him*, he'd quit.

He'd been shunned by his clan. Banned from them.

That had been almost forty years ago.

They'd been the ones to massacre the family of Richard Collins. David had taken no part in it. It was after his time.

But there weren't many Kings left. They'd gone into hiding because they were dying out one by one.

"Throats torn out," David said, wincing as he plucked a small shard of glass from his side. "Blood spread on the walls. A message from the wolves."

"What message?"

David sighed. "That he was coming for all of us."

David had gone into hiding, using old familial connections to stay one step ahead of Richard and the Omegas. Most hunter clans turned him away, not wanting any part of a feud that would surely result in their deaths. But there were some with which old debts were owed, and he was able to go stretches of days, even weeks, without looking over his shoulder.

"There were times when I thought maybe I was good," he said. "Free. Because I didn't have anything to do with my father and grandfather. I didn't take part in that massacre. Grandad was long dead. Cancer, if you can believe that shit. Man goes his whole life fighting against tooth and claw, and gets knocked down by *cancer*."

"What about your father?" I asked quietly.

David laughed. It was a hollow thing. "Old man, he was. Memory long gone. He was in a nursing home in Topeka. Heard they had to scrape what was left of him off the walls."

One month turned into two, turned into three, and David had started to think he'd been forgotten, that he didn't even register on any radar.

"That's all it takes," he said. "Complacency. Just one moment of *complacency*, and you get sloppy. Maybe I showed my face to people who weren't supposed to see it. Maybe I left my scent somewhere it wasn't supposed to be. Don't know, really. But he found me."

Outside Fairbanks. The snows were melting, grass poking through, bright and green, and then *he'd* been there.

"He asked me if I knew who he was," David said. "Just showed up at my door and knocked, neat as you please."

David didn't even need to answer. Richard Collins must have seen the look on his face, because he *laughed* when David tried to shut the door and go for his gun. He'd almost made it, but he thought Richard had let him. "It was a game," he said. "I think it was just a game to him. The big, bad wolf had huffed and puffed and then he knocked my fucking door down."

The next thing David knew, he was strung up in his own temporary home, arms tied and stretched out above his head, legs bound together.

"He cut me," David said, lifting up his shirt. His torso was a mass of scars, some still mottled pink, most thick and rigid and white. They crisscrossed his chest and stomach, wrapping around his sides to his back, where I couldn't see. It looked like he'd almost lost a nipple. "With his claws. For hours. The thing about pain is that you can take a lot of it before you pass out. I took a lot of pain that day."

He'd been delirious by the time it had ended.

"One minute there was Richard, Richard, Richard, and the next he was gone, and there was a red-eyed wolf in front of me. An Alpha."

"Joe," I whispered.

"Joe," David agreed. "Joe Bennett. I'd heard what had happened to Thomas Bennett. Never met the wolf myself, but I'd heard about him. Most everyone had, if you were in the know. He was this . . . *legend*, you know? The closest thing to a dynasty the wolves ever had. I have no love for wolves, okay? Some of them are fucked up, some of them are *monsters*, but humans can be too. I should know. I've seen it. But Thomas . . . he was always off limits to most people. Sure, there were those who said they'd hunt him down one day, just so they could say they'd hunted the Alpha of all the wolves, but no one ever did. It was just shit they spoke to make themselves seem better than they were."

Apparently Richard had been gone a good hour before Joe had found David. There were two other wolves and a witch. They'd patched him up, asked him questions. Joe had been angry.

"Why?"

"Because he'd been so close to Richard," David said. "Apparently, it'd been the closest they'd gotten to him. Or so they said."

They'd left almost immediately. But not before Joe had pulled him aside, eyes burning red, asking him to deliver a message.

Not yet.

I scowled at him. "And it took you three months to get here?"

"You try being almost gutted by a crazed werewolf," David snapped. "I needed time to recover. *And* I needed to make sure he wasn't going to find me again. I didn't *have* to come here."

And he was right, of course. Though part of me almost wished he hadn't. Because *not yet* wasn't enough.

"How did they look?" I asked. "Did they look . . . were they okay?"

David smiled sadly at me. "Tired," he said. "They looked tired. Didn't talk with the others, not really, but they were all tired."

I nodded, because I couldn't think of anything else to say.

Then, "He doesn't know. Does he?"

"What?" I asked.

"About you. How you're an Alpha."

"No. I don't think so." Then, "How did you?"

"I grew up in this life, kid. There are some things you learn. Tricks of the trade, I guess. The red eyes give it away, mostly."

"I don't have red eyes."

"That's why I said *mostly*. When you're in the presence of an Alpha, you just know, okay? There's this sense of . . . *power*. Of something *more*. Especially with an Alpha in his own territory. I've met one other Alpha, aside from you and Joe. Back when I was a kid. You all felt the same." He cocked his head at me. "How did you do it?"

"I didn't do anything," I said, feeling scrubbed raw. "It just . . . happened."

"Jesus, kid. I don't envy you."

"Why?"

"Because people won't understand." He sounded like the gruff man.

"I don't give a shit about those people."

"They don't care about that either."

"As long as they leave us alone, they can do what they want."

"Do you really think they'll do that?"

"Let them come," I said, voice low and dangerous. "We've dealt with worse."

David squirmed in his chair, just enough that I knew he'd gotten the point.

"Do you have a place to stay?"

He laughed. "Not here," he said. "Never here. Especially in an Alpha's territory. I'm leaving just as soon as we're done here. He found me once, which means he can find me again. Gotta keep moving. For as long as I can."

"That's no kind of life."

"Maybe," he said. "But it's the only one I have now."

"He'll end this. Joe will."

"Kid, I don't doubt you believe that. And maybe he will. But I'm not going to take any chances. I'm a ghost now, you see. And maybe one day I won't have to be anymore, but until the day I hear that Richard Collins has had his head separated from his body, I'll just be haunting the roads."

He stood up slowly, wincing as he did.

"Sorry about that," I said.

"About what?"

"The whole . . . window. Glass. Thing."

He snorted. "I came into an Alpha's territory unannounced. I think I got off pretty easy."

He had. "Still."

"It happens," he said. "Been through worse, though I can't say I won't feel this tomorrow. Ain't as young as I used to be. I'll show myself out. It's been . . . interesting." He turned to walk away.

"You shouldn't talk about me," I said quietly.

He paused. "How's that?"

"About what you've seen here. About . . . me."

He snorted. "Nobody to talk to, even if I could. It's better that way. I ain't going to be ratting on you, Alpha. No worries about that."

I didn't stand. I felt heavy, weighted.

He made his way to the office door. His hand was on the doorknob when he stopped. "You know," he said without turning around, "there was something about him. When he said your name. There was this . . . light. In his eyes. I thought maybe he was all rage and anger, lost to his wolf. An Alpha Omega, maybe. Violet and red mixing together. But he said your name and . . . I don't know. There was something different about him, then. It felt . . . green? I don't know if that makes sense. Thought you should know."

Then he was gone.

.   .   .

stand down. false alarm. just some kids. broke a window.

The pack responded immediately with messages of relief.

are you sure? Elizabeth asked.

yes

She didn't respond.

I stayed in the office long into the night.

Not yet, I thought.

Not yet.

.   .   .

I didn't tell them about David King.

It seemed easier that way.

.   .   .

Robbie kissed me toward the end of the third year.

I wish I could say I saw it coming.

I didn't, though. That one was on me.

One moment we were walking through the woods, just him and me, as I tried to do with each of my Betas, laughing and talking about nothing in particular, and the next his lips—clumsy things—were on mine, his hands against my chest, his breath on my face. He was warm and sweet, and I hated myself for not pushing him away. I could say that I was startled. I could say that I hadn't expected it, but the fact remains that I didn't push him away, not at first.

I didn't kiss him back.

I just stood there, laughter dying in my throat.

Hands at my sides. Eyes wide.

He didn't move much, just a press that held for one and two and three and *four,* and then he stepped away, heart jackrabbiting in his chest, lips slick. His tongue darted out quickly, like he was chasing the taste of me.

We stared at each other.

I didn't know what to do.

He said, "Ox, I—"

I held up my hand.

I thought on it. I really did.

Because it'd be so easy.

To take. Right here. Right now.

I hadn't been with anyone since before Joe.

I hadn't planned on it, either.

But I wasn't sure where I fit with Joe's plans anymore.

And it would be so easy.

And I liked him. Robbie. I really did. He was nice. And kind. And handsome. Anyone would be lucky to have that.

And I could.

But I could never give him what he wanted. What he deserved. Because Robbie deserved someone who could give their whole heart.

And I'd given mine away a long time ago to a blue-eyed boy who'd stood on a dirt road and waited for me.

"Robbie," I sighed.

"I shouldn't have done that," he mumbled, looking down and scuffing a boot in the dirt.

"Maybe," I said. "But it's not a bad thing."

"It's not?" A faint glimmer of hope.

"Because it can't be a thing at all."

He sighed, shoulders slumping. "Because of Joe?"

"Because of Joe."

"He's not here."

"No. He's not."

"Ox."

"He's not here. But that doesn't matter to me. Maybe one day, it will. But not now."

"I just . . . I just wanted—"

I said, "Hey. It's nothing to worry about. It's okay. It happens."

He was getting frustrated. "You're my friend," he said, "and my Alpha. I just . . . I want to *be* something. For you. I know you had Jessie . . . before. And I thought . . . maybe I could be after. If there could be an after."

"You already are something to me." I reached out and hooked my fingers under his chin to tilt his head up. "You're more than I could have hoped for."

He gave me a pained smile. "But not enough."

"It's not about being enough," I said. "It's about what's right. I'm not right for you because I'm right for someone else. You'll feel the same one day. When you meet them."

He gave a short bark of laughter. "Maybe. But . . ." He shook his head. "No one has believed in me like you have. I don't know if I want to feel any different."

"You're my friend," I told him quietly. "And that is good enough for me. I hope it can be good enough for you."

He nodded, and I dropped my hand.

We continued walking through the trees.

After a while, he said, "You must really love him. To do what you've done."

"He'd do the same for me," I said, knowing it was true. No matter how else I felt, I believed that with everything I had.

And we walked on.

.   .   .

That night, I dreamt of him.

He was waiting for me on the dirt road, the sun filtering through the leaves, little splashes of light on the ground like puddles of rippling water. He smiled so brightly as I reached my hand for his, our fingers curling together like they always had.

We walked slowly toward the house at the end of the lane.

We didn't speak.

We didn't have to.

It was enough just to *be*.

.   .   .

Robbie was awkward around me for a few weeks after that. He stammered and blushed and avoided me when he could.

Elizabeth smiled and said it happened every now and then.

"He'd be very lucky," she said to me as we sat on the porch, watching the sunset. "Both of you would."

"I belong to someone else," I said.

"Do you?"

"Yes."

"I'm glad for that."

And she never brought it up again.

.   .   .

More Omegas came.

We were stronger then.

Better. Faster.

More complete.

They prowled along the edges of the wards, teeth snapping. There had to be at least fifteen of them. Maybe twenty.

"Human," one spat at me.

I said, "I'll only tell you once."

Violet eyes flared.

"Leave. While you still can."

They snarled at me.

I tapped my crowbar against my shoulder. "If that's the way it's going to be."

My pack roared behind me, humans and wolves alike.

The Omegas took a step back, suddenly unsure.

But that was as far as they got.

                         •   •   •

Three years.

One month.

Twenty-six days.

HOME

I t was a Wednesday.

We were at the garage when I felt the wards change. Like they were shifting. Like they were breaking.

I was in the office, and it felt like I'd been struck by lightning.

"The fuck was that?" I heard Tanner say out in the shop as he dropped something metal to the floor.

"Jesus Christ," Rico muttered.

"Ox?" Chris called out. "You—"

The door to the waiting area slammed open, Robbie skittering through the garage as he ran toward the office. "Did you feel that?" he demanded as he came through the door. "Are you okay?"

"I'm fine," I said through gritted teeth, even though it felt like my skin was electrified. "It was the wards. Something happened to them."

Robbie paled. "More Omegas?"

I shook my head. "Something different. Something else." The others crowded in the doorway, Chris's phone already to his ear even as mine rang. I heard Chris say something to Jessie as soon as she picked up. "Elizabeth," I breathed as I put my own phone to my ear.

"You felt it," she said.

"Yes. What is it?"

"I don't know," she said. "Something is coming."

"Were the wards broken?"

"No. I don't think—It's like they changed. Somehow."

"Robert?"

"I don't know, Ox. I think it's coming this way."

"You stay there," I growled. "With Mark. We're coming."

"Be careful."

I hung up the phone.

"You hear that?" Chris said to Jessie. "Get to the house."

"Keep her on the phone," I told Chris. "I don't want her there before us." Chris nodded as I stood. "Robbie, Tanner, with me. Rico, go with Chris. You follow behind us. We get to Jessie, she leaves her car there and gets in with you. Understood?"

They nodded, eyes narrowed, teeth bared.

. . .

We reached the dirt road without seeing anyone, though the electric feeling intensified the closer we got. I gripped the steering wheel, knuckles turning white. My teeth were clenched and I was *angry*.

Jessie was already waiting for us and she didn't hesitate, moving from her vehicle in with Chris and Rico, hair pulled back, staff clutched in her hands. I watched in the rearview mirror until she shut the door, then took off down the road, dust kicking up in plumes behind us.

We passed the old house first. It stood as it always did.

The house at the end of the lane was the same. Elizabeth and Mark were waiting for us on the porch, half-shifted, eyes bright even in the sunlight.

"Anything?" I demanded as I threw open the door to the truck.

"No," Mark said. "No one has approached the house."

"They will," Elizabeth said, looking off into the trees.

I walked backward toward the porch, scanning the tree line. Everything looked the same. The trees swayed, the birds sang. The territory felt like *mine*, like *ours*. But there was something else there, sliding along on top of it, not quite fitting, but close. I didn't know if it was Richard and Robert, trying to trick us. Because even though my skin was crawling, it felt like something I should recognize, but it was making me anxious. Snappish. I wanted to prowl in front of the house, warning any intruders away.

The others gathered behind us on the porch, spread out in the formation we had trained in so many times. They didn't need to be told. They just knew. The wolves were spread out among the humans, claws out and ready. I could feel their strength at my back, all of them, and I hoped whoever was stupid enough to come at us felt it too before we made sure they wouldn't do it again.

The electric feeling intensified.

"It's coming from the north," Mark muttered. "From the clearing."

It was also moving.

"What is it?" Rico asked, sounding nervous.

"I don't know," Mark said. "It's almost like—"

The wolves all tensed, hearing something that we couldn't.

"Four of them," Robbie growled. "Moving fast."

"Stand together," I said. "Whatever it is, we stand together—"

I heard it then. In the forest. The footsteps, the running strides. A flash of color through the thick trees, something red and something orange and it—

"Oh my god," Elizabeth said, because she understood first.

.   .   .

Once, when it was just the two of us at the house, she'd decided it was time to play Dinah Shore again. Joe and the others had been gone for almost two years.

She put the old record on, and while the singer crooned about being lonely, she looked at me and asked me to dance.

"I don't know how," I said, trying not to blush.

"Nonsense," she said. "Everyone can if they can count."

She took my hand.

She moved slowly with me as she counted out the steps, my hand dwarfing hers. She moved us in a circle, the song repeating over and over again.

When she no longer needed to count, when I felt the song seep into my bones, she said, "We stayed behind because we had to."

I stuttered in my step, but caught myself before it got out of control. She smiled quietly at me as I counted under my breath.

Then, "Did we?"

We moved and swayed.

She said, "We did. They didn't want to leave us, Ox. None of them. Joe. Gordo. Carter and Kelly. Thomas. Your mother. None of them wanted to leave."

"They did, though. All of them."

"Sometimes," she said as we spun lazily, "the choices are taken out of our hands. Sometimes, we don't want to leave, even though we feel we must."

"He didn't *have*—"

"You think him selfish," she said. "And you may be right. But never forget that everything he does, he also does for you. And there will come a time when you will see him again. It'll be up to you what happens next."

"I'm angry," I admitted. "So angry."

"I know," she said, squeezing my hands. "It's why we're dancing. I find it hard to be angry when I'm dancing. There's just something about it that doesn't foster rage."

"Do you think . . . ?"

"What, Ox?"

"Do you think he'll come back?"

She said, "Yes, I do. He'll always come back for you."

And we danced.

And danced.

And danced.

. . .

"Oh my god," Elizabeth Bennett said.

"What is it?" Rico asked, voice higher than normal. "Is it the bad guys? Is it *the bad wolves*—"

"No," Mark said. "It's not. It's an Alpha. It's—"

Robbie's hand dropped onto my shoulder, claws piercing through my work shirt and dimpling my skin. It grounded me, made me realize I wasn't dreaming, that I was awake, since I couldn't feel pain in a dream. There was pain. Sharp pain that was mostly bearable.

"Ox," Tanner said in a low voice. "What do we do? What do we—"

They didn't need to do anything.

Four men walked out from among the trees. All of them had had their heads shaved. The one in the front, the Alpha, had a beard, dirty blond and full. He was the same size as the other two wolves, large and intimidating, moving with a grace he hadn't had before. The fourth man moved with them, smaller than the others, but his tattoos were as bright as they'd ever been, the raven fluttering on his arm.

They all looked similar to each other. They wore dusty black jeans, scuffed boots. Worn jackets. The man with the tattoos had his sleeves pushed up, exposing the bright colors on his arms.

The other two wolves moved like they were orbiting their Alpha, never more than a foot or two away.

They approached slowly but surely, only stopping once their feet touched dirt. They took a formation much like our own, moving in sync with each other, the witch next to the Alpha, the two Betas on either side of them. It was practiced. They'd done it before. Many, many times.

They stopped.

We breathed.

Joe.

Carter.

Kelly.

Gordo.

Hey! Hey there! You! Hey, guy!

None of my pack moved from behind me, though I could feel how much Elizabeth and Mark wanted to. They were waiting.

For me.

Who are you?

Because we weren't one pack.

We were two.

Ox? Ox! Do you smell that?

Robbie's hand tightened on my shoulder.

Joe, whose eyes had never left me from the moment he'd broken the tree line, glanced at Robbie's hand. His hands twitched slightly and the skin around his eyes tightened briefly, but nothing more.

No, no, no. It's something bigger.

The others were there. I understood that. My brothers Carter and Kelly. My friend and brother and father Gordo. They were there. I hadn't seen them in thirty-eight months. They'd disappeared into the wild and left us behind.

But at that moment, I only saw Joe.

It's you! Why do you smell like that?

He was larger than he'd ever been in the life I'd known him. Before. He was roughly my size, and carried the weight of the Alpha well. He'd once been tall and lean, still growing into the man he'd become. Now he was thick, the muscles in his arms and legs straining against the coat and sleeves. His chest was broad and wide. We were probably the same height now.

Where did you come from? Do you live in the woods? What are you? We just got here. Finally. *Where is your house?*

This wasn't the boy I'd known, the one I'd first found on the dirt road. This was an Alpha, pure and true. He was road worn, the dark circles under his eyes stark against his pale skin, but his strength showed even as he stood there. The clumsy boy I'd known was gone, at least physically. I didn't know how much else of him remained.

We have to go see my mom and dad. They'll know what this is. They know everything.

I didn't know what to do.

I didn't want to speak first.

Because I was sure I'd say something I'd regret.

Because I was so goddamned angry.

Seeing him here. Safe. Sound. Alive. It should have made me happier than I'd ever been. And it did.

But the anger was stronger.

My pack sighed behind me as my fury washed over them.

And then, like he could hear the memory in my head of the day we'd first met, Joe Bennett said, "I'm sorry." His voice was deep. Rough. Strong.

I played my part. "For?"

He said, "For whatever just made you sad."

"I dream. Sometimes it feels like I'm awake. And then I'm not." And I had to remind myself we were not who we'd been then, the little boy on the dirt road and the big dumb Ox who was gonna get shit all his life.

His voice cracked when he said, "You're awake now. Ox. Ox. Ox. Don't you see?"

"See what?"

He whispered, as if saying it any louder would make it untrue, *"We're so close to each other."*

And it wasn't the same as before, as what he'd said when he'd been the little tornado on my back, but it was enough. Because we *were.* We were so goddamn close to each other, closer than we'd been in over three years, and all I had to do was take that first step. All I had to do was open my arms and he could be there. If he wanted to be. If *I* wanted him to be.

I didn't move.

But he wasn't done. "Mom," he said, though his eyes never left mine. "Mom. You have to smell him. It's like . . . I don't even know what it's like. I was walking in the woods to scope out our territory so I could be like Dad and then it was like . . ." He closed his eyes for a moment. We all held our breaths. He continued, "And then he was all standing there and he didn't see me at first because I'm getting so good at hunting. I was all like *rawr* and *grr* but then I smelled it again and it was *him* and it was all *kaboom*." He opened his eyes again. They were filling with the red of the Alpha. "I don't even know. You gotta *smell* him and then tell me why it's all candy canes and pinecones. All epic and awesome."

His voice died out.

A lark sang from the trees.

The grass swayed in the breeze.

He said, "Ox."

I said, "Alpha," and my voice barely contained my anger.

He winced the slightest bit before nodding in return. "Alpha," he said.

It wasn't repetition. It was acknowledgment.

Because this wasn't his territory anymore.

Somehow, it'd become mine.

Robbie flexed his hand gently on my shoulder.

Joe's eyes darted to Robbie again. To his face. Where he was touching me. Back to me.

He growled. A warning. This was a strange wolf he did not know touching me.

Everyone tensed.

Robbie snarled in response and, before I could stop him, vaulted over me, landing in front of the pack, crouched down and teeth bared at the others.

Carter and Kelly popped claws and fangs in response, crowding around Joe, waiting to see what Robbie would do. The others began to move behind, assuming tactical poses, ready to fight if need be, to protect their Alpha should the others come after me.

This wasn't how it was supposed to be.

None of this was.

I wasn't dreaming.

I wasn't dreaming.

I said, "*Enough.*"

Robbie sagged.

As did Carter and Kelly.

They stepped back, away from Joe.

Gordo still hadn't moved, either to attack or to defend.

Robbie looked sheepish, rubbing the back of his head as he stood. "I would do it again," he muttered.

"I know," I said. "But you won't have to."

He brushed against my shoulder as he resumed his place behind me.

I looked back at Joe. "You're here." Short. To the point.

"I am. We are."

"Did you do what you set out to do?"

A brief hesitation. Then, "No."

That . . . I didn't know what to do with that. "Why not?"

"Things change."

"So all of this was for nothing."

"I wouldn't say that. Look at you."

"Look at me," I echoed.

"Are we welcome?" he asked, and that was the most important question. Because an Alpha of the territory had to give his consent to another pack. It was how things worked.

But it shouldn't have to be like that with him. With them.

"This is your home," I said through gritted teeth. "You don't have to ask that."

"We do," Joe said, the red in his eyes fading to their normal blue, bright and wide. "You know that as well as I do, Ox. Especially now that you're . . . you."

For the briefest of moments, I thought about saying no. *No, you aren't welcome here. No, we don't need you. No, we don't want to see you. Because you've been gone so long. You left us alone. You put others in front of us. You were selfish. And cruel. We needed you. I needed you. I fucking needed you and you left—*

I said, "You're welcome here. All of you."

Everyone relaxed the smallest amount.

Except for Joe and me.

"For how long?" Joe asked.

A crack in the wall. "As long as it takes for you to decide to run again."

It was out before I could stop it.

The four of them looked as if I'd slapped them.

I should have felt better about that.

I didn't.

"You can go to them," I said.

And Elizabeth and Mark surged forward, brushing past me to get to their family. Gordo took a step back as Elizabeth grabbed her sons, holding them as close as she could, her arms barely able to reach across all three of them at the same time. She rubbed her face against each of their cheeks, wanting her scent on them and theirs on her. The Alpha in me bristled at the thought of my pack smelling like another, but I pushed it away. It wasn't about that. Not for her.

Mark ran his hands over their shorn heads, mingling his scent on top of Elizabeth's.

Carter and Kelly were crying as they clung to their mother.

Mark moved toward Gordo. Gordo didn't move. They stood staring at each other, speaking a silent language I didn't know.

Joe still hadn't looked away from me, even as his mother held him close.

I said, "Your rooms are still yours. I expect you'll want to get some rest."

And because I couldn't take it anymore, couldn't take his proximity anymore, I walked away.

.   .   .

I closed the door to the old house behind me and sagged against it, trying to breathe.

I hadn't been in here in the longest time. The house was in my name. Robbie had moved into the main house a while ago, so this one usually sat empty. We kept it, though, in case it was needed. In case we needed more room. If the pack expanded. If people came seeking sanctuary.

If others came home.

Elizabeth and the rest of the pack took turns cleaning the house. Made sure it was aired out. While we usually shared responsibilities, this was one thing they wouldn't let me do. They knew how I felt here. About this place.

Because even though it'd long since been scrubbed away, I knew my mother's blood had soaked into the bones of the house.

She was everywhere here.

Most of her clothes had been donated after I'd given the okay.

But there was more to her than what she'd worn.

She was in every corner of this house.

There were soap bubbles on my ear.

She was nervous, because the Bennetts were coming over and they were so fancy.

She'd signed her name and dissolved her marriage.

She'd stood with me in the kitchen, asking why I was crying. I'd told her I couldn't be crying, because I had to be a man now.

She'd pointed on a map, showing where my friend had moved, saying no one ever really stayed in Green Creek.

She'd been my pack. My first pack.

"Ah," I said, trying to take in another breath. "Ah. Ah."

I slid down to the floor, my back against the door.

I put my head on my knees.

From where I sat, I knew I could look up and see the spot where she'd died. Where she'd looked up at me with such steel in her eyes. She'd known she was going to go, and she went out on her own terms, giving me the smallest of chances to escape and howl for our pack.

The shadows lengthened as the day wore on.

I could feel the others. My pack. Their joy. Their confusion. Their sadness. Their anger.

I couldn't feel Carter and Kelly like I used to. I didn't feel tied to Gordo like I had once been. Even if he hadn't been pack for most of the time I'd known about wolves, there'd always been *something* there between us, especially after he'd gifted me the work shirts when I'd turned fifteen.

Joe, though.

I could feel him.

Because he was an Alpha. More than I ever was.

This place, this territory, was rightfully his.

And since (*if if if*) he was back, it should be his again.

I should have felt relieved at that.

That the responsibility wasn't mine alone to bear anymore.

And I did. Mostly.

But there was a part of me that said *mine, mine, mine.*

That this place, these houses, these people were *mine.*

I banged my head against the door, trying to clear my thoughts.

The shadows stretched farther.

And that's when he approached.

Even before I heard him, I felt him.

I didn't focus on the bond, the thread. I didn't want to see how tattered it was between us, if it was even there at all. Something once growing stronger every day now in shreds.

I tried to keep my breaths even. My heart calm.

I tried to make him go away without even saying a word.

My breaths were short. My heart was stumbling.

He didn't go away.

He didn't speak, but he didn't go away.

The porch creaked as he slowly climbed the steps.

His hands were on the porch rail, fingers dragging along the chipped paint.

He reached the top step and stood there for a beat.

He took in a great breath and let it out slowly.

Taking in the scent of the territory.

Of this house.

Of me.

I wondered if he could tell that I hadn't spent more than a few hours here since he'd left.

I wondered if he could still smell the blood of my mother.

He didn't speak.

He took another step forward. And another. And another, until he was standing in front of the door.

He didn't knock.

He didn't touch the doorknob.

Instead, the door jerked slightly as he turned and leaned against it, sliding down like I'd done.

He sat on the other side, our backs separated by three inches of oak.

It wasn't very long before our breaths and hearts were in sync with each other.

I tried to fight it. To stop it.

It didn't work.

I hated the peace I felt. The relief, the goddamned green relief that *bowled* over me, as if I ever really stood a chance against it. I held onto my anger as hard as I could.

He stayed until I fell asleep.

·   ·   ·

I woke as morning sunlight filtered in through the windows.

I was warm and had a crick in my neck.

I opened my eyes.

I was still sitting against the door. My back hurt.

Two wolves rested their heads on my thighs. They both opened their eyes as I did, as if they'd been waiting for me to wake.

A third wolf lay curled against my side, feet twitching as he dreamed.

Elizabeth. Mark.

Robbie.

The others were there.

Jessie was snoring softly, her arms wrapped around one of my legs.

Tanner, Rico, and Chris were sprawled out around me, each with a hand touching me somehow. My foot. My hand. My stomach.

No one else.

Joe wasn't against the door.

I hadn't heard him leave.

I hadn't heard the others come in.

Mark had closed his eyes again, breathing deep and slow.

Elizabeth still watched me.

I ran my fingers over her ears.

She flicked them at me, huffing quietly.

"I don't know what to do," I said quietly, so as to not wake the others.

She blinked.

"I'm angry. And I don't know how to let that go."

She sneezed.

"Gross," I said.

She nosed against my hand.

"Needy," I said, rubbing the skin between her eyes.

She snorted.

"You're here," I said. "With me."

She looked at me as if wondering how I could say something like that while sounding stupidly shocked. And she probably was. I'd had years to get used to the facial expressions of wolves.

"You should be with them."

She bit my hand gently between her teeth, shaking her head back and forth.

All I got from her was *PackSonLove*.

I knew what she was doing. She and the others were showing where their loyalties lay. It made things better. And that much worse.

I didn't want this. This divide. And as long as I felt this way, as long as I let my anger spiral out of control, my pack would suffer for it. Thomas had taught me that the pack was an extension of the Alpha, and that whatever he felt, they did too. More so when it came to a particularly strong emotion.

All I felt now were strong emotions.

She closed her eyes again and sighed, resting her head on my leg. Soon, she slept again.

I didn't move for a long time, surrounded by my pack.

LIKE A WOLF / THEY BLED HERE

It'd been three days since they'd come back, and I'd done my damnedest to avoid, avoid, avoid, at least until I could sort out my own head. I stayed in the old house while Joe and the others stayed in the main house. Elizabeth and Mark went between, but when night fell, we stayed in our separate houses.

I didn't know what was going to happen at the full moon, which was only a few days away.

Hopefully, I'd have made a decision on how to proceed by then.

Or gotten my head out of my ass.

Same difference.

Robbie had called back east to let Alpha Hughes know Joe and the others had returned. She had questions that needed to be answered, but Robbie couldn't. He hadn't really spoken with Joe, aside from their initial confrontation outside the house on the first day. He spent most of his time at home with me in the old house. The rest of the pack came and went, as they normally did. They felt the pull toward me, but not as strongly as the wolves. While it was common for the human members to be gone all at the same time, I usually had a wolf or two with me.

But I hadn't spoken with them. Hadn't even really seen them aside from a glimpse or two. There was a moment when I was coming back from the garage when I came face to face with Carter near the old house, and all I could think about beyond his rough exterior was the way he'd laughed after Joe had found out Carter had kissed me first. The way they'd run through the forest. The way Kelly had called me Dad in that wry tone of his.

Everything had seemed so simple then.

Carter had opened his mouth to say something, but I'd just nodded and sidestepped around him. I thought he was going to reach out and stop me, but he didn't, though I could feel him staring after me as I went inside and closed the door behind me.

I didn't see Joe, but that didn't mean he wasn't watching.

I didn't ask Elizabeth or Mark about them. They didn't volunteer anything.

But if they weren't in the old house, I knew where they were.

"Looks good," Gordo said, and I froze over the expense invoices I'd been staring at for the last hour because I hadn't heard him approaching.

I looked up at him slowly, a weird déjà vu washing over me to see him standing there, like he was coming in to check on me to see how my homework was going. He wouldn't let me out on the garage floor unless I could list off seven facts about fucking Stonewall Jackson, and it's not *that* hard, Ox, you can do this, come on.

Except *this* Gordo wasn't *that* Gordo. *This* Gordo was harder than the other Gordo had ever been. There were lines around his eyes, more pronounced than before. He was thirty-eight years old now. The last three years hadn't been kind, though he was bigger than he'd been before. I didn't know if that had to do with the pack he was in or if they'd done nothing but work out the entire time they were gone.

It was his eyes, though, that threw me the most. They'd always been vibrant. Bright. Quick to flash in anger, quick to light up when he was happy.

Now they were dull and flat, slightly sunken. This was a Gordo who'd lived hard the past three years. I didn't want to know the things he'd seen. The things he'd done.

This new image of him wasn't helped by what he wore. He wasn't in his usual shop gear, no work shirt with his name stitched on the breast, no navy Dickies. He wore jeans and a tank top stretched tight across his chest. A beat-up brown leather jacket, the collar curved up around his neck.

"Yeah," I said, because I didn't know how else to start. "We've done all right."

The *no thanks to you* was left unsaid, but he heard it. Even if I hadn't meant for it to be out there like that.

He nodded, running a hand up the frame of the door, fingers picking at a little sliver of paint. "Better than that, I expect."

"We haven't gone under, if that's what you were worried about."

"No. Didn't think you would." He cracked a smile that I didn't return. "Never worried about that, kiddo."

I looked back down at the invoices, unsure of what to say next.

He sighed and moved into the office, dragging his hands along everything he could reach. I recognized it as the habit of a wolf when they wanted to get their scent on something or someone. The Bennetts had done it when they'd come into my house the first time, sprawling over and touching everything they could. Joe, especially. When he'd gone to my room. When he'd seen the stone wolf sitting on my—

No. I wasn't—

"You act like them," I said rather than follow that train of thought. "Like a wolf. Move like them too."

He arched an eyebrow at me. "Pot, kettle."

"That wasn't an accusation."

"I didn't say it was one."

"I don't . . ."

He waited.

Gordo wasn't wrong. If anything, I was more wolf than he was, even though he'd been immersed in it more, especially over the last three years. He'd been entrenched and I'd . . . well. "I did what I had to."

"And you won't hear anyone say otherwise."

This was surreal. I wondered if it was the same for him. "They've told you. What we've been through."

He paused, fingers barely touching the photo on top of the filing cabinet. It was old. Me and Gordo. Tanner, Chris, and Rico. My sixteenth birthday, when I'd been given keys to the shop. The day I'd met the Bennetts. I didn't remember who'd taken the picture, probably someone in for an oil change, but Gordo's arm was around my shoulders as I grinned at the camera. Rico stood on his other side, and Tanner and Chris were next to me. Gordo had a cigarette behind his ear.

He let his finger rest against the glass of the picture frame, tracing the faces of everyone in the photo aside from himself.

"Some," he said. "They were vague. Purposefully. It wasn't their place. It needs to come from their Alpha. Much like we haven't said much to them. Or you. Because it needs to come from Joe."

"Why hasn't he said anything?" I would have thought he would have at least spoken to Elizabeth. To Mark. At least to update them as to what had happened. I'd been too wrapped up in my own self-pity to approach him. It wasn't fair, but I needed to be selfish for my own sanity.

Gordo snorted. "Ox, that was the first time we'd heard him speak in almost a year, barring the few words he said to that idiot David King to get him here. Which . . . I assume he came?"

Gooseflesh prickled along my arms.

Not yet.

"What the hell," I whispered.

Gordo shrugged as he pulled out the chair on the other side of the desk and sat down. He sighed and rubbed a hand over the stubble on his head. It rasped under his fingers. "He just stopped, Ox. Carter and Kelly said it was like he was after . . . well. After Richard Collins. And before you."

"But how—He is the *Alpha*. How the hell did He—Oh, Jesus. He didn't even need to talk, did he? The bonds. The pack bonds between all of you."

Gordo sighed. "Yeah. It was . . . intense. Feeling them the way we did. It was like that when I was . . . after my father, I guess. I was twelve when I was made the witch of the Bennett pack. It wasn't like it is now. Or has been for the last few years. Everything is more . . . I don't know. Just *more*."

"So he stopped talking," I said flatly.

"Mostly. If he ever did speak, it was one word or two. Nothing more than a grunt, really."

"And you all just allowed it."

"We didn't *allow* anything, Ox. It's just how it was. You think you could make a grieving Alpha do *anything*? Go ahead. Be my guest."

"Really," I snapped. "Because I wouldn't know anything about being a grieving Alpha."

That stopped him cold. Whatever anger had been building in him died, and he just looked tired. And older than I'd ever seen him look before.

"Ox," he said quietly.

"And not to mention, you left your goddamn *mate* here."

His face grew stony. "You leave him out of this."

"At least you're acknowledging it now."

"I don't want to talk about him."

"Does he know that?"

"Ox."

"Three questions."

He blinked. "What?"

"I am going to ask you three questions."

"Leave Mark out of this."

"Not about Mark. About everything else."

"Ox, I told you. It needs to come from—"

"Gordo."

"Fine." He sounded slightly irritated. It reminded me of the Gordo I'd used to know. "Three questions. And I get to ask the same of you."

My skin itched. "Fine. I'll go first."

He nodded. For some reason, the tattoos on his arms flared.

"Why did you ditch the phones?" I asked.

Gordo stared at me. He obviously hadn't expected that.

I waited.

"Joe thought it'd be easier," he said slowly. "He thought if we cut ties, we could focus on what we needed to. That being reminded of home, of all of you, made things harder."

"And you all went along with it."

"Was that a question?"

"Statement."

"We went along with it. Because he was right. Because of what we had to do. Because every time he picked up that phone, every time we saw a message from you, it became that much harder to not turn around and come right back. We had a job to do, Ox. And we couldn't do it while being reminded of home."

"So instead of letting us know you were okay, that you were alive, you decided—excuse me, *Joe* decided—you'd all be better off keeping us in the dark."

Gordo winced. "Joe said Mark and his mother would know. That they'd still feel—"

I slammed my fist down on the desk. "*I* didn't," I snarled at him. "I didn't feel a *goddamn* thing. And don't you tell me I had them to know, because it wasn't the same."

"You think we wanted this?" he snapped back. "Any of this? Do you think we *asked* to be put in this position?"

"Was that your question?" I said, throwing his own words back at him.

The ghost of a smile, long since deceased. "Why did you tell them?"

Rico. Tanner. Chris. Jessie.

"Because they needed to know," I said. "Because they didn't understand why you'd left them. Because whether you knew it or not, they were your pack too. They needed to understand that they weren't alone, even if you were already gone."

He closed his eyes.

"Why did you come back?" I asked.

"David King."

I frowned. "What about him?"

"What was left of him was found in Idaho."

"What was left," I repeated.

"Pieces, Ox," Gordo said, opening his eyes. "He was found in pieces outside Cottonwood. In a shitty Motel 6. His head was placed in the middle of the bed."

"When?"

"A few weeks back."

"Richard."

"Probably. There was a message written on the wall in his blood. I saw the photos. Four words. *Yet another fallen king.* Joe . . . well. Joe lost it. Just a bit. It had been a long time coming. There were deaths in Washington. Nevada. California."

"All around Oregon," I muttered.

Gordo nodded. "David was the last. It was like Richard was taunting us. Joe. He—We headed home after that. We needed to make sure—" He shook his head. "You need to talk to Joe. He'd tell you that . . . Just talk to him. My turn. When did you become an Alpha?"

Not *how* but *when*, like he knew that it had been only a matter of time. "Omegas came," I said.

"The wards."

"Jessie was outside them. She smelled like us. Like me. They took her. Tanner, Chris, and Rico were already part of us by then. We went to the Omegas. We fought. They lost. The others, they looked to me. And since there was no one else here to lead them, I did what I had to do."

"You always did," he said.

"I'm not a wolf."

"No," he said. "But you're something. Last question."

So many things I needed to ask. About the last three years. About where we stood now. About the state of his mind. If he was the same Gordo he used to be. If that Gordo was dead and buried. If we could ever again be what we'd been to each other.

But there was only one question, really.

"Am I still your tether?"

His eyes widened.

His hands shook.

His bottom lip trembled.

He took a great shuddering breath.

When he spoke, his voice was cracked and wet.

He said, "Yeah, Ox. Yeah. Of course. You always have been. Even when things got dark, even when we were hundreds of miles from home, sleeping on the side of the road, yeah. Even when I was tired and didn't think I could take another step. Even when I found places in my magic I didn't think were possible. Yeah. You were. You are. I thought of you because you're my home. You're my pack too, okay? I don't care if you're an Alpha. I don't care if you're *my* Alpha. You're my pack too."

I nodded, not trusting myself to speak.

He said, "My turn. Ox. *Ox*. Am I still your friend? Because I don't know if I can stand not being your friend. And your brother. Please say that I'm still your brother. Because I need you to be. I need it so bad. I don't know what to do if you're not. Ox, just please say I'm—"

And I put my head down on the desk and cried.

. . .

They found us sometime later, Gordo crouched down at my side, rubbing his forehead against my shoulder, both of us sniffling and wiping our faces.

"Jesus Christ," Tanner muttered.

"It smells like feelings in here," Rico said. "Is that what I would say if I was a werewolf?"

"Are you guys *crying* all over each other?" Chris demanded. "I thought we could still be angry at him! Ox, you traitor!"

I laughed wetly. At the rate I was going, I'd never be a man like my daddy said a man should be. I didn't think that was such a bad thing anymore.

Gordo muttered something darkly, still pressed against me, hand gripping mine. I didn't know that I was ready to let him go just yet.

"*We* can still be mad at him," Tanner said. "Even if Ox caved already."

"Three days, *alfa*," Rico said with a glare. "You lasted three days."

"I'm still going to be mad," Chris said.

"Twenty-five years, we've been friends," Tanner said.

"And you kept this shit from us," Rico said. "*Brujo.*"

"You told us things were just *weird* sometimes," Chris said.

"That your tattoos didn't move," Tanner said. "That we were just crazy."

"Or that when you broke up with Mark, that's all it was," Rico said. "*Just a breakup.*"

"And that your father was in jail for murder," Chris said. "Not that he had murdered people with *magic*."

"In hindsight, it kind of makes sense." Tanner frowned.

"Now that we're saying all this out loud, I feel kind of stupid." Rico scowled.

"Like, why did we even believe him when he disappeared on full moons sometimes?" Chris sighed.

"But we're still mad at you," Tanner said.

"Because you're an asshole," Rico said.

"The biggest asshole," Chris said.

They crossed their arms over their chests and glared at Gordo.

"I missed you guys," Gordo said hoarsely. "More than you could possibly know."

"Goddammit," Tanner said.

"*Mierda*," Rico said.

"We need to hug now," Chris said.

And they piled on top of us.

. . .

I walked home that night.

The stars shone overhead.

I reached the dirt road that led to the house at the end of the lane.

Joe was there.

I hadn't seen him since the first day.

He was dressed normally now. A pair of jeans. A soft sweater.

He'd shaved the beard off. I saw the boy in him that he'd once been.

Barely, but he was still there.

Just . . . more, now.

He wasn't the seventeen-year-old boy he'd been.

Bigger. Stronger. A man. An Alpha.

He didn't say anything as I approached.

We were the same height now. I was sure of it.

I wondered how big his wolf was now. If he shifted and looked like his father.

I had so many questions.

But I couldn't.

I said, "Not yet," knowing full well that it would burn.

He flinched but didn't speak.

I walked by him without stopping.

. . . .

Two days later, Carter and Kelly kidnapped me.

Technically.

I came out of the diner after I'd finished up a sandwich for lunch. Before I could even take a step to cross the street back to the garage, a familiar SUV squealed to a stop in front of me. I barely had a chance to react before the passenger door was thrown open and two wolves glared at me.

"Get in," Carter said.

"Or what?" I said.

"Or we'll make you," Kelly said.

"Really. You want to try that again?"

"Sure," Carter said. "Get in *now*."

"Before we drag your ass along," Kelly said.

I contemplated walking away.

"Fucking werewolves," I muttered.

I got in the SUV.

They looked surprised when they turned back to stare at me.

"Well?" I asked, arching an eyebrow.

"I didn't think that would actually work," Carter said.

"Seriously," Kelly said with a frown. "I thought there'd be a lot more posturing."

I shrugged. "I don't know what that is."

"He means he thought we'd actually have to drag your ass," Carter said.

*   *   *

"Oh. So you were going to kidnap me—"

"Not *kidnap*. You can't *kidnap* someone your size, what the fuck—"

"—*kidnap* me, and what? Sit here and stare?" I shook my head. "Jesus, how the hell did you guys survive this long on your own?"

They glared at me.

I glared right back and felt something settle in my chest. Like a crack filled.

I gave them an out. "Right. So. I have work to do. If we could get this started, so it'll be finished?"

"You're not going back to work," Kelly said. "Not today."

"Gordo's already there," Carter said, turning back around and pulling away from the curb. "Decided now would be a good time to get back to the shop. Lucky us, because now we have all the time in the world."

"Did he?" I asked, unsure whether to be amused or irritated. A little of both seemed right. "Seemed he forgot to mention that to me." Probably for good reason, too. While we were on the mend, I don't know if I'd have agreed to this had I known ahead of time. And I think everyone knew that. I was a stubborn ass when I needed to be.

"Well, the shop *is* called *Gordo's*," Carter said. "I'm sure he didn't think he had to."

"He'll probably need to relearn a few things," I said. "Three years is a long time to be away."

They both winced at that.

"He's been doing it for years," Carter muttered.

"It's not like he would have forgotten," Kelly mumbled. "It wasn't *that* lo—"

"Don't," I said, my voice deeper than it normally was. "Don't you *dare* say it wasn't that long. You have no idea what it was like here. So don't you say that."

The rest of the trip was silent.

*   *   *

I was surprised when the SUV stopped and I found we were out by the old covered bridge. It was in the middle of the day on a weekday, so we were alone. Carter got out first, slamming the door behind him. We watched as he paced in front of the SUV, glaring at the bridge. He was growling, something I could hear even though the windows weren't rolled down.

"We can smell them," Kelly said. The Omegas.

"There was a lot of blood."

Kelly watched his brother. "Mark told us. Not everything. Some parts. Said the rest needed to come from you. Joe wasn't too happy about that."

I snorted. "I don't expect he was."

"It was hard for him. For all of us."

"Just as hard for us who were left behind."

"We didn't want to leave."

"You did."

"Joe . . . no. That's not fair. We all made the same choice. He didn't make us." Kelly sighed. "I can smell your blood too. Here. And my mother's."

"It happens when you're fighting against fang and claw."

"Do you understand?"

"What?" I asked, watching Carter as he stalked the area where we'd fought, stopping every now and then to glare at the dirt.

"Why we made the choices we made."

I could lie, but he would know. They both would, because I knew Carter was listening in.

"No," I said, "I don't. You kept shit from me. After. You acted like I wasn't a part of this. A part of you. You made decisions without me."

"You'd just lost your mother—"

"So you all decided the best thing was for me to lose the rest of you too?" I asked. "Because that's what happened. I lost my mother. And my Alpha. And then my brothers and my . . . Joe. That's what I lost. Because you all decided to—"

"We just wanted to keep you safe," Kelly said, frustration bleeding through. "I know you don't like it, but I sure as hell hope you can understand at least that."

I laughed. "Understand? Sure. Why not. Do you understand why I'm so angry I can barely think straight? Do you understand why just the sight of you makes me happy and sick all at the same time? That I don't know whether or not to hug you or kick your fucking ass?"

He bowed his head.

"Of course you don't. Because you chose the path of least resistance. All you could think about, all *he* could think about, was revenge. Not the consequences of staying here. Of dealing with the grief of losing pack. Of losing your goddamned *Alpha*. And since the *new* Alpha made this decision that you all went right along with, we were forced to make good with all we had left. So yes. There is blood here. *My* blood. And your mother's. And Mark's. And every single other person in *my* pack. Because they bled here. For me. For you. And for *him*."

Carter had stopped, hands fisted at his sides, shoulders tensed. Listening.

"We tried," Kelly said in a broken voice. "We wanted . . . Just . . . There wasn't a day that went by, Ox. Okay? That we didn't think of you. That we didn't wish we were home with you. And Mom. And Mark. I know you lost your mother, Ox. And we lost our father, but when we . . . when we left, it was the hardest thing we ever had to do. You think we didn't grieve? We did. We grieved for our father. For our *Alpha*. But it was nothing compared to the grief of leaving you all behind."

"You should have come home."

"We should have."

"You shouldn't have cut us off."

Kelly reached up and wiped his eyes. "Yeah," he said. "I know. But I also know why we did. Gordo, he . . . uh. He fought against that. Said it was stupid. That you . . . you wouldn't understand. But it was different. For us. For the wolves. Because we were all tethered to you then, Ox, okay? And it hurt. It *hurt*. And we couldn't do what we needed to do by being tied to you. By seeing your words on his phone. By—"

"Was it worth it?"

He looked out the window at his brother. "Some days, I think it was. Some days, I don't. Most days, I don't know what to think. Because I don't know how we fit. You can feel it, can't you?"

He opened the door and got out.

I watched them both through the window.

Kelly went and stood next to his brother, shoulder to shoulder.

Carter looked tense. They both did.

I thought maybe they could be mistaken for twins now, not just because of how they looked, but because they both wore the same haunted expression. Because of the way they wore their guilt.

It had hurt when they'd left.

When my mother had died. When Thomas had died.

But we'd grieved. For them. For all of them.

And it *still* hurt. But maybe not as sharply as it had before.

They hadn't gotten that.

Because they'd been *surrounded* by it. By Richard Collins, and all that they'd done.

They'd made their choices, yes.

Whether by family or obligation.

And they'd never had a chance to stop. To rest. To mourn everything they'd lost.

It hurt my heart.

I followed them out.

They looked up at me as I walked slowly toward them.

"I don't know how to forgive you," I admitted. "To forgive Joe."

"You forgave Gordo," Carter said, sounding bitter. "That seemed easy enough."

"I didn't forgive him for shit. Just because I talked to him doesn't mean anything. Trust me, he's in no different position than any of you."

"I would do it again," Carter said.

Kelly made a strangled noise.

"Would you?" I asked.

"If it all happened again, if we had to do every single thing again, I would." He was defiant. Angry. Scared.

"Why?"

"Because we had to go."

"You could have taken me too."

Carter looked frustrated. "You don't understand."

"I think we've established that."

"Dad knew."

Kelly said, "*Carter.*"

Carter ignored him. He kept his gaze on me.

I glanced between them. Then, "Knew what?"

"He didn't say it. Not in so many words. Not straight out."

Kelly said, "Carter, maybe he should hear this from—"

Carter said, "He told us to protect you. That you were special. That you were different. That if something ever happened to him, we needed to make sure you were safe. Just like we would keep Mom safe. Because you were *important*. But it was different with you."

I felt gut-punched. My heart was breaking all over again.

"And something *did* happen to him. He *died*. And Joe became our Alpha. And all he could think about was stopping this once and for all. All *we* could think about was keeping you safe. Because if Osmond knew what you were, then Richard did too. And if Richard knew, then you *weren't* safe."

"So you left," I said.

"Maybe not the best choice," he said. "But it was the *only* choice."

"It sure as hell *wasn't*," I snapped at him. "You could have—"

"We left to end this. To draw attention away from you and find him ourselves," Carter said. "We left to keep you safe, and by warding you in, we hoped we could keep the others out. We did our *best*, Ox. Was it the right thing to do? I don't know. But I would do it again if it meant keeping you safe. Because I don't think any of us were surprised to come back and see what you'd become. I think Dad knew before all of us that this is who you would be. You made a *pack*, Ox, out of *humans*. No one could have done that but you. I'm sorry we left. I'm sorry you felt like we'd abandoned you. I'm sorry we didn't tell you any of this. But you are my *brother*. You are Kelly's *brother*. We would do *anything* for you."

"You can't leave again," I said, voice rough. "Not again. You can't. You would do anything for me? Good. Fine. Don't leave."

Carter and Kelly exchanged a look before shrugging almost in unison.

"Sure," Carter said.

"Fine," Kelly said.

I stared at them. "That's it?"

They tackled me even before I knew what was happening.

     .   .

We lay tangled on the ground, Kelly with his head on my stomach, rising with every breath I took. Carter clung to my arm and hand, palm to palm, fingers gripped tight.

The anger was melting away.

I struggled to hold onto it, because I thought it was too easy to let it go.

That there should be more to it than this.

But it was green in its relief.

I hadn't forgiven them—Gordo, the two wolves curled against me—but I would. Not today, and probably not tomorrow.

But eventually.

Joe, though. I didn't know about him. Everything was wrapped up in him. It didn't seem fair that I could find forgiveness in the others but not in him.

Kelly sighed and buried his face against my chest, rubbing his nose back and forth.

"Okay," Carter said. "I gotta ask, just because someone has to."

That didn't sound good.

"Jessie," Carter said.

"Oh," I said. "What about her?"

"You banging her?" Carter asked.

"Banging," I repeated.

"You smell like her," Kelly said.

"I smell like your mother too, I'm sure."

They both scowled at me.

"Holy shit, that's not what I meant! Jesus, don't tell her I said that. And no, fuck, I'm not *banging* Jessie. There hasn't been anything between us in a very long time. She had a date the other night. With a history teacher."

"So you didn't bang her while we were gone?"

"Stop saying *banging*!"

"Seriously, Carter," Kelly said. "That's gross." Then, "Are you banging Robbie?"

"Oh my god," I muttered.

"That's not a no."

"*No.*"

"He's protective of you," Carter said.

"I'm his Alpha."

"Seemed a little more than that," Kelly said.

"I hate you both."

"Still not a no."

"It's not . . . Look. It's—"

"He has a crush on you!" Carter said, sounding rather gleeful at the prospect.

"It's not a *crush*—"

"Dude," Kelly said. "You didn't build a pack. You built a *harem*."

"Kelly!" Carter yelped. "Mom is in his harem!"

Kelly paled. "Oh my god. And Mark."

"Working your way through the whole family, eh, Ox?" Carter said. "You kissed me first and it couldn't quench your insatiable thirst for Bennett."

"At least you're both still idiots," I muttered.

They laughed at me.

It was a nice sound, even if it hurt to hear it after so long.

"Joe's not a fan," Carter said easily.

"Of?"

"Jessie being in your pack. But mostly Robbie. That was quite the statement he made when we got back, his hand on you. Like he was keeping you calm."

"He was."

"Well, shit," Kelly said. "That's not going to go over well."

"What isn't?" I asked.

"Robbie," Carter said, as if I was stupid. "He's your tether."

"I'm not a wolf."

"You're an Alpha," Carter pointed out. "I don't know that it matters."

"You feel just like we do, just without the change," Kelly said. "It's close enough. He keeps you grounded."

"Joe has no right to be pissed about that," I growled. "He doesn't get a say."

Carter and Kelly tensed.

Carter said, "He's just—"

"No," I said. "I don't have to explain anything to him. Not yet. And even if Robbie was my tether, I don't have to justify myself to him. Or to you. You were *gone*. You cut us *out*. You say it was to keep us safe, and you say you would do the same thing again. That's *fine*. But don't expect to come back here and have things be the way you left them. We did what we had to do in order to survive because that's now how life works. We don't put ourselves on hold because *you*—"

"No one asked you to," Carter said, gripping my hand tightly. "And I don't know that we expected you to. But I know Joe. He hoped, Ox. Even if he never said anything, even if he turned into a broody Alpha asshole, he hoped. I know he did. So cut him some slack since you've moved on from—"

I sat up, knocking the two wolves off me. "Moved on?"

Kelly and Carter exchanged another of their looks. "With Robbie," Carter said slowly.

"There is *nothing* between me and Robbie. Sure, I mean, he *kissed* me. Oh, for fuck's sake, stop *growling*. I told him no, okay? And he *understands*. It's not like that between us. It won't ever be, for me."

"Because of Joe," Carter said, far too smug.

I said, "*Not* because of Joe," and they both grinned when they heard the lie.

"You need to fix this," Carter said.

"You need to go fuck yourself," I said.

Kelly squinted at me. "Does being an Alpha automatically make you a douchebag? Because between you and Joe—"

I punched him in the shoulder. Hard.

He laughed at me and pushed me back down so he could lie on me again. I didn't fight it. I didn't want to fight it.

Carter moved closer so his head was in the crook of my arm.

It didn't feel like giving up. It felt green. The both of them.

I didn't know what to do about Joe.

I said, "It's not just him."

They waited.

I tried to find the right words. "Robbie. It's all of them. It's the pack. They're my tether."

Silence.

Then Carter said, "Like it was for Dad."

"That's how it always was for him," Kelly said. "Always pack."

I touched their arms. Their shoulders. Their necks. Their faces. They leaned into the touch and all I thought was *packpackpack*.

As the sun began to set, I asked, "Do you really think he knew?"

"Who?"

"Your dad. About me."

"Yeah, Ox. We think he knew. I think maybe we all did."

They dropped me off back at the shop.

Gordo was the only one still there.

It was strange, seeing him sitting behind his desk again.

He said, "It was their idea."

I snorted and leaned against the doorframe. "Throwing them under the bus?"

He shrugged. "They'll survive."

"How's it feel? Being back."

He ran his hands over my—his—desk. "Like I've been gone too long."

"Sounds about right."

"Tanner let me back into my house. He had the keys."

"We cleaned it. Once a month or so. Making sure it was good for when you came back."

"Did you?"

"Yes."

"You said when."

"What?"

"You said *when* I came back. Not *if.*"

"Oh. I guess."

"Did you think . . . ?"

I looked away. "Maybe. I hoped."

Gordo cleared his throat. "It felt weird, standing in there. Like I didn't remember how I'd got there. Like I was dreaming."

I knew about dreaming. "That's how I feel anytime I step back into the old house. Like . . . I'm not awake. Like it's not real. But it is. It'll take some time, before it's real again for you."

"Is it real for you?"

"Most of the time," I said honestly.

We were quiet for a little while.

He said, "Joe patrols at night. For hours."

"I know."

He drummed his fingers on the desk. "Of course you would. Because you can feel it now. Like he can. Maybe even better. You knew, didn't you? The second we stepped back into Green Creek."

I nodded. "You touched your wards. To see that they were still up."

"I don't understand how this is possible."

"I don't either." I didn't know if we ever would. It seemed odd to be considered a strange thing among people who could change into wolves on a whim.

"You need to talk to him."

"Are you saying that as my friend? Or as his witch?"

He stiffened slightly. "Does it matter?"

"I don't know."

"What *do* you know?"

"I was yours first." I smiled. "Though I think Mark would disagree with that."

He glared at me.

I stared right back.

He looked away first. "Then Joe probably would too."

And he had me there. "For which one of us?" I countered.

"You going to fix this?" he asked, ignoring my question.

"You've been home for less than a week," I said, "after three years. Things change."

"We noticed."

"Meaning?"

"Meaning we came back and you had your own pack. With people we didn't know. It sucked, Ox."

"I made do with what I had. You left us in pieces. I had to try and put us back together. You don't get to blame us for anything. Not after what you did. All of you."

"And you did good, kiddo," he said. "It's just going to take a while to get used to it all again. We don't blame you, Ox. None of us do. You made the choices you had to, and no one can fault you for that."

I almost believed him.

      . . . .

I turned down his offer for a ride.

I walked home.

Joe was waiting again in the shadows on the dirt road.

I couldn't do this now. I'd already been through too much today.

I made to walk past him again and—

He reached out and grabbed my arm, stopping me.

His nostrils flared.

"My brothers," he said. "And Gordo."

I said nothing.

"You can't do this," he growled. "With them. And not with me. Not forever."

"Not yet," I spat out.

He let me go.

I didn't look back as I walked away, though every step was harder than the one before it.

.　.　.

That night I ran along the edges of the territory, making sure we were safe.

Thomas said, *You're different, Ox. I don't think even I know how different. It will be truly a sight to behold. And I, for one, can't wait to see it.*

My mother popped a soap bubble on my ear.

Somewhere on the other side of the territory, a wolf sang a song for all the forest to hear.

It was blue, everything about it was *blue*.

HOWLED FOR YOU / ALWAYS BEEN MINE

How would this work?" I asked Mark and Elizabeth. It was seven days since the others had returned and one day before the full moon. We walked through the woods, brushing our hands against the trees, leaving our scent on the bark. They'd chosen not to shift, knowing I needed advice.

"What would that be?" Mark asked.

I rolled my eyes. "You know."

"Maybe, but it helps to hear you say it," Elizabeth said.

I held back the retort and just said, "Joe."

"Between the two of you?" Mark asked.

"No. Well, yes, that too. But that's not what I meant. Between all of us."

Mark chuckled. "Of course that's what you'd be thinking of. Everyone else but yourself."

"It's my job," I said.

"That may be," Elizabeth said, "but there's a time to be selfish, Ox."

"I can't," I admitted. "Not yet." I hated those two words more than anything.

"You're angry still," she said, touching my arm.

"It's not something I can just get over."

"But you have already," Mark said. "With Gordo. Carter. Kelly. Maybe not completely, but you've started."

"And?" I asked, trying to play dumb. "That has nothing to do with—"

"Why should Joe be any different?"

"Because *he* is different." It was petty, but I didn't like feeling cornered. "He's not the same to me as everyone else."

And they knew that. But they'd also talked to him since I'd been back. Every day. They went back and forth between the old house and the main house. They spent the day with him while I was at work with the rest of my pack. They hugged him, they touched him, they listened to him breathe. They didn't wake up from nightmares where Joe was gone again, that he hadn't said anything, he'd just been *gone* like he never was at all.

"You're not dreaming, Ox," Elizabeth said quietly, and again I wondered just how connected we all were. Because sometimes I thought they were always in my head. "I know it seems like you are. The edges are fuzzy and you can't quite make sense of what's happening, but I promise you, this isn't a dream."

"What do you talk about?" I asked, not looking at either of them. "When I'm not there."

Mark sighed. "Not much. Carter and Kelly do most of the talking. Joe . . . doesn't say very much."

I felt guilty at that, even though I didn't know if I should have. Apparently, he'd been like that for a long time now. I didn't know what else had changed. I didn't know how to ask.

"I have to let this go," I said. "But I don't know how. I've tried. I have. It's killing me to know he's *right there* and I'm not doing anything about it."

"Then *do* something," Elizabeth said. "You've never been indecisive before, Ox. Don't start now."

I snorted. "That's bullshit. There's plenty of times I haven't been able to make a choice."

She slapped me upside the head, and I glared at her. "Fix this," she said. "Before I lose all my patience and take care of it myself. You don't want that to happen."

"You really don't," Mark said. "She'll become like a little gnat, always buzzing in your—"

"Don't even get me started on you," Elizabeth said. "You're in the same boat, Mark, I swear to God. You just wait until this is finished, and I'm going to start on—"

Mark raised his hands in surrender. "Hey, all right. All right. I hear you."

"Either end it or don't," Elizabeth said to me after glaring at her brother-in-law. "Forgive him or don't. Just don't make him wait. It's not fair. To either of you. Men. Useless. All you do is make things difficult just because you can."

"Could a pack have two Alphas?" I asked, trying to distract them.

She narrowed her eyes at me, knowing what I was doing. But she allowed it. "Who's to say we couldn't? We already have a human Alpha. We're not exactly orthodox here. We never really have been, even when we were supposed to be. There's tradition, and then there are the Bennetts."

I was still learning that. "And if I say no," I said slowly. "If I rejected him. If I kept the packs separate."

"It would be your choice," Elizabeth said. "And we would know you thought you were making the right one."

"But you wouldn't agree."

"Maybe," Mark said. "Maybe not. But it's not about that. You have . . . instincts we don't."

"I could say the same about you."

"True," he said. "But our instinct is to trust you to make the right decision for the pack."

"Even if you disagree?"

"Even then."

"That feels like I'm controlling you. That you're not getting a choice in this."

"We are," Mark said kindly. "We chose you."

"They're your sons. Your nephews."

"And you're our Alpha," Elizabeth said, eyes flaring orange. "This is the way things are."

This wasn't how I wanted things to be. "I don't want to come between you."

"You couldn't, even if you tried," she said.

And that was that.

. . . .

He was waiting for me on the dirt road.

Looking hopeful. Scared. Angry. Tense.

Because I'd talked to all of them except him, and he knew that.

I was tired. Of all of this. Something had to give. And it needed to come from me.

I just needed to find the words.

I reached him, and I *knew* he thought I was going to walk by, maybe say *not yet* again, throwing those words into his face like I'd been doing since he'd come home.

His shoulders were already starting to slump.

So I said, "Hey, Joe," and hoped it was a start.

He was startled. He opened and closed his mouth a few times. He made a growling noise deep in his chest, a low rumble that made my skin itch. It was pleasure, that sound, like even just me saying his name was enough to make him happy. For all I knew, it was.

It cut off as quickly as it had started. He looked faintly embarrassed.

I scuffed my foot in the dirt, waiting.

He said, "Hey, Ox." He cleared his throat and looked down. "Hi."

It was weird, that disconnect between the boy I'd known and the man before me. His voice was deeper and he was bigger than he'd ever been. He radiated power that had never been there before. It fit him well. I remembered that day when I'd really seen him for the first time, wearing those running shorts and little else.

I pushed those thoughts away. I didn't want him sniffing me out. Not yet. Because attraction wasn't the problem right now. Especially not right now.

I cleared my throat, and he looked back up at me.

Our eyes met like a car crash, colliding and breaking away.

It was awkward in a way it'd never been before.

But it was *something*. More than we'd had in a very long time. I couldn't help but think of the single kiss we'd shared, the driest brush of his lips against mine as we'd lain side by side. *I will come back for you*, he'd said, and hadn't I believed him? Hadn't I believed every single thing he'd told me?

I had.

And he had come back. Like he said he would.

It'd just taken longer than we thought.

"You—" he said as I said, "There's—"

We stopped.

He coughed. "You first."

I nodded, because it had to be me. "Tomorrow. It's the full moon."

"Yeah? I guess it is." He knew, but he was humoring me.

"What are you doing for it?"

He shrugged and scratched the back of his neck. "Hadn't really thought about it."

Which I thought was possibly a lie.

"If you're not busy, we could . . . run. Your pack. And mine."

He looked surprised. "You'd do that?"

"You were here first, Joe. It's your land."

"But it's—"

"Just . . . Will you do it?"

He nodded furiously. "Yes. Yeah. I can. *We* can. It'll be—"

"Good," I said. "It'll be good."

And I didn't know what else to say after that, because I had *too* much to say.

So I said nothing at all.

We stared at each other for a little while. Taking each other in. I tried to force myself to take a step closer to him, just to . . . *be*. But I couldn't.

"Okay," I said finally. "Tomorrow, then."

He frowned as I moved to walk around him down the dirt road to the old house.

"Ox," he said quietly as we were shoulder to shoulder.

I held my breath and waited.

"Are we—" He stopped. Shook his head. Let out a frustrated groan. "We have to talk. About everything I need you to know. Everything. There are things you have to hear. From me. I need you to . . . just . . . I need you."

I tried to ignore the heat along my skin to focus on what was important. "Is he coming?"

He knew who I meant. "I think so."

"Are we safe for now?"

"Yeah. Yes. It can wait a few days. But—"

"Then the rest of it can wait too."

"Ox."

I said nothing.

He sighed. "Okay."

Somehow I was able to walk away.

. . . .

The sky was darkening the next day when my pack gathered at the old house, standing in the kitchen. I still avoided the living room whenever possible. Elizabeth and Mark still slept in the house at the end of the lane, but Robbie had moved back to the old house, taking over the spare bedroom, knowing Mom's room was off limits. Apparently, him being there didn't sit well with Carter and Kelly, and they told me as much. I didn't know what Joe thought.

"Are you sure about this?" Robbie asked me. "We don't even *know* them."

"I'd like to think I do," Elizabeth said lightly. "I gave birth to most of them."

Robbie grimaced slightly. "Sorry."

"For giving birth?" she teased.

He blushed and mumbled something incoherent.

"He's got a point," Jessie said. "Full moons with you are different. We know these wolves. Most of the humans here don't know them. Are you sure they're in control enough? Have you even seen them shift since they've been here?"

I hadn't and said as much.

"They broke away," she said. "How is that different from them being Omegas?"

"They had an Alpha," Mark said. "They still do. They may not have . . . been here, but they still had an Alpha to draw strength from. They tethered themselves to him."

"Just as long as there are no wolves gnawing on my ass, I'm okay," Rico said.

"Succinct as usual," Tanner said, smacking him upside the back of the head.

"*Pendejo*," Rico muttered.

"No one is gnawing on anything," I said.

"Really?" Chris said innocently. "I'm sure Joe's going to be disappointed to hear that."

I glared at him as most everyone in the room snickered at that.

"We're going to be fine," I said, trying to get the conversation back on track. "We'll run with them, there will be no gnawing on anyone—Chris, keep your mouth shut—and we'll figure this out. Okay?"

They nodded.

"Okay," I said.

This was going to be fine.

.   .   .

It was not fine.

It *had* been fine, for the most part.

When we arrived at the clearing, the moon was rising and Joe and his pack were already there. The eyes of the wolves were flashing at the pull of the moon. Gordo's tattoos were glowing, and I realized this was the first time I'd ever seen him as part of a pack on a full moon. It hurt dully to think he'd been a part of something for so long and I hadn't been there to see it. There hadn't been enough time to ask him about it after everything had happened.

Like they did when they first came back, they all moved together, watching us as we walked into the clearing. I was sure that if I were a wolf, I would have heard their hearts beating in sync.

It felt tense as we approached, a little bit off, but I didn't think it was too bad.

It might have been wishful thinking.

"Ox," Joe said, but not before his gaze flickered over my right shoulder, where I knew Robbie stood.

"Joe," I said.

"Thank you for allowing us to join you tonight."

I nodded, hating how formal this was. "Thank you for being here."

"Oh my god," Rico muttered. "They are so awkward."

"Shut up," Tanner hissed. "They're *werewolves*. They can *hear* you."

"I *know* what they are. Stop whisper-shouting at me!"

"They are really awkward, though," Chris whispered.

"They were always like that," Jessie mumbled under her breath.

If I hadn't been watching Joe, I would have missed the way his lips quirked for just a second, like he was fighting back a smile.

"This is my pack," I said, trying not to snarl at all of them.

"And this is mine," Joe said.

Carter and Kelly were snickering to each other. Gordo looked like he was ready to roll his eyes.

"Shall we run?" Joe asked.

"We can," I said.

"And here comes the part where really attractive people get naked," Rico said. "And most of them are related. Which isn't weird. At all."

"Rico," I said.

"Yes?"

"Shut. *Up*."

"It's *weird*. Just because *you* don't see it as weird doesn't mean it's not."

"Talking about it doesn't make it any *less* weird."

"I feel like we should at least *address* the weirdness—"

"Rico!"

"Shutting up now."

Carter and Kelly had already disrobed by the time Rico had closed his mouth. Carter winked at me before he shifted, the familiar snap of bone and muscle loud in the clearing. Kelly followed quickly, and then there were two wolves standing in the moonlight, eyes orange and teeth bared in canine smiles.

They weren't all that much different than they'd been years before. Same coloring as they'd always been. But they were bigger and heavier. They would never be as big as Thomas had been, but they had grown noticeably. I didn't know if that had to do with age or Joe. Probably both.

Mark and Elizabeth followed suit, Rico muttering about everyone being way too calm with the nudity and Chris calling him a prude.

Soon, there were four wolves in the clearing, and they rubbed up against each other, Carter and Kelly crowding on either side of their mother, wriggling excitedly like puppies.

"Go ahead, Robbie," I said, feeling Joe's eyes on me.

"I don't have to," he said through a mouthful of sharpened teeth. "I can stay with you. I can run like this. Or half-shift. It's fine."

But it wasn't fine. I knew the moon was pulling at him, his wolf clawing just under the surface to break free. Mark had told me once a long time ago that it physically *hurt* not to change with the moon, and that if a werewolf denied it for too long over too many moons, it could cause a mental break.

"It's fine," I said lightly. "You should get used to the others."

He didn't look happy about that, glancing between Joe and me. He let out a huff and started stripping. I averted my eyes as a courtesy.

Joe was still watching me with a blank look. He didn't use to be able to do that. I hated it.

Robbie shifted somewhere behind me. He was ganglier than the others and smaller, with long, thin legs and a narrow body. His tail twitched as he came to stand next to me, watching the wolves from his pack mingle with wolves from another pack.

He looked tense and unsure. I ran my hands over his head, tugging gently on one of his ears. He nuzzled into my hand and I felt a pulse of warmth along the thread that stretched between us.

"Go on," I said.

And I thought he would. I thought he'd join the other wolves, but instead he turned back to the humans behind us and started rubbing up against their legs, snapping playfully at their heels to get them moving toward the trees to run through the woods.

Then it was just Joe and me, listening as the wolves sang and the humans hollered.

He spoke first.

He said, "You did good, Ox."

I didn't know what to do with that, so I just said, "Thanks." But that didn't sit right, so I added, "It wasn't just me."

"Oh?"

"It was all of us. They did as much for me as I did for them."

"I know. That's what pack does."

I bit back the retort and pushed away the familiar curl of anger. Joe probably knew it, could probably taste the bright spark of rage before I caught it, but he didn't say anything about it.

Instead, he said, "But don't think it wasn't you, Ox. If it wasn't for you . . ."

I waited to see if he would continue.

"Ox."

I looked over at him. He was closer to me than he'd been in over three years. I didn't understand why it felt like he was still so far away.

"Thank you," he said.

"For what?"

"For doing what I couldn't."

I shouldn't have had to! I wanted to shout at him.

You shouldn't have put me in this position!

You left us. You left me.

"I didn't have a choice," I said instead.

He snorted, eyes bleeding red. "You always had a choice, Ox. And you still chose us. You always did."

"That's what pack does," I said, throwing his words back at him.

He smiled at me. He had many teeth.

"Are you going to shift?" I asked, suddenly feeling very warm.

He took a step toward me.

My feet wouldn't move.

Another step. And then another.

He stopped within arm's reach but didn't move to touch me. It was odd, knowing I didn't have to look down to meet his eyes anymore.

"When I was gone," he said, playing with the hem of his shirt, "when *we* were gone, every day was hard."

I watched his fingers as he started to tug on his shirt, pulling it up.

"But the full moons were the hardest," he said, and there were *miles* of skin. He wasn't a little boy anymore, or even a teenager stumbling in his father's footsteps. No, he was a man now, and an Alpha. And it showed in the cut of the muscles in his stomach. The breadth of his chest, and the way it was covered with a smattering of lightly colored hair. The way his biceps bunched as he pulled the shirt up and over his head before dropping it to the ground beside him. "They were the hardest," he said, "because I would be howling for my pack and only some of them heard me. Only some of them howled back."

His hands moved toward the fly of his jeans, fingers trailing along his waist, curling into the hair on his stomach. He lifted one foot behind the other, toeing at his boot. It slid off and he pushed it to the side. "I was howling for you," he said quietly as he slid off his other boot. "Even if you didn't hear me, even if you couldn't feel it, Ox, I swear I howled for you."

He unbuttoned the top button of his jeans, and I told myself to look away. I told myself this wasn't right. That I was still so angry at him that I could barely stand it, that we had so fucking much to talk about to even see *if* we could get back to the way we once were. Or even close to it.

He knew what he was doing to me.

And for a moment, I hated him for manipulating me like that.

But if I thought about it, *really* thought about it, I didn't think he'd do something like that. Use his own body to get what he wanted. Granted, I didn't know this Joe. I didn't know what he'd done while he was away. How many people he'd fucked, if he'd fucked anyone at all. He was innocent and kind, the boy I once knew. I tried to fit him with the man before me, tried to reconcile the differences between the two.

The second button was undone, then the third.

I didn't think he'd be wearing underwear, and the moon was bright enough to see his pubic hair, the base of his dick.

I looked back up at his face.

The blank look was gone, the mask of the Alpha slipped and discarded, even though his eyes still burned red.

He looked younger, almost. Softer. Unsure of himself.

He said, "There was never anyone else the entire time I was gone. There was never anyone else for me. Because even if you couldn't hear me when I called for you, the howl in my heart was always meant for you."

I wanted to tell him to get out of my head, because *somehow* he'd known what I was thinking. He shouldn't have been able to see that. To hear that. To *know* that.

I wanted to tell him I hadn't been with anyone else either.

That I had waited. And waited. And *waited* for him until I thought my skin would break apart and my bones would turn to so much dust. That I did what I had to do to keep us *alive*, that even though we had become something more than what the pieces of us should have made, there was an ache in my head and a hole in my heart and it was because of *him*. He'd done this to me.

He hadn't fucked anyone else?

Well, good for him.

I didn't even *think* about it.

There was a yip in the trees, louder than the others.

I looked over.

Robbie stood at the tree line, watching me, head cocked in question.

"He cares about you," Joe said from behind me.

"I'm his Alpha."

"Sure, Ox," Joe said, and I knew from the sound of it that he'd stepped out of his jeans. I told myself not to turn around. I'd already seen too much and I wasn't going to break down that easily, even if he was all I'd ever really wanted.

Robbie yipped again and turned back toward the forest.

"We still need to talk," Joe said, and he was *right behind me*.

I closed my eyes but I could still feel the heat of him. His breath on my neck. All I had to do was lean back and—

I took a step forward.

"We will," I said. "Tomorrow." Because I didn't think I could go another day like this. It was choking me, and I was struggling to breathe through it.

"Tomorrow," he said, and it came out like he was acknowledging a promise I didn't know I'd made.

He shifted behind me.

The sound of it seemed to go on forever.

There was that heat behind me still, but it was different now.

Something pressed against the middle of my back.

His nose, from the feel of it.

He took in a long, slow breath.

Exhaled low and hot.

Something tugged near the back of my head, buried in the bonds of my pack.

I thought to reach out for it. To test it. To taste it.

But before I could, the Alpha wolf circled me.

And my breath was knocked from my chest.

He was big. Bigger than Thomas had ever been. The top of his head reached almost to my neck. He was still completely white aside from his nose and paws. His lips and his claws. And his eyes, which were like fire. I wondered if this was how my mother had felt that first time, when Thomas had shown her that she would never be alone again.

And like he could hear every single thought in my head, Joe leaned up and pressed his nose to my neck and I said, "*Oh.*"

. . .

It started out fine.

Mostly.

I felt like I was caught in freefall, my stomach swooping up in my chest to the back of my throat. I felt like I was stuck in that moment when you miss the last step and land hard on your foot.

We ran in the woods.

Through the trees, jumping over logs and creeks, our feet splashing in the water when we didn't make it far enough.

The wolves were howling around me, but it was off, the harmonies too far off key to be really singing together.

My wolves sang like they always did, in time and in sync.

Joe and his wolves did the same, but a step above or below mine.

It grated, the mixing of the two, but there was something *there.* Something that was *thrumming* just below the surface. It crawled along my skin, and I ran toward it, to escape from it.

The humans laughed as the wolves chased them.

Gordo hung back, mostly watching, eyes on the perimeter, arms alight as his tattoos fluttered and flew.

I thought we were close to something as we moved in the forest.

Something that was just out of reach.

Joe ran at my side, the muscles under his white coat moving like water. Like smoke, fluid and rippling.

I wasn't a wolf. I didn't think I'd ever *be* a wolf. I didn't feel the pull of the moon.

But I felt different now.

I wanted to howl out a song. I wanted to sprout claws and fangs and tear into the flesh of a rabbit. I wanted my eyes to burst red, to feel the grass on my paws.

There were thoughts, some my own, some coming from all directions.

They said, *PackLoveBrotherSon* and *safe here we are safe here* and *together oh my god we're together we run together* and *home we're finally home look here this tree i know this tree* and *he's gone FatherHusbandAlpha he's gone but i can still feel him i can still smell him i can still love him* and so much more. It was all of them at once, the wolves, and maybe the humans of my pack. They were skittering along my thoughts, tying themselves to me and each other, the threads tangling.

But it was the wolf who ran with me that I heard the most.

He said, *here.*

He said, *i'm here.*

He said, *with you finally with you.*

He said, *i can feel you.*

He said, *i know you can feel me.*

He said, *that little voice at the back of your head that little tug you feel that you've always felt that has never left you has always been me it's always been me because you've always been mine i gave you my wolf because you are pack pack pack you are mate you are you are you are—*

We were so distracted, running under this euphoric high, this fever dream that couldn't have possibly been real, that we didn't see him coming. One second Joe and I were side by side, and the next there was a flash of gray and black in front of me and Joe was knocked off his feet onto his side.

The fever broke.

There was loud snarling, a snapping of teeth.

I kept running for five steps before I remembered I had to stop.

I turned and—

Robbie was on top of Joe, teeth buried in his throat. Joe was kicking up at him, the claws on his back legs shredding into Robbie's sides, his stomach.

There was an angry roar behind me as Carter and Kelly burst out from the trees. Robbie let out a high-pitched whine as Joe got in a vicious kick, knocking him off and into a tree.

Elizabeth and Mark came from the other direction, eyes orange and teeth bared. They stood in front of Robbie as he tried to pick himself up, blood dripping from the lacerations on his sides.

Joe was already on his feet, the hair around his throat stained red. Carter and Kelly came up on either side of him, growling, backs arched as they crept toward Robbie, who had managed to get himself to his feet.

There was too much going on in my head.

I was being pulled in different directions.

There were threads pouring out of me, latching onto Robbie and Elizabeth and Mark, and these threads were strong and true and they said *pack* and *protect* and *mine*. They only grew stronger as humans ran through the trees toward us, spiked with fear and thoughts of *attack are we under attack remember the training remember what the Alpha taught.*

There were other threads too, shredded and thin and weak, and they pulled toward the white wolf, the Alpha, even as the thought of another Alpha in *my* territory made me want to bare my teeth in anger. *These* threads spread to him and, through him, out to the others, to the other two wolves by his side, to the witch that came to stand next to them. He ran his hands over the Betas, arms flaring, the raven's mouth open in a silent call as it flew up along his arm and out of sight onto his back.

They were protecting him.

Much like my pack was protecting Robbie, idiot that he was.

It didn't matter that family was spread out among two packs.

All that mattered was the bonds between us telling us that nothing touched pack, that nothing harmed what was ours. If it came down to it, they would fight each other.

Joe, though.

Joe wasn't moving. By rights, he could. Robbie's attack had been unprovoked.

And was his pack really advancing? Or were they defending?

I couldn't do this. I couldn't have this.

Not like this.

Robbie took a step forward, spittle dripping down onto the grass as he rumbled deep in his chest.

Carter crouched low.

And I said, "*Stop.*"

My voice was a crack in the air.

All the wolves stopped at once, ears flattening to the backs of their heads.

Except Joe. His eyes grew brighter.

Even the humans took a step back, reacting to their Alpha, eyes wide, shoulders tense.

They waited.

There was an order here. No matter how much I wanted to go to Joe, wanted to make sure the wounds in his neck were closing, that the red on his throat was nothing serious, I couldn't.

Because I had to tend to my own first.

His eyes tracked every step I took.

I knelt in front of Robbie.

I cupped his face in my hands. His eyes were wide and wet. One of the wolves behind me—Carter, I thought—growled, but was cut off with a low bark from Joe.

Elizabeth and Mark nosed along Robbie's sides and stomach, licking at the bloody hair, while he kept his eyes on me. I tightened my grip, just slightly.

"I know what you were doing," I said in a low voice, though all the wolves could hear me. "But you can't do that."

He whined and tried to lick my hands, but I held him still.

"I don't need you to fight for me," I said. "Especially when there was no need to fight at all. Not against each other."

He shifted then, and I felt it under my hands, the way his bones broke and reformed, the way the hair receded, the muscles jumping. It was like I was holding a bag of writhing snakes, and I shuddered at the feel of it.

I didn't hold a wolf's face in my hand. It was now a man's.

And he was furious.

He snapped, "He was in your head. I could *hear* him. He had no right to—"

"What the hell are you talking about?" I asked, dropping my hands.

Robbie gritted his teeth and shook his head, eyes darting over my shoulder in a glare.

"Robbie, I asked you—"

"He's right," Rico said. "We could . . . hear him."

I looked back at the others. They stood nervously behind me, well away from the wolves, but ready to attack if needed. They weren't angry like Robbie, but they were spooked.

"What do you mean?"

Rico glanced at Tanner, who nodded once. "Like, when we hear you. Just . . . You're our *alfa*, okay? Big boss man. We can feel the others, we can, but not like . . . not clear. Not like we can hear and feel you. And Joe was . . . loud. Everything. It was overwhelming."

Elizabeth and Mark shifted too, their bodies straining.

"I will *never* get used to that," Rico muttered. "Hi, Mrs. Bennett. How lovely to see you. You're naked. Again."

Elizabeth ignored him. "We could hear him too."

"I thought you always could," I said. "You told me that you—"

"Not like this. The bond between a mother and her sons is different than this."

I looked to Mark, who nodded.

"Shit," I muttered.

"Ox," Elizabeth said. "This isn't forcing an issue you're not yet ready to face. If anything, it's *re*inforcing the fact that there is something between you two. That there always has been since the day you first met. That's nothing new. You've known that for a very long time."

"It shouldn't be like this," Robbie said. "He's pushing himself back onto Ox and—"

"Robbie," Elizabeth said. "Enough."

"But he can't *do* that—"

Carter and Kelly snarled at him.

Robbie looked to me.

I didn't want to hurt him. Nor did I want to embarrass him any more than he probably already was. Not in front of everyone.

"I can take care of myself," I told him quietly.

"I know," he retorted. "But you shouldn't have to. I don't know them. I don't know what they'll do—"

"I do," I said. "I know them. I've known them for a very long time."

"Not what they've become," he said. "People change, Ox. You know that. You knew them a long time ago. You don't know what they've done in the last three years. Where they've been. What they've seen."

"Do you trust me?"

He blinked. "Of course I do. You're my Alpha."

"Then you have to trust me on this," I said, trapping him neatly. And probably a bit unfairly.

He took a step back, glancing between me and the other pack. Joe stood between his brothers, not making a single sound, just watching. Waiting. He was letting me handle this, but I also knew he was trying to figure out just how close the bond between Robbie and me was.

Robbie scowled at me. "That's not how this works."

"Maybe not. But nothing about us is how normal things work. We're not like everyone else. And then there's the fact that he could have killed you."

"I can handle myself."

"He's an Alpha, Robbie."

"But—"

"Stop," I said, my voice deepening the smallest amount.

He flinched.

Carter and Kelly whined.

"Go," I said. "All of you. Run. Robbie, stay here."

He groaned.

The others left, Mark and Elizabeth shifting back into wolves. She pressed her nose against my hand before she followed Mark into the trees. Carter and Kelly waited at the tree line for Joe, who hadn't yet moved. They glared at Robbie, daring him to make a move.

"I'll be right behind you," I told Joe.

His eyes flashed red before he turned toward his brothers and disappeared into the dark.

"You love him," Robbie said as soon as they were out of earshot.

"Does it matter?" I asked. "He's an Alpha, invited here tonight, and you *attacked* him. What the hell were you thinking?"

"He shouldn't have been—"

"Robbie. That wasn't for you to decide."

He looked hurt at that. "How am I supposed to protect you if you—"

"He gave me his wolf. When he was ten years old. Did you know that?"

Robbie made a choked noise, face slackened by shock.

"I didn't know what it meant. Not at the time. But he gave it to me. The day after he met me. Because he *knew*. And when I found out what it meant, I tried to give it back. I tried to tell him he was wrong. That he'd chosen the wrong person. That I wasn't good enough for someone like him, someone brave and smart and kind. And he wouldn't hear any part of it. Because I was it. He'd already decided that I was it for him."

"I didn't know that," Robbie said quietly. "Not that it went back that far."

"There has always been him and me," I said. "And I think there always will be, no matter what we decide to do. Even if we're just friends, or allies, or something more, there will *always* be him and me, because that's what we chose."

"You love him," Robbie repeated.

I didn't have it in me to deny it. "For a very long time," I said, staring out to where Joe had disappeared.

"I'm sorry," Robbie said, sounding hurt and confused. "I shouldn't have—"

I held out my arm for him, and he rushed over, curling into my side, his head near my chest as he wrapped his arms around my waist, claws prickling my skin. He trembled as I dropped my arm onto his bare shoulders, running my hand through his hair.

We were quiet for a time.

Eventually, he sniffed. "So," he said. "Kelly is kind of cute."

I tilted my head back and laughed.

We found the packs in the forest late into the night.

I pushed Robbie toward them. He shifted and fell onto four legs. He looked back at me once and nodded before turning and trotting toward Rico and Elizabeth.

Carter and Kelly watched him warily but didn't make any aggressive movement toward him. Gordo arched an eyebrow at me. I shook my head. Nothing further needed to be said.

Joe sat along the outside of the group, looking at his mother as she gnawed on what had been a rabbit at one point. His ears twitched as I approached, but that was all the acknowledgment I got. I didn't think he was upset, but I could have been wrong.

I sat next to him, leaving enough space between us that we didn't touch.

His throat was still red, but the blood looked tacky. The wound had healed.

I said, "He didn't mean it."

Joe huffed.

I said, "You don't understand how it is for him. You weren't here."

Joe growled low in his throat.

I ignored it. "He didn't mean it. Not like you think."

Joe didn't look at me.

"Tomorrow," I said, and this time, it was a promise.

I didn't say anything more.

We watched our packs as they ran together. As they lay together. As they bickered and laughed and howled out their songs together.

We sat there for the rest of the night.

And I didn't say anything as Joe moved closer to me, pressing up against my side as the sky began to lighten in the east.

LOVE

I went into the garage later in the day so Tanner and Chris could go home and get some sleep. They blinked at me blearily before yawning and heading out toward the SUV where Elizabeth waited to take them away.

Before I'd gotten out of the car, she'd stopped me with a hand to the arm and said, "Whatever you decide, make sure it's the right choice for you."

Rico nodded at me as I entered the garage. "Gordo's in the office," he said quietly. "Is it weird to be surprised every time I see him here again?"

I shrugged. "We'll get used to it. It's not like he's going anywhere."

Rico snorted. "That's what I would have said three years ago."

And yeah. That stung, because he was right. I would have said the same thing. And I didn't know if I could trust my own words.

Gordo was sitting behind his desk, hunting and pecking at the keyboard as he frowned at the computer screen.

"What is this?" he growled. "None of this makes any sense."

"We had to upgrade to a new system while you were gone," I said. "The old one was outdated."

"It wasn't outdated. It worked just fine with what I used it for."

"You weren't using it."

He glared up at me. "This going to be a thing now?"

"Probably," I said easily.

"For how long?"

"As long as I think it's necessary."

He scowled at the monitor. "Fucking Alphas," he muttered.

"You okay in here?"

"Peachy. I'll just sit here and try to figure out how to use something that we *don't even need*."

"Pain in my ass," I said as I went out to the shop floor.

. . .

Rico was right. It was weird to see him there.

To see him leaning against the office door, arms across his chest, as he listened to Rico singing a song in Spanish.

To hear him growling into the phone at a supplier, telling them they were out of their goddamn *mind* if they thought he was going to pay that much, he was running a *business* and he could go somewhere else.

To feel his hand on the back of my neck, squeezing once as he walked by.

It was weird.

Good, but weird.

. . .

"You want a ride?" he asked as we closed the garage. We waved at Rico as he drove off in his old Corolla. It was only three, but we were slow today.

I shook my head.

"He waiting for you?"

"Probably."

"You gonna fix this?"

"Why?"

"Why what?"

"Why do you care?"

He scoffed. "Right. Why the fuck do I care. I wonder why the fuck I care about you. And Joe. And your bullshit. Huh, Ox? I don't know."

"It's good to know some things don't change."

"Use your fucking head, Ox. I care about this because I care about *you*."

"Yeah, Gordo. I know."

"Then fix this," he said. "We didn't risk our lives for this long just to come back and have both of you pussy out. That's not how these things work."

I couldn't help but feel a little awed by him. "That's different."

"What is?" he asked, locking the front doors.

"Used to be, you didn't want me in this. With them. With this."

He tilted his face toward the heavens as he rolled his eyes, like he was asking the Good Lord for the strength to deal with someone like me. I'd seen that look a lot in my lifetime. But coming from him, it didn't feel like it did with others. He was my friend. Still.

"Used to be," he said, slightly mocking, "I hadn't been through what I've been through now."

"You didn't care about them before."

He looked pained. "Things were . . . different. Okay? I didn't know then what I know now."

"Which is?"

He shook his head. "It doesn't matter. Not in the long run. And you shouldn't be talking to me about this, Ox. You know that. He's waiting for you. He's *been* waiting for you. It's time for you to pull your head out of your ass."

"Ah," I said. "I suppose I could say the same for you, then. If things have changed. If you've been through shit. If you can pull your head out of your ass."

"Ox, I swear to—"

"Chickenshit."

"Fuckhead."

I grinned at him.

He reached out and cupped the back of my neck and brought our foreheads together. We kept our eyes open. He looked blurry this close up. I swore I felt little tendrils of his magic arcing along my skin, little pricks of electric light.

We stayed like that for a moment. Then he pulled his head back and kissed my forehead, a firm press of lips. He pushed me away and stalked toward his truck. "Fix it, Ox," he called over his shoulder. "Or end it. Let him explain to you or don't. Just do something, because the longer you draw this out, the more I want to punch you in the face. Your ridiculous feelings are spreading through all of us and it makes me want to vomit."

I loved that man more than I could ever say.

. . .

He was waiting for me on the dirt road, just as I knew he would be.

I couldn't spit out *not yet*. I couldn't walk by him and pretend he wasn't there.

I couldn't pretend like my heart hadn't been broken for a very long time.

That I was indifferent to him standing in front of me.

Not now. Not anymore.

He said, "Hey, Ox."

I said, "Hey, Joe."

He smiled, but it was a tremulous thing.

I tried to smile back. I don't know how good it was.

He said, "Guess we have to talk."

I said, "Yeah. Guess we do."

We sounded ridiculous.

He sighed. "Look. Hey. Just . . . Whatever happens, okay? Whatever you . . . decide, I need you to know that I meant what I said."

"When you said what?"

"Everything I've ever said to you. Everything, Ox."

My throat closed just a tad.

"Yeah, Joe," I said roughly. "Okay."

He nodded before turning and walking down the dirt road.

I fell into step beside him.

My hand brushed against his. I didn't know if it was on purpose or not.

I cursed myself for not having enough courage just to reach out and take hold of his hand. We'd done it countless times before. Before he'd—

Just before.

But he decided for us, since the next time we touched, he latched on, curling his fingers against my own. My thumb pressed against the pulse point in his wrist, feeling the nervous, erratic beat that bounced under his skin.

I held on as tightly as I could.

· · · ·

The old house was empty when we arrived. The house at the end of the lane was lit up, wolves moving around inside. The humans were in their own homes. I thought maybe Robbie was out in the woods somewhere, but I couldn't be sure. I was too overwhelmed by Joe.

It was thoughtful, leaving us alone, but they weren't being subtle.

But then, I didn't know if werewolves knew *how* to be subtle.

I didn't know if I did either, for that matter.

He hesitated briefly, looking up at the house, and I remembered the day he'd jumped on my back, that little tornado who said he was sorry for whatever had just made me sad. He hadn't been in the house since that night. Since Thomas and my mom died.

I dropped his hand and he sighed as we moved up the steps to the porch.

The door was unlocked. I pushed it open, and he followed me inside.

His eyes flashed red as soon as he crossed the threshold, claws and teeth popping out like he had no control over them.

He said, "Shit. Oh Jesus. It's not . . . It's not the same. It's not like—"

"Joe," I said sharply, making sure I stayed a careful distance away.

"I can smell him," Joe snarled through a mouthful of sharp teeth. "He's been here. He *stays* here. He's in the *wood*. He's in the *walls*. He's—"

It hit me then. "Robbie."

Joe looked over at me and I thought, for the briefest of moments, that I wouldn't reach my crowbar in time, that regardless if I was an Alpha, I was still a *human* Alpha, and Joe was anything but.

"I almost tore into him," Joe said, taking a step toward me. "The first time I saw him. The way he stood by you. The way he *touched* you. He knew you. He'd known you for *years*. I knew that before either of us even said a word. And you were just standing there. You were just *allowing* it to happen. I come home and I find him . . . and he's *touching*—"

He was standing right in front of me, blood dripping from his hands in little drops where his claws had pierced his palms. His eyes were wide and wild, each breath sounding like it was being forcibly pushed from his chest. His words were spoken in a low growl, and he was big, so very big.

But I wasn't afraid of him.

I'd never been afraid of him.

I said, "Joe."

"Ox," the wolf growled, and I could feel his breath on my face.

"He lives here. He is part of my pack and he *lives* here. He lived here for a long time before he moved into the main house. You *know* this. I know you've been told this. Your mother. Mark. The others. They *told you*."

Joe blinked rapidly, eyes flickering red, then back to their normal blue. He took a step back, looking horrified. "I didn't . . . I didn't mean to—"

"Stop," I said. "It's not—"

"I would have hurt him," Joe blurted, sounding impossibly young. "If I'd thought I could have gotten away with it, I'd have hurt him. That first day. When he came at me, it took every piece of me to hold back. And even then it almost wasn't enough. I would have killed him without a second thought."

"I know."

"You *don't* know," Joe snapped. "You *don't* know what it felt like. Coming home, *finally coming back home*, and finding . . . *him*. And all of you. Just like you were . . . Just like you didn't even *need* the rest of us."

I nodded, taking a step back, trying to put a little distance between us before I reached out and clocked the fuck out of his face. "So that's how it's going to be," I said, gritting my teeth. "That's how it is. We're going to do this. Now. This way."

This startled him. "What? What do you mean? What way?"

I took another step back, just to be safe, because I might have cared about him and I might have been waiting for this day, but sometimes, oh *sometimes*, Joe Bennett could be so fucking stupid.

"My mother *died*," I said as evenly as I could. "My Alpha *died*. The boy I lo—The decision I made, my *choice*, turned into an Alpha. And a little over a week later, he was *gone*."

"Ox," Joe said. "You know why I had to—"

"No," I said coolly. "I don't. I don't know *shit* about what you had to do."

He narrowed his eyes. "You *told* me he couldn't get away with this. You *sat* there next to me and told me Richard Collins had to pay for what he'd done to you. To us. To our *pack*."

"My mother had just been *murdered*," I growled at him. "I wasn't thinking clearly."

"And I was?"

"Clearly enough that you made a fucking decision *behind my back*."

"You *just said* your mother had been murdered. That you weren't *thinking* clearly." He started pacing in front of me. "Do you really think I wanted to put any more weight on your shoulders? That I wanted to drag you into this further than you already were? Ox, I was a seventeen-year-old Alpha who had been tortured by the man who had just killed my father. I wasn't thinking about the pack. I wasn't even thinking about my *mother*, God help me. I was thinking about *you*. And the only way that I could protect *you*."

"So you kept everything from me until the last minute," I said. "And then disappeared for three years. Because that was the best way to protect me."

He stopped pacing and stared at me as if I was stupid. For a moment, I hated him because I remembered my dad giving me a similar look. "I didn't *disappear*—"

"Bullshit," I snapped at him. "Don't you try and tell me otherwise, Joe Bennett. Because anything else would be a lie."

His jaw tensed and he fisted his hands. He took a breath, visibly trying to calm himself down. I tried to do the same, because if things went any further like this, they'd just end before they even began. I hadn't meant for it to get like this. At least not yet.

"Look," he said. "I . . . made choices. Because I had to. They may not have been the best in the long run, but they were the best at the time. You can't fault me for that."

I laughed bitterly. "Yeah, Joe. Funny thing is that I can. And I do. That's the problem." I walked toward the kitchen, trying to get as far away from him as I could. I leaned against the counter. He stayed near the door.

"Ox—"

"Did you know?"

"What?"

"About me."

"I don't understand."

But I thought maybe he did. "That I'd become . . . like this. Like how I am now."

"An Alpha."

"A *human* Alpha."

He started to shake his head, but then stopped and sighed. "Maybe."

"Maybe," I repeated.

He rubbed a hand over his face. "Dad thought . . . well. Dad thought a lot of things about you. You know that, right? That you were his in all but blood. I don't think he saw any difference between Carter and me and Kelly and you. You were his just as much as we were."

It hurt, but in a good way, like pressing against a loose tooth. A bittersweet ache that clawed at my heart. "Yeah, Joe," I said hoarsely. "I saw that. Maybe not at the time. But now? I know now."

Joe nodded. "Sometimes when we went out into the woods, just me and him, we'd talk, you know? About the pack. About what it meant to be an Alpha. About you. We talked a lot about you. Things I've never told you about. Things he never got the chance to tell you himself."

I waited, not wanting to interrupt.

"After you left," he said, looking down at his hands, "that first day I found you, they just stared at me. For a long time. Especially him. They hadn't heard me talk since . . . well. Since Richard. Because of the things he'd done to me. The way he'd broken me. But you, Ox. It wasn't like anything I'd ever felt. Okay, just . . . Look. They stared at me. They listened to me. They smiled at me. They hugged and laughed and cried, but I kept saying *Ox. Ox. Ox.* And I *knew* then what it meant, even if I didn't quite understand. When I told them I wanted to give you my wolf, they were *scared*, okay? Because they *understood*. We'd come home, trying to find a way to help me, to *fix* me, and the very first day, I'd found you, brought you home, spoken for the first time in over a year, and then told them what you were to me, even if I didn't use the right words."

He looked back up at me, expression stark and pleading. "They were scared, Ox. But I was sure. I was so goddamn sure about you. I wanted you to have the thing that mattered the most to me, aside from my pack. When you're little, you're given your wolf and taught that one day, you will find a person to give it to, that it will be a token of everything they are to you. Dad, he . . . Mom. She didn't want me to, not then. She wanted to wait. She told me it would mean more if I knew you better. If you knew what you were getting into. She told me that I didn't have to do anything. That you weren't going anywhere. I didn't care. And Dad. Dad knew that. He could see it, okay? I told him that it was my choice. Because that's what we're told. That it always comes down to choice."

"And you chose me," I said quietly.

He laughed and rubbed his eyes. "Yeah, Ox. I did. You know I did. And Dad, he knew I would. He knew I wouldn't *not*. So he told Mom it was all right. That when a wolf knows, he knows. But that's the thing. I *didn't* know. Not about you. I always knew something about you, but I didn't know what he meant, okay? I didn't. All I heard was *yes, Joe, yes you can give the one thing you want to give to the one person you want to give it to.* He helped me, too. He brought out the box I put it in. Gave me the ribbon to tie it with. And I never asked him. I never asked her. But I think it's the same one he used when he gave his to my mother."

The house creaked around us. I couldn't find a single word to say. That wasn't unusual. Sure, I'd gotten better over the years. An Alpha couldn't be silent, not really. But I still had trouble with words sometimes. It wasn't that I didn't have any. It was that I had *too* many, and they all got stuck trying to come out at once.

But that was okay. Because Joe had plenty.

"He knew," he said. "Even then, I think he knew something was different about you. That you were wonderful and kind and amazing, but that there was something *else*. Not something *more*, because what you were was already enough. It was already a part of you. He recognized it. I don't know how. But . . . Ox, he knew, okay? I really think he knew."

He was watching me. I knew I had to say something, anything, to fill the silence that followed his words. I owed it to him. To myself.

I said, "I still have it."

He nodded and gave a wobbly smile that quickly disintegrated. "Okay," he said in a choked voice. "Okay. Yeah. You do? That's real good, Ox. I know—"

"Things aren't the same."

He stopped whatever he was going to say.

"I'm not the same," I said.

"I know," he said. "I knew that the moment I got here. Even before. I stepped back into the territory and knew."

"Did you know? That I was an Alpha? Here, after you left?"

He shook his head. "I hadn't heard about you."

"Alpha Hughes knows."

He looked surprised. "Why? Did they—"

"Robbie."

Joe scowled. "Robbie."

"He came here to . . . spy on us? Maybe. I don't know. He was the new Osmond."

"And you let him in the *pack*?" Joe demanded.

I watched him coolly. "He doesn't belong to Hughes. He belongs to me."

He recoiled like I'd slapped him. "Ox, you know what Osmond did. He *betrayed* my father. For all we know, Hughes was in on it too! They could have wanted him dead for *years*."

"He's not," I said. "It's not like that."

"You don't know that," Joe spat. "They said the same thing about Osmond."

"Is this because of Robbie? Or is it because of you?"

"What the hell?"

"He is my friend, Joe. That's it."

"Right," Joe said, giving up all pretense. "And nothing more. He doesn't want anything more."

"*I* don't want anything more."

"He can't . . . He's not—"

"I told him. He knows."

"Knows what?"

But I wasn't ready for that. It would be too easy to let him off the hook. And part of me wanted to. I was already tired of this. Of the anger.

I said, "You cut us out."

He took a step back. "Ox."

"You said *I'm sorry*. In the middle of the night when you knew I wouldn't see it. Like a coward. You said *I'm sorry* and then I didn't hear anything from you. *We* didn't hear anything from you. For *years*."

He was revving himself up for another fight. I could see it in his stony expression. But I wasn't going to let this one go. He had been wrong about a lot of things, but I thought this had been his worst mistake.

"I did what I had to," he said, voice even.

"What you had to," I echoed. "And why was that?"

"We couldn't have the distraction."

I snorted. "Right. We, meaning all of you. Meaning you all agreed."

He hesitated.

"You didn't," I said, "did you? All of you didn't agree."

"It doesn't—"

I slammed my hand against the countertop. "Don't you say it doesn't matter. It matters. All of it *matters*. I understand what it must have been like for you, Joe. I get it—"

"You don't get *anything*," he exploded. "You *don't* get it, because you weren't there!"

"And whose choice was that?" I said coldly. "You made it perfectly clear that—"

"Don't," he said, pointing a claw at me. "You don't get to say I didn't need you. You don't get to say that when it's not true. I needed you. I needed you too fucking much."

"That was the problem, wasn't it?" I said, answers slowly locking into place. "I was your tether. And you couldn't have me be your tether. Not with what you set out to do."

"Every time I saw your words," he said, "every time I wrote back to you, the more I wanted to come home. To you. To the others. And I couldn't, Ox. I couldn't, because I had a *job* to do. He had taken from me, and worse, he had taken from *you*. And I couldn't do what needed to be done while being reminded of home. So yes, I stopped. I cut you all out. I did it because I cared too much about you to be able to do what I needed to do. I told myself that if I kept you separated from me, from *this*, I'd be keeping you safe."

"You were wrong," I said. "We weren't safe. Not all the time."

"I know," he said, deflating. "They told me. The others. I didn't think—"

"No, you didn't. You only had one thing you focused on."

"Revenge," he said. "Rage. The need to find him and make him suffer."

"And you didn't." I didn't mean it to come out like it did, like I was accusing him.

His shoulders slumped. "No. We . . . were close. So many times. But he always managed to be one step ahead. I tried, Ox. I tried to make things right. But I couldn't. So I just kept going."

"Would you even be here?" I asked. "If you didn't think he was coming for us again?"

He said, "I don't know," and the honesty *hurt*.

I nodded. My head felt stuffed. I didn't know what else to do. "Why would he come here now? Why, after all this time, would he come back? Why not before?"

"I don't know."

"When is he going to get here?"

"I don't know."

"What do we need to do?"

"I don't know."

"What the fuck *do* you know?" I snarled at him. "Have you wasted three goddamn years of our lives for *nothing*?"

He flinched, eyes on the floor.

I couldn't stop. Not now that I'd broken open.

"Tell me, Joe. Was it worth it? Was it worth keeping me safe like you think you did? Was it worth leaving us all behind so you could go after a fucking ghost?"

"I don't—"

"*Don't tell me you don't know!*" I roared at him. "Tell me one fucking thing you *do* know!"

"That I love you." His breath hitched in his chest.

And I just.

I couldn't breathe.

Everything felt too loud. Too real. Too bright. I wanted to hurt myself to know if I was dreaming or awake. Of all the things he could have said, I'd expected that the least.

And it wasn't *fair*.

I croaked out, "What?"

He didn't look up at me, eyes trained on the floor. When he spoke, he sounded smaller than I'd ever heard him. He said, "I don't know a lot. Not anymore. Everything changed. You did. The pack. The people in it. This place isn't like it was when we left. And Carter and Kelly, they just . . . They fit again. Like it was nothing. Like we hadn't been gone at all. With Mom. With Mark. With all those *strangers*. And with you. And Gordo. Gordo, Ox. He didn't even need to worry. Because he always had you. Even though he'd tied himself to me somehow that night, even though he became mine, he was always yours. They all are. And I'm here just . . . I don't know why I'm here. I messed up, Ox." He wiped his eyes and something shattered in my chest. "I thought I was doing the right thing. I thought I was keeping you all safe. But I was selfish. Because I just wanted to keep *you* safe. To keep *you* away from the monsters. If you didn't know me, if you had never met me, you wouldn't be here right now. Your mom would be alive. And you would be happy. I thought you'd want it that way. The longer I was gone, the easier it would be to forget me and everything I've done to you. I wanted to come home, Ox. All I wanted to do was come home, because without you, I don't *have* a home."

"Joe—" I said.

He raised his hand, cutting me off. "Just . . . let me. I know you have a choice. Still. And I know I've done nothing to make you still choose me. And I'm okay with that. Because if there's"—his voice was strangled and harsh—"*someone* else, or if there *could* be, I don't want to stand in the way of that. I just want to be wherever you are. As your friend. Or packmate. Or just me and you like it was before all of this.

"You don't have to keep the wolf, Ox. You don't have to. I just needed to be near you, because I'm *tired*. Okay? I'm so tired of this. Of running. Of not getting what I want. I just want you. Please just let me have you. Please. Nothing else matters if I can't have you. Just let me—please, just let me. You're the Alpha here now, but please don't make me leave."

His face was wet by the time he'd finished. He had shifted partway, close to losing it to the wolf completely. I didn't know how strong his control was anymore, given that I'd seen him shift only once on the night of the full moon.

And it wasn't that I didn't trust him, at least with this. Joe would never hurt me, not physically.

I didn't want to fight this anymore. I didn't want to fight him.

I took a step toward him.

His eyes flared again.

"Don't," he said. "You can't. Ox, I'm slipping."

"You won't," I said.

"You can't know that," he pleaded. "It's not the same. I can't find my way back because *it's not the same.*"

I knew that. We both did. Some might have seen us and wondered how we'd gotten this far. After everything we'd been through. After everything we'd both done. He'd left. I'd stayed. I took his place, whether I'd meant to or not. I'd spent a good while angry at him. He'd spent the same time angry at himself.

None of that mattered, though. Maybe it would again, and soon, but right now, I just couldn't take the thought of not touching him one second longer.

"No," he said, "no, no, no, you *can't*—"

I stood in front of him.

His back was against the door.

Our knees knocked together.

My hands brushed his.

It felt like such a tremendous thing, after all this time.

He growled at me, more wolf than man, and I took his face in my hand, that half-shifted face, white hair sprouting and receding, like he was stuck somewhere between the two. As soon as my fingers touched his skin, he shuddered against the touch and there was a moment when I thought it wouldn't be enough. That too much had come between us for him ever to find his way back again.

Because I understood now what his choice had cost him. He might have been an Alpha and he might have had his brothers and Gordo with him to keep him sane, but he was almost an Omega too, having cut ties from his tether in order to give himself to his wolf. He hadn't been able to focus on me because I kept him human. He'd given that up for the wolf. To become the predator. The hunter.

It couldn't have all been for nothing.

These past three years couldn't have been *nothing*.

They weren't.

Because I was here, standing tall, even though I felt like crumbling.

My daddy had told me people were gonna give me shit and that it was gonna hurt.

My father was a liar.

Everything had been shit.

But I was still fucking standing.

I said, "Hey, Joe."

And he looked up at me with fire-red eyes, the skin of his face rippling with the shift.

He said, "*Ox*."

My mother took me to church once. After my daddy had left.

She'd thought maybe we could both use some Jesus.

Joe said my name like the preacher spoke about God.

Reverent, filled with awe. Terror and adoration.

I didn't know what to do with that.

I didn't know that I deserved that.

I did the only thing I could think of.

I kissed Joe Bennett. There. In the old house.

And for that moment, everything was all right.

.   .   .

It was like before.

Only not.

We lay side by side in my old bed, facing each other.

We didn't fit in it like we used to.

I hadn't changed much. Maybe gotten a little wider, but not much else.

Joe, though.

Joe had changed.

He took up more room than he ever had before.

It was a tight fit, but we made it work.

One of his legs was pressed between mine. I held it in place.

We shared the same pillow. I told myself it was just because we couldn't have him falling off the bed. But really, I just wanted him as close as I could get him.

He didn't mind. I thought maybe he wanted to be close too.

We didn't speak much, at least for a little while. I felt like all I'd been doing was talking lately and it was nice to have a break. To not need words. It wasn't going to last, but that was okay. It was enough for now.

He'd walked into the room, and it was much like the first time he'd ever done so, eyes darting everywhere, taking everything in. I didn't know what he saw, what differences were here. What differences there were in me. But I saw the exact moment he found the little stone wolf, still sitting atop my old desk. He froze, and the whine that came out was more wolf than human, a low, wounded noise that hurt my heart. He hadn't made a move for it, hadn't even reached an arm out to touch it, but he knew it was there all the same. What it meant for me. And for him.

He didn't take his eyes away from me as we lay in that bed. They roamed over my face like he was trying to memorize me all over again. I can't say I wasn't doing anything different. I wondered what I'd see if he couldn't heal like he could. What kind of scars there'd be. What stories they'd tell. I had my fair share. My stomach. My right arm. My back was the worst, from when that Omega had gotten me the night Thomas had died. They told my stories. I couldn't read Joe's.

The world moved outside of my room, but we ignored it.

He reached out and ran a finger along my eyebrows. My cheek. My forehead. The tip of my nose. He brushed it against my mouth and I kissed it, the barest press of my lips.

I wanted . . . more from him. More than I'd wanted from anyone else before. And it would be easy to take, because he'd give me his everything.

I couldn't do it, though. Not yet. I thought maybe I was on my way to forgiveness, if there was still anything left to forgive, but I wasn't there yet.

And I still had a pack to think of. A territory to protect.

I didn't want to speak.

But I had to.

I said, "Joe."

He said, "Yeah, Ox," and for a moment my breath caught, because all the times I'd imagined him finally back with me, here, in my bed, I'd never really expected it to feel like this.

He must have heard the tripping of my heart, because he pressed a hand against my chest. The angle was awkward, not really enough space for him to press too hard, but I knew what he was doing.

My heartbeat slowed. Calmed.

"I need to know," I finally said.

He gave a little hum, eyes glinting.

"He's coming here."

"Yes."

"Again."

"Yes."

"Why?"

His teeth were sharper. "Because that's what he does. He's no lon-ger rational. He has lost himself to his wolf. I don't think he even remembers what it was like to be human. The wolf, it . . . thinks differently, Ox. It's still us. We're still here, but when we change, when we shift, it's not about rational anymore. It's about base instinct. Things are more black and white. It's the human side that deals in shades of gray. He's lost that way of thinking. He gave up his humanity because he blames humans for destroying his family. It doesn't need to be more complex than that."

"Why now?"

I felt his claws prick my chest through my shirt, but his eyes never left mine. "Because he knew it would bring me back here. He needed time to recover. To heal. To put himself back together. He changed course, but the endgame is the same. He made sure to send us that message with the Kings. Killing David was the last sign. Everything pointed back to Green Creek."

"He's circling."

Joe smiled bitterly. "More like ensnaring. By pointing threats in your direction, he knew I'd have no choice but to come home."

"You always have a choice."

His smile softened. "Not when it comes to you."

I couldn't take much more of this. My skin was buzzing and I felt the need to *touch* and *mark* and *bite*, but I had to finish this first. I had to make sure.

"What do we do?"

He sighed. "What we have to. I'm tired of running, Ox. I'm tired of chasing shadows. All I want is to dig my feet into this earth because it once belonged to my father. And I know he meant it for me, too. This was his home. It's yours now, and I'm okay with that. I'm okay with you and this. What you are. But I want it to be mine, too. I want it to be ours. If you'll let us. If you'll have me."

Doubts, then. "I'm not—"

"No," he growled. "You don't get to say that. You don't get to say you're not *anything*."

Of course he knew. Those residual fears that I couldn't ever be rid of, a holdover from when I didn't think I'd amount to much. Maybe I could see now that I meant something to someone. Or someones. Maybe I could see it in their eyes when they looked at me. But that didn't mean I didn't feel like I was still a kid playing dress-up. Or a sheep in wolf's clothing. It was a mask, this thing I was, and I wore it well.

Funny thing was, I almost believed it.

"Ox," Joe said, sounding frustrated. "How can you not see it?"

I said, "I'm human," as if that explained it all. To me, it did.

He smiled. "I know. And that's the best part of all."

We were whispering now, as if saying this any louder would stop it from being real.

I said, "What do we do?"

He said, "Whatever we can."

I said, "I don't know if I can do this, by myself."

He said, "You won't have to. Ox, don't you see? I'm here now. If you'll let me."

I said, "You can't leave again. You can't. You *can't*. Even if he comes. And even if he runs again. Joe, you can't leave us again. You can't leave *me* again."

He said, "I won't," and I heard the *promise* behind those two words, the *intent*. Joe Bennett was many things to me, but he wasn't a liar. He might have had my anger, however much of it was still left. He might have held the remains of my trust in his hands. But Joe Bennett wouldn't lie to me. Not about this. Not when it meant so much.

I believed him.

So I don't know that I can be blamed for surging forward then, thinking *now* and *finally* and *JoeJoeJoe*. He grunted once, but I swallowed it down, my mouth on his, frantic and harsh. His hands came up and cupped my face, holding me close, and aside from the taste of him, all I could think about was the last time we were like this, side by side. We'd been saying good-bye then, and now it was *hello, hello, I can't believe you're here, hello.*

It was clumsy at first. The angle was off, the rhythm filled with teeth and too much saliva. It hit me that I was only the second person he'd kissed in his life, if what he'd said was true. Frankie had been nothing but a passing thought, and I never wanted to know just how far they'd gone.

So I gentled it down as well as I could, slowing the pace, dragging it out. He was already breathing heavily as I swiped my tongue along his lips. He let out a little gasp, the smallest of noises, and his lips parted and my tongue touched his.

One moment I was leaning over him and the next I was flat on my back with an Alpha werewolf on top of me, a growl vibrating from his chest as he dragged his nose along my neck up behind my ear, inhaling as he went. His lips trailed after, wet against my throat, huffing out little breaths on my skin, trying to get his scent to mix in with mine.

He stretched out on top of me, and if there had been any doubt we were now evenly matched, that was long gone given how we met perfectly from head to toe. He ground down onto me, and I felt the hard line of his cock pressing against mine.

I reached up and wrapped my hand around the back of his head, holding him close against my neck. He was panting now, like it was overwhelming, like all of this was crashing over him. He trailed his lips and tongue up my jaw until he kissed me again. He was still unsure, the kisses shy and unpracticed, but it felt more real than any other person I'd been with.

I let go of the nape of his neck and slid my hand down the wide expanse of his back, trying to find skin, trying to feel the heat of him.

His shirt had risen up, and I touched his back, pressing my hand flat against him, pushing him down as I pushed myself up, wanting the rough friction. He groaned into my mouth as our cocks lined up briefly before sliding next to each other.

He was pulling back, just the smallest amount, his lips still brushing mine, saying, "I don't know what to do, I've never done this, I don't know what to *do*," and his eyes were the brightest red I'd ever seen, like he was burning from the inside out.

"I know," I said. "I know. I do. I'll take care of—"

Which, really, I should have known to never tell a current bed partner of my past sexual experiences while in bed with him, especially if he happens to be an Alpha on a hair trigger. The moment I said *I do*, because I *did* know what to do, my hands were pinned over my head and Joe was snarling in my face, teeth sharp and eyes flaring impossibly brighter.

"You said you *didn't do that while I was gone*," he growled, hips stuttering against me like they hadn't caught up with the fact that he was pissed.

Not that he had any right to be. "I didn't," I snapped back. "I told you I—"

"No one else," he said and then rolled his hips deliberately, like he wanted to see my reaction up close.

I couldn't stop my eyes from fluttering shut, my tongue darting out to wet my lips. I said, "*Joe*," and he did it again, harder this time.

"Say it," he said hotly, pressing his forehead to mine, circling his hips again and again. "You say it, Ox."

It was fucked up. It really was. Because I knew what he wanted, what it meant to the wolf, and it was possessive and not who I was. I wasn't a *thing*.

But goddamn, did that do more for me than anything else.

There was the Alpha part of me that gnashed its teeth at the thought.

But there was the even bigger part, the part that was all Ox, that said, *yes yes yes*.

"*Say it*," the wolf said near my ear.

"Yeah," I said hoarsely. "Yours, Joe. I'm yours."

He shook above me, inhaling sharply like he was surprised, like he hadn't expected me to agree with him, to do what he said. I didn't know how deep his insecurities ran or how far his instincts were taking him, but he hadn't expected it.

It was the start, I thought. For both of us.

Because even though he was still clumsy, even though he didn't know what to do, he sat up and straddled my waist, legs bent on either side of me. He rolled his hips again as he took his shirt by the hem and pulled it up and over his head, revealing that wide chest of his, the sparse hair, the cut of his stomach. He tossed the shirt to the floor and leaned back on his hands as I traced along his stomach up to his chest. His nipples were dusky, little whorls of hair around them. I took one between my fingers and gave it a sharp twist, watching his stomach clench, mouth falling open.

And because I could, I rose up, wrapping my arms around his back, holding him close to me, licking where my fingers had been. His nipple hardened under my tongue, and I scraped my teeth against him just to feel him tremble.

His dick was pressing against my stomach through denim, but I wasn't ready for it yet. He leaned over behind me as I worried his flesh with my teeth, pulling at my work shirt until he got it and the tank top I wore underneath up to my shoulders. I leaned slightly to let him pull them off. I didn't see where they went because there was so much skin pressed against mine. He burned hot, almost feverish, as he tilted my head back and kissed me again, sloppy and wet. He tasted like I thought he would, clean and powerful. He gripped the sides of my face with his hands as I dropped my own down to cup his ass, squeezing to pull him against me even more.

He muttered my name against my lips before I tilted my head back again. His teeth found the skin near my throat and began sucking a mark. Something in me shifted, growling at the idea of him marking me, trying to get him to suck harder, to use more teeth. I wanted it there for everyone to see, so no one would make a mistake as to who put it there. These weren't thoughts I'd ever had with anyone else, but then I'd never been with someone like him.

I reached between us as he continued marking me, trying to grab the front of his jeans. I missed the fly and my knuckles dragged against the hard outline of his cock. It was an accident, but I did it again when he whined against my neck. I pressed harder, with purpose. He rutted against me as I did my best to grip him, but the denim was too soft between my fingers, the friction too light.

I reached up and pushed against his chest, leaning him back again. His eyes were red and heavy-lidded as he looked down between us, slack-jawed. His lips were swollen and slick and I had the savage thought that *I'd* done that. *I'd* made him look that way.

I flipped the button of his jeans with a practiced twist of my wrist, something that caused him to growl. I ignored him. He didn't need to be upset with my experience, especially since he was going to benefit from it.

"Jesus," I muttered. "What is with you and not wearing underwear?"

He grinned sharply down at me. "I had hopes."

I snorted and trailed my fingers along the base of his cock, his wiry pubic hair scratching against the back of my hand. His breath caught in his chest and I was almost struck dumb at the fact that I was *teasing* him, that he was here, that we were together, and I was *teasing* him. The thought that I was the only one that had done this to him (and I was certain of that now) only made me feel more powerful. That I was the only one who'd seen him like this.

(*And the only one who will get to*, a little voice whispered in my head, but I pushed that away because it was too much, too much for me to even think about, even though the lizard part of my brain said *yes* and *yes* and *yes*.)

I pulled his dick out of his jeans, careful of the zipper. He was uncut and half-hard, his dick slimmer than mine and maybe a little longer. The weight of it in my hand short-circuited my brain a bit. Wolves burn warm, and it felt hot in my hands. I gripped it, squeezing as carefully as I dared, watching the foreskin slide as he grunted and thrust into my hand.

"Ox," he said, sounding breathless and strangled.

"I know," I said gently as I tightened my grip on him.

"You gotta—"

"I know."

"Do something!"

I let go of his cock and he exhaled heavily, like he'd been punched in the stomach. Before he could protest, I raised my hand toward his face and said, "Lick."

He didn't even question it. He grabbed my hand and brought it to his mouth, tongue rasping over my palm, up between my fingers, before sucking two of them into his mouth, getting them spit-slick and wet. I ground my teeth together to keep from shoving him back and taking what I wanted right then and there. This wasn't about me, though. Not yet. I needed to make this good for him.

I pulled my hand away, and he whimpered, reaching up and wiping his mouth with the back of his hand. "What are you—"

The rest of it was choked off when I grabbed his dick again and, using his spit, slid my hand up and down. His hands came down to my shoulders, claws out, but not digging into my skin as I jacked him off. His stomach muscles tensed as I leaned forward and licked up to his chest. He wrapped his arms around my neck, pulling me close, barely leaving enough space for my hand between us. He was growling near my ear, a continuous purr that I was going to make fun of him for later.

I swiped my thumb over the tip of his dick, and his hips jerked. I groaned, my cock pressing painfully against my zipper, trapped under his ass. I couldn't get off like this, and I didn't want to. I wasn't a kid anymore. I didn't need to nut in my jeans.

I nosed my way up to his neck and it wouldn't be until later that I realized he never froze, never pulled away. He bared his throat to me as if it were nothing, as if he weren't an Alpha who was unused to doing such things. The throat, I knew, was a vulnerable place for a wolf. It showed rank, especially for an Alpha. Betas always bared their throats to the Alpha as a sign of submission. Even the humans in my pack had taken to doing it whenever they saw me, an unconscious action I didn't even think they were aware of anymore.

But his neck was back like he'd never been threatened before, like he'd never been hurt before, and I knew what it meant. I latched my teeth onto the skin and I *bit*, not enough to draw blood, but enough to make him feel it. His wolf was close to the surface, if the noises he was making meant anything, and I felt more animal than man, words like *mine* and *mate* and *claim* running on a loop through my head.

It wasn't enough.

I pushed him back. He went without protest, bouncing on the bed, his dick displayed obscenely, jeans low on his hips. I jerked them down, fingers grazing against his strong thighs. He was jerky in his movements as he helped, trembling in his excitement. He tried to kick his jeans off, grunting in frustration when they caught on his feet. I pressed a hand against his leg, trying to get him to calm. He raised his head from the bed, looking at me. His eyes were blue again, back to normal, but he was flushed, a sheen of sweat on his forehead.

I reached down to where his jeans had bunched around his feet, and pulled them off. Joe Bennett was nude, spread out in my old bed, waiting for me to move. His cock was curved and jutting up toward his stomach. His balls lay against his thigh, shifting when he moved his leg. His thighs were hairy, and I wanted to run my hands and tongue on them. To touch. To taste.

He was the most precious thing I had.

And, at least for the moment, I *did* have him. Whatever happened later, this could not be taken from me.

"What is it?" he asked, sounding nervous.

"Nothing," I said, voice rough. "I'm just . . . You're here."

"Yeah," he said. "Yeah, Ox. I'm here."

He lifted his foot and poked a toe against my chest. I caught his ankle, holding it in place. I leaned down and pressed a kiss against the bone, and he sighed, squirming slightly as I exhaled against him. I kissed his calf as I reached down and unbuttoned my own jeans. The pressure eased some, and it was enough for what I wanted to do. There could be a good pain, and I wanted to push against those boundaries.

I continued up his leg, reaching his knee. He huffed a laugh when I kissed the inside of his knee, and I grinned. I arched an eyebrow at him, but he just rolled his eyes and made an impatient noise.

"You need something?" I asked, not moving, but still holding his leg up.

"You bastard," he said. "You know what you're doing."

"I have no idea what you're talking about."

"Fuck you, Ox," he said.

"We can do that."

He gaped at me.

I shrugged.

He tried to pull his leg back.

I couldn't have that.

So I grabbed his other one too, pushing my weight against the back of his thighs. His knees came to his chest as his eyes widened.

He was exposed to me. His dick pressed against his stomach, his balls drawn up between his folded legs. His asshole was surrounded by soft hair and I wanted to bury my face in him, to take in his scent, the smell of him.

"Ox," he said, panting again, like he *knew* what I was thinking, like he *knew* what I was going to do.

"It's fine," I said. "You'll like this."

He cried out when I licked him from his ass to his balls, trying to pull away and push toward me all at the same time. I'd never done this before, not really, but I knew the idea behind it, the mechanics of it. I didn't know if he wanted me to fuck him or if he was going to fuck me, but I wanted him loose and wet with my spit.

"Hold your legs," I said, putting more Alpha in my voice than I should have. He didn't hesitate, reaching up under his knees and holding himself in place. His claws were still out, and I placed his fingers to make sure he wouldn't hurt himself.

It was a heady thing when I pulled back, to see him as he was.

There was a sense of power rushing through me, to have someone like him on his back and waiting for me. I didn't know if it was because he was an Alpha or if it was because he was Joe, or a combination of the two. It made me light-headed, the edges of my vision going fuzzy.

He was starting to twitch under my gaze, the flush spreading down his neck to the top of his chest.

"You're good," I told him, and he inhaled sharply. "You're doing so good."

"Ox," he pleaded.

"I will." I leaned down to just above his asshole. I let a thin string of spit fall onto it. He groaned as he watched me from between his legs. I reached up and rubbed the spit into his asshole, not breaching, but enough pressure that it was close. I held his asscheeks apart when I leaned forward, tongue in a flat stroke against him. He started making little noises in the back of his throat as I pressed my tongue against him and in. I wanted to eat him out for hours.

He said my name again and again, and I dragged my tongue up his perineum to his balls, mouthing at them, taking one in and then the other. I knocked his hands away from his knees, pushing his feet flat against the bed.

I didn't give him a chance to question it, just licked from the base of his dick to the tip. He gave a hoarse shout, trying to arch up against me, but my weight against his hips held him down. I tongued his slit, tasting the bitter precome. I sucked down the head of his cock, giving in to experience. It bumped against the back of my throat before I stopped moving, breathing through my nose. Joe was crying out above me, hips stuttering like he was holding back. I rose up slowly, looking up at him through my eyelashes. His eyes were red and his teeth had lengthened, like he couldn't stop the shift from happening.

I pulled off with a wet pop. He looked down at me, mouth open. I said, "You don't have to hold back," and he shuddered at the words.

I went back down on him, working him over, tugging at his balls, giving them the slightest of twists. My own dick was out over the top of my underwear and I ground my hips against the bed.

He took the permission I gave him and thrust tentatively up into my mouth. I reached up and grabbed his hand, putting it to the back of my head. He grunted and the claws shrank until there was nothing but blunt human fingers gripping my hair.

He fucked my mouth harder then, pushing up awkwardly until he found a steady rhythm. His fingers tightened in my hair, giving the right amount of pull to hurt, but not enough to distract me.

I hollowed my cheeks, spit dripping down the sides of his cock as he used my mouth. I choked briefly, but pushed it away even as my eyes watered.

"So good," he babbled, punctuated with growls. "So fucking good, Ox. I knew you would be. I fucking *knew* you'd be so—" He tilted his head back, baring his neck yet again, and it only made me want this more.

I pulled off him. I didn't want him to come yet. Not like this.

He looked back down at me, bleary-eyed and with a mouth filled with fangs.

Making sure he was still watching, I rose up on my knees, pushing my jeans and underwear down my hips. My cock sprang free, slapping against my stomach. He snarled at me and fisted the comforter. I pushed my jeans down as far as they could go before I leaned forward, hands on either side of his chest. He brought his arms down, biceps holding me in place. We were almost eye level, and neither of us blinked as I leaned forward enough to get off my knees and push my jeans down with my feet. One leg was free and then the other, and he leaned up to kiss me. I pulled away slightly, just out of reach. He snapped his teeth at me. I grinned down at him.

"Ox," he said. "Just come here."

I leaned down slowly. He strained forward. I licked his lips as they parted but remained just out of reach. We both knew he could easily hold me down, that he would always be the stronger of the two of us, but it didn't matter right then. Right then, all that mattered was that I was in control, and he was allowing it.

I gave him the kiss he wanted. He laughed into my mouth, but it turned into a moan when I lay flush against him, chest to chest, cock to cock. His legs were bent up on either side of me as he chased my tongue with his own. I trailed my hand down his hairy thigh and gave a slight push with my hips, our cocks rubbing together.

He said, "Come on, come on," into my mouth and I pushed harder.

We rutted against each other and my name fell from his lips in a sigh, in a moan.

He said, "Ox, I want—" and I kissed it away, tongues sliding together as he anchored his feet to the bed, trying to find more friction between us. I gave it to him as best I could, feeling the drag of his dick against mine.

There was a zing at the base of my spine and I knew if we kept going like this, we'd come. The thought of him covered in my spunk was almost enough to continue as we were. He'd be marked by me. They'd be able to smell me on him.

Yes and yes and yes.

"Ox," he gasped into my mouth. "I want more. Please, just let me have more."

We were sweating, the room almost stifling.

He wanted more. I did too. But I didn't know if I was ready for that. To be mated. Because if we fucked, we wouldn't be able to stop it. I wanted it so bad, I could taste it, but not with everything else hanging over our heads.

But there was more we could do. I'd make it good for him.

I pulled back and he growled at the loss of my weight against him.

He tried to pull me back down, but I pushed his hands away.

I reached over to the table beside the bed and opened the drawer. There was an old bottle of lube in there, half-empty from all the times I'd used my fingers on myself while he was gone. I could do the same for him.

"Yeah," he breathed when he saw what was in my hand. "Yeah, that's real good. You should do that. You can fuck me, Ox. I promise I'll make it so good for you."

I shook my head. "We're not doing that."

He looked hurt, even as his eyes dilated. "But—"

"Not yet," I said. "You know why."

"Mate," the wolf said.

"Do you trust me?"

He didn't hesitate. Not like I thought he would. Even after all this time, after everything we'd been through, he said, "*Yes.*"

"I'm gonna make you feel good," I promised him. "And one day soon, I'll fuck you till you can't walk anymore. Then you can do the same to me."

His dick twitched on his stomach. He reached down to stroke it, eyes on me. "You promise?" he insisted.

I said, "Yeah, Joe. I promise."

I opened the lube and poured some on my fingers, getting them slick. I dropped the bottle and reached between his legs. He saw what I was doing and spread them farther. My fingers touched his asshole, still wet from my tongue. He lifted his hips slightly off the bed as I pressed a finger against him.

"You ever done this to yourself?" I asked him in a low voice.

He snapped his head up and down. "Yeah."

"You fucked your fingers?"

"Yeah," he whined at me, trying to push his ass toward me.

"Feel good?"

"Never could get enough," he said, breathing heavily. "Never could get the right—"

I pressed a finger in to the first knuckle. His hand stilled on his dick.

"You just breathe," I told him. "Just breathe and it'll feel all right."

He nodded at me as I pushed in slowly, just the one finger for now. The muscles in his stomach contracted as I pulled the finger almost all the way out.

He was tight around me, and like a furnace.

I pushed in again. His eyes rolled in his head.

"Touch yourself," I told him. "I want to watch."

He shook his head frantically. "No. I don't want to get off. Not like this, Ox. I need you to—"

"I know what you need," I said, and he *moaned* at that, trying to take more of my finger, pushing back and pulling away. "I'll give it to you. Just not today."

His eyes were glassy when he looked at me. His tongue darted out as he licked his lips. "But, I just . . . Ox."

"We'll get there," I told him, pushing my finger all the way into his asshole again just to watch his chest hitch. "After all of this is done, I don't want anything hanging over our heads. When you claim me. When I claim you."

He grunted as I added a second finger. His balls were drawn up tight. He said, "You promise. You promise me, Ox. You *promise me.*"

"I promise," I said, because I did. There wasn't any chance it wouldn't end that way. Joe and I were always heading in that direction, even if there'd been a three-year detour. I'd just needed to get over myself and the anger I felt before I could realize that.

He grabbed his dick again and started jacking off, slow, even pulls, swiping his thumb over the head of his cock. It was a practiced move, something he knew he liked. Just the thought of him doing this by himself, sitting on his own fingers, rubbing his cock, hit me hard. My own dick throbbed at the thought, at the sight of him spread out before me. I looked down and watched my fingers disappearing into his ass. I barely had to move my hand as he rocked his hips down and then away, down and away.

He started tensing as I fingered him, his hand moving faster on his dick. His nipples hardened, and I knew he was getting close. He kept chanting my name, little grunts that rolled out of his chest. His eyes started flashing red again, and I added a third finger almost brutally. He growled at me, teeth sharp. His ass clenched around my fingers, and just when I knew he couldn't take much more, I knocked the hand on his cock out of the way and swallowed him down to the root, gagging slightly as he bumped the back of my throat. He cried out from somewhere above me, hands going to the back of my head, claws pricking my scalp. My nose was in his pubes when I pushed my fingers harder into his ass. He came down my throat, heavy spurts that tasted bitter on the back of my tongue. I choked on it, pulling off, his spunk dribbling down my chin, the last bit going onto my cheek.

He looked thoroughly fucked out below me, still chasing his orgasm as he tried to push himself farther onto my fingers. I pulled them out, and he gasped, eyes flashing open, looking up at me. I rose to my knees above him, and all I could think about as I licked my lips to taste him was that he needed to be marked. And kisses I could suck into his skin would fade. But the smell of me wouldn't.

I used the hand that had been in his ass on my own cock. It wasn't soft or gentle. I stripped it furiously, wanting him to be covered in my scent.

"Yeah," he said, voice hoarse and wrecked. "I want it. Ox, I want it." He reached over and grabbed my balls as I jacked myself off above him. He held them in his hands, squeezing tightly enough to make me grunt, twisting them into bright *pleasurepain*. I felt it building at the base of my spine, little bolts of lightning arcing along my skin. My toes curled underneath me.

I shot off on his chest as he pressed two fingers against my taint.

I snapped his name out like a curse. My spunk landed on his chest, his nipples. It rolled down over his clavicles and pooled at his throat.

He looked ruined. Owned. I'd never felt so primal. I didn't know if it was the Alpha, or if it was just me. It didn't matter. Everyone would know. And that's all I cared about.

He reached up and ran his fingers through the jizz on his chest. He looked delirious and rubbed his wet fingers over his right nipple.

I collapsed down next to him, the bed creaking under the weight of two grown men. We were both breathing heavily as we lay side by side, shoulders touching, faces turned toward each other, just inches apart. He kept touching the spunk on him, kept running his fingers through it like he was spreading it around. I leaned over and kissed him, and he whimpered into my mouth as I sucked on his tongue, letting him taste himself.

I pulled away, and his eyes were red again.

He said, "I want to bite you."

I said, "I know."

He said, "I want to claim you. I want to give you scars with my claws. I want my teeth embedded in your neck."

I said, "I know."

He said, "You're mine. No one else can have you. No one else can be with you. Not like this. Not ever. You hear me, Ox? Not *ever*. You're mine, and I'll kill anyone who thinks they can take you away from me."

And I said, "*I know*."

. . .

It wasn't until later, much later, long after night had fallen, the sky outside black and littered with stars that burned coldly, that we spoke again. It'd been a strange sort of contentment just to lie there and watch each other.

I might have drifted in a doze, but every time I opened my eyes, Joe was still next to me, face so close I could see individual eyelashes. He hadn't moved much, still sprawled out, comfortable in his nudity. His cock was soft against his thigh. My spunk had dried on his chest, little flecks of white sticking against the hair. It was going to be a bitch to get out later, but he didn't seem to care.

I was the one that broke the silence.

I didn't mean to.

One moment I was opening my eyes, and the next I said, "You shouldn't have left."

And it wasn't what I'd meant to say.

He sighed. "I know."

"We should have done this. Together."

"I know, Ox. But it's done. There's nothing I can do to change that."

I wanted to be angry with him at that. Still. I wanted to be so angry.

But I just couldn't. Not when he was here next to me, still looking like he'd just gotten fucked.

I nodded slowly. "Okay." I wondered if it was just as simple as that.

"Okay?" He arched an eyebrow.

"Okay."

He grinned at me, wide and bright, for just a moment before it faded slowly. Then, "Do we even need to talk about Jessie?"

"What about her?"

"Just . . . why, I guess."

"Why what?"

He scowled at me. "Why is she in your pack?"

I barely restrained the eye roll. "Why, Joe Bennett. You jealous?"

"No."

"Okay."

"I just don't see *why* she needs to be near you. Or in your pack. Or alive."

I rolled over on top of him, causing him to laugh under me, squirming, and there were just *miles* of naked skin. "She helped us heal," I said.

He searched my face, looking for I didn't know what. "And did you?" he asked.

I kissed him instead of answering, because I didn't know quite yet how to put into words that I hadn't healed, not completely, because part of me had been missing.

I wondered at all the things we'd missed. Everything he'd been through when he'd been gone. Maybe one day I'd get to hear everything that had happened to him. To them. I thought maybe it didn't matter right at this moment. There were bigger things coming for us. We'd have time. After.

Because regardless of what Richard Collins would bring, I wouldn't let him touch Joe Bennett. Not again. Not ever.

HURT YOU / OUR FUCKING PACK

The two packs were spread out before us in the house at the end of the lane. My pack was on the couches, on the sofa. On the floor. Looking like they belonged, casual and easy. Most of them, anyway. Robbie was tense.

Joe's pack stood off to the side, Carter and Kelly leaning against the wall near the bay windows and Gordo standing at parade rest next to them.

There was a divide. It was visible.

But Joe. Joe stood next to me. Side by side, close enough that we brushed against each other with every breath. The wolves knew. Of course they did. They could smell the previous night on us. I took some strange, savage satisfaction at that. Until I looked Elizabeth in the eye, that is, and flushed horribly, even though she looked nothing but amused.

They were all waiting for us to speak first. Even the humans.

"So," I said, trying not to be nervous. "We have some things to discuss."

"Like your lack of showering," Carter said, sounding like he didn't have a care in the world. "Seriously, Joe. We get it. Jesus Christ."

Joe refused to be embarrassed, which was fine, because I was embarrassed for the both of us. "Damn right," Joe said, sounding smug.

"What the hell?" I muttered.

He winked at me.

"No shit," Tanner said. "Seriously?"

"Oh boy," Rico said. "This is probably going to get awkward."

"Only if we make it awkward," Chris pointed out like a reasonable adult. Then, "We should make it really awkward."

"We could compare stories, I guess," Jessie said because she was evil.

"Yeah," Chris growled while glaring at his sister. "Let's not even go there, because I really don't want to have to punch my Alpha in the face."

Jessie rolled her eyes. "Please," she said. "He's bigger than you."

"*Anyway*," I said pointedly, before this sunk down into something I couldn't control anymore. "We've talked—"

Carter and Kelly started coughing obnoxiously.

Joe snarled at them with red eyes. They smirked at him like it didn't matter. It probably didn't. It was the closest I'd seen to them acting like they had before they'd left. I wondered if this was because they already knew what we were going to say.

"—and we've decided to see if this could work," I finished.

"To see if *what* could work?" Robbie asked with a frown.

"Us," Joe said before I could answer. He cocked his head at Robbie, but didn't flash the Alpha eyes. "The pack. Trying to be . . . one."

My pack was mostly silent. The humans looked curious. Mark and Elizabeth looked happy. Robbie had a blank expression.

"How would that work?" Tanner asked. "Both of you would be the Alpha?"

I nodded.

"We don't know him," Rico said. "We only know you. And you want us to . . . what? Treat him like you? No offense, Joe," he added hastily.

"None taken," Joe said easily. "And you're right. You don't know me. Not like you know Ox. This isn't going to be something that happens right away. It's an endgame. It'll take time for you to trust me."

"Trust you?" Robbie said. "How can we trust an Alpha that left his pack behind?"

"Robbie," I barked.

Joe put his hand on my arm. I looked over at him. He didn't say anything, but I didn't think he had to. He wanted to handle this. He wanted me to trust him.

And I did. To an extent. Maybe not like I had before, but we'd get there. Eventually.

He said, "Robbie, I know this might be hard for you."

"Do you?" Robbie said coolly. "Because you know the first thing about me."

I gritted my teeth. Because as much as I understood his frustration, he didn't need to be acting this way.

"You care about him," Joe said simply.

"He's my Alpha."

"And I'm not going to take that away from you."

"No?" Robbie snorted. "Because it seems like you've already started."

"I've . . . made mistakes," Joe said. "Ones that I'm going to have to live with for the rest of my life. I hurt people here. My mother. Mark. My brothers. Ox, though. I think I hurt him the worst."

Robbie narrowed his eyes. "So you can see why I—"

"But I've never hurt you," Joe said. "Because, like you said, I don't know you."

"You hurt Ox," Robbie said. "He's my Alpha. Therefore, you hurt me."

Joe said, "Okay. Then I apologize to you too. For hurting him."

Robbie blinked. "It's not that easy."

"And is that for you to decide?" Joe asked.

"Ox," Robbie said to me. "You can't be buying this bullshit."

"You don't know him," I said quietly. "Not like I do. He means it, Robbie."

Robbie looked hurt at that. And I felt bad, I did, but I didn't know what else he expected of me. Robbie was pack. Joe was my mate. I would fight for both of them, but I couldn't have them fighting each other.

"Look," Joe said. "I don't expect you to believe me. Or trust me. Or even *like* me. And I know respect is earned. You care for Ox. He's your Alpha. But *I* care for him too, because he's more than that to me. And I would do anything for him. If you have a problem with me, then come to me. Either we'll hash it out or we'll find some way around it. But don't hurt him or yourself by hating me."

Robbie, for once, was speechless.

I was a little impressed.

Joe could probably smell how impressed I was.

Which probably wasn't the best thing to have happen in this first meeting together. In front of his blood relatives.

Even though they probably already knew.

Kelly coughed quite loudly.

I tried hard not to blush.

"Sorry," Kelly said. "Something in my throat."

"That's what Joe said," Carter muttered under his breath.

They fist-pounded each other without taking their eyes off me.

"He'll be like you are to us?" Jessie asked, staring at Joe. "We'll be able to feel him like we do you?"

"You should have told me about that the moment we got back," Gordo said, glaring at Rico, Tanner, and Chris.

"Hey!" Rico said. "We had to be careful. We didn't know if you were the enemy or not."

"The enemy," Gordo repeated flatly before slowly turning to look at me.

"I didn't say anything," I said.

"You could have gone Dark Side," Tanner said.

"Like full-on Darth Gordo," Chris said.

Gordo put his face in his hands. "I *told* you guys. I'm a *witch*. I'm not a *Jedi*."

"Um, excuse me," Rico said. "Can you or can you not shoot Force lightning from your fingertips."

"*It's not Force—*"

"We rest our case," Tanner said quite loudly.

"The humans feel the bond too?" Gordo asked Elizabeth and Mark.

"Curious, isn't it?" Elizabeth said, smiling faintly. "I dare say even extraordinary."

"It's because of Ox," Mark said, "and all that he is. He responded to the territory's need for an Alpha, and the pack's desire for one. He grew up here."

Everyone turned to stare at me.

"Mystical moon magic," Jessie whispered.

I tried not to squirm under the attention. "It's not—"

"It makes sense," Gordo said thoughtfully.

"Mystical moon magic makes sense?" I asked incredulously.

Gordo rolled his eyes. "No, Idiot. It's not mystical moo—I'm not even going to say that. Look. There was always something about you. Even before all of this. The fact that I was able to tie myself to you as easily as I did should have been my first clue, but I think I was just so relieved to have that again, I didn't think of anything else. I could feel you because of that connection. The wolves could feel you because of their pack bond. But the humans? I didn't think that was possible. Not to the extent it seems to be. How far does the bond go?"

"He has to push for it," Jessie said. "It's not like it is with the wolves. We know he's there when he's reaching for it."

"Can you push back?"

The humans looked at each other. Then Jessie said, "Sometimes?"

Gordo frowned but didn't say anything.

"Have you heard of anything like this before?" Carter asked his mother.

She shrugged. "Rumors, mostly. Unsubstantiated stories. But never proven. Not like him."

"And who else knows besides the people in this room?" Gordo asked.

Everyone paused.

"Alpha Hughes," Robbie said finally.

"And the gruff man," I added.

"The who?"

"Philip Pappas," Robbie said. "He serves under Alpha Hughes as her second. He came here when you were gone, to . . . assess, I guess. I don't think they told others, or at least not many. I don't think they know what to make of him."

"They wanted me to register," I said. "If Joe didn't come back."

Joe grabbed my hand and squeezed. He didn't let go. Robbie looked at us briefly, then away.

"You can't make other wolves," Gordo pointed out.

"But I can make a pack," I said. "And I've shown you don't need it to be just wolves. I think it worries them."

Gordo shook his head. "You just had to be a special snowflake," he muttered, but there was a small smile on his face.

"That's it?" Kelly asked. "No one else knows about—"

"David King," I admitted.

"Who?" Chris asked.

And shit. I'd forgotten I hadn't told them about him.

"King," Elizabeth said slowly. "As in the hunter clan King?"

"He came here," I said. "Months ago. That night I sent out the alert."

My pack stilled.

"We saved him from Richard," Joe said. "Barely. He was running, but Richard caught up with him. Richard escaped, but David . . . I sent him here. With a message for Ox."

"And you didn't think to tell us?" Mark asked. He didn't sound angry, just confused.

Not like me. I'd succumbed to anger, multiple times, and I'd let it get the better of me.

"And he knew," Elizabeth asked, letting me off the hook for now, "that you were an Alpha?"

I nodded. "Said he'd been around them enough to know."

"Where is he?" Mark asked. "If he's still on the run, we need to make sure he's not talking about—"

"He's dead," Joe said. "A few weeks ago. Not that far from here. Idaho."

"Richard?" Elizabeth asked her son.

Joe nodded.

"That's why you came home, isn't it?" she asked. "Because you think he's coming here again."

"Maybe," Joe said. "And maybe I just wanted to finally come home."

"They said you didn't speak," Elizabeth said. "That you stopped talking again."

He looked down at the floor. It was quiet in the house.

"Do you know why?" she asked him.

"It hurt," he said in a low voice, sounding like the tornado who'd once waited for me on the dirt road, wide-eyed and demanding. "Being apart from you. From him. I couldn't . . . find the words. To say anything. I just wanted to find the monster so I could come home again."

"And here you are," she said. She rose from her feet and approached her son. I didn't know what, if anything, they'd discussed since Joe's return. I had a feeling she'd been waiting for me to talk to him first.

She was so much smaller than him now. It was oddly endearing, the way she had to reach up to cup his face. He leaned into her hands, even as he still held onto mine.

"Your father would have been very proud of you," she said.

"I don't think—"

"Joe," she said.

He wrapped an arm around her and pulled her close, his nose on her neck as she ran her fingers over the stubble on his head. She glanced at me and smiled.

Eventually, she pulled away and took a step back. "I think we should try," she said. "Because we are so much stronger together than we could ever be apart."

"Is it going to be bad?" Rico asked. He looked tired. They all did.

"Maybe," I said. "But it's been bad before, and we've always gotten through it. Because of the pack. But if you don't think you can do this, I won't hold it against you. But I need to know. Because if you stay, I have to be able to count on you. So tell me now."

No one spoke.

I hadn't thought they would. They were brave, all of them. Foolish, but brave.

"Then we do this," I said. "As a pack."

I wondered if this was what it felt like to heal.

· · ·

Two days later, Robbie said, "She wants to speak to you. Both of you."

Joe glanced at me before looking back at Robbie. "Alpha Hughes?"

"Yes."

Joe sighed and rubbed his hand over his face. He stood at my side as I chopped peppers for Elizabeth, who was humming lightly near the stove. Mark, Carter, and Kelly were off somewhere in the woods. Gordo was still at the shop, though he was supposed to be over later. I'd given the others the night off. They had lives beyond the pack, and I didn't want to take away from that, even if they looked at me funny when I said so.

"When?" I asked.

Robbie snorted. "Now, probably. She doesn't like to wait."

"She never did," Elizabeth said, not looking up from the stove. "This will hold. Just try not to take too long."

I scooped up the sliced peppers and placed them on a plate next to Elizabeth. I kissed her cheek before looking at Joe.

He shrugged at my unasked question. "No time like the present."

"What does she want?" I asked Robbie as we followed him to the office.

"I don't get to ask questions like that. Not of her. Most people don't."

"I'm not most people," I said, because I wouldn't be cowed by anyone.

"Yeah, Ox," he said, sounding fond. "I know."

Joe kept a blank expression.

A laptop was open on the desk. I thought it was Robbie's. I didn't have one. I dealt too much with the computer at the garage ever to want one at home. Joe sat in the desk chair, and I pulled a second chair over next to him.

Robbie pulled out his phone and typed a message. It was a moment before his phone pinged and he sent a response. He shoved the phone back in his pocket before turning the laptop toward himself. He clicked on Skype and said, "She'll call you in a minute." He put the laptop back in front of us and left the office, closing the door behind him.

Joe waited a beat before saying, "It's going to be a long time before he sees me as anything but an enemy."

I rolled my eyes. "He doesn't think you're an enemy."

"He thinks I'm *something*."

"You *are* something."

Joe smiled. "Probably thinking of two different things, Ox."

I took his hand in mine, still marveling that I could do this. We'd stayed in the old house, Joe in my bed every night. It was cramped and small, but it gave us the excuse to sleep on top of each other. I didn't need distance from him now. I probably wouldn't for a long while.

"He'll get there," I said. "I told you what he said about Kelly. Maybe we could—"

The computer chimed. A little flashing screen popped up.

"Ready?" Joe asked.

I kissed him once, brief and sweet.

I said, "Yeah, Joe."

He squeezed my hand and then connected the call.

I didn't know what I'd expected her to look like. If I were being honest, I hadn't given much thought to this Alpha at all. She didn't know me. She didn't know my pack. Not really. She might have been the big Alpha, but what she did meant nothing to me in the long run. She hadn't come after me and mine, but she hadn't done anything to protect them either.

But she was young—younger than I thought she'd be. Maybe in her late thirties, early forties. She looked calm, relaxed even, her dark hair pulled back in a loose ponytail, the white collared shirt she wore opened a few buttons at the throat. She didn't scream Alpha, but I'd only met a few in my life that I could compare her to.

She didn't smile when she saw us on the screen, but instead flicked her gaze between the two of us. I realized this was the first time she'd seen us, though she'd probably heard about us plenty. We probably weren't what she'd been expecting either.

For some reason, I didn't think that speaking first was going to be right for Joe and me. Joe must have thought the same thing, because we both waited.

"You won't remember me, Alpha Bennett," she said, voice even. "You were probably only five or six the first time we met. But I remember you. Your father was . . . well. He was a good man. My condolences."

"Thank you," Joe said, rather stiffly. "That's kind of you to say."

She nodded at him, then looked back at me. I refused to be intimidated by her. I don't know how much I succeeded in that. "Alpha Matheson," she said. "Curious thing."

I didn't know if I should be offended or not. "How so?"

"I've never met someone quite like you before," she said. "To all intents and purposes, you appear to be one of a kind."

"I don't know about that," I said honestly. "And you don't have to call me Alpha. It's just Ox."

"Really." She sounded amused. "Just Ox."

"It's a sign of respect," Joe said to me.

"I know," I said. "But nobody else calls me that. I don't need her to either."

"Curious," she said again. "We could dispense with the pleasantries, I suppose. I was never one to stand on ceremony."

"What did you want, Michelle?" Joe asked.

She smiled at him, but it didn't quite reach her eyes. "That list is a mile long."

"Why don't we just start with the things you want from us," Joe said. "Seems like it'd be easier that way."

"I don't recall saying I wanted anything from you."

"You didn't have to," Joe said. "It was implied."

"Fair," she said. The smile dropped off her face. "Where have you been the last three years?"

Joe tensed next to me. "You know where we were."

"Not the specifics."

"Specifically, we were everywhere. We didn't stay in one place. Funny how that worked."

Her fingers tapped on the desk as she leaned back in her chair. "But you never caught up with him. Richard, I mean."

"No," Joe said stonily.

"And Robert Livingstone? Osmond? Anything from them?"

"No."

"Why is that?"

"I couldn't tell you," Joe said. "Why don't you ask the teams you sent out? They didn't seem to have any better luck."

"Yes." She frowned. "That. That . . . was disappointing, to say the least. Why do you think that was?"

"Because he's smart," Joe said. "And ruthless. Something your people could never be."

"And you could?" she asked, and I squeezed Joe's hand out of sight, because *careful, careful.*

He knew what I was trying to say. I couldn't feel him yet, not like I used to, but I didn't think it would be long. The packs were going to come together. They had to. I didn't really see any other way it could be.

"I did what I had to do," Joe said.

"And your pack," she said.

"They did as well. We were all in agreement."

She glanced at me. "Were you?"

"Yes."

"Where is Richard Collins?"

"I don't know."

"But you came back."

"It was time."

"It had nothing to do with the King clan, then?"

Joe said nothing.

Michelle sighed. "I can't help you if you don't tell me what's going on."

"We didn't ask for your help," Joe said.

"You'll need it if he comes again."

Joe snorted. "He's already come twice. He's already taken from me. Where were you then?"

She didn't even flinch. She was very good. "Things are different now."

"They are," Joe agreed. "But that doesn't change anything between us. You and I both know that my desire to lead ended when my father was taken from me. I don't care about that. Not anymore. You can have it. Do with it what you will."

"You don't trust me," she said.

"No," Joe said coolly. "I don't. I don't trust any of you. You did nothing to help my father. And, in fact, you sent someone who betrayed us. So forgive me if appeasing your guilt isn't one of my first priorities."

"I'm not asking you to appease *anything*," she said, that hardened exterior cracking just a little. "This doesn't affect just you, Joe. Richard Collins is an enemy to *all* of us. We're supposed to work together. To stop him. To *end* this."

Claws pricked my fingers as Joe's grip tightened. "You should have thought of that when you had the chance to end this after he took me when I was a kid. You *had* him and you—"

"I wasn't even *part* of this then—"

"It doesn't matter," Joe interrupted. "You are the Alpha of the wolves now. Everything that has come before you now rests on *you*."

"I could send someone there," she said. "Multiple someones, if I was inclined."

"Actually, you couldn't," I said.

She glared at me. "And why is that?"

"Because I'm the Alpha of this territory," I said. "And you are not welcome here."

She laughed. "Mr. Matheson, I assure you, I don't *need* your permission. If anything, you answer to me now."

"I don't answer to anyone except for my pack," I said. "And I *assure* you, if you think otherwise, you're going to be sorely disappointed."

She looked back and forth between us, her mask slipping just a bit further. "Can't you see that I'm just trying to help you? You don't have to be alone in this."

"We're not alone," Joe said. "We have each other. Our packs."

Her eyes narrowed. "You can't both be Alphas and lead the same pack. It doesn't work that way."

"You don't know *how* we work," I said.

"And you'll listen to him?" she asked Joe, ignoring me. "The *human*? After everything they've done. After everything they *could* do?"

"Speciesist," Joe said. "Unfortunate. I never thought you of all people would think that way. Osmond did. And so did Richard."

Her eyes flared red. "I am nothing like them."

"Maybe not," I said. "But it doesn't matter. Not now. Not with what could happen."

"Which is all the more reason to let us *help* you."

"Three years," I said, "and this is the first time I've heard from you. Why is that?"

She hesitated.

"You knew Joe was gone. You knew some of us remained. And yet you *never* contacted us. Not me. Not Mark. Not even Elizabeth. Why is that?"

"There was no need," she said stiffly. "You were grieving. Robbie was there telling me what I needed to know."

"And yet," Joe said, picking up on the thread, "I've been back two weeks and here you are."

"I figured it was time—"

"No," Joe said. "You didn't."

"Because you didn't want us," I said. "You want Joe."

"He is the Bennett Alpha," Michelle snapped. "He's *supposed* to be—"

"My father told me that in order to be a good Alpha, I always need to put the good of the pack first," Joe said. "Above anything else. Because an Alpha cannot lead if he doesn't have a pack who will follow him."

"What good will it be when your pack is gone?" she asked. "Because that's the risk you run. Joe, I am asking . . . no, I am *begging* you. Let us help you."

Joe looked over at me. I made sure my gaze didn't waver, that he could see every single part of me that I'd built up for him. We still had a long way to go. Those hurts and burns that had scarred my skin over the last three years would take a long time to heal. But I'd given my heart away years ago to a blue-eyed boy who loved and trusted me enough to keep his family safe.

He made a little choking sound, deep back in his throat, like he hurt. There was a burst of warmth in my head and chest, and it was *there*, however small, however young, this thread, the tiniest thread, and it said *pack* and *love* and *mate mate mate*.

Michelle was right. Joe was the Bennett Alpha.

But she hadn't expected me. She didn't know about me. Whether or not she believed what I was or not, she still thought me weak.

Yes, Joe was the Alpha.

But so was I.

And I would do anything for him. For our pack.

I turned back to Michelle. "You aren't welcome here. Not now. Not until this is over. Not until we can be sure we can trust you. I'm human, but I am an *Alpha*, and I will do anything for our pack."

"Even die?" she asked quietly.

Joe froze.

I didn't. "Even that," I said, "if it means keeping them safe."

She nodded. "I hope it doesn't come to that. Truly. I am sending teams to Oregon. You can't fight me on that. If they find Richard first, well. We will do what we can. But if he makes it through, if he comes for all of you, I . . . I hope you know what you're asking of me."

"We do," I said.

"I hope we'll talk again soon," she said. "We have much to discuss. Alpha Bennett, Alpha Matheson."

The screen went dark.

"That didn't go like I thought it would," I muttered.

He didn't say anything, so I looked over at him. His face had paled slightly.

"What?"

"You were serious."

"About?"

"Dying for them. For us."

"No one's dying, Joe. I was making a point."

"But you would," he insisted.

I didn't know where this was going. So I said, "Yeah, Joe. Yes. For you. For all of you."

He reached up and gripped the back of my neck, pulling me forward. He pressed his forehead against mine. "You can't," he said. "You can't die."

"Joe—"

"*Ox,*" he growled.

I sighed. "I can't promise you anything."

"Then you stay by my side," he said. "No matter what happens. You don't leave my side."

"You knew this. You know what I would do for them. For you."

His grip tightened, and he shook me a little. "I don't *care*," he said, sounding desperate. "You don't get to do that. You stay by me."

"You think he's coming."

"I *know* he is." His eyes burned. I saw a flash of fangs.

"With others. Omegas. Osmond. Robert."

"I don't know. It doesn't matter. He'll come either way. Alone. With an army. He'll *come*."

"For you. Because you're the Bennett Alpha."

"Yes."

"This is our territory."

"Yes."

"It belonged to your father."

"Yes."

"He can't take this." I bared my teeth. "Not from you. Not from us. Not from our fucking *pack*."

"*Yes*," the wolf said, all snarls and fire.

I kissed him then. Because it was the right thing to do. Because it was the only thing I *wanted* to do.

He kissed me back, urgent and harsh. A single fang pricked my lip, and I tasted the sharp tang of blood, *my* blood, between us.

"Alpha," he whispered against me.

And I thought *yes* and *yes* and *yes*.

THIS EMPTY SHELL / HEARTBEAT

Aweek after the call with Michelle Hughes, I stood watching Elizabeth sashay through the kitchen. It was a Sunday. And I'd told her we should have dinner with everyone. Because it was tradition.

Her eyes got very bright at that. She patted my hand, and we both ignored the roughness in her voice when she said, "That'd be nice, Ox. That'd be really nice."

The humans in my (*our our our*) pack were outside setting the table. Or rather, Jessie was, and Tanner, Rico, and Chris were drinking beer and sitting in frayed lawn chairs they'd pulled out of nowhere.

Gordo was with them, and I could see him trying. Trying to find his way back to them. Trying to forge the bonds that had been there before. Because even if they hadn't known, even though none of them were wolves, they'd still been his pack longer than anyone else. He needed them. Like he needed me. It was slow going, given the long history between them, but they understood. Mostly.

Carter and Kelly were manning the grill. Robbie was trying hard not to shadow Kelly too much. After that first meeting when Joe and I had told them about combining the packs, Robbie had pulled back, had softened slightly around the others, less bristling and sharp edges. It helped that he had started to divert his attention away from me. Joe, possessive bastard that he was, was amused by the whole thing, especially seeing the bewildered look on Kelly's face.

Joe was walking in the trees somewhere. An Alpha needed to be in touch with his territory. I'd told him I'd go with him, but he'd shaken his head. "It'll be fine, Ox," he'd said before he disappeared into the woods.

And so it was just Elizabeth and me. The salad I'd tossed was ready in the large plastic bowl. She hadn't given me another task, so I waited. It felt like the right thing to do.

Eventually, she stopped dancing to the song that only she could hear.

She said, "Ox."

"Yeah?"

"It's nice, isn't it?"

"Yes." Then, "What is?"

She smiled but didn't look up from the potato salad she was stirring.

"This. Us. You and me. All of them."

And it was. So I told her so.

She said, "I didn't expect this."

"What?"

"That we could have this again."

"I wanted you to," I said. "I wanted you to have all of this again. After."

She nodded. "I know you did. But you couldn't. Not right away."

I shrugged, trying to keep cool. "I don't know."

She glanced up at me. "You did," she said. "I know you."

She did. Very well. If I'd thought my heart could take it, I would have called her Mother. But hearts are funny things: they beat strongly in our chests, even though they can shatter at the slightest pressure.

She heard all I couldn't say. Part of it was the threads between us. Most of it was because she was Elizabeth Bennett. She just knew.

She said, "He needed to come home. For me. For us. But for you most of all, I think."

"He missed us all the same," I said.

She rolled her eyes, something she did so rarely that it still always made me smile every time it happened. "Sure," she said. "I know *that*. I am aware of *that*. But it was for you, Oxnard. Even if you don't believe it. Even if you don't understand it. He came here for you."

She stared at me as if daring me to contradict her.

I said, "Okay. Yeah. Maybe."

She huffed. "You've settled into your skin since he's been back. You were the Alpha before. But it's different now."

"Is it?"

"You know it is. And Joe, he . . ." She sighed and looked away. "One day, a very long time ago, my son was taken from me by a monster. I'd always told him that there was nothing to fear. That I wouldn't let anything hurt him. But I lied, because he *did* get hurt. Badly. Over many weeks. I heard him crying when . . . when the monster called us. I heard him crying for me. I wanted—" She broke off and shook her head.

"You don't have to do this," I said hoarsely.

Her eyes flashed orange as she looked up at me. "I *do*," she snapped. "I *do*. Because you don't see your own merit. Still. After all this time. We found him, Ox. We found Joe and he was *broken*. He was weak and starved and *broken*. He flinched at *everything*. And for a while, I don't think he even knew who we were. And when he *did* know, when he remembered us, he cowered away because that . . . *that man*, that *terrible man* had told him we didn't love him, that we'd never wanted him, that he was never meant to be an Alpha."

Her claws came out as she gripped the countertop.

She said, "And I *despaired* over him. Because I didn't know what to do. I loved him more than I had ever loved anyone. I thought maybe that alone would be enough. To bring him back. To put his pieces together again. But it wasn't enough. It took Richard Collins only weeks to destroy the little boy I'd known. He was this *shell*, okay? This empty *shell*, and I didn't know how to fix it. And then, Ox . . . oh, and then there was *you*."

She was crying, and I didn't know how we'd gotten here. I knew the other wolves could hear her too, but they weren't busting in through the door. They were waiting. For what, I didn't know.

"You came," she said. "And he brought you home, like something he'd found in the woods. And the look on your face that first day. You were so nervous. So sweetly shy. You didn't understand what was happening. You couldn't. But I did, Ox. And Thomas did. Because Joe spoke. He spoke to *you*. He made the choice, even if he didn't know what it meant. You were his, Ox. Even then. And he was yours."

I couldn't speak. I had no words left. Because this was the first time I'd seen her cry. Even after Thomas's death, she'd grieved as a wolf. So this was new, and I didn't know how to deal with it. It didn't help that her words were hitting me hard in the chest and I almost couldn't breathe.

"And he had to leave again," she said, wiping her eyes. "Whether or not it was right, whether or not he should have, he did. They told me about him. Carter and Kelly. How he closed down like before. How he gave himself over to the wolf. How he didn't speak for months and months. And yet, the *moment* he comes home, the *moment* he sees you again, he finds his voice like he'd never lost it at all. So don't you say that you're not worth it. Don't you think you're not good enough. Because you have brought my son back to me again and again, and even if you weren't my Alpha, even *if* you weren't the one my son chose, I would be indebted to you for that. You've given him back to us, Ox. And no one can take that away from you."

She laughed then, her cheeks wet, eyes red, but only in a human way.

I said, "I" and "I just" and "I want to be who you think I am."

She said, "Ox. Ox, can't you see? I don't think. I *know*."

She was light on her feet—three steps and she was pressed against me, hands curled between us, her head pressed against my chest. I wrapped my arms around her shoulders and held her close, and there were those threads between us, and she pushed her way through them, singing *pack* and *son* and *love* and *home*.

After a time, I said, "It's tradition, I guess."

She rubbed her face against my shirt. "It is," she said.

"Everything okay?" a voice said from the doorway.

She laughed again and stepped away from me.

"Everything's fine," she told Joe. "Ox and I were . . . well. I suppose that's it. Ox and I were."

Joe nodded, looking concerned.

"I should get this out there," Elizabeth said, a smile on her face. She took the potato salad and went out the door without looking back.

Joe moved toward me slowly, like he was worried I'd be spooked. And maybe, in a way, I was. Because even though I knew what I meant to him, sometimes I didn't think I knew *everything*. It was a weight on me, but I had strong shoulders. I could take it.

"All right, Ox?" Joe asked.

I said, "Yeah, Joe," and I couldn't keep the awe out of my voice.

"You sure?" He sounded amused.

Maybe I wasn't. And maybe that was okay. Because Elizabeth was right. He'd given himself to me. All of him. I just had to make sure I kept him safe. Because sure, he'd chosen me. Out of everyone. He'd given me his wolf. Which was essentially the heart of him.

I said, "I love you, you know?"

And how he *smiled*.

.   .   .

It took time. It really did.

Things weren't always going to be good.

They'd left us, and there had only been three of us.

They'd come back, and now there were eight and I was the Alpha.

There were clashes trying to merge them together.

To see if there were pieces of us that fit.

Sometimes they did, and we could move in sync with each other. Other times they didn't.

Robbie yelped in pain when Carter knocked him into a tree.

It was an accident. They were roughhousing. Wolves did that.

But all I heard was the crack of bone and the sound of one of mine hurting.

Robbie whined in the back of his throat, trying to lift himself up onto four legs.

I was in front of him even before I knew I was moving.

Carter had shifted back, standing nude, bare toes digging into the grass and dirt.

"Hey," he said. "I didn't mean—"

"Back the fuck off," I snarled at him.

Carter's eyes went wide, and he took a step back.

I turned and knelt beside Robbie. His ears were flat against his head, and he trembled slightly, reacting to my anger. I took a breath and let it out slowly.

There was a sharp knob of bone where one shouldn't have been near his shoulder, bulging the skin and hair. Robbie grimaced, teeth gritting together as it slowly snapped back into place.

"Okay?" I asked, running my hand along his snout.

He nipped my finger gently.

"Sorry, Ox," Carter said from behind me. "It was an accident."

I grunted at him, unsure of why I felt this way. "Not me you should apologize to."

"Sorry, Robbie."

Robbie yipped and pushed himself to his feet, rubbing against me as he walked past. He butted his head against Carter's hip and all was forgiven.

"You're still thinking of them as separate packs," Joe told me later that night. We lay side by side in my bed in the old house. The room was dark and the moon was a sliver in the sky. "You saw that as an attack on your pack, not as two packmates roughhousing with each other."

"I don't know how to switch it," I admitted quietly. "It's been this way for so long."

Joe sighed.

"I'm not blaming you, Joe."

"Maybe you should," he muttered.

"I did. It's done. I just need to figure out how to work through it."

"Maybe . . ."

"Maybe what?"

"My dad," Joe said. "He . . . taught me things. About what it meant to be an Alpha. What it meant to have a pack. I could . . . show you. If you wanted."

I took his hand in mine.

I said, "Yeah, Joe. Sure. That sounds fine."

Once, when I was seven, my father came home from the garage.

He sat on the porch, opened a beer, and sighed.

I sat near him because he was my father and I loved him.

He looked at the house at the end of the lane. It was empty. It had been for a long time.

The sun was setting when he was on his fourth beer.

He said, "Ox."

I said, "Hi, Daddy."

He said, "Hey" and "Ox" and "I'm going to give you some advice, okay?" the words tripping all over each other.

I nodded, though I didn't know what he was talking about. I just liked the sound of his voice.

He said, "You think you're gonna get somewhere. You think you're gonna do something great with your life. Because you don't want to be like wherever you came from. But people are gonna shit where you walk. They're not going to give a damn about what you want. All they want to do is knock you down. Trap you in a job you hate. In a house you can't stand. With people you can't even look at. Don't let them. Okay? You don't fucking let them do that to you."

"Okay," I said. "I won't."

He grunted at me and took another sip from the red and white can.

He said, "You're a good kid, Ox. Stupid, but good."

I wondered if that was what true love felt like.

. . .

Joe took me to the trees, to the woods, walking the path of his father. His Alpha.

He said, "Dad told me that there have always been these threads that connect us. They bind us to each other because we're pack. The better we work together, the more we trust and respect each other, the stronger the bonds become."

He reached out and ran his fingers along the bark of a tree.

His father had done the same many times when we'd walked through the forest together.

I told him as much.

He smiled at me. "It helps."

I didn't know what that meant, not really, but I let it go.

"You can feel them, can't you?" he asked as he stepped over a rotting log that burst with flowers and long blades of grass.

"Most of the time," I said.

"Carter? Kelly? Gordo?"

I shrugged. "It's getting there, I think. I don't know. Gordo, maybe. Only because I've known him. I'm tied to him."

"You're tied to everyone else, too."

Until you broke that away, I wanted to say. *Until you snapped those threads like they were nothing.*

But I didn't. Because I was moving beyond it. For the most part.

"It was my fault," he said, and I *hated* werewolves right then, *hated* being tied to them as I was, because there were so many times that my thoughts didn't seem to be my own anymore.

"It's not like that," I muttered.

He rolled his eyes and there were whispers of *who are you* and *where did you come from*, spoken in the voice of a little tornado. It was that disconnect again. The little boy I'd known, the teenager he'd been, the man he was now. He was gruff and quieter than he'd been before, but little flashes broke through the cracks every now and then. Joe was Joe was Joe.

I could live with that. For him. Because of him.

"It's a little like that," he said. "But I'm fixing it."

"How?"

He shrugged. "It's hard to put into words."

"Try."

He narrowed his eyes at me but took my hand in his, our fingers meshing together. "I guess it's like . . . Okay, it's probably stupid to say *instinct* and that you wouldn't understand because you're not a wolf, but it's not like that. I think you're more wolf than man these days."

He sounded proud about that. I didn't understand why.

"This is my home," he said. "It's where my father grew up, like his father, his *father's* father. We were meant to be here. There's a certain . . . magic in it, I guess. Not like Gordo's magic, but something that runs through the ground beneath our feet. It recognizes me. The pack. The Alphas. When things get frayed—broken—it feels it."

"And you broke it," I said without meaning to. "When you cut us off, you broke it."

He winced, but nodded. "Yeah, I guess I did." Then, "You felt it, didn't you?"

I remembered that feeling in my head and chest when I'd woken up that morning. The two words on my phone.

I'm sorry.

Yeah. I'd felt it.

"There was something," I said as levelly as possible.

He looked pained at that. "Ox, I—"

I didn't want to hear it. I was done with apologies. They didn't help us, not anymore. "We're good, Joe."

"Are we?"

"We're getting there," I amended, because it was closer to the truth.

"Which is why it's up to me to fix it," he said. "It's not you, Ox. Why you can't feel them. Not yet. It's me. I divided us. And I'm trying to fix it."

"How?"

He grinned. "Communing with nature, of course."

"I still don't get it," I said, thinking about my father.

He said, "Hey, Ox. That's okay. I get it enough for the both of us. I'll fix this. I'll fix everything. You trust me, right?"

Most might not have heard the doubt in his voice, the little sliver that pushed its way in at the end. But I'd known him since he was ten years old. We were just Ox and Joe and I knew him, probably better than anyone else. Even if he wasn't the boy who'd left that day years ago.

There really was only one answer to his question.

So I said, "Yeah, Joe. I guess I do."

. . .

Sometimes when I couldn't sleep, even with Joe beside me, I'd walk out into the trees. Gordo didn't like that I did that, but I told him I wasn't worried, because I had faith in his wards. I had faith in him.

He'd said he would deny it till his dying day if I told anyone that he got choked up over that.

On nights like that, I'd put on some shorts and one of Joe's shirts. I'd kiss him on the forehead as he slept on. I'd head outside into the dark, the air cool on my skin.

And I'd just walk.

It usually took less than an hour before a white wolf would catch up to me, padding along beside me, brushing up against me. We didn't speak much, but he was always there until we crawled back up into bed. Sometimes, he'd shift back. Other times, he'd stay as a wolf and we'd lie on the floor since the bed was too small. I'd take the blankets down and he'd curl up next to me, his gigantic head on my chest, rising and falling with every breath I took, red eyes watching me until I drifted off back to sleep.

. . .

Nothing came for us in that first month.

Or the second.

There were rumors. Whispers.

"They tracked him north," Michelle Hughes told us over Skype, "toward Canada."

I frowned at the screen. "That doesn't make sense. Why would he be heading away from us?"

"He's not," Joe said, a faraway look in his eyes.

"No," Michelle said. "I don't think he is."

"A distraction," I said.

"Misdirection, more like," Michelle said. She looked tired, dark circles under her eyes. "I don't know what he's planning, but it's not anything good. My teams went north, but the trail just . . . ended.

One moment they thought they were close, and the next there was nothing there."

"How can he do that?" I asked. "Can you fake a specific wolf's scent?"

"Magic," Joe said.

"Robert Livingstone," Michelle agreed. "Most likely. Joe, are you sure we can't come to—"

"We've already talked about this," Joe said, eyes flashing crimson.

"And you're being stupid about it," she growled right back.

"I have the people here I trust," he said. "That's all we need."

I hoped he was right.

. . .

There *was* trust there. However small. However fragile.

But it was starting to build.

I saw it in the way the humans began to relax around Carter and Kelly. They looked less tense, less suspicious.

I saw it in the way that Gordo laughed at something Rico said. Or the way he bumped shoulders with Chris as they walked side by side. Or the way he hugged Tanner wherever they said good-bye.

I saw it in the way Robbie grew shy anytime Kelly walked into the room, blushing slightly, eyes darting toward the ground. Kelly would always look confused at this, but he never pushed it.

I saw it in the way we moved together. We weren't in sync, not yet, but we were getting there. We were finding the rhythm, the cadence we needed. I didn't quite understand it myself, but their eyes were always on whatever doorway I walked through, like they were expecting me. They did the same with Joe.

It was in the way they spoke.

Carter said, "You can feel it, can't you? The bonds. The threads. I've never had this, Ox. I've never had a pack this big."

Kelly said, "I don't understand. Why does he keep making those faces at me? Why does he stutter every time I try talking to him? I didn't *do* anything to Robbie. I don't get why he's acting weird."

Robbie said, "I don't even know what to say to him! I don't even *know* him. Any time I try and talk to him, I forget how to talk and— oh my god, are you *laughing* at me? You're a fucking bastard, Ox, I swear to God."

Jessie said, "I tried going out with some girlfriends. We were at dinner, and they were laughing about . . . I don't know what. And all I could think about was how they weren't *there*, you know? They weren't . . . in my head. Like the others. And it was *empty* for me. Ox, I swear to God, if you've ruined a normal life for me outside of this, I will punch you in your spleen."

Chris said, "She'll do it too. Trust me. When she was seven, I accidentally—ow, *fine*, it was on purpose, stop *hitting* me, for fuck's sake—left one of her Barbies on a heating vent. It melted its face and looked . . . well, it looked just awesome. But she didn't think so. I still have a scar on my elbow from where she attacked me with her fingernails."

Tanner said, "He's different. Gordo. Maybe it's just because I know about the whole witch thing now. Maybe that colors it. But I don't know if that's *all* of it. He's different, you know? Since he came back. He's . . . quieter. And more centered, maybe. I think he needed a pack, Ox. I know he had us, but I don't think it was the same. I think his magic needed someone."

Gordo said, "I couldn't breathe. When we were gone. Not like I can here. Not like I can when I'm with you. I know you get it. I know we don't really . . . talk. About stuff like this. Feelings or whatever. It's not who we are. But, Ox, you let me breathe. I never wanted to leave you. I just . . . I'm . . . I had a pack. That night, something . . . I did what I had to. Or my magic did. I bound myself to him. To Joe. But I need you to know, I was always bound to you first."

Rico said, "If you had told me five years ago that I'd be in a werewolf pack with a kid half my age as my *alfa* who was also butt-fucking the other *alfa*—don't you glare at me like that, Ox, you know it's true—I would have asked if I could have some of whatever you were on. Life is . . . strange. Green Creek is strange."

Elizabeth said, "I started painting again. First time in three years I picked up a paintbrush and it didn't scare me. Oh sure, the idea of creating something new is *always* scary, but the act itself is cathartic. Liberating. I don't know what phase I'm in now, Ox. But I'm going to do my best to find out. Maybe green. I feel green, Ox. Do you feel it too?"

Joe said, "I can feel them."

Joe said, "I can feel all of them."

Joe said, "Little pinpricks of light."

Joe said, "My father taught me an Alpha is only as strong as his pack."

Joe said, "Ox. *Ox.* Don't you see? Can't you feel it? Our pack is *strong.*"

Joe said, "And it can only get stronger. I think—"

Joe said, "I think he would have been proud. Dad. I think he would have been proud of me. Of you. Of us."

Mark said, "It's your heartbeat."

.   .   .   .

"What?" I asked, glancing up at Mark, who sat across from me in the diner. Mark had wandered into the shop, telling me he was taking me to lunch. I wasn't surprised when we sat in the same booth he'd sat in the day I'd met him. Things always seemed to work out that way.

He was watching me with those same eyes I'd first seen when I'd barely been able to grasp the scope of the world. "How they move. How *we* move."

I frowned. "Did I say that out loud?"

"No."

I sighed. "Of course not. Fucking werewolves."

He grinned. "I know these things."

"I know you do. At what cost, though, Mark? I'll *tell* you the cost. My sanity. And my fucking *privacy.*"

"Should have thought of that before you became an Alpha."

"Like I had a choice in the matter."

His smile softened. "You had a choice, Ox. You know that as well as I do."

"Yeah," I said.

The waitress came over and took our orders. She smiled flirtatiously at Mark, but he just ordered a tuna melt and didn't react.

"I'm also your second," he said as she walked away. "The enforcer. That's how I know these things."

That . . . gave me pause. Because we'd never discussed that.

He waited.

And, really, it made sense. "Okay, then."

"You really didn't know that."

"I never really thought about it."

"You still don't have to," he pointed out. "It doesn't change things."

"Who is Joe's . . . Never mind. Carter."

Mark looked pleased.

"Heartbeats?" I reminded him.

"It's how a pack works," he said. "How we move in sync with each other."

"I don't understand."

"It's your heartbeat," Mark said. "And Joe's. We move with you because we listen to the sound of your heart."

"But the humans—"

"They follow our lead," he said. "And yours. Until it becomes second nature."

"That's what we did with Thomas?" I asked quietly, because suddenly things made much more sense. How we'd been with him. How they were with me. How Carter, Kelly, and Gordo were with Joe.

Mark said, "Yes. You didn't hear it. Not like we could. But you moved with us, over time. And now we do it with you. And Joe."

We became lost in our own thoughts then. The waitress eventually brought out our food. Mark's foot was pressed up against mine, touching, always touching.

I looked down at my soup and said, "I'm glad we're friends. Still. After all this time."

He didn't say anything, but he didn't have to. I think the pounding of my heart spoke for the both of us.

. . .

At some point during the third month, we became cohesive.

There were still times where we clashed. You couldn't have twelve people together like that and always get along.

But the clashes were few and far between, and they were always shut down before they could escalate into something more.

Most stayed at either the Bennett house or the old house more often than they didn't. Joe and I didn't think to move from my old bedroom, even though the bed was too cramped. We fell asleep together, we woke together. We would rise in the mornings, him to take the wolves out into the woods, me to lead the boys to the garage, Jessie to work, a line of cars rolling through Green Creek in the early hours.

No matter what, though, every morning Joe would touch the wolf he'd given me, that little stone wolf that sat on my desk. He'd run his fingers over it, over the head and down the back to the tail. There would be a look of such reverence on his face, like he couldn't believe I'd kept it, that I still wanted to keep it.

Without fail, we'd be late, because I'd have him pressed up against a wall, groaning as I sucked on his tongue.

He'd push for more. For me to fuck him. For him to fuck me.

But I couldn't. Not yet.

I'd seen what had happened to Elizabeth when Thomas had died.

I'd seen how far she'd gone into her wolf.

If something happened to me now, well. I knew they would be upset. They'd feel it down to their bones. Joe might not recover. Or he would, and be stronger for it.

But if we were *mated* and something happened to me?

I didn't think Joe could come back from that.

Because being mated meant being more than we were now.

He wanted it. I knew that. *I* wanted it more than anything else.

But I couldn't do that to him. Just in case. I couldn't take that chance.

Most likely we'd always have something over our heads. But I couldn't think of anything worse than Richard Collins.

I told myself again and again that once he was gone, I would take everything Joe would give me.

Because Richard *would* be gone. He *wouldn't* take this from me. From us. We were stronger than we'd ever been before. We were together. We were a *pack* like we'd never been before, all of us. We worked together. We lived together. We ate together. We were a family, and I'd already lost too many people to ever allow anyone else to be taken from me again. If it meant giving up my own life to make sure they were safe, then fine. So be it. As long as they were safe, I would have done my job as Alpha.

I didn't want to die. But I wanted them to live more. And there was guilt with that.

Because I was there at night when the nightmares came. Joe Bennett was twenty-one years old, but he still dreamed of the things that had been done to him. Whenever he would start thrashing and whimpering, caught in the claws of whatever was in his head, I would wrap myself around him, holding him tightly, whispering in his ear that he was safe, that he was home, that I would never let anything happen to him. Not while I still breathed.

He would always sleep deeper after that. Safe, while I watched over him.

This was my family.

These people were my pack.

I would have done anything for them.

Which is why, when Richard Collins came again, he came for me.

BEAST

The beast said, "Hello, Ox."

My grip tightened on the phone.

I tried to keep my heart from racing.

The wolves were in the woods, running in the early-afternoon sun. The full moon had been six days before and they were working off excess energy that still coursed through them.

The humans were sprawled out around me. Gordo was farther away, sitting cross-legged, eyes closed as he took in deep, slow breaths, his fingers curling in the grass below him.

It was a peaceful day. Soon, we would go back home to start dinner. It was a Sunday. It was tradition. Elizabeth had found a new meatloaf recipe she wanted to try. I was going to make a cucumber salad.

I said, "Hello."

Richard Collins laughed quietly. "I can hear them. The way they breathe around you. The wolves are . . . farther, but if I strain, if I listen *hard* enough, I'm sure I can hear Carter and Kelly. Mark. Elizabeth. Robbie, is it? The new one. The new Beta *bitch* of yours. And Joe, of course. The prodigal son returned home to the land of his father. A prince and the kingdom of the fallen king. Tell me, Oxnard. Does it burn knowing I put my hands on him first? Does it just *curdle* your stomach to know my fingers traced his skin before you ever could?"

I said, "Maybe. But never again."

Richard said, "Oh, Ox. Tell me you don't really believe that. Listen. Are you listening?"

"Yes."

"I want you to leave them. Now. We have much to discuss, you and I."

"Ox."

I snapped my head up.

Rico was looking at me. "Everything okay?" he asked.

I nodded and gave him a tight smile. "Just gotta take this," I said, trying to keep anything from leaking through the bonds. Alphas, I'd been taught, could dull even the strongest of their emotions so as to not put them on their Betas, their pack.

I thought, *My mother was a wonderful woman.*

I thought, *She was great and very kind.*

I thought, *I love my family.*

I thought, *Joe came home, he's home and he's here to stay.*

I thought, *I won't let anyone hurt them because pack, because love, because home.*

My heartbeat slowed.

The back of my neck was slick with sweat.

My skin felt tight.

But my heartbeat still slowed.

Rico cocked his head at me. Jessie looked up with a frown.

"I'll be right back, okay?" I said. I even smiled, a terrible, false thing that felt too wide.

They nodded.

I pushed myself up to my feet, keeping the phone at my ear as I walked away from all of them.

In the opposite direction of the wolves.

I could hear every breath he took.

The scrape of his tongue against his teeth.

I thought of calming things, like how the cucumber salad would taste, crisp and sweet, like tradition, even. The sweat trickled down my back. The sunlight burned through the trees. I thought all the birds had fallen silent, that the entire *forest* had fallen silent, but it was just the blood rushing in my ears.

I felt like I'd been walking for days through the trees.

It had been only minutes.

I said, "I'm alone. And away."

"Are you?" he asked. "I'll be honest. I expected a bit more . . . resistance from you."

"I could be lying."

"You could be," Richard said. "But you're not. Your heart is remarkably steady. In fact, the control you seem to be exhibiting is extraordinary. How is it that you can do what you do?"

"I don't know what you're talking about."

"*No,*" he said harshly. "You *don't* get to do that. You *don't* get to play me like that, Oxnard. Not today. Not *ever*. You think you know what I'm capable of, but you have no idea. I told you, Ox. I *am* the monster."

"I don't give a *damn* who you are. You will *never*—"

"Do you know Mr. Fordham?"

That stopped me, because I didn't understand. Mr. Fordham was an old guy that came into the garage every now and then. I remembered when Gordo had given him a reduced price on a catalytic converter because Mr. Fordham hadn't been able to afford it. That was just the type of person Gordo had been—still was, even—and the look on Mr. Fordham's *face* had been something extraordinary, so sweet and kind and just *grateful* at what Gordo had done for him. When he'd heard Gordo was back in town, he'd come in and shook his hand and just *talked* to him.

"Ox," Richard said softly. "I asked you a question."

"Yes," I said, feeling detached. "I know him."

"Did you know that he had a doctor's appointment today? One he needed to leave Green Creek for. He's an older man, you know. The heart tends not to *tick* like it used to. He's also rather fearless, if you ask me. Especially in light of all my teeth."

No. No, no, no.

"What did you do?"

He laughed. "Ox. I haven't done *anything* yet. But I will now. Here. Say good-bye."

The phone was shuffled for a moment as I gripped my own tighter. The sun was too bright. Everything felt too real.

Then, "Ox," a wavering voice said.

"Mr. Fordham," I breathed.

"You listen to me, boy," he said, like he had a spine of steel. "I don't know who he is or what he wants, but you don't give it to him. You hear me? You don't give it to him. His eyes, Ox. His *eyes* are colors I can't even imagine. He can't get in, *they can't get in*, so the only way is for you to come out. So don't you do it. *Don't you do it*—"

There was a wet slap against the phone.

I knew that sound.

The sound of the skin on a neck separating.

The sound of blood spilling.

Mr. Fordham, eighty years old if he was a day, choked as he died. I could hear the rattle in his throat.

"Ox?" Richard said. "Are you still there?"

"I'll kill you," I said. "I will find you. And I will kill you."

"Well, you'll certainly *try*," Richard said, sounding amused. "I must admit, Ox, I've never really met one such as yourself. I may have underestimated you the day when I killed your mother. That's not something I'll do again. And, ah, *there* it is. Oh, Ox. Your *heart*. It's beating so *fast*."

It was. It was. It was, and I couldn't stop it. The anger. The rage. I thought maybe I understood now why Joe had done what he had. Why he'd left. What he knew he needed to do even if it meant tearing himself from everything and everyone he knew. I got it now. Because I could do the same.

I was not a wolf.

But I wanted to give myself *over* to the wolf so bad.

I said, "What do you want?"

"That's better," Richard said. "Because it *is* about what I want. It's simple, Ox. You will come to me. And you will come alone."

"I won't let you use me to bring Joe. I will never let you have him."

"It's not *about* Joe. It's about *you*, Ox."

A meadowlark sang out somewhere overhead, a thin and aching song.

"What about me? I'm nothing. I'm not—"

"They kept you from me," Richard said. "And it might have stayed that way. But they didn't count on David King. They never even *thought* about him. Do you know what he told me, Ox, while I spilled his blood? He was *begging* me to stop, *begging* me to just let him go, please, to please just *stop*, I'll do anything you want, *please, please, please*." His voice had gone high-pitched and mocking before he chuckled. "He did tell me things, Ox. Before I tore his head from his body. He told me things about *you*."

I said nothing, because I knew where this was going. I closed my eyes and wished it wasn't so.

"*Alpha*," Richard breathed in my ear.

.   .   .

"There you are," Elizabeth said.

I stood in the doorway to the kitchen. I could hear the others moving around outside. And upstairs. And in the living room.

"Sorry," I said. "Phone call I had to take. Work thing."

I kept my voice even. I kept my heart steady. I was in a house of wolves and they would know everything if I let the mask slip even the littlest bit.

"Everything all right?"

I smiled at her. "Everything is fine."

Her gaze lingered a moment before she nodded. "Well. This dinner won't cook itself. Get to work, Ox. There's much to be done."

. . .

"Hey."

I looked up from the onions I was dicing.

Joe arched an eyebrow at me, leaning against the counter. He crossed his arms over his chest, muscles bulging from the residual pull of the moon. He was beautiful because he was Joe. He was beautiful because he was mine.

"Hey," I said, and it was getting harder already. I didn't know how I was going to get through this.

"Where'd you go?"

"Phone call," I said as I shrugged. "Took longer than I thought."

"Yeah? Work thing?"

I nodded, not daring to speak. I looked back down at the onions.

"Joe," Elizabeth scolded. "Stop distracting my help. He's going to cut something off if you keep posing like that. Don't be gross in my kitchen. Go find something else to do."

Joe blushed and started spluttering.

I tightened my grip on the knife and swallowed through the lump in my throat.

"I wasn't *posing*," Joe said.

"Totally posing," Elizabeth said.

"Ox—"

"Totally posing," I managed to say.

"Fine," he said. "I can tell when I'm not wanted."

No, I almost said. *You're always wanted.*

I always want you.

I never want to leave you.

I never want to say good-bye.

I'm sorry, Joe.

I'm so sorry.

I said, "For just a little while."

"Yeah?" Joe said. "And then you'll want me? I feel so used."

I nodded.

"Hey," he said, and he was right by my side, pressed up against me, nose pressed against my neck. "I was just joking. You know I don't mean it like that."

"Yeah," I said.

He kissed my jaw. "I'll leave you to it, then. And later, I'll let you show me how much you want me."

He smacked my ass and cackled as he left the room.

. . .

We sat down to Sunday dinner, all twelve of us. Because it was tradition. It was what the pack did.

I sat at the head of the table. Joe was at my right. I'd told him before that he should have his father's chair. He'd shaken his head and said I looked good where I was. No one tried to say he should have sat at the opposite end of the table like his mother and father had. It felt better to have him at my side.

The table was cluttered with food. Our pack laughed and smiled as they served themselves and each other. They fell silent, one by one, waiting.

The Alphas always took the first bite. For the wolves it was instinct. For the humans it was now routine. No one ever complained, because it was just how things where.

I picked up my fork.

I could do this.

I had to do this.

I put down the fork, because I couldn't do this. Not without saying good-bye.

Joe's hand covered mine.

I looked up at him.

He was watching me, concern on his face. "Ox?"

I said, "Sorry. It's just . . . It's been a long day. I'm a little tired."

"You sure?"

I gave him a small smile. "Yeah," I said. "I'm sure."

I hoped it was enough for him to believe me.

I turned away from him to the others.

I said, "I, uh. I don't talk. Very good. Or a lot. It's . . . It's something my dad broke in me, I think. Sometimes it's hard for me to think of the right thing to say. I get worried that I'll just make things worse."

Joe squeezed my hand.

I said, "So I don't say what I should. Like how much I love you. All of you. How much I need you. How there are days I can't believe you put your trust in me. Your faith. Because I'm just Ox, you know? My daddy told me once that I was gonna get shit. All my life. And for a long time, I did. And I thought maybe that's all there was. But then, I . . . I found people. People who didn't care that I was a little slower than others. That I was bigger. That I said stupid shit. And I just . . . You're my family. Okay? You're my family. My pack. And whatever happens, whatever comes our way, I need you to remember that. That you have each other, no matter what."

My mouth felt dry, my tongue thick. Joe's grip on my hand would leave bruises if he kept it up. Elizabeth was wiping her eyes. Mark had that secret smile on his face. Robbie looked at me like he was in awe. Carter and Kelly smiled dopily, like they were teenage boys again, like they hadn't been to hell and back. Rico, Tanner, and Chris had their heads bowed. Jessie had her arm around her brother's shoulder, pressing her forehead against his cheek. And Gordo. Gordo, Gordo, Gordo.

He was frowning.

I said, "And now that it's awkward . . ."

People laughed.

I made a show of taking the first bite.

Joe's hand never left mine.

And Gordo never looked away.

.   .   .

The Bennett boys were doing the dishes. The humans were on their way to their own homes. Robbie and Mark were in the library. Elizabeth was painting and it was green, green, green.

Gordo said, "Walk with me, Ox."

I hesitated.

He jerked his head toward the front door.

I sighed but followed him out.

He waited until he knew we were out of earshot of the wolves.

He said, "I know you."

The day was beginning to darken.

"Long time," I said, unsure where this was going.

"And we tell each other most things. Because that's the way we are."

"Sure, Gordo."

"Is there anything you want to tell me now?"

I forced myself to look at him. "What do you mean?"

He narrowed his eyes at me. "I'm not stupid, Ox."

"I never said you were."

"Something's wrong."

"With what?"

"You."

I snorted. "Many things."

"Ox," he warned me. "Don't be flip."

"I'm not trying to be. Gordo, there's always something wrong. But nothing more than usual."

"I need you to tell me, Ox. I can't help you if you don't tell me what's wrong."

I sighed. "It's nothing. Okay? I'm just tired. The full moon, work, everything. It happens every now and then. Shit just comes back and piles on. I just need to go to bed early tonight. I'll be better tomorrow."

"And you'd tell me, right? If something was wrong."

Not if it meant keeping him safe. Keeping all of them safe. "Sure, Gordo," I said, the lie tasting like ash on my tongue.

He watched me for a moment longer, his gaze cool and calculating, before he shook his head. "Fine. Just don't do that shit to me, Ox. For fuck's sake, you sounded like you were saying good-bye at dinner. I just . . . Just don't do that to me."

"Yeah." I coughed. "Just tired. All those things come out when I'm tired."

He rolled his eyes. "Well, go put your feelings all over Joe where they belong. Ah, God, I wish I hadn't said that."

I laughed, real and true. Gordo tried to push by me to head back to the house, but I grabbed his arm and pulled him into a hug. He let out a grunt of surprise, but his arms wrapped around my back immediately and he gave just as good as he got.

.   .   .

"What did Gordo want?" Joe asked me as we walked toward the old house.

The sun was almost gone. The stars were coming out above us. The wind blew through the trees. They swayed back and forth.

"Shop talk," I said.

"Shop talk," Joe said. "Sounds exciting."

"Ass."

He grinned fondly at me, taking my hand in his. "Just giving you shit."

"I know."

"You gotta keep it up, anyway, if I'm going to be your kept boy."

"That's a terrible plan. You should just get a job."

"GED first, Ox," he said, like we hadn't talked about it a million times already. "Then online college. Then probably pick up where Dad left off. We don't need the money right now."

"I know," I said. "You'll do good."

"Yeah?"

I leaned over and kissed his cheek. His stubble scraped against my lips. "Yeah. Maybe then *I* could be the kept boy."

He laughed and shoved me away.

. . .

My phone went off.

Just a single beep.

Joe lay on the couch, his head in my lap, eyes closed as I ran my fingers through his hair. He'd started growing it out again and there was almost enough there for me to hold on to. The TV was on, the sound muted.

I picked up the phone where I'd set it next to me.

I had one new text message.

It was from an unknown number.

You've had enough time.

I didn't let my hands shake.

I said, "Shit."

Joe opened his eyes. "What?" His voice was rough and wonderful.

"Jessie."

"What about Jessie?"

"She got a flat tire, and she doesn't have a jack."

"Shit. All right, give me a second, and we can—"

"Nah," I said. "Don't worry about it. It won't take long."

"You sure?"

I nodded, looking down at him. "You'll see. I'll be back before you know it."

He opened his mouth to speak, but then frowned. "Weird."

"What?"

"Your heart just skipped when you said that. Like—" He shook his head. "Never mind. I'm just tired, I guess. As long as you don't plan on running off with her, I'll let you go. This once."

"Never," I said, though I thought I was breaking. "I'll never want anyone else but you."

He smiled up at me. "You're such a sap today. Hurry up and go so you can come back. If I'm not asleep, I'll suck you off."

"Wow. With an offer like that, I should be running out the door."

"Damn right."

He let me lift up his head and move from the couch, putting one of the pillows under him to take the place of my lap. I knelt down next to the couch, cupping his face in my hands. I leaned forward and kissed him. He sighed happily, hand coming up to scratch at the back of my head. He pressed his tongue against my lips, just once, and I pulled away.

I ran my thumbs over his eyebrows. His cheeks. His lips. He hummed softly. Safe. Content.

"I love you," I said, because if there was one thing I hated, one thing I blamed myself for more than anything else, it was that I hadn't told him this every day. Multiple times a day. It was a rare thing between us. We didn't need to say it out loud to know how we felt, but that shouldn't have stopped me.

"Yeah?" he asked, kissing my thumb before taking it between his teeth and biting gently. He let it go and said, "I love you too, Ox. You're my mate. And one day soon, I'm going to show you that."

I had to go before I couldn't.

I kissed him again.

Stood.

Picked my keys up off the coffee table.

Took a step back.

His eyes were already closing. "I'll wait for you," he mumbled.

My throat closed.

I turned and left before he could see the shine in my eyes.

·   ·   ·

Alpha.

What?

I know you're an Alpha.

I'm not. I'm human. I am nothing—

Don't. Lie. To me. I don't know how you did it. I don't know what makes you different. But you are an Alpha, human or not. An Alpha in the Bennett territory, no less.

What do you want?

I have six more people from your town.

You fucking asshole.

I will kill them, Ox. I will kill each and every single one of them. I will make you listen while I tear their arms from their bodies. Ox, one of them is a child. *Surely you wouldn't want to be responsible for the death of a* child.

You goddamn animal.

Oh, Ox. I know this about myself. And if you're just now figuring that out, you're a bit late to the game.

You won't get away with this.

I won't? Ox, I already have.

What do you want!

You. I want you. If I can't take the Alpha from Joe, I will take it from you. You will come to me. Alone. And I won't harm these people. This child. Can you hear them, Ox? They're crying because they're scared. Because I've already made the child bleed. Just a scratch, but enough to show them how serious I am. To them. To you. Can you see now, Ox? How serious I am?

You won't ever get to Joe. The wards will keep you out. Even if you're an Alpha. It doesn't matter who you have with you. Gordo won't—

Ox, Ox, Ox. You are missing *the entire* point. *I don't* care *about Joe. I don't* care *about your territory. All I care about is that you are a Bennett in all but name. All I care about is taking from you the one thing Thomas Bennett never wanted me to have. Hell, let me have this and I won't harm a single member of your pack.*

And you expect me to believe you?

You said it yourself, Ox. I can't pass the wards. Frankly, whether or not you believe me isn't a concern of mine. Can you really go on, knowing these innocent people will die because of you?

I . . .

Ox. You were never meant to be an Alpha. I can take this all away. Your pack will be safe. These people will be safe. Green Creek will be safe. And Joe. It'll hurt, I'm sure. At first. Loss always does, that sharp stab of pain that guts you. But he's strong. Stronger than even I gave him credit for. He'll live, because he'll have a pack that will need him. One day, he'll smile again at the thought of you, at the memory of you.

I can just . . . can't I just give it to you—

Ah. I'm afraid there isn't time. I know of only one way to truly take the power of an Alpha. It's an unfortunate side effect, death is, but I'm sure you can understand. I can promise I'll even make it as painless as possible.

I can't. I can't just leave *them. They're my—*

Do you hear her screaming? She's the mother, Ox. Her child is watching as I cut her.

Stop it! Oh my god, stop it. You fucking bastard. Leave them alone!

I'll give you the remainder of the day. I know how much . . . tradition . . . meant to Thomas. So have it. Say your good-byes. But, Ox, I swear to you, if I even catch the barest of hints that you've deceived me, I will kill them all. And then I will find a way to break these wards. No matter how long it takes. I will break *them, and I will slaughter every single person you love. I will save you for last. I will make you watch as your pack dies in front of you, and all the while, you'll be mired in the knowledge that it's because of you, that you could have prevented this. And when I get to Joe, I will* fuck *him until he's broken. I will* fuck *him until he smells of nothing but me. And then I will rip his heart from his chest. You'll watch as I eat it. And then, and* only *then, when you are* shattered *at the loss of your pack, at the way every single one was* torn *from you, I will begin on you. I'll start at your feet and work my way up, and by the time I get to your fucking knees, you will be* begging *me to kill you. And I will say no. Do you believe me? Do you believe I'll do that?*

. . . Yes.

Good. That's real good, Ox. Have your last hours. Not a single word. I won't touch the people here. Not unless you make me. Your pack will never be safe if you do. You can't keep them locked in Green Creek forever, Ox. One day, someone will slip and I will be waiting. You do this now, and I promise *you they will be safe from me.*

When?

When I summon you. I'm a monster, Ox, but I'm not that bad. I'll give you time. With those you love.

Where.

The wooden bridge. Where I can smell the spilled blood of Omegas. Mine, maybe. Or they could have been. Was this you, Ox? Did you defend your territory like a good Alpha? It's buried in the dirt, but I can almost taste the fear. The pain. The anger. It tastes like Joe did. When I had him. I licked the sweat from his head. Did he ever tell you that? I didn't go further, but it was a close thing. Every time I snapped one of his little fingers, I wanted to stuff him full of my—

That's. Enough.

Ooh. I can feel it. You are an Alpha. The goose bumps, Ox. They are crawling along my skin. I wish there was time to find out how you did it. How you became an Alpha on your own, but alas, there isn't. I would just hate to prolong the inevitable. It would sour the taste of you.

Take the time you need. I will let you know when to come. Remember, Ox: not a word, or I will make them all suffer. I'll see you soon.

. . . . .

Foolish, yes.

But if there was even the *smallest* chance Richard was being truthful, that he wouldn't hurt them, wouldn't hurt *Joe*, I had to take it.

And I couldn't let innocent people die when I could do something to stop it. Thomas had taught me that there was value in all lives, that it was an Alpha's responsibility to care for those in his territory, even if they didn't know what an Alpha was.

Green Creek was mine.

The people here were mine.

I had already failed Mr. Fordham.

I couldn't let that happen to anyone else.

I waited until I'd left the dirt road, the truck's tires kicking up dust until they rolled onto asphalt, before I started to mute the bonds between myself and the pack one by one.

We did that sometimes, when we wanted privacy. When we were being intimate. When we wanted to be alone. When we wanted not to be overwhelmed by the continuous feeling of *pack pack pack*.

When we wanted to keep secrets.

I rarely did it.

And I knew it wouldn't be long before questions were asked.

Green Creek was almost empty this late. The moon was half full. The street lamps along the main drag burned softly. I didn't see any other cars moving.

The diner was lit up almost like a beacon. I saw a waitress moving around inside as I passed by. She held a pot of coffee in her hands. She was smiling, about what, I'd never know.

My mother sat in the seat beside me.

She said, "Are you sure about this?"

I said, "For them? Always."

She said, "I thought as much" and "I love you" and "I am so proud of you" and "You've got a soap bubble on your ear" and she *laughed*, and it was a beautiful sound, a joyful sound, and it was so much like her that my eyes burned and my throat closed.

But she wasn't really there at all.

I passed out of the lights of Green Creek.

Red eyes looked at me from the passenger seat.

Thomas said, "An Alpha is only as strong as his pack."

I said, "I know."

Thomas said, "You are one of the strongest Alphas I've ever met."

I said, "Am I strong enough to do this?"

Thomas said, "Are you going to do this?"

I said, "Yes."

He said, "Then you're strong enough" and "You're my son just the same as the others" and "We'll sing together soon and I promise you, it'll fill your heart" and his eyes flashed red again, because even in death, he would always be an Alpha. *My* Alpha.

The bridge was a couple of miles away when I pulled over to the side of the road.

I had one last thing to do.

The seat was empty next to me.

They hadn't really been there, I knew that, but I thought maybe I wasn't alone.

I picked up my phone.

I typed two words to Joe and two words only.

Because I knew he'd understand.

He'd find it in the morning when he woke, since I'd turned his phone off before I'd left.

I stared at the screen, hesitating.

I didn't think I could do this, what if I couldn't do this, *what if I couldn't keep them safe—*

I hit Send.

The message disappeared, relayed into towers and then the ether.

I turned off my phone.

I hoped he didn't hate me for this.

I hoped he could forgive me one day.

I hoped he would find happiness again.

He'd know what the two words meant. Because he'd sent the same thing to me when he'd known what had to be done.

I pulled back onto the road and continued toward the old bridge.

And I thought those two words over and over again.

I'm sorry.

I'm sorry.

I'm sorry.

. . . . .

The road to the bridge was empty as I approached.

There were no street lamps out here.

Only the moon and the stars.

It was very dark.

My headlights lit up the bridge, thirty feet away.

It was empty too.

But I could feel them.

A poison on the land that had somehow become mine.

It was a blight against the grass and the trees and the leaves that shuddered in the wind.

A wound that was festering.

I turned off the truck. I left the lights on.

The engine ticked. I breathed evenly and slowly. Thomas and Mom didn't come back.

I wished they would, even if they hadn't been real.

I didn't want to walk this alone.

The pack bonds were completely cut off.

I felt cold and empty. I hadn't felt like this in a long time.

I took the crowbar out from underneath the seat. It felt smaller than it'd ever felt before.

I opened the door of the old truck. It screeched in the quiet night.

I stepped out onto the dirt road.

I did not tremble.

I did not shake.

I gripped the crowbar tightly and closed the door to the truck.

I moved toward the front of the truck, the headlights stretching my shadow until I looked like a giant against the wooden bridge.

I felt the moment I passed through the wards, like walking through a spiderweb. They brushed along my skin, and then the moment was over.

There were crickets in the grass, and they creaked.

I did not falter. The crowbar was cold in my hands.

A flash of violet off in the trees. Blinking once. Then again.

Then another pair. And another pair. And another.

They came then.

Out of the shadows.

There were ten of them.

Omegas.

More feral than I'd ever seen before.

Their eyes were continuously violet.

They were half-shifted, slobbering through fang-filled mouths.

Six humans were pushed out in front of them.

Their hands were bound behind them.

They had gags in their mouths.

Five adults, one child.

They all looked terrified, eyes wide and cheeks streaked with tears.

Two men. Three women. A little boy.

I recognized them. All of them. I'd seen them in Green Creek. They came into the garage. I ran into them in the grocery store. We passed by each other on the street. We waved hello. We waved goodbye. We said things like "Have a good day" and "It's nice to see you again" and "I hope everything is well with you."

Mr. Fordham wasn't with them because Mr. Fordham had been murdered while I'd listened.

They looked relieved at the sight of me, the humans.

I wasn't their Alpha—not before—but I would be now. At least, for as long as I had left.

The little boy—William, his name was. His mother, Judith.

I said, "Hey, it's okay. It's all right. I know it's scary. I know. But

I'm here now. I'm here now and I promise I will do everything I can to make it okay. Just have faith in me. I will take care of you."

The Omegas snarled as they laughed. They scraped their claws against human skin, leaving welts but not drawing blood.

The humans cried, tears and snot on their terrified faces.

The Omegas stopped in front of the bridge, standing behind the humans.

They forced them to their knees in the dirt.

Claws curled on the humans' shoulders.

The one behind William was bigger than the others. And meaner looking. He curved his claws around the boy's face, fingers hooking under his chin. He caressed the claw on his thumb along William's cheek, dimpling the skin. It wouldn't take much. Just the slightest pressure and William would be—

Another man came out.

I wondered at the dramatics of werewolves.

These ones especially, revealing themselves slowly.

It was probably Richard's idea, to come out one by one.

He knew what seeing Osmond's face would do to me.

He was playing a game, and I was falling for it.

Because it was taking all I had not to launch myself at Osmond.

The years hadn't been kind to Osmond. He looked haggard, smaller than I remembered him. Thinner. There were dark circles under his eyes. He seemed twitchy, hands flexing and then curling into fists again and again.

I remembered the first time I'd met him, the look on his face when he'd realized Joe had given me his wolf. The disgust. The *disdain*. He'd probably gone right to Richard after. Told him everything. Told him how Thomas had held him up against the side of the house at the end of the lane, snarling in his face, telling him that I was *worth* something. That I *mattered*. That just because I was human didn't make me any less than the wolves that surrounded me.

Thomas had stood up for me.

And then Osmond had *betrayed* him.

I thought how easy it would be to bring the crowbar down upon his head.

Just to see the skin and skull split, the spray of blood.

I'd be torn apart, sure. I probably wouldn't even make it over to him before I was surrounded by Omegas.

But I could try. I really could.

His eyes flashed like he could hear my thoughts. They were violet, just like the others'.

I said, "Your eyes."

He flinched, like he hadn't expected me to speak.

"Was it worth it?"

The Omegas laughed again.

Osmond said, "It doesn't matter." His voice was quiet. "What's done is done."

What's done is done. Like my mother. Like Thomas.

Oh, the rage I felt.

The *anger.*

It must have been radiating off me, and even though the Omegas weren't mine, even though I was not their Alpha, I was still *an* Alpha, and their shoulders tensed and they whimpered and they *whined* at the sight of me.

Osmond looked to cower, but stopped himself at the last moment. "Enough," he said harshly to the Omegas. They barked and yipped at him in return.

"How did you do it?" Osmond asked me. "How did you become an Alpha?"

"How do you sleep at night?" I asked him. "Knowing you did what you did?"

"I sleep very well."

"Lie," I said. "You don't look good, Osmond."

"This isn't going to end well for you. You have to know that by now."

I smiled at him. He flinched again. "Maybe not," I said. "But I know who I am. Can you say that?"

"We looked into you, Matheson. No wolves. No one in your family was ever a wolf."

I said nothing.

"We thought that it could be the witch. You were part of his coven, his pack, even before you knew the wolves. But there isn't magic strong enough to create an Alpha. Believe me, he looked."

Robert Livingstone. I wondered if he was here. I thought not. Gordo would have known, even without the wards.

"No magic," Osmond said. "No wolves. And yet here you are."

"Here I am," I agreed, waiting for the monster to show himself, to slink out of the dark with fang and claw.

"How?" he asked again. "How can you be the Alpha if you can't feel them?"

"Does it matter?" I didn't touch the last part. Because it sounded like he didn't know about the bonds. About the threads that tied us all together. And if he didn't know . . .

Osmond narrowed his eyes. "If you could do it, there could be others."

I knew what it was. For the most part. But he didn't need to know that. He didn't need to know that it came from grief and need. That it came from trust and belief. That there were wolves and humans alike who believed in me so much that I couldn't be anything *but* their Alpha. That even though I wasn't a wolf, they trusted me to care for them. To love them. To give them a home and make us a family.

It was something Osmond could never understand.

It was something Richard *would* never understand.

Because even if he took this from me, even if he ripped it from my chest, he would mangle it and twist it into something unrecognizable. He could be an Alpha, but he would never get what it meant to *be* an Alpha.

I said, "Where is he?" I was done with Osmond. I was done with waiting.

Osmond said, "He'll come when he's ready."

I snorted. "Drawing this out, then. Listening as you try and get as much information from me as you can. You're his bitch, Osmond. You've never been anything more than his bitch."

Osmond growled, eyes flashing as he took a step forward. "Chaney," he said coldly, eyes never leaving mine. "Just a little bit."

The mean wolf, the large wolf, the wolf holding onto William, grinned, his chin wet with saliva that leaked from his mouth. He dragged his thumb harder against the boy's cheek, splitting it cleanly. The boy shrieked into his gag, blood spilling. It was a thin cut and probably wouldn't even scar, but the wolves smelled the blood and began to gnash their teeth. William's mother tried to lunge for him but was snapped back by her hair, the Omega behind her jerking it none too lightly.

"Don't," I said hoarsely. "Just—"

I was distracted. By the wolves. By the humans. By the blood dripping down William's face. It made sense. It was overwhelming. I was surrounded by Omegas who were shifting further and further into their wolves, by Osmond, who looked both defiant and nervous.

I was distracted.

Which is why I didn't hear him coming up behind me.

Which is why I didn't anticipate his arm coming up around my chest, pulling me tightly against him.

Which is why I didn't expect his other hand to latch itself around my throat, claws digging into my neck.

His breath was on my ear. It stank of flesh and blood.

Richard Collins said, "Hello, Ox."

I closed my eyes, and even though I tried to force it down, my heart tripped and stumbled in my chest.

He felt it. He heard it.

He chuckled at the sound, the rapid beat.

He sounded amused when he said, "You don't stink of fear. Curious, that."

"Because I'm not afraid of you," I said even as he tightened his grip around my throat. His front was pressed against my back, his lips near my ear. It was the furthest thing from intimate I'd ever experienced.

"Maybe," he said. "If you aren't, it's only because you've convinced yourself of it. But I can make you scared of me, Ox. Very quickly, if I choose to."

The Omegas in front of us grinned and ran their claws over the heads of the humans at their feet. Osmond watched us warily, eyes flickering violet.

"It's quiet?" Richard asked.

Osmond nodded. "Only him."

"Good," Richard said. "It's a start." Then, "Thank you, Ox. I knew I could count on you."

"Fuck you."

"Such kindness. Now for your next trick, I need you to drop the crowbar. You won't be needing it."

I didn't move.

"Ox," he said, voice filled with regret. "I can do this as easy or as hard as you make me. Really, the power is in your hands as to how this can go. Don't you want this to be easy?"

He lied, I knew. His words were filled with promise that died in my ears. Nothing about this would be easy.

"Ox. Drop. The. Crowbar."

I was an Alpha. I was a goddamn *Alpha*—

I didn't have time to move or even react when he dropped the arm around my chest, his hand snapping to my wrist. He twisted it brutally, the bones grinding, then breaking. A wave of pain shot up through me, glassy and sharp. My stomach rolled as the crowbar fell to the ground. It kicked up a plume of dust as I gritted my teeth together, trying to swallow back the cry that wanted to fall from my mouth.

"That was . . . unfortunate," Richard said, and he shoved me down into the dirt.

I tasted dirt in my mouth.

And, for the first time, panic.

It started in my chest, a slow roll that crawled through me, little pinpricks that turned into something so much stronger than I'd ever felt before. It wasn't *just* panic. Or, at least, not just my own.

It was the panic of the pack.

The bonds had reopened.

No, no, no, no.

Thomas whispered, *The Alpha's greatest gift to his pack is sacrifice. Because he must protect them above all others, at all costs. Even if it means his own life.*

They would come.

As soon as they recovered from the anger, the rage, the pain, they would come.

I tried to push the threads down, but they were bright and electric, like live wires. I couldn't push them away because they were *aware*.

They were coming.

And Richard didn't know it.

I couldn't take the chance.

I couldn't let any of them get hurt.

It would take time for them to find me. They thought I was at the garage.

Maybe there'd be enough time to—

But there was one, one that was brighter than all the others. Closer. Angrier.

I felt his fury. I felt his magic.

Gordo.

Gordo was here.

Gordo was here.

I rolled over onto my back. The crowbar was off to my left, within reach.

Richard towered above me, a look of disgust on his face.

I said, "If I give you this, if you take this from me, you give me your word that you'll leave them alone. All of them. The pack. The people. Green Creek."

"I don't know that you're in a position to ask me for *anything*, boy," Richard growled. "You are *human*. You may be an Alpha, but it was *never* yours to have. I will take it from you and you will—"

"Don't you want to know how I did it?" I asked, clutching my wrist to my chest. "How a human became an Alpha?"

He paused. Then, "I'm listening."

"They'll hear," I said. "The Omegas. They'll hear and they'll try to do the same. They'll take it from you. They'll try to become Alphas themselves. You don't want that."

He crouched down next to me. Stupid man. I hated him more than anything in the world.

"You should speak now," he said in a low voice. "Before I run out of patience."

And I said, "Fuck you."

I moved quicker than I ever had before. I was fueled by sorrow and despair, by ire and that feeling, that goddamn feeling of my *father*, my daddy saying *you're gonna get shit, Ox*, because here he was, here was Richard fucking Collins proving my dad right. He was giving me *shit*, and I wasn't going to take it now. I shouldn't have to begin with.

But most of all, it was pack that pushed me, pack that allowed me to move as I did, it was pack and pack and *pack*, these people, these wolves that were my family. And Joe, who I could feel rising within me, Joe who was scared and furious and *coming*, oh God he was *coming* for me.

I pushed along the thread toward Gordo, stronger than it had been since he'd come back, saying *the humans the humans the humans you can't let them hurt you have to help them save them help them,* even as my fingers curled around the crowbar in the dirt.

Richard's eyes flickered to my hand.

I swung the crowbar in a rising arc. It smashed into the side of his head with an audible crunch, the breaking of bone jolting down the bar into my arm. He grunted and started to drop to the side.

Gordo came then.

He stepped out from behind the truck, tattoos blazing brighter than I'd ever seen them before. The raven flapped furiously, and I swore I could actually *hear* its cry when it opened its beak, a loud, shrill call that vibrated deep into my bones. I felt the *thrum* of his magic on the ground as it pulsed deep within the earth. It called to me, saying *AlphaAlphaAlpha,* and I *pushed* into it, grabbing the thread between Gordo and me as tightly as possible.

Even before Richard hit the ground, a snarl already forming on his broken face, the ground around the humans and the Omegas shifted and broke apart. Great columns of earth rose up with a loud roar, knocking the humans forward and the Omegas back.

Osmond was moving forward as I pushed myself to my feet. His focus was on Gordo, claws outstretched, snout elongating as he ran toward the witch. I flipped the crowbar until the curved end faced away from me and swung it down at Osmond's legs as he tried to run by. The crowbar smashed into his shins as I put my all into that hit. He cried out at the crack of bone, the sizzle of skin, but I pushed through the swing as hard as I could, sweeping his feet out from under him. He fell forward into the dirt, his momentum causing him to skid along the road facedown, coming to a halt near Gordo's feet.

I didn't stop, turning away from them, trusting Gordo to have my back. I ran toward the broken earth, sliding in the dirt as I fell to my knees in front of the humans. They were dazed and unsure. I started with Judith, ripping the gag from her mouth.

"You have to help me," I said, cupping her face as the earth continued to crack behind her. "You have to get them out of here. Untie them and take the truck. Go to Green Creek. Don't stop until you're at the garage. You stay there." I let go of her a moment and dug the keys out from my pocket. She started to lose focus, whimpering and looking around with a dazed expression. The others were moving slowly.

"Hey!" I snapped at her. "Listen to me. Are you listening?"

She whispered, "Ox?"

I held up two keys in front of her, inches from her face. "This is the key to the truck. This is the key to the garage. Do you understand?"

"I . . . Ox, their *eyes*, it's—"

"Judith, your son will *die* if you don't get him out of here."

She recoiled, but the fog in her eyes began to clear. She steeled herself, automatically reaching for the keys and William at the same time. She undid his bindings while I helped the other three. "You follow her," I told them. "She'll keep you safe. You don't stop until you're at the garage and *lock the doors behind you.*"

I hoped the wards would be enough. They had to be. We had no other choice.

Judith picked up William, who clung to her, arms around her neck. I pushed the keys into her hands, even as the Omegas began to growl. She turned back to me, and said, "Thank you, thank you, we'll—*watch out!*"

I was slammed into the ground by something heavy that landed atop me, crying out as pain lanced across my back where four sets of claws dug in. I had a mouthful of dirt as the wolf on my back growled near my ear.

The weight was suddenly lifted off me, and the wolf yelped in pain.

I was pulled up, hands on either arm. A woman was on my left (Megan?), a man on my right (Gerald—I thought his name was Gerald). Another man stood in front of me, breathing heavily, my crowbar in his hands. His name was Adam, and he worked at the hardware store, a kind man with terrible acne scars.

He said, "Holy fucking shit."

I stumbled forward, grabbing the crowbar from him. "Thank you."

He nodded at me, eyes wide.

"Ox!" Gordo shouted. "You need to get them moving. *Now.* Osmond's gone, and I don't know where he is."

I spat onto the road, blood and dirt mixing together. "Go," I snapped at them. "Get out of here. Hurry!"

They didn't wait for me to tell them again. They pushed each other toward the truck even as there was another low growl from behind me.

I turned.

Richard Collins was full wolf now, snout bloody, nose split. He pushed himself up on four legs, eyes violet, lips curling up around his fangs. He pulled himself to his full height, smaller than Joe and Thomas had ever been, but still a big fucking wolf.

"Omega," I said. I wasn't surprised at that. He was too far gone into his wolf to be anything but.

He snarled at me.

I took a step back, tightening my grip on the crowbar.

He coiled down, preparing to jump.

Then, a wolfsong rolled over us, echoing as loud as it'd ever been. It was howled with rage and terror.

It was the song of an Alpha.

"No," I whispered.

He'd found us. Already.

I couldn't let this happen. Joe couldn't be here. Not when there was a chance that Richard would hurt him, would take him away from the pack. A pack needed an Alpha to survive, so they wouldn't become Omegas. Thomas had been our Alpha. Then Joe after Thomas's death. Then me, because of necessity.

But Joe had come back.

And he was the true Bennett Alpha.

They needed him.

And I had to make sure he survived.

I looked back at Richard, who'd been distracted by the call of the Alpha.

"Hey!" I shouted at him. "I'm right here, you fucking asshole!"

And then I ran. Away from our territory. Away from the wards.

Away from my pack.

Away from Joe.

"Ox!" Gordo cried out behind me. "*Don't do this!*"

There was another song then.

It was deep and guttural, more scream than howl.

The song of a predator having found its prey.

I headed for the bridge, no real destination in mind, just *away away away.*

There were piles of writhing earth ahead where Gordo's magic had called up the rock and soil to cover the Omegas. I jumped over them, Omega claws breaking through and trying to grab me. A single claw scraped against my calf and there was a moment when I thought I wouldn't make it. I felt the scrape against my skin, a small flare of pain, but the Omega couldn't grab me in time.

I landed on the other side of the Omegas, glancing over my shoulder in time to see them rise from the earth, teeth bared and eyes violet. Gordo was farther behind them, staring after me, horrified. A large wolf prowled between them, waiting for me to get enough distance away to make it a good hunt.

The Omegas went for Gordo before he could trap Richard. His tattoos flared to life again as they rushed toward him. The ground under his feet shifted, rocks rising from the earth and spinning around him. He flicked his wrists and they shot toward the approaching Omegas, knocking them back and down.

Richard ignored them.

He only had eyes for me.

I ran because I had people I loved to keep safe.

I ran because Richard had shifted his attention from Joe to me, and I would do everything to keep it that way.

The bridge was dark. I could hear the wood creaking.

Then, the pounding of a wolf's paws against the dirt.

He was coming for me.

For a moment, I swore there was another wolf running with me, a great wolf, an Alpha wolf, a wolf I knew had died years before.

For a moment, I swore my mother ran with me, arms pumping, feet stomping upon the earth, hair trailing behind her.

I pushed myself harder.

I wouldn't be able to outrun Richard forever, but if I could get far enough away, then I'd—

I was close to the old bridge.

I would cross it and hope it was stable enough. The drop was only ten feet to the creek below, but I didn't want the whole thing coming down on top of me.

I hit the bridge, feet against the wood.

It groaned under my weight, the beams above me shuddering with every running step I took.

I was at the middle, sure I was going to make it. I didn't know where I'd go next, but I was going to fucking *make it through*—

Osmond dropped down from the shadows on the far side of the bridge, half-shifted, face smeared with blood and dirt. I skidded to a halt, almost falling forward. I caught myself at the last second.

A wolf snarled behind me.

I glanced over my shoulder.

Richard Collins stood at the other end of the bridge. He took a step toward me.

"It's over," Osmond said. "You've lost."

I nodded. "Looks like."

"You would never have won."

I chuckled darkly. "Jesus Christ. Fucking get on with it."

Osmond narrowed violet eyes. "What?"

"Don't fucking talk at me," I snarled at him. "You want me? Come and fucking *get me*."

Osmond growled.

Richard roared.

And they ran toward me.

The bridge shifted and groaned.

There was a crack of wood from up above.

They leapt, just like I knew they would, but flying toward me.

I waited until the last possible second, hearing the sound of claws slicing the air before I dropped to my knees.

I threw my arm up, crowbar in hand, ends facing toward Richard and Osmond.

Their momentum was too great to change direction midair.

Richard struck the crowbar first, the point end impaling his chest, snapping bone and muscle even as the silver started to burn. My arm jerked the opposite direction with the force of the impact. The curved end of the crowbar smashed into Osmond's throat. The silver scalded, and the pressure from Richard's impact forced the curve *into* Osmond's neck, stabbing and tearing through his throat. Blood sprayed out on either side of me even as their claws cut into my arms and chest, seizing and skittering along me as the pain from getting speared with silver started rolling through them.

My arms were drenched in blood, mine and theirs. I couldn't hold the weight of both of them up, and the crowbar slipped from my bloody hands. They fell to the floor of the bridge with a loud crash, arms and legs kicking as they both gagged and flashed their teeth, each trying to pull away from the bar lodged in his neck and chest. The bridge shook and creaked.

I scrabbled away, kicking out when Osmond reached for me, pushing my back up against the wooden wall of the bridge.

They were collapsed just out of reach, connected by the crowbar.

Both sets of violet eyes were on me.

There was pain, but it was distant. I couldn't tell what blood was my own.

The bridge groaned again, louder than it had before.

The cracking of wood became louder, the struts starting to shake.

The whole goddamned thing was going to come down.

I almost didn't care.

I wanted to close my eyes. Maybe sleep for a little while.

There was a low growl.

I looked down in front of me.

Richard was trying to stretch toward me, but the heavy weight of the crowbar in his chest, pinning him to Osmond, didn't allow him to move much. He craned his neck, jaws frothing as they snapped near my foot. His teeth were only inches away.

I pulled my foot back before kicking out viciously. There was a crunch of bone as he howled and pulled back, shaking his snout.

The bridge lurched nauseatingly to the left. It was only inches, but it felt like miles.

Dust filtered down from the wood above.

I laughed. Because I could.

I tilted my head back and against the wall and laughed.

"You'll die here," I told them as Osmond's legs kicked weakly, hands burning as he tried to pull the bar from his throat. "Both of you. You'll fucking *die* here. You failed. You didn't get Joe. You didn't get *me*."

Richard began to drag himself toward me, more bloody than not.

I had to move.

It'd be easier not to.

But I'd never taken the easy way out.

I pushed myself up the wall, using my legs instead of my shredded arms.

Richard snapped his teeth at the movement, struggling to move faster.

Osmond was starting to seize, eyes rolling up in the back of his head, mouth open, shifting between human and wolf, hands into claws and then fingers, scraping along the floorboards. His neck was pulled at a sharp angle as Richard continued toward me.

I stood above him. Above the wolf. He glared up at me, tongue lolling as he bared his teeth near my foot.

I said, "You'll never have him. You'll never be an Alpha. You lost. And now you'll die. For *nothing*."

The bridge began to break apart, the floorboards splitting, a large crack running up the wall as the wood splintered off. The walls and ceiling began to shift to the left, the bridge about to collapse.

And with all that I could, I ran again.

Every step hurt, my arms useless at my sides.

But I didn't want to die in here. Not with them. Not like this.

I had protected my pack from them. Joe would find me. Everything would be all right.

I tripped near the end.

A floorboard had snapped up, hitting me in the shin.

I crashed to the ground, turning to land on my shoulder to avoid hitting my face.

A wolf roared behind me as the bridge broke down.

A voice whispered in my head.

It said, *get up.*

It said, *we're almost there but you need to get up.*

It said, *AlphaBrotherLoveSonPack get up get up get up.*

It said, *we love you.*

It said, *we need you.*

It said, *you're our Alpha and you need to GET UP.*

It said, *GET UP GET UP GETUPGETUPGETUPGET—*

I got up, because I would do anything for them.

Everything hurt, but I got up.

The bridge was tilting now, the roof coming down around me, so close that I could have reached up and touched the ceiling.

I took those remaining steps, and the moment, the *second* my feet touched dirt, the bridge crashed into the creek below in a cloud of dust.

There was a loud cry through the bonds, the threads that stretched between us, a call of horror, of *no no no* and *OxOxOx DON'T YOU DO THIS OX—*

And I said, "Hey, Joe," because there was no one else that would have screamed for me like that, no one else who would have sounded so desperate to hear my voice.

And the song he howled was a wondrous thing, filled with such green relief that it caused my eyes to burn.

It echoed in the trees around me. He was close. So close.

I needed to see him. To make sure he was okay. To tell him how sorry I was. That I never wanted to leave him. That I never wanted to be anywhere but by his side. All I'd ever wanted was to keep him safe. Ever since that first day on the road, when he spoke and moved like a little tornado, all I'd ever wanted was to make sure nothing ever happened to Joe Bennett.

He was coming for me.

I tried to focus on the rest of the pack, to make sure they were all right, but Joe was overwhelming. Everything was him. He was all I could hear and see and taste and smell.

I stumbled my way down into the creek bed as carefully as I could. The debris from the bridge lay spread out in the water, piles of boards and nails strewn everywhere. I didn't feel them—Richard, Osmond, the Omegas. Not anymore. The poison was gone.

My feet hit the water, boots and pant legs soaked.

I could hear them now.

The pack.

Joe.

I started to climb up the side of the creek bed. Blood dripped down from my arms into the dirt, but it was okay. It was all right. I was almost home.

I reached the top.

And there he was. The white wolf with the red eyes. Only yards away.

There was the familiar shift of bone and muscle. And he stood there, watching me with wide eyes and not a stitch of clothing.

He said, "Ox." His voice was hoarse and broken. "I thought . . . I *thought—*"

So I took a step toward him and said, "No, it's okay. It's okay, I promise you, he's done, it's done, I promise, Joe. I'm sorry. Please don't be mad. Please don't be mad at me. I'm sorry, I'm sorry, *I'm—*"

There was an explosion from behind me.

I whirled around.

The remains of the bridge were blown apart as a half-shifted Richard Collins rose from underneath and landed in front of me, body bloodied and broken, claws extended.

One hand landed on my shoulder and pulled me toward him.

"*Alpha*," he snarled in my ear.

And then I was impaled by his other hand, claws slicing into the skin of my stomach, punching in until his whole hand was inside me.

Joe screamed behind me.

I'd never heard him make such a sound before.

It broke my heart even as Richard Collins tore his hand out of me.

I coughed, unsure of what had just happened.

I looked down.

Blood was gushing out of me.

Part of me was hanging out, a wet and red meaty-looking thing.

I looked back up. I felt like I was moving in slow motion.

I was very tired.

Richard took a step back as I fell to my knees. Blood began to pour from my mouth.

Richard tilted his head back. Popped his neck from side to side.

The lacerations on his body started to heal.

He opened his eyes.

They burned the red of an Alpha.

For those next long few seconds, he had gotten what he wanted. What he'd started so many years before had finally come to an end.

He roared.

I felt it down to my very bones.

It was a strong sound.

A powerful sound.

But it was cut off when Joe Bennett placed his hands on either side of his face, claws extended, and then tore Richard Collins's head from his shoulders.

Richard sank to his knees, mirroring my own pose.

Except I bled from the wound in my stomach.

He bled in great bursts from the ragged stump of his neck.

It was fuzzy. My everything.

I couldn't swallow.

I didn't think I could breathe.

Joe dropped Richard's head to the ground, and I wanted to ask why he was moving so slowly. He was an Alpha, but it was like he was underwater and I didn't understand why.

Richard fell backward.

I did the same.

Before I hit the ground, arms came underneath me, breaking my fall.

I blinked up as I was lowered the ground. The stars were so very bright above.

And the moon. Ah, God, the *moon*. I wished it was full. Because full moons were my favorite kind of moon.

Joe's face came and blocked it away. I decided that was okay, because I loved his face more than I could ever love the moon.

I tried to tell him as much, especially since he was crying, but I couldn't seem to find the words.

But we were underwater. I didn't think I should talk when we were underwater.

His lips were moving, he was shouting and crying, but I couldn't make out the words. I could *hear* him, but it was in my head and chest and he was saying *no* and *please* and *you can't do this i won't let you do this do you hear me do you hear me Ox you're my Ox and i can never let you go i will never let you go i need you i need you more than anything because i love you i love you Ox mate pack love home you are my home home home and without you i won't ever be okay.*

There were others too.

I could see them, crowding around along the edges of my vision.

They were crying too, yelling for someone to do something, to fix this, please *fix this we can't lose him it can't end like this not like this.* There were so many of them, all their voices running together saying *why is he bleeding so much oh god he can't die he can't leave us AlphaAlphaAlpha we need you here we are your pack how can you leave us OxOxOx don't go please don't go you are my son you are my brother you are my friend you are my love.*

They said, they said, *they said*—

Alpha.

Alpha.

Alpha.

One voice broke through the rest. He rose above the storm, my little tornado.

He said, *i won't let it end.*

He said, *not like this.*

you hear me

OxOxOx

this isn't our end

it'll hurt

and you'll feel it

but you have to fight

fight

for you

for your pack

and for me

OxOxOx

i need you to fight for me

I had so many things to tell him.

So many things I should have said.

So many things I'd never gotten to be for him.

He needed to know.

What he meant to me.

Everything he'd done for me.

I forced my eyes open.

I took in a gurgling breath, blood spraying from my mouth. I choked, but pushed through it.

I looked up at him and garbled out, "Thank you for choosing me."

A tear fell down his cheek.

He said, "No."

He said, "Please."

He said, "You can't, you can't, you can't."

He said, *"I will always choose you."*

And then his eyes were so red, I thought he was burning up from the inside.

Hair sprouted along the sides of his face, white like the snow.

He lowered his head, mouth open, fangs descending from his gums.

I'd never seen a more beautiful wolf.

I closed my eyes.

There was a bright splash of pain between my shoulder and my neck, but it was green, so fucking *green* that I couldn't be bothered to take another breath.

So I didn't.

And as I died, I smiled a bloody smile.

WOLFSONG

I opened my eyes.
  The moon was full and fat overhead.
  I raised my head.
I was in a clearing in the middle of the woods.
I knew this place. I knew it because it was mine.
It was home.
I sat up in this clearing.
The grass was warm under my fingers. It felt vibrant.
It felt green.
I took in a deep breath.
I could smell the trees.
I could hear the leaves fluttering on their branches.
I dug my fingers into the earth.
A rabbit moved a half mile away, running through a thicket.
I didn't know how I could hear it, but I did.
I rose to my feet.
Something was coming.
I could feel it in the vibrations in the air.
The way the forest seemed to bow around it.
Whatever it was, it was the king of the woods.
From the trees came a howl like I'd never heard before.
The song it sang caused my bones to quake.
It was love. And hope. And anguish. And every terrible, beautiful
thing that had ever happened to me. To mine.
I tilted my head back and sang in return.
I put everything I had into it.
Because I didn't know if I was dreaming.
I felt pain, but it was an ache in my heart.
Our songs intertwined. Harmonized. Became one.
I'd never howled like that before. I hoped one day I could again.
There was a tug in the back of my head.
It hooked itself in and *pulled*.
I felt my eyes sharpen. My gums itched. My hands shook.

The pull became stronger and I wanted to run.

To hunt.

To feed.

To feel my paws on the earth, tasting the wind on my tongue.

I raised my hands in front of my face.

As I watched, that *pull* in the back of my head became sharp, and claws slid out from the tips of my fingers, wicked black hooks that glistened in the light of the moon.

The king was closer.

I could hear him now. The steps he took. The breaths through his nose.

Soon he would appear.

I dropped my hands back to my sides.

The noises around me died and all was silent.

I said, "Hello?"

The forest held its breath.

A great wolf moved into a clearing.

He was white with black spattered along his chest and back. He was poised, holding himself regally, every step he took deliberate. He was larger than he'd ever been in life. My eyes burned. My throat closed off. That ache in my heart grew larger.

It wasn't that I was dreaming.

It wasn't that I was awake.

It was that I was either dead or almost there.

Thomas Bennett stood in front of me, face level with mine.

I choked out, "I'm sorry."

The wolf huffed and leaned forward, neck on my shoulder, head curling around my back, pulling me close.

I fell against him, pushing my face against his chest.

He smelled of the forest. Of pine and oak. Of a summer breeze and a winter wind. I'd never smelled that on him before, not like this. Not this strong.

He let me stay against him, waiting for me to stop trembling. He was warm. I was safe.

Eventually, I calmed.

I pulled away, the side of his head trailing against my ear.

He sat in front of me, tail thumping against the ground.

He waited.

I looked down at my hands. What could I say to him? What could I possibly say to let him know how sorry I was? How I should have done more to keep his pack together? How I thought I'd done my best. How I only wanted to keep them all safe. How I did what I thought was right. How angry I was that a monster could come and take everything away from me, could steal me from the people I loved the most. How his son was the only person I could ever see myself with.

And how, when I'd needed him the most, he'd been there for me.

As my friend.

As my packmate.

As my Alpha.

As my father.

I looked up at him.

If a wolf could smile, then I thought it would look like he did right then.

I said, "I have a choice, don't I?"

He cocked his head at me.

I said, "To go with you."

He looked back behind him, toward the woods. There was movement there now. In the trees all around us I could hear the sounds of other wolves. Yipping. Barking. Singing. Howling. There were dozens of them. Maybe hundreds.

They called to me. They sang, *we're here we're ready when you are pack and son and brother and love we're ready and we can wait for as long as you need.*

Thomas turned toward me.

I said, "Or I could go back."

He huffed again.

I said, "My daddy told me I was gonna get shit. Before he left. Did you know that?"

He whined low in his throat.

"He told me that. He said I was just a dumb ol' ox who was gonna get shit all my life. But he was wrong."

The wolves in the forest howled.

"He was wrong," I said. "Because Joe found me. And brought me to you. You gave me purpose. You gave me a home. A pack. A family."

The wolf's eyes were wet and bright.

"You are my father," I said, though my voice broke. "In everything but blood."

And I felt it then. The bond. The thread that stretched between us, even in death. It wasn't as strong as it had been, and it probably would never be while I still lived, but it was there.

And there was a whisper along it.

The quietest of voices.

It said, *Take care of them for me, my son.*

Thomas Bennett leaned forward and pressed his nose to my forehead.

And I said, "*Oh.*"

.   .   .

I opened my eyes.

I was in a darkened room.

There was heat on all sides of me.

I felt safe and warm.

And more. Because there *was* more.

There were soft *thumps* overlapping in the room.

Some were in time with each other.

Others were not.

But they were all slow and sweet.

It took me a moment to figure out what they were.

Heartbeats.

I could hear hearts beating.

Picked them out one by one.

There were ten of them in the room with me.

There should have been eleven.

There should have been *eleven*.

There should have been—

"Hush," a voice whispered near my ear. A cool hand came to my heated brow and brushed my hair off my forehead. "You'll wake the others."

"I wasn't even talking," I muttered weakly.

"I know," Elizabeth said. "But you don't have to. Not anymore."

I knew what she meant. Why she meant it. It didn't seem possible.

And I knew the heartbeat that was missing.

"Joe?" I asked.

"Close your eyes," she said near my ear. "Because things are

different now and you must find a way to hold onto your humanity.
Close your eyes, Ox. And listen."

I did.

I heard many things.

I felt even more.

There were the heartbeats of my pack, lying around me on the
living-room floor at the house at the end of the lane. Pillows and
blankets had been placed around us, and everyone had curled up
against each other, reaching and touching in some way, the wolves
curled around the humans. I was at their center. Elizabeth was somewhere near my head. There was an empty space to my right.

I heard their breaths.

The little sighs they made in their sleep.

I smelled them too, sweat and dirt and blood, but underneath that
it was the forest and the trees, sunlight filtered through a canopy of
leaves, and that smell right before a thunderstorm, ozone-sharp and
earthy.

But there was another smell. A baser smell, embedded into each
of them.

I recognized it as my own.

They all smelled like me.

Like their Alpha.

It wasn't just mine, though.

Because inlaid with my own scent, there was the heavy scent of
another.

And this one, oh *this* one sunk its claws into me at the base of my
neck and the base of my spine and *yanked*.

I growled, more animal than human.

The pack stirred around me but did not awaken. I heard their
heartbeats elevate slightly at the sound that crawled up from my
throat.

I let it pull me farther.

There was the house at the end of the lane.

There was the smell of pack that had sunk into the wood.

There were voices, echoes of the past, people gathering on a Sunday because it was tradition.

There was the scent of another Alpha, but it didn't rankle.

It was built into the rest of the house.

Every board. Every wall. Every tile.

He was here, with us.

And he always would be.

Farther.

There were the grounds around the house at the end of the lane.

A little tornado demanding that his parents tell him of candy canes and pinecones. Of epic and awesome.

There was another house.

An old house.

A house once saddened by the cowardice of a father.

A house made whole by the love of wolves.

The blood on the floor, hidden from sight but buried in the bones.

She had laughed here.

She had popped soap bubbles here.

She had sat at a table and told me we'd be all right. She'd showed me that we'd both *be all right.*

There was a line, a connection between these two houses, a thread stronger than I'd ever seen, that bound them together. They weren't separated. They were one and the same. They had been for a very long time.

Farther. I had to go farther.

It pulled.

I pushed.

Through the grass. Through the trees.

I heard every bird.

I heard every deer.

I heard the possums hidden in the brush.

The voles underground.

The squirrels up the sides of the trees.

There was a town in the mountains.

There were people who lived in this town.

I couldn't feel them, not like I could feel the pack.

But I was *aware* of them.

Like I was on the outside, barely looking in.

There was a sense of them.

My pack were bright beacons in the darkness.

The people of Green Creek were fuzzy stars at the edges of space.

But they were *there.*

I pushed.

It pulled.

The pack shifted around me, heartbeats syncing up one by one, both human and wolves.

Elizabeth sighed.

There was a clearing in the middle of the woods.

It tasted of lightning and magic.

Of claw and fang.

And in the middle of this clearing sat a man who had once been a boy.

A boy whom I had loved.

Then a monster came to town with murder on his mind and tore a hole in our heads and hearts.

The boy chased after the monster with revenge in his bloodred eyes.

The monster was gone now.

And so was the boy. Because a man had taken his place.

And this is where it *pulled* me, this is where I *pushed* it, because there was a thrum under my skin, the movement of an animal wanting to burst out of me.

The people of Green Creek were fuzzy stars.

The pack around me were lights in the dark.

This boy, this *man,* was the sun, bright and all-consuming.

The animal in me roared to be freed.

Elizabeth Bennett whispered, "*Go.*"

I went.

. . .

I was out of the door and stepping onto the grass when it happened.

There was a great ache in my body, a pain I'd never experienced before. My muscles seized as I stepped off the porch and dropped to my hands and knees. I couldn't find a way to draw in a breath. Everything was too loud. The heartbeats. The forest. Green Creek. They were all *screaming* for me, they were screaming *OxOxOx* and I opened my mouth to scream back, but the sound that came out was low and guttural, a snarl no human could have made.

My bones began to crack and break, the pieces rearranging themselves. Hair began to sprout along my skin, and it was *black* like the deepest part of the night, and I couldn't stop it, I couldn't fight it.

Claws popped out from underneath my fingernails, the strain of it tremendous.

There was a brief moment, a *human* moment, when I realized what was happening, that it shouldn't have been possible, that I had *died*, Richard's hand *in* me, my guts spilling *out* of me. I believed in magic. I believed in the impossible. I believed in werewolves and the call of the moon.

I almost didn't believe this was happening.

It's a dream it's a dream it's a—

It wasn't a dream, though, because the pain was extraordinary. It had to be, with the way everything inside me was breaking and shifting. I cried out again, my voice even less human than it'd been before. It came out garbled, and there was the thought of *I'm turning, oh my god I'm turning I'm—*before it dissolved.

The pain faded.

I was I was I was I was I was I was I was I *AM*

a wolf

colors there are

blacks and whites

blue there is blue i see blue it's

in the moon it's in the moon

it's green

everything is green

there are *others*

here i can feel the *others*

it's pack it's home it's mine it's ours ours ours *ours*

they're here

in pack house they're they're standing there standing there and watching

i am

Alpha

i am their

Alpha

eyes

my

eyes

are

Alpha

yes they are mine

all of them

oh my god the woman said the young woman the human woman who i

knew because she was mine

not mine

both pack but nothing else because of him because of him because of

he's turned the wolf mother said *he's turned because he feels him calling*

holy shit alfa one of the human men said *that is a gnarly fucking wolf*

yes

i am wolf i am gnarly am gnarly wolf

uhhh other human man said *why is he growling at us like that*

can't you feel it in the bonds the witch said laughing my witch my witch *he's being a smug fucking bastard he liked when you called him gnarly*

yes because i am

Alpha

i am big

and strong

i take care of my pack they are mine they are

mine to protect because i am

Alpha

oh jesus the last human man said *he's going to be insufferable after this*

i show them my teeth

they are not afraid they laugh because they are not afraid

good i don't want them to be

afraid of me because they are mine

and i am theirs theirs theirs but

but

where is mine

where is mine

where is mine mine mine

sing for him

i need to sing

loud song so he can hear me in the trees
i sing
the trees they *shake* with it with my song they shudder and shake
my song is
the trees are mine
the grass is mine
all of this is mine
my territory
answer me
sing me home sing for me sing it—
song song song song song song song song song *song songsongsong-
songsongsong*
in the clearing
i hear it i hear it it's for me it's calling me he's calling me because
he is
my
pack
my
mate
my
Alpha
i sing for him i sing back for him i sing for him to hear i am coming mate i am
i run
toward the song he sings for me
i run
toward the heart that beats for me
i run
because he has called me
because he is singing me home
through the trees
i sing
my song is
i sing
i'm coming
please don't leave
please wait for me
please love me

i am wolf
i am Alpha
i am yours
you are
mine mine mine mine
i see you
do you see me
are you angry
are you scared
are you mad at me
you smell sad
you smell like me but sad please don't be sad why are you sad i am
here with
you and you don't have to be
boy man wolf Alpha
please
ox he said *ox ox*
why won't you look at me
why won't you see me i am here with you i am
your skin tastes like salt
crying
are you crying
don't cry
you can't be sad
i don't like it when you're sad
he said *i thought*
he said *his hand*
he said *it was in you ox*
he said *you bastard*
he screamed *how could you*
he screamed *how could you leave me*
he is angry at me
please don't be angry
i am here i am wolf Alpha pack mate
and i can feel it
it's clawing at me
my wolf
it wants to bite

and kill
i am so angry now
you are angry
i am *angry*
you can't stop me
you can't stop this
this is
i am wolf
i am
Alpha
he said no no ox no i'm sorry
he said that's not how this is supposed to be
he said i am here
 i am here with you for you ox because you have always done the
same for me you are candy canes and pinecones you are epic and awe-
some you are the only reason why i was able to get through the years i
was gone i cut us off and tried to push you out of my mind but when it
was late when it was dark i would think of you of coming home to you
of being with you being happy being home because ox you're my home
without you i am nothing i am no one you are my love my life my pack
my mate so i need you to focus *i need you to* listen *to my heart to my*
voice to my breaths i am your Alpha and i can't do this without you so
you come back you come back you fucking come back to me ox
 i listen
his breaths
his voice and words
his heart
and i
i am
i am
I AM OX I AM OX I AM—
shifting and
"Holy fucking shit," I gagged as I fell to my human knees. There
was a hand on my back, the fingers warm against my skin, as I fought
back against my churning stomach. The world was too loud around
me, like I could hear every single thing in a ten-mile radius. I was
assaulted by the smells of the forest.
 The shift tried to push its way forward again, my claws digging

into the dirt. My gums itched, and I wanted to *push* for it, I wanted it to come.

He said, "Ox."

I growled at him.

The Alpha said, "*Ox.*"

Everything paused.

He knelt in front of me.

He took my face in his hands and tilted my head up until I could see his eyes.

They were red, a burning fire red, and they *called* to me, even now, even through the storm in my head, the wolf clawing just underneath the surface.

He said, "Listen to me."

He said, "You're here.

He said, "With me."

He said, "And I will never leave you."

I said, "I don't believe you."

"Do you trust me?"

Yes. Yes. Yes. I grimaced as my muscles tightened. "I can't—"

"Ox," he said sharply. "*Do you trust me?*"

"Yes," I bit out. "Yes. *Yes.*"

"Then I need you to trust me now," he said. "I am your Alpha. But you're also mine. Ox, I bit you to save you. You've turned. You're no longer human. You're a wolf, Ox. Like me. And Carter and Kelly. Mom. Mark. You're a wolf, okay?"

"My eyes," I managed to say. "What color are my eyes?" Because I couldn't help but think they were violet, that I didn't have a pack anymore, because I was never part of the pack to begin with. Joe was the Alpha. He'd come home and he would be in charge and they'd have no place for me, they wouldn't need—

"Red," he said quietly. "Your eyes are red."

"Fuck," I breathed and everything snapped into place.

.   .   .   .

I never thought about control.

Before.

I never thought about how much it took to actually *be* a wolf. Thomas and the others had always made it look so easy.

The only time I'd ever seen anything close to a lack of control had been the night Joe had first shifted.

Years. It'd been years since that night.

So I hadn't thought about it much.

Now it was all I could think of.

I lay in the clearing with my head in Joe's lap, his hand in my hair, both of us unconcerned with my nudity. The grass was cool against my heated skin. I was listening to his heartbeat, taking a breath for three beats, letting it out for five.

The wolf in me still gnashed, its hackles raised, but it was calming under the touch of the Alpha.

We didn't speak for a long time.

I didn't know what he was thinking. I didn't understand the smells coming off him. They were bright, these smells. Kinetic. They burned my nose. But underneath them was Joe. It was smoke and earth and rain. It was the smells I'd always associated with him intensified a thousand times over. I wanted to bury myself in them, roll around in them until his scent covered me.

But the silence ended. It had to. There was too much to say.

He said, "Osmond is dead."

I grunted, having figured as much.

"Gordo killed him. The others in our pack took care of the rest of the Omegas. The humans that were taken made it to the garage. They were safe. We found them huddled together in the back of the garage underneath one of the lifts. Gordo . . . did something to them. Altered their memories. They weren't hurt by it. They just . . . won't remember. This. The Omegas. Us. You. None of it. They'll heal. They thought they were in a car accident. It was odd, really."

Convenient. Maybe too convenient. I didn't know just how far Gordo's magic ran or what he'd had to do in the years since he'd been gone, but there'd be time. Later. Now I just needed to hear Joe. To be near him.

I tried to find words, any of them, to say something. But all that came out was a garble of sounds, more wolf than man. Joe's hand stilled briefly in my hair, but then resumed, blunt fingernails scratching my scalp.

He said, "I should have known that something was wrong."

His voice was even. Carefully restrained.

"I should have known," he said again.

I wanted to ask how he'd found out, but—

He heard it anyway. Somehow. "You closed the bonds. For everyone. I called you. Your phone went to voicemail. I called Gordo. He didn't answer. I went to the shop. The others followed me because they *knew*, Ox. They *knew* something was wrong."

A slight crack in the tone. Anger spilled through, tinged with something that tasted like pain. Or sorrow. I didn't know if there was a difference between the two.

I pressed my face into his lap, trying to stay calm.

"Gordo knew," he said. "He followed you. Said something wasn't sitting right. And he just . . . He knew. I didn't, but he did. He—"

My hands were claws.

"You foolish man," he whispered. "You stupid, foolish man."

I whined at him, begging him not to push me away. Not now. Not ever.

"How could you think this would ever be okay?" he choked out. "How could you ever think . . . ? I couldn't get to you in time. I couldn't . . . And then he was *there*, the monster from my dreams, he was *there*, and his hand was *inside you*—"

He broke off as he began to shudder.

I wrapped my arms around his waist, pressing my face into his stomach.

"I couldn't stop him in time," Joe said, no longer even and smooth. His heartbeat had skyrocketed. He gripped my hair. He was speaking through fangs. "I couldn't reach you in time. I had to watch you, when he . . . did what he did. And all I can remember, all I can remember *thinking*, is how this was a dream. That it was all a dream. But it wasn't, because you'd told me once that you can't actually feel pain in your dreams, that that's the difference between dreaming and being awake. Ox, I wasn't dreaming because I *felt* it. Everything. He tore into you and he tore into me and then his head was gone and you were *bleeding*."

He hunched over me, as if trying to protect me from everything around him.

His breath was ragged in my ear.

He said, "You fucking bastard. How dare you die in front of me."

It was then I found my voice.

Because I needed to speak.

And because he needed to hear me.

I should have said *I'm sorry.*

Or *Everything will be okay now.*

Or *The monster is dead and I'm here and I'll never leave you.*

I didn't say that, though. Any of it.

When I spoke, my words were muffled against him.

My voice was deeper than it'd ever been, like I was trapped somewhere between man and wolf.

I said, "I would do it again. If it meant keeping you safe."

He inhaled sharply.

And it was the truth. I would gladly give up my life if it meant Joe would live another day. Or any of them in our pack. Because that's what an Alpha did. Thomas had taught me that. An Alpha put his pack above all else. It was an Alpha's job to keep his pack whole. To keep them safe. To keep them alive.

Richard Collins might have tried to come after them, even after he'd given me his word.

But that was a risk I'd had to take.

Because it meant they'd be safe.

I turned, lying on my back to stare up at him.

He looked down at me.

A single tear fell, landing on my forehead.

"I hate you," he whispered.

I nodded, because I knew he did. For this one thing. "You would do the same. For me. And for that, I hate you too."

He laughed wetly. "Goddamn you."

The angle was rough when he bent over to kiss me. His back was curved as much as it could, and I raised my head slightly to meet him. It was just a graze, a brush of his lips against mine. But it felt like more than any time that had come before. There was desperation in it, and longing, and hurt, so much goddamn hurt, but there was green too. So much green shot through it because we were *here*. We were both here and not even a monster could tear us apart.

.   .   .

He traced his fingers over the skin of my stomach where Richard's claws had gutted me. There wasn't a mark, the skin completely healed. There wasn't even any pain. It was like it'd happened to someone else.

I wondered then if all my scars were gone, the marks that made up the map of my life. If they'd all healed too. The thin line on the back of my neck where I'd caught it going through a barbed-wire fence when I was six. The small divot on my cheek from when I'd had chicken pox when I was nine. The mark on my right forearm from when my daddy had been drunk and had thought it'd be funny to toss a brick at me to catch. That one had gotten me six stitches and an apology.

I couldn't look. I didn't know how I'd feel to see them gone.

I was more myself now. The wolf was pushed back. I thought it was because Joe was near. I could feel all the others, more than I'd ever felt before. Two days ago, they'd been there, but the edges had been blurred. Now, they were all crystal clear. They were waiting for us. We'd get there. Soon.

Joe said, "I turned you because I couldn't let you go." It was the first time he'd spoken in almost an hour.

I sighed. "I know."

"Are you angry?"

"No. I'm not angry at being a wolf."

"But you're angry."

"No."

"Ox."

"Not really. I don't know. I can't tell what's my anger and what's yours. It's like . . . it's going through me and—"

"Feedback loop," he said.

"I don't know what that is."

"It's a circuit. A circle. Completed between you and me. Everything I feel is everything you feel."

I nodded slowly. "Is it always going to be like this? It's . . ."

"Overwhelming?"

"Yeah."

"No, it won't," he said. "You're newly turned. Everything is dialed up. Once you get the hang of it, you can control it better."

I thought that sounded right, but it didn't help me now. "So we're both angry, then."

He snorted, hands pressing harder against my stomach. "Nah. It's just me right now. I'm pissed off."

"At me."

"Damn fucking right I am."

"Oh."

"Why?"

I didn't play dumb. I didn't think I'd be able to anymore. "Because if there was a chance he wouldn't hurt you, then I had to take it. And the others. The humans. I couldn't . . . I couldn't leave them, Joe. I just couldn't."

"You should have told me."

"Kinda makes the whole heroic thing moot if I tell everyone about it."

The breath he let out then was more of a sob than anything else, but we waited until he was okay again.

"You can't do that again," he said finally.

"If it means—"

"Ox. No more secrets."

I squinted up at him. "Is that because you can read me now like this?"

He snorted. "I could always read you, Ox. We're . . . I just could. You're Ox."

"You're Joe."

"Right," he said.

I looked up at the stars. "Do they know?"

"Who."

"Alpha Hughes. The others. Back east."

"No. I told Robbie to wait."

"Until?"

"You."

"Why?"

"We're a team, Ox. You and me. I can't do this without you. And you shouldn't have to do this without me. Not anymore."

"I can," I admitted. "Do this without you. I just don't want to."

He chuckled, and it was a nice sound to hear. "Good."

"Hey, Joe?"

"Yeah?"

"What do I look like?"

"You look like you."

"As a wolf."

"You look like you," he repeated. "I would have known you anywhere. And I will."

The sky was starting to lighten.

Birds were beginning to call out.

I was overwhelmed by the sheer *everything* of it.

He said, "You're big, Ox. Bigger than I've ever seen before. Bigger than me. Than my father. But it makes sense, you know? Because that's how you've always been to me. Bigger than anything else. That first day I saw you, I knew things would never be the same. You're all-encompassing. You dwarf everything else. When I see you, Ox, *all* I see is you."

He said, "Your eyes are red, like mine. But your wolf is black, Ox. Black like the dark. All of you. Not a single variation. Your tail is long, and your paws are big. Your teeth are sharp. But I can still see you in the wolf. I can see you there, in the eyes. I know you, Ox. I would know you anywhere."

He said, "You didn't shift because of the moon, but because you had to. Because your wolf knew it had to find me. So I could prove to you that I could bring you back. Once upon time, there was a lonely boy, a broken boy who didn't know if he could shift, and it took one person to show him how. And now I've done it for you because *that's what we do for each other.* That's what pack is. That's what this all means."

He said, "You're mine, Ox."

He said, "I'm yours."

He said, "And I can't wait to show you how I'm made for you just as much as you were made for me."

I reached up and cupped his face. He leaned into my touch. There had never been anyone such as him before. From that little boy on the road to the teenager with red eyes, to the hardened man who stood before me at the house at the end of the lane and said the *same words* he'd said to me all those years before. There was never one like him. And he was *mine.*

I pulled him down to me.

The kiss was warm and wet. His lips worked over mine, my hands holding him close, and I thought that even though the monster had been brought to an end, this was only the beginning. I didn't think

I could let him go. Not anymore. Not again. We weren't fixed. There was a chance we never would be. My daddy had told me once that people were gonna give me shit all my life. The monster had told Joe that his family didn't want him anymore. We'd have to live with that, those things that were whispered in our ears. Maybe we'd never be free of those shadows. Not completely.

But we'd still fight like hell.

And maybe that's all that mattered.

.   .   .

The sun had started to rise when the rest of our pack found us, wolves and humans both. I could hear them coming through the trees the moment they stepped into the forest. I had felt them wake up shortly before that.

I knew that when they got to us Rico, Tanner, and Chris would probably shriek at my nakedness, accusing me of trying to use my position as Alpha to make a harem. They would be all wind and bluster, but I would see the relief in their eyes as they saw no gaping wounds on me.

Gordo would roll his eyes fondly at them before handing me a pair of sweats. He would lean down and whisper in my ear that I was never allowed to scare him like that again, and I could sure as shit bet we'd have words later over my actions. He would cup the back of my neck and he'd press our foreheads together and we would *breathe*.

Jessie would look a little unsure, maybe a little teary-eyed as she watched me. She'd be the first to yell, to tell me how stupid the choices I'd made were and just who the fuck did I think I was, did I have a fucking *death wish*?

Robbie would be a wolf, and he'd rub up against me, trying to get his scent on me, hating the stench of blood that still clung to my skin. He'd tell me later it smelled like death, that *I* smelled like death, and he couldn't deal with that. He couldn't lose me. I was his *Alpha*, goddammit, and I needed to take better care of myself, because he didn't know what he'd do with himself if I was gone.

Carter and Kelly would also be wolves, and they would yip and prance around Joe and me, backsides wiggling as they pressed themselves against us, trying to act aloof, but their eyes would be just a little too wide, the whines in their throats a little too panicked to fool anyone. Eventually, they would collapse on either side of us, curling into their Alphas and closing their eyes, finally breathing steadily.

Elizabeth and Mark would bring up the rear, both of them in human form. They'd watch the others descend on us, Mark with that secret smile on his face, Elizabeth closing her eyes and letting the sounds of *pack pack pack* wash over her. They'd join us after the others had started to settle down, Elizabeth next to her sons and Mark sitting next to Gordo, both of them avoiding each other's gaze but their hands in the grass next to each other, pinkies touching, and there would be a sense of *rightness*, of being *complete*, finally, finally, *finally*.

We had lived.

We had loved.

We had lost. Oh, God, had we lost.

But we were here now. Together. And maybe this wasn't over. Maybe there were still other things to come. Robert Livingstone. Alpha Hughes. All the monsters still out there in the world.

That was fine. That was okay.

Because we were the goddamn Bennett pack.

And our song would always be heard.

EPILOGUE

He said, "You ready?"

He towered above me, a look of such reverence on his face. My skin was sweat-slicked, heated. I felt flushed and over-warm.

I almost couldn't find the words, but I managed to say, "Yeah. Yeah, Joe."

He leaned down to kiss me as he pressed slowly in. I gasped as he fucked into me, and he swallowed it down, tongue against mine. My dick was trapped between us, dragging against his stomach.

He sank down as far as he could go, his hips pressed against my ass, my legs up over his shoulders. We breathed each other in, eyes open, noses brushing together.

He said, "Oh *fuck*," against me as his hips stuttered.

And he waited, holding himself in place, like he couldn't move, like he didn't *want* to move.

I said, "It's okay, Joe. Please. It's okay and I need . . . Oh, God, I fucking *need*—"

He said, "Yeah, Ox. I'll give you what you need. I'll fuck you, okay? Just let me fuck you and—"

And he pulled away, then pushed back in. The bed creaked below us and he did it again and again, and we were both snarling at each other, my claws digging into his back, not caring if they pierced flesh.

He rolled his hips into me as he sat up, pushing my legs back against my chest until I was almost folded in half, just so he could look down and see his dick in me. He slowed, eyes wide as he watched me come apart beneath him. We'd been at this for hours, and I was too worked up to make this last much longer. For all his inexperience, he was a fast learner, doing things to me that caused my eyes to roll back into my head and my mouth to go slack.

But this wasn't about fucking or just getting off.

This was about more.

So much more.

I could feel it building in the base of my spine. I didn't try and stop the shift as it rolled through me.

Joe was the same above me, half-shifted and crying out as I clenched around him.

He said, "Ox, it's almost time."

I said, "Yes, okay, yes. Please, yes."

Because we'd been building to this. This moment.

Ever since the day he'd handed me a box that held a little stone wolf inside and promised himself to me.

I snarled, *"Do it."*

His eyes flashed red.

His fangs descended.

I came messily between us, tilting my head back, exposing my throat.

He whispered my name, said my name, shouted my name as he came in me.

And then he bit. Right in the space between my neck and shoulder.

There was pain, bright and glassy.

Then it faded, replaced with something different.

Something so much larger.

My eyes snapped open as I gasped.

Because it was *more* than I ever thought it could be.

It was *everything.*

His teeth slipped from my skin.

I could feel the blood oozing.

He was panting as he pulled back, lips as red as his eyes.

He said, "Oh my god."

He said, "Ox."

He said, "Ox, can you feel it? This is . . . I can't believe we . . . After all this time we—"

He said, "Ox."

He said, "Mate."

The wolf snarled, *"Mine."*

Read on for an extract from

RAVENSONG

BOOK TWO OF THE GREEN CREEK SERIES

BY TJ KLUNE

PROMISES

The Alpha said, "We're leaving."

Ox stood near the doorway, smaller than I'd ever seen him. The skin under his eyes looked bruised.

This wasn't going to go well. Ambushes never did.

"What?" Ox asked, eyes narrowing slightly. "When?"

"Tomorrow."

He said, "You know I can't leave yet," and I touched the raven on my forearm, feeling the flutter of wings, the pulse of magic. It burned. "I have to meet with Mom's lawyer in two weeks to go over her will. There's the house and—"

"Not you, Ox," Joe Bennett said, sitting behind his father's desk. Thomas Bennett was nothing but ash.

I saw the moment the words sank in. It was savage and brutal, the betrayal of a heart already broken.

"And not Mom. Or Mark."

Carter and Kelly Bennett shifted uncomfortably, standing side by side near Joe. I wasn't pack and hadn't been for a long, long time, but even I could feel the low thrum of anger coursing through them. But not at Joe. Or Ox. Or anyone in this room. They had revenge in their blood, the need to rend with claw and fang. They were already lost to the idea of it.

But so was I. Ox just didn't know it yet.

"So it's you," Ox said. "And Carter. Kelly."

"And Gordo."

And now he did. Ox didn't look at me. It might as well have been just the two of them in the room. "And Gordo. Where are you going?"

"To do what's right."

"Nothing about this is right," Ox retorted. "Why didn't you tell me about this?"

"I'm telling you now," he said, and oh, Joe. He had to know this wasn't—

"Because *that's* the right— Where are you going?"

"After Richard."

Once, when Ox was a boy, his piece-of-shit father had left for parts unknown without so much as a glance over his shoulder. It took weeks for Ox to pick up the phone and call me, but he did. He'd spoken slowly, but I'd heard the hurt in every word as he'd told me *We're not doing okay*, that he was seeing letters from the bank talking about taking away the house he and his mom lived in down that old familiar dirt road.

Could I have a job? It's just we need the money and I can't let her lose the house. It's all we have left. I'd do good, Gordo. I would do good work and I'd work for you forever. It was going to happen anyway and can we just do it now? Can we just do it now? I'm sorry. I just need to do it now because I have to be the man now.

That was the sound of a boy lost.

And here in front of me, the lost boy had returned. Oh sure, he was bigger now, but his mother was in the ground, his Alpha nothing but smoke in the stars, his *mate*, of all fucking things, digging his claws into his chest and twisting, twisting, twisting.

I did nothing to stop it. It was already too late. For all of us.

"Why?" Ox asked, voice cracking right down the middle.

Why, why, why.

Because Thomas was dead.

Because they'd taken from us.

Because they'd come to Green Creek, Richard Collins and his Omegas, their eyes violet in the dark, snarling as they came to face the fallen king.

I had done what I could.

It hadn't been enough.

There was a boy, this little boy not even eighteen years of age, bearing the weight of his father's legacy, the monster from his childhood made flesh. His eyes burned red, and he knew only vengeance. It pulsed through his brothers in a circle that never ended, feeding each other's anger. He was the boy prince turned furious king, and he'd needed my help.

Elizabeth Bennett was quiet, letting it happen in front of her. Ever the muted queen, an afghan around her shoulders, watching this goddamn tragedy play out. I couldn't even be sure she was all there.

And Mark, he—

No. Not him. Not now.

The past was the past was the past.

They argued, baring their teeth and growling at each other. Back and forth, each cutting until the other bled out before us. I understood Ox. The fear of losing those you loved. Of shouldering a responsibility you'd never asked for. Of being told something you never wanted to hear.

I understood Joe. I didn't want to, but I did.

We think it was your father, Gordo, Osmond had whispered. *We think Robert Livingstone found a path back to magic and broke the wards that held Richard Collins.*

Yes. I thought I understood Joe most of all.

"You can't divide the pack," Ox said, and oh Jesus, he was *begging.* "Not now. Joe, you are the goddamn *Alpha.* They need you here. All of them. *Together.* Do you really think they'd agree to—"

"I already told them days ago," Joe said. And then he flinched. "Shit."

I closed my eyes.

.   .   .

There was this:

"That's shit, Gordo."

"Yeah."

"And you're going along with it."

"Someone has to make sure he doesn't kill himself."

"And that someone is you. Because you're pack."

"Looks like."

"By choice?"

"I think so."

But of course it wasn't that easy. It never was.

And:

"You mean to kill. You're okay with that?"

"Nothing about this is okay, Ox. But Joe's right. We can't let this happen to anyone else. Richard wanted Thomas, but how long before he goes after another pack just to become an Alpha? How long before he amasses another following, bigger than the one before? The trail is already growing cold. We have to finish this while we still can. This is revenge, pure and simple, but it's coming from the right place."

I wondered if I believed my own lies.

In the end:

"You should talk to him. Before you go."

"Joe?"

"Mark."

"Ox—"

"What if you don't come back? Do you really want him to think you don't care? Because that's fucked up, man. You know me. But sometimes, I think you forget that I know you just as well. Maybe even more."

Goddamn him.

.   .   .

She stood in the kitchen of the Bennett house, staring out the window. Her hands were curled against the counter. Her shoulders were tense, and she wore her grief like a shroud. Even though I hadn't wanted anything to do with wolves for years, I still knew the respect she commanded. She was royalty, whether she wanted to be or not.

"Gordo," Elizabeth said without turning around. I wondered if she was listening for wolves singing songs I hadn't been able to hear for a long time. "How is he?"

"Angry."

"That's to be expected."

"Is it?"

"I suppose," she said quietly. "But you and I are older. Maybe not wiser, but older. Everything we've been through, all that we've seen, this is just . . . another thing. Ox is a boy. We've sheltered him as much as we could. We—"

"You brought this upon him," I said before I could stop myself. The words were flung like a grenade, and they exploded as they landed at her feet. "If you'd stayed away, if you hadn't brought him into this, he could still—"

"I'm sorry for what we did to you," she said, and I choked. "What your father did. He was . . . It wasn't fair. Or right. No child should ever go through what you did."

"And yet you did nothing to stop it," I said bitterly. "You and Thomas and Abel. My mother. None of you. You only cared about what I could be to you, not what it would mean for me. What my father did to me meant *nothing* to you. And then you went and left—"

"You broke the bonds with the pack."

"Easiest decision I ever made."

"I can hear when you lie, Gordo. Your magic can't cover your heartbeat. Not always. Not when it matters most."

"Fucking werewolves." Then, "I was *twelve* when I was made the witch of the Bennett pack. My mother was dead. My father was gone. But still, Abel held out his hand to me, and the only reason I said yes was because I didn't know any better. Because I didn't want to be left alone. I was scared, and—"

"You didn't do it for Abel."

I narrowed my eyes at her. "What the hell are you talking about?"

She finally turned and looked at me. She still had the afghan around her shoulders. At some point she'd pulled her blond hair back into a ponytail, locks of which were loose and hung about her face. Her eyes were blue, then orange, then blue again, flickering dully. Most anyone who looked at her would have thought Elizabeth Bennett weak and frail in that moment, but I knew better. She was backed into a corner, the most dangerous place for a predator to be. "It wasn't for Abel."

Ah. So that was the game she wanted to play. "It was my duty."

"Your father—"

"My *father* lost control when his tether was taken from him. My *father* has aligned himself with—"

"We all had a part to play," Elizabeth said. "Every single one of us. We made mistakes. We were young and foolish and filled with a great and terrible rage at everything that had been taken from us. Abel did what he thought was right back then. So did Thomas. I'm doing what I think is right now."

"And yet you did nothing to fight your sons. To not let them make the same mistakes we did. You rolled over like a *dog* in that room."

She didn't rise to the bait. Instead she said, "And you didn't?"

Fuck. "Why?"

"Why what, Gordo? You have to be more specific."

"Why are you letting them go?"

"Because we were young and foolish once, filled with a great and terrible rage. And that has now passed to them." She sighed. "You've been there before. You've been through this. It happened once. And it's happening again. I'm trusting you to help them avoid the mistakes we made."

"I'm not pack."

"No," she said, and that shouldn't have stung like it did. "But that's a choice you made. Much like we are here now because of the choices we made. Maybe you're right. Maybe if we hadn't come here, Ox would be . . ."

"Human?"

Her eyes flashed again. "Thomas—"

I snorted. "He didn't tell me shit. But it's not hard to see. What is it about him?"

"I don't know," she admitted. "I don't know that Thomas knew either. Not exactly. But Ox is . . . special. Different. He doesn't see it yet. And it may be a long time before he does. I don't know if it's magic or something more, but he's not like us. He's not like you. But he's not human. Not completely. He's more, I think. Than all of us."

"You need to keep him safe. I've strengthened the wards as best I can, but you need—"

"He's pack, Gordo. There is nothing I wouldn't do for pack. Surely you remember that."

"I did it for Abel. And then for Thomas."

"Lie," she said, cocking her head. "But you almost believe it."

I took a step back. "I need to—"

"Why can't you say it?"

"There's nothing to say."

"He loved you," she said, and I'd never hated her more. "With everything he had. Such is the way of wolves. We sing and sing and sing until someone hears our song. And you did. You heard. You didn't do it for Abel or Thomas, Gordo. Even then. You were twelve years old, but you knew. You were pack."

"Goddamn you," I said hoarsely.

"I know," she said, not unkindly. "Sometimes the things we need to hear the most are the things we want to hear the least. I loved my husband, Gordo. I will love him forever. And he knew that. Even in the end, even when Richard—" Her breath caught in her throat. She shook her head. "Even then, he knew. And I will miss him every day until I can stand at his side again, until I can look upon his face, his beautiful face, and tell him how angry I am. How stupid he is. How lovely it is to see him again, and would he please just say my name." There were tears in her eyes, but they didn't fall. "I hurt, Gordo. I don't know if this ache will ever leave me. But he *knew*."

"It's not the same."

"Only because you won't let it be. He loved you. He gave you his wolf. And then you gave it back."

"He made his choice. And I made mine. I didn't want it. I didn't want anything to do with you. With *him*."

"You. *Lie*."

"What do you want from me?" I asked, anger filling my voice. "What the hell could you possibly want?"

"Thomas knew," she said again. "Even at the brink of death. Because I told him. Because I showed him time and time again. I regret many things in my life. But I will never regret Thomas Bennett."

She moved toward me, her steps slow but sure. I stood my ground, even when she placed a hand on my shoulder, squeezing tightly. "You leave in the morning. Don't regret this, Gordo. Because if words are left unsaid, they will haunt you for the rest of your days."

She brushed past me. But before she left the kitchen, she said, "Please take care of my sons. I'm trusting you with them, Gordo. If I find out you have betrayed that trust, or if you stood idly by as they faced that monster, there will be nowhere you could hide that I wouldn't find you. I will tear you to pieces, and the regret I feel will be minimal."

Then she was gone.

Read on for a

WOLFSONG

SHORT STORY

As the children run ahead of her, the wolf mother thinks in green, green, green. Laughter reaches her, the sound of joy under a sky so blue it takes her breath away. Summer again, the leaves verdant, the grasses swaying in a gentle breeze. Not too hot. Next week, though. Next week is supposed to be a scorcher.

The children reach the clearing first, and she's not surprised when the oldest of the children—ever the protector—pulls the younger two apart as they wrestle on the ground.

"No fair!" the youngest cries. A boy, towheaded, with bright eyes that have yet to change color. Soon enough. He has on only shorts, refusing to wear anything else. He's a *wolf*, he's said time and time again. Wolves do not wear clothing. They run with their paws in the earth, the wind whipping through their hair, noses twitching at the scent of prey. Wolves don't have time for clothing—it gets in the way, it tears, and isn't it better to be naked?

All arguments she's heard before. The shorts were a victory, temporary though it probably will be. She's amused at the fact that boys are so . . . well. Boys.

The child in the middle—both in age and height—lies on his back, stretching his arms above his head. Quieter than the other two, he is not a mystery, at least to the wolf mother. He is like his father, in a way. Contemplative. Grounded. He sees the big picture, even if he tends to get a bit lost in it, and is worldly beyond his short years. His light-colored hair is in need of a cut, legs and arms a bit too gangly to be anything but adorably awkward.

"You just wait," the youngest says with a semi-ferocious growl. "One day, I'll be the biggest and strongest wolf. Everyone will say, *Wow! Holy crud! Look at the size of him!*"

The oldest boy snorts fondly and rolls his eyes. "I know you will be, but that won't happen for a little while yet. Give it time."

The little boy listens. They both do, to the oldest. Always. They defer to him in most things. Strange, then, that he is not an Alpha. But the wolf mother has seen many strange things in her life. Magic has a way of muddying the waters in ways she doesn't always understand.

But if there is one thing she *does* understand, it's children. "Hush," she says, motioning for them to sit on the ground before her. They do, pressed together, linking hands so they're connected. The scent that contact leaves behind is important. It strengthens the bonds between them. "Close your eyes. Clear your minds. Breathe in. Can you smell the grass? The pine needles? The wildflowers?"

The boys do as she asks, eyes closed, nostrils flaring as they inhale. She covers her smile with her hand as the oldest boy turns his head toward the forest. If he were shifted—an awkward thing with slim, long legs and oversized paws that cause him to stumble—she has no doubt his ears would be twitching. A herd of deer, half a mile to the north. At least a dozen of them. The full moon is still a week away, and she feels the pull of it, soft, insistent. For the boys—at least the older two—it will be stronger. Not painful, but there's a reason she has brought them here. A distraction meant to calm the wolf inside.

"There," she says as the children relax, their shoulders slumping just a little. "Isn't that better?"

The youngest boy opens one eye, the other squeezed shut. "I think I can hear my wolf!"

"Can you? That's wonderful. What does it say?"

He opens his other eye and frowns. "I don't . . . know?"

"And that's okay," she says as the remaining children open their eyes. "You are learning. So is your wolf. Though you are one and the same, there is a duality behind it: Human. Animal. Balance is important. Human, wolf, you are both."

"How can we be both?" the middle boy asks.

"Because one cannot exist without the other," she explains. "If there were only the wolf, you might run the risk of losing everything that makes you who you are. Our humanity is what grounds us, reminds us that we are capable of rational thought, of empathy."

"The thread," the oldest says. "Tethers, holding us together."

"Yes," she says. "To ourselves, and to each other. A wolf's tether to their humanity, be it a person or an event or even a feeling, is a necessity. Without it, we would be lost."

"Monsters," the youngest whispers.

A low, cold trill crawls up her spine. Memory, ever present. She has known monsters. Many of them. "Oh, yes," the wolf mother says. "Though, fear not, little cubs: there are no monsters here today, at least not any real ones."

This is not a lie, though it feels like it should be one. She has known pain, she has known death, she has known the evils of men and wolves alike. Rage as black as the deepest night, all in the name of what? Power? Control? Entropy, at the very least, descending into chaos, fire, and blood. She thinks herself a hypocrite, telling the cubs about the importance of humanity when it is a fickle thing, capable of great triumph and equally great horror.

But regardless of what she's seen, regardless of what she's been through, she believes what she's saying, for the most part. She has to. Anything else would mean giving in, and she's come too far to do that. Not now, not ever. She is a mother, she is a wolf, she is—as some whisper with great alacrity—a queen. Silly, that. She was never one for fealty, for subservience, but woe to anyone who stands in her way. Some have learned this lesson firsthand, and she refuses to feel regret.

The children look at her expectantly, and she says, "Now, I promised you a story, one I haven't told you before. This story is very old; not the oldest I know, but it is just as relevant as any other I've told you."

"Like the sun and the moon," the middle boy says.

"Yes," she replies. "Always in search of each other. I've told you about the First Wolf, and how they were made. I've told you about the clearing upon which you sit, a place of great power. The people lost and found. You know our history, and how we came to be in this place. But I have never told you about how Omegas were made. And why."

Their eyes widen, and the wolf mother hopes they never lose their sense of wonder, a prize effortlessly stolen by age and cynicism. No matter what else they are, they are still children, and she will do what she must to ensure that they are prepared for how sharp the teeth of the world can be.

My queen, a beloved voice whispers in her ear as a hand rests briefly upon her shoulder. And then it's gone. It's enough.

She says, "Listen."
She says, "Hear me."
She says—

.   .   .

Once upon a time, the world was feral with magic. It poured down from the sky in fierce electric storms, lightning changing soil to cloudy glass. Mountains rose higher than should have been possible, jagged cliffs of black rock covered in a snow that never seemed to melt. There were caverns that stretched to the center of the earth, caves with glittering crystals that looked like the winter sky. Flowers that bloomed in impossible colors, many of which have been lost to time.

Rivers that cut their way through the landscape, water crashing against stone.

At the base of the biggest mountain sat an endless wood with trees so large their tops touched the clouds, misty halos that seemed to glow from within. Great beasts lived in the woods, lumbering creatures with sharp teeth and dark eyes as they shuffled through the undergrowth. Some had never been seen, only heard in the deepest parts of the night as they moved with low, wet snorts and hypnotic mewls.

People lived there, too, people in houses made of wood and stone, roofs thatched with heather and water reeds. Many people who worked the land, who climbed the trees, who told stories of their beliefs, of their history. They sang songs of loss and mourning, of triumph. They lived and they died, a never-ending cycle that fed the earth in recompense. Life is a debt that must always be paid in full.

For generations, the people of the forest lived in harmony with nature. They never took more than they could use, maintaining the delicate balance with the woods. They prayed to the old gods for fertility, for the crops, for peace and love. They prayed for hope, they prayed for courage, they prayed for tenacity and perseverance. They prayed to survive because that was what tradition had taught them: the old gods—cranky, ornery things—took and took and took and, sometimes, gave in return when one least expected it.

But there was one god who was placed above all others, one god whose name was spoken with both reverence and fear equally: the God of the Forest.

The oldest god: the world was created because it willed it so. The oceans, the mountains, the grassy plains, the snowy trenches, all of it existed because of the God of the Forest.

Some even thought the humans came from the god, that it had broken off one of its ribs and fashioned a man out of grass and mud and magic—though that was the old way, and the old way was dying.

But even the humans with all their knowledge, their beliefs, their skills learned from generation after generation, even they could not stop darkness from spreading.

When it was discovered, no one knew where it had come from, or why it came to be. All they knew was that an infection was spreading unfettered through the forest they called home, growing stronger as the days passed. The people of the villages that dotted the forest came together in large gatherings, wondering aloud how such a thing could exist. Magic, they whispered. Deep and dark magic, the kind that made the shifters, people who could change their shapes into beasts with glowing eyes—though none had been seen for longer than anyone could remember. Perhaps it came from them. Or perhaps it was a way to be tested, the gods needing to be sure humanity was capable of survival.

They called it the rot.

It started in the trees: trunks cracking, a caustic black liquid spilling out, dripping to the ground. The rot spread through the forest, consuming trees and bushes, turning them into twisted and gnarled abominations covered in sharp thorns and dripping poison capable of causing death in a few short hours.

It spread to the animals, this wild darkness, turning even the most docile creatures into fearsome predators. Some deer had three eyes and horns that dripped with rot. Birds sat in the trees in large numbers but made no sound, their beaks gummed together by infection. Little animals—voles and squirrels and foxes and badgers, once thought harmless—became frightening nightmares capable of causing death.

And all the creatures infected had one thing in common: eyes of violet.

The people of the village came together and prayed to the God of the Forest. They sang. They wailed. They begged the forest to hear their calls, to tell them what must be done to return things to the way they once had been. They danced, they threw their hands toward the sky, they sobbed, they fought, they turned on one another, blood spilling, teeth bared.

And still, the forest did not listen.

After weeks of attempting to call upon the God of the Forest, it was decided that if it would not hear their pleas, then one of them must go to it in the deepest parts of the wood to make their case. Many men volunteered, each proclaiming their strength, their ingenuity, their desire to stand before the God of the Forest and prove themselves worthy.

Given that the minds of men are fickle things, they began to argue with one another, all demanding the right to be chosen. It was their destiny, it was their fate, and the longer the fighting went on, the louder and angrier they became.

But that was the thing about fate, destiny: it too was fickle, indiscriminate, and it had already made its decision.

Because there was one in the village, one who had yet to speak, one who knew that silence allowed one to watch, to listen.

And now she was done listening.

"I will do it."

Silence fell. The people turned to her as one.

The woman was young. Headstrong. Barely in her nineteenth year, and yet she thought more clearly than anyone else, her mind free of fanatical dogma. She believed in gods, yes, but that was not where her faith lay. She wanted to believe in humanity, in a purpose for their existence that had nothing to do with the gods.

But that did not mean she wasn't afraid. Oh, was she frightened. And yet, she refused to let it show.

She was tall and lithe, her feet covered in mottled scars from her time in the trees, hands coarse and rough. Her hair was as black as the crows in the sky, her skin brown, with dark summer freckles on her face forming constellations that mirrored the night sky in the dead of winter.

Which was why it had to be her.

"You?" one of the men said with a scornful laugh. "What can you do?"

She stared at him, barely blinking. "What you cannot. While you sit here and argue among yourselves, the rot is spreading. It has already reached the boundaries of our territory. It won't be long before it consumes us all."

Another man—the elder, their leader, skin wrinkled and sagging, one eye covered in a milky sheen—said, "Sen is worthy of consideration. I seem to remember a time very recently when she returned from a hunt victorious when others came back empty-handed. Or was it the time before that?"

"You would trust her with our future?" a man demanded.

"I am not afraid of death," she retorted. A lie? Perhaps, but one she was willing to tell.

The elder smiled, a brittle thing. "There are some things much worse than death. You have seen what the rot has done to the creatures of the forest. Who's to say the same thing won't happen to you?"

"Then it does," she said. "And there will be one less mouth to feed. What are you going to do when the rot infects all that remains? Pray more? Pray harder? You said if the God of the Forest won't come to us, then we must go to it. There is no one here more suited than I."

"Careful," the elder said. "Your hubris will be your undoing."

"Challenge," a third man called. "I challenge Sen for the right to be chosen as emissary to the God of the Forest."

She turned her head.

Tek. Older by a few years, corded with thick muscle. His black hair was pulled tight in a braid down the center of his back. Mean and, even worse, stupid. He thought himself better than almost everyone and, unfortunately, had the tracking and hunting skills to back it up. Headstrong and callous, he made Sen wary, their history fraught with tension. Months ago, Tek had made his intentions known. He wanted Sen for a wife.

But she already had her sights set on a pretty girl who traveled among the villages with her father, trading wares. The girl—woman, really—had eyes the color of mud and a smile that, while shy, caused Sen's heart to trip all over itself. Slow going, but Sen would see it through.

Tek hadn't taken the news well. A formidable opponent, he would surely try to use this moment to prove that he would be her best choice.

But she would not back down.

The village formed a ring around them, the elder sitting with his arms crossed on a wooden stump, hands resting in his lap. "First blood," he said. "Tek, since you are the challenger, Sen has the right to choose her weapon first." He nodded toward a rack of spears, long blades, a corded whip, mallets of stone with sharp spikes around the crowns.

Sen did not move toward the weapons. Instead, she crouched toward the ground, scooping up soil, bringing it to her nose and breathing in.

It smelled alive, not yet infected by rot. Letting it fall between her fingers, she stood slowly. From her side, she unsheathed her knife, a gift from the elder on the eve of her fourteenth year. The blade itself was made of hardened black stone so shiny, it looked as if it would be slick to the touch. Half the length of her forearm, the blade was an extension of her, the wooden pommel familiar in her grip.

She raised the knife above her head and said, "I have chosen."

The elder nodded slowly. For a moment, Sen thought she saw a funny little smile on his face, there and gone before she could be sure. He turned to Tek and waved his hand. "Make your choice."

Shoulders squared, Tek approached the weapons, others from the village calling out to him, saying he'd make quick work of this challenge. Tek grinned, waving them off.

Even before he decided, Sen knew what he would pick. She was not disappointed when he picked up the whip, letting the length fall to the ground. Made from animal hide, the whip was ten feet in length and could slice skin with a single flick, if held in expert hands.

And Tek was nothing if not an expert.

Tek turned toward her as the villagers quieted, and the elder stood and raised his hands. "No interference. No assistance. First blood, and you will stop the moment it happens."

Tek attacked before the elder had finished speaking. With a heavy grunt, he swung the whip out in a flat arc. Taking a stumbling step back, Sen felt the tip of the whip slice the air inches away from her nose. Before she could recover, Tek brought his arm back again.

The whip hurtled toward her. Sen dove to the right, rolling on the ground as the whip scored the earth where she'd just stood. She didn't stop, rising from her roll swiftly, on her feet before Tek could pull the whip back once more. In her right hand, the blade. In her left, a palmful of earth.

Stepping on the end of the whip to keep Tek from pulling it back completely, she flung the dirt at his face. He cried out as it hit his eyes, right foot sliding back. He rubbed his eyes with one hand, the other still holding on to the whip.

Near silent, Sen rushed toward him, running on top of the whip, holding it down beneath her feet. With only a short distance remaining between them, she leapt, knife above her head.

But Tek must have heard her coming. Dropping his hand from his face, he crouched low, and it was too late for Sen to correct herself. As she collided with him, he thrust his shoulder up and into her stomach, breath knocked from her lungs in an excruciating burst between her lips. The impact caused her aim to miss, her blade glancing off his shoulder as she flew up and over him, landing on her back. The impact was jarring, painful. Dazed, she could only blink up at the blue above her, her weapon on the ground beside her, just beyond her fingertips.

Until a shadow blotted out the sky.

Tek, standing above her. He grinned. "Close, but not close enough."

He raised the whip above his head, and in his face, she saw that he would not stop until she was no more.

Without thought, she snapped out her arm, the socket groaning. The blade, the knife, her knife, and her fingers tightened around the pommel as Tek prepared to strike. Before he followed through, she slammed the knife down through his right foot. It sank to the hilt.

She breathed in. She breathed out, teeth and tongue gritty.

The whip fell from Tek's hand as he began to scream, blood gushing around the blade. He bent over, teeth bared as a string of spittle descended toward the ground. "You snake," he snarled. "I'll kill—"

In one smooth motion, Sen pulled the knife from Tek's foot with her left hand, her right curled into a fist. She rose quicker than Tek could react and punched him underneath the jaw. Her knuckles split in a bright flash of pain, but it was negligible compared to Tek landing on his back, dazed, blinking with unfocused eyes.

Sen spat on the ground, then wiped her mouth with the back of her hand. She looked down at Tek, then to her people, all of whom watched her with a mixture of awe and fear.

The elder, though. He seemed almost . . . amused. "First blood," he said mildly. "It would seem as if Sen has proven herself more than worthy." He stood as Tek rolled on the ground holding his foot, blood dripping to the ground. "See to him immediately. The wound looks painful. Sen, to me, please." And with that, he turned and headed away from the people.

Sen followed, glancing down at Tek. He snapped his teeth at her, eyes wet and furious. She did not give him the satisfaction of a response.

Away from the others, the elder stopped next to a flowering bush, the petals yellow and thin. Touching one of the budding flowers with the tip of his finger, he said, "A knife to the foot. Interesting choice. How like your father you are."

She looked off into the trees. "You taught me well, Grandfather."

"He would be proud of you," the elder said. "Both of them would. Taken far too soon, but you are their legacy, their history, their hope for the world. And I know you, Granddaughter. I know your heart, your mind. Which is why I will ask you this only once: Are you sure?"

She did not hesitate. "I am. I will find the God of the Forest. He will listen to me."

The elder's hand moved almost quicker than she could follow, his fingers biting into her wrist. She didn't try to pull away. "Do not think an audience with a god means they will hear your words. Gods are capricious, unpredictable. It would be within their rights to eat you for daring to stand before them."

"I'm not scared of the gods," Sen said.

Her grandfather dropped her wrist, looking as old as she'd ever seen him. Ancient, really, the valleys of his face deep. "You should be," he whispered.

ABOUT THE AUTHOR

Natasha Michaels

TJ KLUNE is the *New York Times* and *USA Today* bestselling, Lambda Literary Award–winning author of *The House in the Cerulean Sea, Under the Whispering Door, In the Lives of Puppets,* the Extraordinaries series for teens, and more. Being queer himself, Klune believes it's important—now more than ever—to have accurate, positive queer representation in stories.

Visit Klune online:
tjklunebooks.com
Instagram: @tjklunebooks